About the author

Son of a Fleet Street journalist, Paul Timblick has travelled and taught English in numerous countries over the last fifteen years. One of them – Peru – inspired his first book *Perune Juice*, a humorous ramble through the highs and lows of Peruvian culture. Completed in 2011, this was the year he met his wife-to-be, Fasika Sorssa, in Ethiopia. She recounted her horrifying experience as a domestic worker in Lebanon, under the Middle Eastern 'kefala' system, while also revealing a quirky set of survival skills. The idea for a book that was simultaneously riveting and awareness-raising stirred Paul into writing Fasika's story. *No Lipstick in Lebanon* aims to open eyes, minds and hearts.

NO LIPSTICK IN LEBANON

Paul Timblick
with
Fasika Sorssa

unbound

This edition first published in 2015

Unbound
4–7 Manchester Street Marylebone London W1U 2AE
www.unbound.co.uk
All rights reserved

Typeset by Ellipsis Digital Limited, Glasgow

Art direction by Mecob

A CIP record for this book is available from the British Library

ISBN 978-1-78352-108-1 (trade hbk)
ISBN 978-1-78352-163-0 (ebook)
ISBN 978-1-78352-109-8 (limited edition)

Penguin Random House is committed to a sustainable future for
our business, our readers and our planet. This book is made from
Forest Stewardship Council® certified paper.

Printed and bound in Great Britain by Clays Ltd, St Ives plc

Dedicated to every migrant worker who has suffered in Lebanon, the Middle East and beyond – this book is for you.

Inspired by our Loved Ones:
Soliana, Hermella, Werkitu Delesa, Yohannes and Dejene.

Acknowledgements

Many sincere thanks to: Elizabeth Garner, Bob Truett, Philippa Hill, City Suites (Beirut), Damu Hotel (Addis Ababa), Deji Akande, Luke (for the laptops!), Mum and Dad, and everyone who supported the book's reassuring leaps towards publication, via Unbound.

Gareth Alun Thomas of Blackwood, Wales, you are a true friend.

Dear Reader,

The book you are holding came about in a rather different way to most others. It was funded directly by readers through a new website: **Unbound**.

Unbound is the creation of three writers. We started the company because we believed there had to be a better deal for both writers and readers. On the Unbound website, authors share the ideas for the books they want to write directly with readers. If enough of you support the book by pledging for it in advance, we produce a beautifully bound special subscribers' edition and distribute a regular edition and e-book wherever books are sold, in shops and online.

This new way of publishing is actually a very old idea (Samuel Johnson funded his dictionary this way). We're just using the internet to build each writer a network of patrons. Here, at the back of this book, you'll find the names of all the people who made it happen.

Publishing in this way means readers are no longer just passive consumers of the books they buy, and authors are free to write the books they really want. They get a much fairer return too – half the profits their books generate, rather than a tiny percentage of the cover price.

If you're not yet a subscriber, we hope that you'll want to join our publishing revolution and have your name listed in one of our books in the future. To get you started, here is a £5 discount on your first pledge. Just visit unbound.com, make your pledge and type **lipstick** in the promo code box when you check out.

Thank you for your support,

Dan, Justin and John
Founders, Unbound

An Afternoon Stroll

'We don't have injera today . . . bread instead,' states my mother in mid-sweep, her back leaning hard into the broom at an angle that usually hints at antagonism.

'Why not injera?' I retort in only bra and knickers in front of our cracked mirror.

This bitter-tasting pancake made of the staple grain teff that we all gobble so frantically every day is undoubtedly a national addiction. A roll of injera has the appearance and comfort of a soft roll of beige towelling: Ethiopian hands cannot resist it. I see no rationale for substituting it with bread, not even for a single day.

'Where are you going?' she asks in answer to my question.

'As usual, Mum,' I shrug.

'Wasting time in Bole Road . . .'

'Discussing this with you is a waste of time . . . why no injera today?'

She stops at the door, leans on the broom and sighs deeply.

'Bread today. Go to Shoa Dabu bakery and buy four rolls, okay?'

'Okay.'

'Do you remember when you were young and I threatened to send you abroad if you didn't eat all your injera?' she chuckles.

'Er, no, but it's an interesting idea . . . if I stop eating injera, will you get me a visa for America? I could work in movies, get rich and buy all the things I don't need.'

Mum glares at me for a second, unsure if I'm joking or not, which frustrates her even more than the sabotage of pleasant nostalgia. Her face is frame-worthy, until she assumes it's one of my little jokes and the muscles around her eyes loosen again.

'Meron, these days you *never* refuse injera. You're as addicted as the rest of us.'

'So feed my addiction. Why bread today?'

'For a change. We need change.'

'Oh.'

I slip on a pair of nondescript blue jeans and step into unremarkable pink flip-flops. I pull a baggy black T-shirt over my untended hair, leaving only scrawny arms hanging at my side like two thin table legs of polished chestnut. The table would be complete if I wore shorts, but exposed legs do not invite anonymity in Addis Ababa.

My large playful eyes, poutable mouth and perfectly formed nose will get no enhancement with make-up: let the beauty go disguised as simple plainness, perceptible only to the most astute. It will face towards the dirt ground, two strides ahead, as I nip through my neighbourhood, catching the attention of nobody. Nobody will see

2

anything in me that is worthy of comment. I'm a 'miskin', a humble poor person.

'Bye, Mum.'

I wish I had the confidence to strut around Addis like a supermodel with swinging hips and scarlet lips. Fashion intrigues me but invisibility is safer: I prefer to merge into the background of corrugated iron that forms a continuous battered corridor through the local slums. If I were a chameleon, my colours would be a permanent patchwork of grey and rust. There are absolutely no other colours in our neighbourhood, apart from the dark green door.

I have no idea why *our* door should be dark green, but it is, like a one-in-a-million freak of nature. As it slams shut behind me, the noisy clatter sounds no different from all the other sheets of metal parading as doors. But it instantly creaks open again.

'Meron!' shouts Mum, craning after me.

'What?'

'Don't forget the bread rolls.'

'I'm not stupid.'

From my dark green door to Meskel Square, it takes about ten minutes of quick walking. I suck in our passageway's thin air streaked with aromas of roasted coffee, smouldering incense, freshly baked injera and human detritus. I switch my countenance from care*free* to care*ful*, with tilted head and resolute eyes, my facial armoury set for the usual daily assailants. These include murky puddles that never dry up, persistent street kids that never give up, eye-stinging gusts of dust, throat-choking plumes of exhaust fumes, random herds of stinking goats, roaming dogs of mingled breeds, and redundant packs of men continuously staring at and startling passing girls. *They* are the biggest problem in Addis, not the dirt, not the traffic, not the pollution, not the flies and not the rats. It's the staring, startling *men*.

Addis swarms with *men* sitting or milling around outside, usually a little high from masticating their chat leaves, a mild drug consumed mainly in the Horn of Africa. My mid-afternoon jaunt to Bole Road invariably coincides with the 'reggae timers' stumbling back into the streets after a couple of hours' manic jaw activity, always commencing with the 'Reggae Time' hour on the radio, straight after lunch. Like injera, chat-eating is also a national habit, but not spreading much beyond the idle fifty per cent.

For the majority of men, though, life's chief pleasure lies in the observation and ridicule of passing pedestrians, with unchecked jibes and jeers freely issued to those least likely to fight back, which inevitably means us, the *women*. We mostly lead demanding but meaningful lives supporting families, earning wages and maintaining the semblance of society. We tend to rely on our religion – Orthodox Christianity or Islam – for guidance and strength. The men tend to rely on their tongues for 'chat' and chatter: without tongues, they would instantly lose the will to live.

'Hey, you! Break your neck? Your head is always down!'

This is directed at me from a cactus-hairstyled stump of a man who always tries to catch my attention at the hectic junction where at least one unfortunate is struck down every week, each one probably distracted by this same chat-eating idler.

'Hey, you, Broken Neck!' he yells.

'Broken Neck!' laugh his companions, my new nick-name cemented by their shared joke, which could endure for days or weeks or forever. But I keep my head low and my concentration deep, before the nickname becomes a doctor's verdict.

'Hey, Broken Neck, you've lost weight . . . must be HIV . . .' he tries again.

How can I have HIV? There has been no sexual rela-tionship of any kind, ever. Who *is* this idiot? I twist round to confront him and . . . I suddenly have the bonnet of a blue and white Lada taxi careering towards my waist, the jarring car horn actually causing greater petrification than the fast-approaching machine. I'm completely stationary. *I'm completely dead!*

The taxi stops in time. The driver pounds his car horn again and again until I feel my flimsy legs recommence their march. All passers-by gape at me for a second and quickly move on. Near-death is normal in Addis, but I'd prefer it without the attention.

Yes, I am losing weight. It's due to lack of sleep, not HIV. I spend the nights worrying about my fragile life and how it might be squandered with men like him. My slumber is not the easy drop of childhood: on some nights the subconscious is barely scraped as I puzzle over the possible routes to personal wealth and eternal bliss, without stooping towards a nightmare marriage where simple incompatibility is the least of our problems. How, God, how?

At last, I meet with Tsehay, my old school friend, at our nation's epicentre. Meskel Square is an ugly dusty place without the shade of a single tree. It is one half of a broad amphitheatre looking out over a ten-lane stage of stop-start traffic which pedestrians can only cross by out-running motorised vehicles. Many of the square's gangly masses *can* do this: Meskel's terraces are where budding athletes come to train in the morning.

Remaining on the terraced side of the square, Tsehay and I exchange greetings in Amharic, the official language of Ethiopia. I kiss her on both gaunt cheeks: the cheek-bones go high, her eyebrows even higher. Too skinny for curves, Tsehay's legs look ready to snap off from her body at any moment. Tsehay wears brighter colours than me – orange today – and subtle sweeps of make-up, suggesting she wants attention, and I am happy for her to take it. I am here for the free show; to watch it, not be part of it.

'Some guy shouted a new nickname at me . . . Broken Neck.'

Tsehay studies me for a second and frowns.

'Not bad. Better than mine . . . Stirring Stick.'

'I don't know . . . stirring sticks are more useful than broken necks,' I chirp.

We set off up the Bole ('*Bo*-lay') Road incline, with offices, shopping centres and cafés on either side of us, as well as tiny stores inside untidy shacks doing their tenacious best to maintain a toehold on Africa's most important driveway.

A truckload of around twenty soldiers in cobalt-shaded uniforms empties in front of us and immediately begins to redirect traffic off the Bole asphalt into inconspicuous side streets. After a few minutes, pedestrians are prevented from crossing Bole Road by these mean-faced troops lining the entire three kilometres from Bole Airport to the

African Union headquarters. In the distance, we see the headlights of a fast-approaching motorcade.

'Which mad man is it to be today? Mugabe? Gaddafi?' I muse out loud.

'Shut up, Meron, or they'll hear you,' whispers Tsehay.

When the continent's presidents and diplomats attend AU meetings, they zoom along Bole Road in black limousines surrounded by police outriders carrying guns. The equally spaced soldiers in front of us are ready to batter any onlooker who might hurl a rock or themselves at the convoy.

As the vehicles flash past, we all strain to glimpse an unhinged dictator through the impenetrable, tinted windows. We are allowed to tut quietly at the inconvenience to our insignificant lives but anything more invites a rapid baton-whack to the midriff.

'Madness always afflicts the men,' I announce loudly.

'Meron, shut up!'

A brooding creature with a slender cane gripped in his right hand looks me up and down with desire or disdain: I am not sure which, but I would love to deflect those devouring eyes at the Stirring Stick next to me.

Typically, we manage to spot nobody of any significance, and resume our daily wander along Bole Road as it quickly refills with humdrum congestion, including on the pavement, where familiar faces veer in front of us like the flies.

'Isn't that Grave Boy?' I ask, noticing a young man in an Adidas tracksuit striding with great intent.

'Yeah, it's him . . . still dreaming of dying outside

Ethiopia because the graves here aren't restful enough,' replies Tsehay, shaking her head. '*That* is madness.'

'At least he has a purpose.'

Grave Boy stops abruptly to say hello. But no social exchange in Addis can be permitted to begin and finish so efficiently: there are at least a dozen obligatory warm-up questions before the meat of conversations can be consumed. 'How are you?' is reworded into 'What's up?', 'Everything good?', 'Where have you been?', 'How's work?' and 'How's the family?', followed by the same for all family members. It can take a full ten minutes before anything other than polite enquiry is broached. By then, what really needs to be said has been forgotten, and often there is nothing to say anyway, but we have enjoyed a full and reassuringly long conversation. This etiquette provides a very reasonable explanation for the swift passage of time in Addis: a few sociable chats in the street and the sun is down for another day.

'Anyway, I can't stop,' says Grave Boy belatedly, 'I'm planning my escape into Sudan . . . more peaceful there . . . for the afterlife.'

And he is back on track, dedicating his life to the achievement of a foreign death. We chuckle at him.

Every day there are different stories, incidents and characters, all marching along like a permanent installation, filling us with shock, sorrow and elation in equal measure. If only we could see through the tinted windows of the black limos to mock the presidential mad men, on the same Bole podium as us.

'Who's this coming? Meron! Look, a new character!'

I can't believe it.

'It's not a new character . . . it's Selam! Hi, how are you?' I blabber as she approaches.

It's been more than two years. Last time, Selam looked just like me: standard backstreet Addis, too modest for a smear of lipstick and shoes too flat to avoid the squelchy silt of puddles oozing between the toes. But I remember she knew change was afoot: money was about to land with a reassuring thud in her life and it was her big secret.

Last time, she gave me twenty birr to go to the cinema. Made in Ethiopia, the movie was about a love triangle and the acting was memorably terrible. But I do also recall Selam's generosity.

'Selam!' I try again.

It's definitely her. A swirl of bright blue and glinting gold breezes past us with only the outline of a vibrant crimson heart visible through the perfumed mist of faultless female form. I cannot take it all in.

But via the vibrant crimson heart of lipstick comes half a smile, maybe less, flashed in my direction. Only a corner of her mouth actually moves, so to say half a smile is an exaggeration. It could be a frown or a mouth ulcer or a lump of mutton gristle jammed between the teeth. And certainly no words pour out. Once, we had a daily connection.

'Selam, *Selam*!' I gasp inaudibly. She's passed now and left me in awe. All I see is her back and the gawping of others: men and women alike.

She has the requisite beauty and style, and a body of absolute perfection, but what opens my mouth into a gaping Bole drain hole is something beyond visual splendour. Confidence is to blame. And I need that. It comes from money. Any Addis girl would crave the money and confidence to strut along Bole Road as though she were the Queen of Sheba. Selam has reached the pinnacle, the highest of the high, the eighth wonder of the world, the Ark of the Covenant, the absence of poverty, the Sheraton wedding, the American visa . . .

Tsehay is spluttering with laughter at my fawning.

'You can laugh, but look at us,' I snap. 'Can't you see what's happened to us . . . the spectators?'

'Why? What? We're enjoying the free show.'

'We *are* the free show! We prance along here every day and now *we've* got nicknames. We're as regular as the others . . . we're ploughing the same cesspit as the chat-eating men.'

'*What?*' exclaims Tsehay, unable to comprehend my sudden gravity.

'Selam has turned up after two years and look at her. She's *something* . . . she's above the nicknames, the jeering and the gossip. She's on that higher plane where she can choose what to do, what to be, what to wear, what to marry, what*ever* she likes . . . and what have we done in those two years? We've gone nowhere. Every single day, we kill time . . . we murder the minutes of our lives . . . we're murdering *ourselves!*'

'Tragedy today in Addis as countless innocent minutes are lost forever . . . it's deeply moving,' replies Tsehay melodramatically like a newsreader.

'Tsehay, that's deeply unhelpful. What's the exact time?'

'No idea. Reggae Time plus some more.'

'Uh?'

I check the time on a foreigner's watch: it is three

thirty-five (international time) outside the Dembel Shopping Centre. I jog for a few seconds and follow Selam across Olimpia's traffic lights, past the Purple Café. She skips across filthy rippling lakes of stagnant rainwater and around the screaming youths of the public taxis trying to lure in passengers with 'Bol-lay! Bol-lay! Bol-lay!'

She darts into Shoa Dabu, the bakery. Bread is warm and fresh at this time of day; customers fight to pay the cashier. I linger beside a man selling fried flour biscuits outside. With rolls in hand, Selam is quickly out again, jumping into one of the jam-packed minibus taxis. There, the trail finishes but it's enough. I race home oblivious to traffic, dogs, people and men.

'Where's the bread?' asks Mum as I tramp into the house.

'Eh? Ah! No . . . sorry, Mum, I was distracted . . . and I was standing outside Shoa Dabu bakery only twenty minutes ago.'

'What? You couldn't manage that one simple thing? Is anything *happening* behind those eyes?' asks Mum angrily.

'And where's Tsehay? I don't even remember saying goodbye . . . where did she go?' I blurt.

'This is ridiculous. You need to get a job, Meron.'

'But I saw Selam,' I gabble. 'I want her secret. Where has she been and why has she got the confidence? Money has to be involved. I need an explanation . . . no, I *demand* an explanation.'

Mum stares at me as though I have pledged never to eat injera again.

'What is becoming of—' she starts.

'Ah! I just remembered! They closed Bole Road for

Mugabe . . . that's the reason I forgot the bread. Blame
him.'

'Another of your silly lies.'

'Really, Mum, just call him at the Sheraton and check
his story . . . I'm sure he's a friendly man.' I shrug.

Two days after the first sighting, I am back outside
the Dembel Centre, same time, strolling casually and
un-coincidentally. I feel the mid-afternoon sun silently
burning my skin, as if punishment for my devious loitering.

But today I can tolerate damaged skin. Here she comes.
Got her! Selam has a routine. And this time, I shall be a
little less desperate.

'Oh hi, Selam!' I squeak, feigning surprise. 'Do you
remember me?'

Selam shakes her head dismissively.

'Wow! You look fantastic . . .' I continue.

You know me. Come on, you have to react to flattery,
you *have* to. But maybe she didn't hear my timid peep
above the lick of the sun's flames.

'You look fantastic!' I try again.

A false smile whips back at me, but a smile nonetheless
and no mouth ulcers this time. The acknowledgement
is trapped and bared for the briefest of seconds. We
make progress.

The following day is Sunday. Nobody bothers with confidence at this hour on a Sunday. The confidence is resting
after a busy Saturday night in the Addis clubs.

Monday sees me in Shoa Dabu bakery, similar time.
I'm not buying anything. Instead, I feign urgent texting,
on a mobile that hasn't worked for a year. I carry it for

moments like this, intently bashing away on the buttons as though my whole family has contracted cholera. I nearly miss my target with my eyes engrossed in this worthless slab of plastic.

She's fast. But I get her on the way out.

'Selam! Hi . . .'

'Hi.'

Thank you. Have a good day, because I will.

But next day, there is no Selam. Or the next. Or the next. Her routine has changed and I am left clutching a slab of plastic as useless as my entire life.

The Possibility of Peace

In Ethiopia, Easter, known as 'Fasika', is *the* major religious festival for Orthodox Christians. More than half the country is Orthodox Christian and Mum ensures that I am very much within that majority. Normally, I am unquestionably happy to be part of this great faith, but this year I am too fractious and distracted to enjoy Fasika.

I hardly notice the fifty-five days of Lent fasting, with no meat, eggs, milk, cheese, butter, alcohol, cigarettes or sex. Or the final 'Week of Pains' ban on kissing, crying, hugging, clubbing, dancing and laughing. Even dying is frowned upon in the last few days before the Crucifixion: fully booked priests cannot grant absolution at funerals and those who are fading must hang on till Monday if they prefer Heaven to Hell.

Nor can I concentrate on the hymns accompanied by the plucking of the begena, or the lengthy Bible readings, or the rigorous prostrating throughout Good Friday. Easter Sunday's celebratory meals of richly spiced chicken and uncooked beef – plus Monday morning's gastric agonies – slip by all too easily. That's another Fasika gone and I can picture only the woman with something I want.

No sign of Selam. Her name means 'peace' but I am not feeling it. She was down at my level, now she's on the moon. Of course I'm obsessed with her. She represents possibility. Where do I find her, God? Do you *want* me to find her? Is this part of your plan? Or have you forgotten Meron Lemma?

'Me too . . . I'm as anxious as you, Meron. You've infected me with your worry,' grumbles Tsehay.

We're sitting on the steps outside her modest house, bored.

'Good! Because we've already wasted two school years not inside the school,' I reply.

Cafés, cinemas, street corners, clothes shops and friends' couches have all been preferable to the maths classroom. But now, at sixteen, we need to devise a clever scheme fast, or a life of drudgery awaits us with open arms: vacancies in drudgery are plentiful and the contract is binding.

'Selam holds the key,' I continue.

'Forget about Selam. Maybe we should do waitressing . . . the tips can be good. We could meet rich guys; the Bole boys. What do you think?' Tsehay offers.

'Waitressing? Bole boys?' I reply irritably. 'Don't you think I've thought about that? Yes, I'm interested in sex but I want to earn good money first. The men can wait for me.'

'*Sex?* What's wrong with you? When did I mention sex?' snaps Tsehay. Her name means 'sun', but it doesn't shine on every utterance. Too often in Addis, names are not as self-fulfilling as they should be, hence the nicknames.

'You said rich guys, Bole boys . . . that equates to sex for money, which equates to being a "business girl". I'll keep my body to myself, thank you. I'm saving the first one for true love.'

'Not every waitress in Bole is selling herself like a business girl. You could just serve some drinks and give them a smile.'

'Smile at Bole boys? That equates to sex.'

'Fine. Just take the orders, serve the drinks, look morose and pocket the tips.'

'Look morose? They'll probably take it as a challenge . . . looking morose is an obvious come-on. It equates to sex.'

'Oh, Meron, shut up! We're going to Elephant Walk Café tomorrow, speak to the manager and check what positions they've got. It's the in-place for the Bole boys.'

'So . . . tomorrow I lose my virginity. Thank you, Tsehay.'

Round and black are the tables in Elephant Walk Café, like all the eyes gazing at Selam. As Selam moves quickly between the tables, fifty or so intent pairs of eyes roll around a little faster, like large marbles spinning through the air. If she stops too hastily, those marbles might smash together and shatter. Instead, she brakes slowly at a table and performs a delicate seat-brushing act, all within sight of Tsehay and me. She doesn't see us. We await the manager for a conversation about work.

'There she is. Thank God we came. Now we don't need to be waitresses!' I exclaim.

'What? Don't be crazy. She isn't just going to hand over a pile of money.'

'Tell the manager I've changed my mind.'

'That's up to you. But I need a job before I'm old and . . .'

I have stopped listening to Tsehay.

Selam is waiting for a date: the lines, shades, blushes, highlights of a beauty salon's craft exude her confidence on a toasted fire-clay skin textured like warm chocolate icing. I really like her off-the-shoulder black minidress and heels, with fake diamond brooch, pearl necklace and silver nails. Her hair displays brazen curls complementing facial, breast and hip curves that are gently pushing at the generous. I see money, style and poise.

'Are you interested?' Tsehay is asking me.

The manager is standing beside us, gold wedding ring flashing on his left hand. He may have the smuggest of smiles upstairs, but downstairs his feet are humiliated by the humblest of leather clogs I have ever seen outside an irrigated field. He's one of the 'Habesha', or Ethiopian, types who can easily be mistaken for Indian. Equally, the Indian businessmen in Addis often get mistaken for Habesha, and I am not sure who is more irritated by this ethnic confusion. The Indians have better shoes than Habesha, I know that.

'The manager is saying we can both try it out, but . . .' continues Tsehay.

'But what?'

'Nothing. Are you interested?' Tsehay nags.

'I'll think about it. I've got my mind on other things at the moment. When do you start?'

'Maybe tomorrow, but he wants to see me later, just me and him . . . said it would help with promotion.'

'Promotion? You haven't even started the job yet.'

'Hey, don't be jealous . . . just because he's a manager. This is the way it works, didn't you know?'

I smirk at her for a second. What can I say? Tsehay is happy to play the game with this 'manager'. He can't even manage his own libido.

'Okay. See you later. I'm staying here. I'll *get* her today . . .'

'Meron, you're crazy.'

'Very possibly, but that's my advantage.'

Stroking an empty Coke bottle as I search for the right words to tackle Selam, I delay too long. Her date arrives, a Bole boy nicknamed 'Hyena' because of his appetite for women. Once more, my chance has gone.

Next day, together with Tsehay, I am a waitress in Elephant Walk Café. Luckily, nothing is required of me by the 'Indian' manager. Tsehay paid double last night.

On busy Friday, Saturday and Sunday evenings, the tables are pushed close enough for customers to ambush or steal the conversations from neighbouring tables. This proximity is unpleasant, but it's business.

Selam is here again, effusing confidence and soaking up stares from all corners of the crowded café. Her table number is not within my serving area, but I linger nearby, hoping to catch something. Just a single explanatory word will do. How so rich, Selam, *how*? But all I can hear is a conversation peppered with unfamiliar foreign words.

'Laa!' exclaims a similarly glamorous friend.

'Be-laa!' rebuts Selam.

'Ba-den . . .' says the friend, sipping on lively cola.

'You know Dany . . . Allah!' says Selam, noticing me and quickly reverting back to the friend as though some wind has momentarily blown her gaze off-course and where I stand is open fallow land.

'Dany? Ah! Hyena!' exclaims the friend.

'Aiwa!' continues Selam.

'Allah! I can't believe it!'

This is a waste of time. I'm getting nothing from this nonsensical exchange. I force my mouth open.

'Excuse me . . . Selam,' I stutter, 'but why don't you know me any more?'

Her head juts forward for a second before turning to take aim. Even her gestures are new. She used to tilt her head to one side before firing off a humorous one-liner.

'Who are *you*? If we need service, we'll shout at you.'

Who am I? I am nothing in a gaudy pink T-shirt with coffee stains down the front: she is hot from a Bole fashion boutique. But I remain at Selam's elbow.

'Yes, what?' she demands loudly.

'I can't believe it . . . Selam, you used to be a good person . . . I remember the jokes . . .' I stammer fretfully, beginning to back away but painfully hitting my rear on one of the café's tree-shaped pillars.

Customers are now staring at *me*. I'm trapped; wedged in between tables, people, pizzas and pillars. Sweat is beginning to seep out of my face, as I gulp in the café's steamy air. I wipe a finger along my eyebrows to smear away the perspiration and ease myself through a gap in the chairs, circling round to the other side of Selam.

'Where's the manager?' shouts Selam.

'I . . . I . . . don't . . . *there*! That Indian guy, over there,' I blurt, pointing him out, happy to get the attention off myself.

Selam has no chance to pursue her complaint.

'Who do you think you are? With all the Arabic mixed up with Amharic, you're making me sick. Use your own mother tongue in public instead of putting on the big Dubai act.'

This surprises us both. It comes from my left at table number five. A weather-beaten shapeless woman in a cheap green blouse, oversized jeans and open-toed sandals is leaning towards Selam, confrontationally in my opinion. I study her feet. Where there should be a proud parade of ten polished soldiers, I see ten mangled, mud-spattered paupers, fresh from crawling along the city's mucky byways. The state of women's toes usually tells the truth in Addis. This woman is not even *trying* to beautify her street-battered extremities. I can see she talks as straight as her exposed toes are twisted, like many people who have moved from the countryside to the city – from abject poverty to average poverty – speaking their mind to complete strangers, whatever gibberish the mind generates, no filter sitting between mind and mouth. But she has a good point. Selam is as false as they come.

'I'll speak how I like,' replies Selam, 'and Arabic is obviously a lot more than you can manage. Your Amharic sounds like the squeaky spring of an overused bed . . . probably yours.'

Selam can handle herself.

'Why do you have to be so false?' asks the country woman. 'You were a servant in Dubai, so what? I was a servant in Addis. We're equals. But *you* think you're something special.'

The countrywoman is stubborn. Like obstinate oxen, they always are. There is no backing down now.

'It was Lebanon, not Dubai,' replies Selam. 'And I paid three thousand birr to take a plane out there. I was a professional servant for a rich Arab family. You came to Addis in a dirty old bus and worked for a mediocre little Habesha family that could hardly afford the teff for the extra mouth. Quite a big mouth, in fact.'

Ah! So Selam's confidence is explained. And her money. Lebanon! It's Lebanon!

Selam is now ahead in this intriguing contest. Other customers can serve themselves. I am going to Lebanon! My future injera will be served on a disposable golden platter. A new one every mealtime! Ha, ha, ha, ha!

'You went to Lebanon to be a slave. I was a servant in Addis. I could leave any time I liked. But you? Stuck inside their house for years . . . the Arabs could kill you at their whim. You were *nothing* to them.'

Oh God. That's absolutely true. Girls come back every week in boxes from Lebanon. The newspapers tell us everything. An affair with the master of the house is punished – by his wife – with horrific 'suicides' from the balconies of high-rise blocks. At least, that's what they call the deaths. Calling them 'suicides' allows the Lebanese murderers to go free. It's scandalous. The Habesha girls in Beirut are at the mercy of their masters. I'm not walking into that death trap. Thank God for this conversation. Lebanon is cancelled forever.

Selam looks the countrywoman up and down with the best contempt she can manage.

'But look at me now . . . the risk was worth it . . . good

clothes, beautiful hair, nice company. You? You took no risk and now you're good for goats and not much else in those rags . . . and I mean goats aroused by fashion from Haile Selassie's time.'

Superb comeback! She's right! This woman would be lucky to get advances from frisky goats. I *am* going to Lebanon. Ha! The risk is minimal. I have an escape!

'At least I'm true to myself and my country and my origins,' responds the countrywoman.

'Eh? Who bothers with *truth* these days? It sounds lame and dated. Haile Selassie probably said it. Just stay true to your *own table* and keep out of my conversation,' snaps Selam, clapping her hands in my direction. 'Bill!'

I clap my hands enthusiastically back at her, shouting 'Bravo!'

'Yes, but get the bill,' Selam repeats, not amused.

'Well, this isn't really my serving area . . .'

'Get the bill, Meron!'

Sweet recognition at last! And now look at me running to fetch the bill for her. I'm *her* servant and earning a pittance. If I were a servant in Lebanon, I could earn a suitcase stuffed with American dollars, instead of worthless birr. Otherwise, I'll be bleating to the goats about truth, country, origins and whatever else flits like fruit flies between the underused, overripe hemispheres within my cranium.

There are no monetary tips from either table. But Selam left enough argument to convince me. My mother may not be so easy.

Persuading Mum

In our shared bed, I catch her unable to sleep in the middle of the night. My mother usually lies behind me with one hand on the indentation of my waist. That hand provides the comfort and security that bring my sleep. But on this night, the hand is scratching her head.

'Mum, are you okay?' I whisper.

My younger brothers, Nati and Henok, are only a metre away in their shared bed, both huffing away contentedly.

'Yes, there's something in my hair . . . it doesn't matter. Go to sleep.'

'Mum, I'm not sure about something.'

'What? Men? Sexual diseases? Please, God, no!' she whispers too loudly.

Since I reached puberty, she has been on permanent standby for disastrous news involving me and men. Beautiful romantic love has not occurred to her.

'Keep your voice down, Mum,' I hiss.

'You haven't fallen into the chasm, have you?'

The chasm is her code word for HIV/AIDS.

'No, Mum . . . not men, not diseases. It's about money.'

'Money? But we're poor.'

'So, Mum, it's a problem.'

'Hoh! Not a problem. Money can't buy happiness and peace. You need the Bible for that.'

'So you want us to stay poor?'

'God will decide.'

'Why can't *we* decide?'

'Because we're poor. God said we'd inherit the Earth, but He didn't say when. I trust His word. It *will* happen. It's better to be poor and enjoy the glory of God with all its promise. The rich can only cower in His presence. They know He can take everything away, any time He decides. They're living in fear . . . they have everything to lose! But us . . . we have *nothing* to lose. We can only win.'

'So, Mum, you feel happier being poor?'

'Poor but happy.'

'So rich but happy is not an option?'

'An impossibility.'

'But we *were* rich . . . once.'

'And God didn't like it. He had His reasons.'

'I love you, Mum.'

But it isn't what I want to hear. Can't we sidestep God's reasoning sometimes? It doesn't always make sense.

'I love you too, so much,' she whispers.

'I know, I know,' I murmur.

The hand falls back in place on my waist. But it has temporarily lost its powers of sleep-promotion. To persuade Mum, I need an ally.

*

Nati, fourteen, and Henok, fifteen, are the two boys who trailed down the same narrow canal as me, fortunately a little while after my trip. Mother pushed us all out a year apart. Ouch! Ouch! Ouch!

As first-born, I am the fastest of us, in wit and verve if not sheer speed, while Nati is the slowest of thought and easiest to manipulate but has the athleticism of a leopard. Henok, in the middle, we do not make jokes about. Facially, we are virtually identical; my brothers are *me*, minus the understated natural beauty.

Henok thinks constantly but speaks seldom, perhaps once a day, always deliberately, wisely and with great effort. Should he speak, we stop whatever we are doing and listen intently, enjoying the novelty of his quiet voice. Henok has never said anything funny, ever. Instead, he stews on pointless dilemmas, causing blood to trickle from his nose as though something is broken inside his head. He studies hard and is plainly intelligent but in a secretive way. He hoards his intelligence, like Nati would hoard food if he could restrain himself from eating it.

Unlike Henok, Nati fails to study anything at school. He routinely attains zero in his tests but, as he explains to Mum, 'at least zero is a number'. Nati's simple engine runs on Mum's cooking, Arsenal Football Club and strident chatter: with staggering frequency, his opinion is both unconsidered and improbably accurate. Nati's intellect defies scientific explanation, and mine. He's unsuitable as my potential ally but slightly less so than Henok. So Nati it is.

'Mum! Look at the moon . . . it's so big and bright! I've never seen it like that,' he says to Mum, on the evening of a full moon.

'That's because you're poor. Only the rich hold their heads up proudly and see the moon, while we trudge and traipse. We bear our burdens with bowed heads. The moon is a sight reserved for the rich and the arrogant.'

'So you're telling me *not* to look at the moon?' says Nati downheartedly.

'Look at it, but it won't do you any good.'

Nati's contrary reaction is to walk tall for a couple of days, head held very high, never glancing downwards. Arrogance dallies with absurdity as Nati navigates the track outside our house with its haphazard selection of badly fitting rocks capable of tripping up a snake. Hanging at head-height, the washing lines dangling across our alleyway force us to duck as we watch our feet: Nati's new gait quickly earns him scuffed knees and a nasty rope burn on his neck. He sensibly adopts a different approach: for five minutes every night, he stands outside our door and stares at the moon.

'For five minutes, I stand tall and feel rich,' he explains to me. 'For five minutes, I'm on the same platform as the affluent of Addis. We all have the same view of the same moon.'

I notice the scar on his neck.

'I can still see the rope burn . . . looks like a love-bite,' I chuckle.

'Yeah, Sis, the poor hang their heads because their washing lines are too low . . . it has nothing to do with bearing our burdens.'

Barely into adolescence, this wooden post of a boy is almost lofty enough to hold up our corrugated iron roof with his head.

'You're so tall. What happened to you? Yesterday a boy, today a man, tomorrow . . .'

'A president,' says Nati hopefully.

We slump onto the old sofa. This is my chance.

'President? You'll need more than a few injeras inside you for *that*. I can't believe where the last ten years have gone. What have we done since we moved here?'

'Well, Sis, I played football and ate a mountain of injera, you drank coffee and slept a lot, Mum went to church every day and scraped together a living to feed us, Henok stayed silent and studied . . . oh, and we watched Haile win the Olympic gold on our neighbour's television.'

Nati's summary of our life is horrifically exact. That is it for ten years: a family's life in a sentence.

'But life is *going*,' I say urgently. 'It's too fast! At sixteen in Ethiopia, I'm already through one third of my life expectancy. By breaking up lifetimes into days, lots of days, God has fooled us into thinking there's more of it than there really is. He's engineered time to appear non-threatening, to lull us into dull routines. But step back from it, Nati . . . what do you see?'

'What do I see? Nothing! We're too poor to step back from it, Sis. If we can't even enjoy the moon, how can we look at time? Haven't you noticed, Sis . . . time's *invisible*!'

'Nati, just try it. You'll see people hurtling towards their deaths at a panic-inducing speed. If everyone could see it, there'd be total chaos. Days are good for sedating most people . . . like sleeping pills. Days are sleeping pills. But they don't work on me any more. I see what's happening now . . . at sixteen, I'm practically *dead*.'

'Sis, have you been eating chat?'

'I've drunk too much coffee.'

'There's nothing we can do about time, Sis. Or is there?' asks Nati, unsure whether the passing of time can be manipulated in some way, like the passing of a football. He has the ability to lob it, flick it, whack it, bend it, backheel it or waste it. What tricks can be done with time? All we've done so far is waste it exceedingly well.

'I tried school and now I'm trying work,' I say. 'The pay is only a little more than a damp rag in my hand. Meanwhile, time is running away down the hill, laughing its head off like a crazed lunatic.'

Nati yawns aggressively. I sigh as though struggling for my final breath. Moments bloated on boredom sneak away like nifty babies crawling towards blazing fires when nobody is watching them for a split second.

'It feels like we're waiting for something to happen. Are we going to stay like this forever, Sis?'

'We'll die one day . . . so, no.'

Come on, Nati, *bite*.

'We need money, Sis!' he shouts. 'Not just small money for meat and coffee . . . *real* money.'

Yes!

'Yeah, you're right . . . money. It's all about money. We've never had enough since we came here. But Mum's not interested in getting a load of money. She has the Bible.'

'Maybe I should play for Arsenal,' he suggests with a straight face.

'Maybe I should be a servant in Lebanon,' I say, casually enough.

'That would be easier,' replies Nati, no shock visible.

'How would I tell Mum I was leaving her and may not see her for several years? And it's just for the money . . .'

Nati strokes his slightly stubbly chin. This usually prefaces improbable wisdom.

'My suggestion . . . wait until she's really, really happy so the bad news doesn't sting so much. I'll help you, Sis.'

In Nati, I have my ally.

The Right Moment

Outside, Mum has arrived home from evening prayers, her head and body swathed in the white chiffon netela and kemis that women wear to enter an Orthodox Christian church.

'Stop at the door!' screams Mum from outside, as Henok comes back from playing with friends in the street.

A daily occurrence, Henok *has* to stop at the door. He removes the stinking trainers and socks from his feet. Beside him sits a metal bowl: these bowls are generally used for covering chickens with severed necks, slowly perishing before being plucked, scalded and boiled for dinner. But chickens for most Addis residents, including us, are a treat reserved for special religious occasions only, especially Christmas and Easter.

Holding a lemon to her nose, Mum throws the metal bowl over the trainers and socks in a single swift movement, as though trapping a speedy rat.

'Got you!' she shouts victoriously.

Mum says it's a bone problem. Apparently, a foul-smelling fungus is nibbling away at Henok's metatarsals, particularly voracious during the rainy season, which is now. As one of gangrene's gentler cousins, the solution is happily less painful than amputation, requiring two fresh lemons, sliced in half and squeezed onto the bare feet, before hard scrubbing into the skin. His feet are soon sticky with lemon juice, the citrus tang pleasantly sharpening the air. We can all relax and breathe inwards.

Having completed the lemon-juice treatment, Henok wears sandals to go outside and wash his hands under the tap. Tadelle arrives at the same moment, watching Henok carefully.

Tadelle is becoming as dispiritingly regular as the metal bowl ritual. Inside the doorway, Tadelle instinctively glances at the metal bowl. It all seems so obvious to him. He thinks Henok is washing his hands because he's been slashing the neck of a chicken now twitching away under the bowl. Tadelle theatrically sucks in the air of our house.

'Ah, lemons again!' he says knowingly. Typically, lemon juice is used with salt to clean skinned chickens before cooking. Tadelle's saliva glands are instantly activated.

I often imagine Tadelle has been plucked from the Bible and placed two millennia hence without physical alteration. The shaggy beard, ragged tunic, haggard looks, tattered sandals, cracked staff and shattered body is not an affected image: he is an Old Testament natural, most at ease on Moses' shoulder, forging across the Sinai Desert with a couple of heavy stone tablets under his arm. The Old Testament is for Tadelle a statement of fact, a guide to life. The coming of Jesus was an unnecessary appendix, an anti-climax no less.

'Judaism was already gathering pace. Jesus just rushed things along. His miracles throw doubt on the Bible's authenticity. We don't need the New Testament's superficiality and its easy answers. Before Jesus came along, we had the Testament . . . no silly comparisons of *old* and *new* . . .' Tadelle is explaining to Mum in the doorway.

'You said that yesterday,' says Mum. She says that every day to Tadelle.

'But it's still true today, Werknesh.'

Of course it is. They are inside an eternal loop. Repeated conversations are part of the conspiracy to blind us to the speeding sands of time. God allows us to repeat ourselves ad infinitum: we think we're being fresh and clever while we butcher the precious minutes, shifting life cycles along a notch or two for no particular reason, though He must have His motives. Whatever those are.

'Sit down and drink coffee . . . we'll talk about it a little more,' offers Mum.

Urgh. Again.

Perhaps Tadelle thinks Mum is 'available'. He looks considerably older than her. Mum retains areas of skin where wrinkles are scarce: her cheeks, for example, are as smooth as the neighbours' television screen. Unfortunately, her lack of teeth adds twenty years every time she opens her mouth but, like a television, we can buy a new set when the suitcase of money arrives. Mum can pass for thirty-five outside of fasting periods. Her actual date of birth, like many born outside Addis, is pure speculation.

As for Tadelle, there has to be an Old Testament chapter and verse referencing his birth, but we haven't found it yet.

'Hello, Meron. How are you today?' he asks.

'I'm fine, thanks. And you?'

'Fine! What have you done today?'

Thanks. More seconds of my life butchered in the abattoir of pointless patter.

'Nothing. How's Moses today?'

'Wonderful! He says "hi".'

Tadelle probably hopes my mother will nurse him through his old age, as well as caring for his four children. According to rumours, his wife died from being struck by a bolt of lightning. That strikes me as a decent Old Testament death and carries a strong message that Tadelle should happily accept: God prefers him single. Don't embroil my mother in your sordid plans, Tadelle; she's still nursing us out of childhood.

Tadelle stares at the metal bowl, covering the rank shoes at the entrance. He always does. Only the rich eat chicken *every* day. Maybe this is why he lurks around my mother.

'And what about the love thy neighbour as thyself passage . . . albeit from the New Testament. But what a thing of beauty. It does of course refer to sharing . . . sharing of possessions when a neighbour is needy . . . of food . . . when a neighbour is hungry . . . be it injera, coffee or chicken . . .' continues the crafty old bandit.

'Yes, Tadelle,' says my mother patiently. 'Listen, today, stay for dinner if you're really hungry.'

'Oh, wonderful, Werknesh! Thank you so very much!'

Tadelle nods at the metal bowl, as if to say 'Did you hear that? You're working for *me* today.'

At dinner time, Nati comes home. He's always through the door at the exact moment of dinner: he *has* to be, or the best of our dinner could be lost to another stomach. But seeing Tadelle still sitting on the sofa and Mum not yet preparing the food, Nati makes a logical deduction.

'What's *he* doing here? Mum, I have to eat *now*!' he erupts.

'Sorry about my son, Tadelle . . . really rude.'

'But we have to eat!' shouts Nati again.

In his world, nothing and nobody must be allowed to stop food.

'Tadelle's staying for dinner . . .' starts Mum.

'Your mother very kindly invited me to stay for the chicken,' beams Tadelle, using his wooden staff to tap the metal bowl tunefully.

'Chicken?' exclaims Nati, immediately detecting something awry.

'Yes, it's just like a holiday, eating chicken together. Wonderful!' enthuses Tadelle.

We're all grinning at each other. Even Henok sneaks out a rare smirk.

'Okay. Come and have a look at it . . . a really *big* one today,' offers Nati beside the bowl.

Tadelle clambers to his feet. Within a single short stride, his face suddenly fervent and predatory, he is doubled over, only a nostril whisker from the metal bowl. I have never seen him like this before, certainly not during the Old Testament discussions with Mum.

'And here it is!' declares Nati, yanking up the bowl to reveal putrid footwear.

The stench hits us all hard. Tadelle staggers backwards in shock, hand instinctively cupped onto his nose.

'I'm so sorry! I thought . . .' Tadelle stutters through a nasal muffle. He grabs his staff and reels out of the door. Nati hastily replaces the bowl in its correct position.

Mum roars with laughter strong enough to fan a fire. It's an extraordinary moment. Nati catches my eye. It's a Lebanon moment.

'My own feet are a little itchy,' I say.

'Use some of the lemon juice,' suggests my mother through her snorts.

That subtlety hasn't worked. Cackling away, Mum serves our usual dinner fare of injera and shiro wat, a spicy chickpea stew. I will just have to say it.

'I'm going to work in Lebanon as a maid,' I say loudly.

'Meron, don't spoil it with one of your silly lies,' chortles Mum.

'It's not a lie, Mum. I mean it.'

Absolute silence descends within a second. I have just killed one of the funniest moments in the family's history.

'What are you talking about? You're happy here,' begins Mum.

'I want to do something with my life before it's too late. I'm wasting my time here. The years are passing too fast. I want money, I want confidence, I want to be like Selam,' I blabber. It all sounds so weak. My timing was dreadful. Why did I listen to the advice of a fourteen-year-old boy?

'Habesha girls don't come back from Beirut. Why are you even considering this?' she reasons. 'I try my best to make you happy. Every day I work hard for you, I pray hard for you . . . what's the problem, my daughter? Can't you trust in God to care for us . . . for *you*?'

'I'm not sure any more, Mum . . . maybe His care is overstretched . . .'

A huge well of sadness is opening up. This has been buried for years and here it is again, spreading right across her face: fresh, raw, heartbreaking grief.

'Don't worry, Mum. You're not *losing* me, I promise I'll come back. After two years in Lebanon, I'll probably buy us a condominium . . . ha!'

'Think of the money she'll send back! And more food for us! What's the big deal, Mum? Let her go and we'll be rich enough to stare at the moon all day,' rejoices Nati, supporting me at last.

'Or all night would be more fun,' I correct.

We sit in silence for a minute. A droplet of blood forms on the end of Henok's nose.

'I can't let you go there,' Mum starts. 'It's God-less and dangerous.'

'Mum! I can look after myself now. I'm not a kid! I need to do something outside Addis. You said we need change.'

'When did I say we need *change*?'

'That day we had bread instead of injera . . . the same day I saw Selam.'

'Uh?'

'And you're right . . . we need change. Here it is!'

Henok is clutching a tissue to his nose, the tissue quickly reddening with blood. If only he would say something.

'Yeah . . . Mum . . .' adds Nati slowly, too jammed up with food to speak.

'No . . . no. I can't let her go. Sorry.'

We resume dinner, but the family plate is now bare. Nati has successfully exploited the hiatus, his jaws almost unable to function against the solid ball of injera stuffed into his mouth.

We sit silently for a while. I have lost my appetite anyway. Lebanon is off. Nati chews sullenly. Henok is in danger of losing a head-full of blood. Mum is trying to make conversation with me.

'How are the customers at Elephant Walk?'

'Fine.'

'How's Tsehay?'

'Fine.'

'How's the traffic in Bole Road?'

'Fine.'

'How's the food in Elephant Walk? What's on the menu?'

'Pizzas, injera, firfir, tibs, kitfo—'

'Mum! Let her go!' barks Nati, unable to stand the names of delicious Ethiopian dishes unless he's actually eating them.

'No, I can't,' says Mum firmly.

'Look at us . . . sitting here, bored as always . . . no television, no satellite, no variation in food. At least let one of us *try* for something more. In rich countries, dollar bills just lie around on the street,' pleads Nati, now sounding impressive.

'No.'

'Mum, *you've* done enough. I can get us back to where we *were*. This is for the family, not just for me. I want to see us return to comfort . . . the way it was,' I push, suddenly happening upon a valid motive for Lebanon.

37

'Yeah, Mum!' shouts Nati. 'This is all for *you*!'

'In that case, no, thank you. I decline the offer.'

I groan. Nati has ruined it.

Blood is spurting and bubbling out of Henok's nose with a life of its own. The three of us look aghast at him. It's never been this bad before. Mum holds Henok's shoulders and shakes him violently. I expect to see limbs flying off.

'What are you thinking? Say it! Say it!' she shrieks into his face.

Henok's forehead scrunches in concentration. So rarely do they flow, but words must be squeezed out of that head: words as sharp as the lemon juice dripping from his feet and vital as the blood spitting from his nose.

'Mum . . . will you please let her go to Lebanon before I drop dead?' says Henok steadily.

'Even Henok supports me! And it'll be better than plodding up and down Bole Road every day . . . I'll be *useful* at last!'

'Ishee,' says Mum at last, indicating a non-retractable 'Yes!'

'All of us want her to go, except *you*, Mum. What's your problem?' continues Nati.

'I said ishee! If you push me any more, I'll withdraw my ishee,' says Mum tetchily.

'She said *ishee*!' I proclaim. 'Nati, shut up! I'm going to Lebanon! We'll be rich!'

'But what about your age? You must be too young,' says Mum, detecting a fault line.

'I don't know . . .'

'The minimum age is eighteen, Meron . . . you're sixteen.'

'Nooo . . .' I whine.

'Change your birth certificate!' shoots Nati.

'How can I do that?' I ask. 'How, Mum? Tell me, *please*!'

'I'll talk to the kebelle. I have a contact person there at the local municipal office . . . they can get a false one for you, I think.'

Nati and I cheer as though Thierry Henry has scored for Arsenal. Henok staggers to his bed and lies down for a while, leaving droplets of blood about the place. Mum's face darkens as though she is peering into a blackened oven of sizzling meat. We have no meat. No animal has been slaughtered. At least, not yet.

Mum obtains the falsified birth certificate within days. I am suddenly an absurdly young-looking nineteen-year-old. Coincidentally, Mum stops wearing her wedding ring at this time – a major development for her – but with my head so full of Lebanon, I forget to ask her why. She is hardly talkative anyway. Perhaps her heart is open for business again after a protracted closure.

The agency sends my details to Beirut. A potential employer, the 'sponsor', chooses me on the basis of my photo. The agency arranges a work visa. Vaccinations are acquired, a health check endured. We pay three thousand birr for all of this. Mum now has no savings. The agency books the flight for Beirut. I start packing.

The anticipation electrifies my every thought and movement but I work hard at repressing my urge to giggle at nothing in particular. Nobody else around me has an exit from the grime of Addis; nobody else is in the mood for sniggering like a fool. Now I can ridicule the brazen men and mock the constant morass of the rainy season. I can even tolerate the unrelenting flies. I am sure there will be no flies in Lebanon.

My Funeral

Today sees the end of the thirteenth month on our calendar, and tomorrow is New Year's Day. Every Ethiopian year enjoys a straggle of five or six extra days, ganging together to form what we generously describe as the thirteenth 'month', though it looks more like a 'week' to me. This is not the only unique feature of our calendar: by taking a flight from Addis Ababa to Beirut today, I will instantly jump from 10th September 1996 to 18th May 2004. There is nothing special about the Ethiopian Airways flight. It will not be whizzing through time: merely 2,800 kilometres of space. Seven or eight years – depending on whether it's a Leap Year – always separate the Ethiopian Coptic calendar from the International Gregorian calendar. And whereas we have thirteen months, the rest of the world has twelve. I learnt all this at school.

We tell the time differently too. By travelling to Beirut, I will relocate from an ancient system based on the number of hours passed after sunrise or sunset to Universal Time, previously known as Greenwich Mean Time: in Addis, it is often termed 'international time' in contrast to 'Habesha time'. Nine o'clock in the morning Universal Time is three hours after sunrise in Ethiopia: therefore, it is three o'clock Habesha time, *not* 9am. Fortunately, in Ethiopia, the sun always rises and sets around 6am and 6pm in Universal Time, and the twelve-hour clock recommences at these times. No difference officially exists between Beirut and Addis Ababa, but as an Ethiopian abroad I will soon be aware of the six-hour gap. School also taught me this.

It is unlikely that anything else learnt in school will serve me in any way at all, except hopefully my English. They did *not* teach us how to be domestic servants. Or how to survive two years and three months without my mother. Or how to cope with the Middle Eastern culture. Calendars, Leap Years, time zones and clocks all seem meaningless today. I go *today*. I leave my family, my home, my city, my mother *today*. Whether it's nine o'clock or three o'clock, 1996 or 2004, heart-mangling physical removal is heart-mangling physical removal. School didn't ready me for *this*.

'Auntie Kidist is here to say goodbye,' announces Mum, jolting me from my last-minute brooding.

'Good luck, Meron . . . but it's a big mistake,' says Kidist, trying to pull a smile across her broad, slightly squashed head.

Younger than Mum, Kidist is a sturdy-framed woman with little rolls of fat evenly dispersed about her body, cleverly saved up for another major food shortage. These little rolls also appear in her cheeks, thus softening the blows of her husband's fists when he beats her. It is strange that such a bright, kind face would invite the sharp knuckles of the one who loves her. Kidist is designed for cuddling not punching, but her husband, Desalegn, thinks otherwise.

'I know you think it's wrong, Auntie, but we all make mistakes . . . let me make a really *big* one and I might even learn something,' I say, beaming bravely.

She kisses and hugs me, but there's something missing in her embrace. If she thinks I was hinting at *her* mistake in marrying Desalegn, then she's absolutely right. Or it could be that she is terrified of our family becoming wealthier than hers.

'Bye, Auntie,' I continue, 'and don't be jealous of my escape from Addis, or the riches that I'll gather.'

'Uh? I'm not.'

Kidist baulks and leaves abruptly. Mum rolls her eyes at me, as if to say 'sorry' for her sister.

Sat on his usual step outside our house, like a wizened old timer, bare feet splayed, grubby hands resting on scuffed knees, itching to slap his own thighs at his own jokes, the usual mucky rags hanging from his frame for the sake of modesty, face screwed up into a constant scoff at the harsh midday sun, Abush, a stunted nine-year-old street kid who serves no useful purpose in the world, looks me up and down, licks his lips and makes an utterance.

'Hey, Lemma, you're almost Beyoncé.'

'Thanks, Abush,' I reply curtly, lumbering with my luggage.

He calls everyone by the old countryside names of their fathers. This is to embarrass my neighbours who prefer to forget their rustic peasant pasts. In Addis, only modern surnames will do. Names make no difference to me today. Lemma, Meron, Beyoncé, who cares? I'm almost not here.

'Don't worry, Lemma! Beyoncé's eyes are wonky . . . yours are straight. Where are you going with the suitcase?'

'Lebanon, two years. Will you survive that long?'

'Survive? That's what I do,' he replies, beckoning me closer so he can whisper. 'Listen, I think the government has missed something, something *big* . . . just between you and me, okay? I eat food from everyone else . . . from their garbage. I get all my food from other people's garbage, Lemma. Free food! I pay *nothing*!'

'Eh? But that makes you sick, Abush, eating other people's rubbish.'

'Sick? Never. Stomach adapts, and anyway, no germs in Addis . . . they're all in Germany . . .'

He falls on the ground chortling. Three other boys race over and join in. They have no idea what they are laughing at. All the germs are in Germany. Ridiculous.

'Hey, Lemma, who's going to pay me your one birr every day?' yells Abush.

This is a street kid's way of saying 'I'll miss you'. Abush does not admit to soft emotions like that.

'Payment in advance. One birr per year . . . two years, that's two birr. Bye, Abush.'

'Good girl . . . and don't give yourself to an Arab. You're already spoken for, Lemma. I've got first claim on you!' he shouts threateningly.

I toss the two birr at him. It is expected. The dreadfully poor of Addis live off the generous poor of Addis, an informal safety net to ensure nobody dies of hunger in the streets. Abush nods appreciatively, a pair of lens-less sunglasses flopping down from his forehead onto the bridge of his buckled nose, endowing him with an almost intellectual look from a distance. But close up, he and the gutter run seamlessly.

I hesitate in case there's a 'Bye, Lemma!' but it doesn't come. I glance back. He pokes out the end of his twirling tongue at me, with its disgusting implication. Managing a slight grin, I shake my head; the final enduring memory of Abush, preserved. Two years for a street kid is a long time. I'm sure there will be no street kids in Lebanon.

Twelve of us board the blue and white minibus. There are ten supportive neighbours, my mother, the driver, myself and a black canvas suitcase with the huge white words 'MERON LEMMA' chalked onto it. This is not for reclamation purposes at the final destination: instead, my mother has assured me that nobody will steal baggage with a scrawled name on the side.

'It looks like you're boarding an aeroplane for the first time,' she explains.

'Well, I am.'

'It makes you look poor and ignorant . . .'

'Thanks, Mum . . . I appreciate that.'

'Which means there's nothing of any value in your suitcase.'

'And there isn't . . . except my snack bag of roasted barley and chickpeas, my kolo,' I joke.

'A potential thief might see the suitcase and think it's full of bedbugs,' she continues seriously. 'Open the thing and suddenly his house is infested . . . within a single night his bedlinen is dotted with blood.'

'It should act as a deterrent then, like my tracksuit and trainers.'

The tracksuit I'm wearing is like a mat of slime-green algae draped over my shoulders. The trainers are more orange than oranges. It's Mum's idea for discouraging a new Arab master from love at first sight. My hair is tied up into an unkempt ball: he might think my head is a mouldy cauliflower. Below this, no earrings, nail varnish, make-up or perfume adorn this girl. To be attracted to me will require an addled imagination, immense will-power or some mind-boggling perversion that has yet to reach Ethiopia.

As the minibus pulls away from our neighbourhood, my mother is very quiet. Her face tilts downwards as though unbearably burdened with sadness. The neighbours jabber with excitement behind us. Their eagerness to accompany us to the airport is what I choose to interpret as 'well-wishing', rather than cynical attachment to me in the hope of receiving lavish gifts upon my return. They help to divert attention from the pure awfulness of a mother–daughter parting.

Mum and I are in the passenger seat next to the driver, who is youngish, skinny, bored. At this moment, I envy him his boredom. He knows tomorrow he will be sitting in the same seat, shouting abuse at the same fellow drivers in Bole Road. He will finish work, chew chat leaves, eat injera, try to have sex and then sleep in a hut. Tomorrow, I will be in Lebanon under the charge of a complete stranger, possibly realising I have made the mistake of my life. If the driver should offer a job swap in these long agonising minutes from home to airport, I will embrace him.

Urgh! He's noticed me. Purely because I've looked at him for a second, he assumes I'm drooling over his spectacular driving skills and my heart is a single flutter away from undying love. There will be no men like *him* in Lebanon. He begins to say something.

'I wouldn't mind being a taxi driver . . . I've seen sixteen-year-old drivers before,' I say to Mum quickly, before I'm flooded with his inanities.

'You're a *girl*, not a boy. You can't drive taxis.'

'I wouldn't mind being a boy.'

That would be the easier option in Ethiopia.

'Shut up, daughter, you are what you are . . . an unworldly girl with low blood pressure who has no idea what she is doing. What do you know about cleaning a large house?'

Thank you, God. Bole Airport is suddenly before us, the international hub of Africa. I choose to check the contents of my pockets rather than answer Mum's question. I know nothing about cleaning a large house. Why *would* I?

Today, there's jostle to rival Merkato, the city's great market. Dozens of families are hanging around next to the barriers into the departures lounge, mainly led by wailing mothers.

'Okay, bye, Mum,' I say casually, readying my passport and ticket in my free hand, the downbeat suitcase in the other.

We hug tightly. I can't let go of her white robe. She's crying without sound or shudder. Mum is a passive crier with only the trickle of tears proving her sorrow. I am the same. If anyone can see me from behind, they will see that I am pumping water onto the concourse like a burst pipe silently gushing in the dead of night. Inanimate weeping is a family trait.

'Okay, Mum, it's time . . . time to go now. Tell Nati and Henok I love them . . .'

They stayed at home playing football in the street. Boys! I'm incensed at their indifference to my departure. Winning a game of street football is obviously a serious affair. When I return, I will ask them what the score was, and expect a detailed analysis of every minute of that single crucial game.

'They're just boys, don't be angry,' says my mother.

As though blind, she is stroking my face, hair, neck and shoulders, savouring the last few moments of my physicality. There's dread in her touch. I feel it.

'I'll miss you so much, Mum, I can't . . .' I'm crying again.

'I'll miss you too . . . you're doing a good thing with your life, I respect that. All I ask is that you pray, you remember your family . . . and be a good worker, show them your Habesha spirit, do what they say.'

'Yes, Mum.'

'Remember Proverbs 6:20–23: "My son, keep your father's commandment, and forsake not your mother's teaching. Bind them upon your heart always: tie them about your neck. When you walk, they will lead you: when you lie down, they will watch over you: and when you awake, they will talk with you."'

'Thanks. It's a good one.'

'Your father is still with you . . . we will both be with you whatever happens and wherever you are,' she whispers, another chiffon clinch enveloping my body.

'Oh God, I want to stay!' I moan.

'You can! Let's go home and be happy!'

A security guy smirks across at me suggestively. Stay here and I'm exchanging my adult life in return for *that*, or something a lot like *that*. The alternative to Lebanon is not pretty. The security guy provides the little push that I need to walk away into my new future. Is this why the airport employs him?

'Mum, I'm really going now . . . I'll be in touch, I promise.'

'Put your trust in God and He will deliver you back to me.'

'Yes, Mum,' I splutter.

One final frantic hug and I run from her. I don't even see the barriers. But I take one last quick glance back.

No! She's adopted her funeral posture: hands behind back, standing to attention, head bowed slightly, fending off the frown of grief before it folds in upon her entire head. Does she think her daughter is as good as *dead*? The face collapses with catastrophe as everything beneath and behind seeps into a hidden drain that can never be closed. Is this how it is to die in front of your own mother? Because I have never seen anything so terrible.

I want to shout at her. Mum, I'm not dead! But it's too late.

I must concentrate on catching the flight. I race towards passport control, rubbing tears from my face. Maybe I *will* die. Oh God, how can a 'goodbye' turn into a presumption of death? *Mum! I'm so sorry!*

Ah! No photo! I have no photo of my mother, my brothers, nobody. But there's no turning back now. I'm through too many barriers. Final call for Beirut. I try to hold the image of my mother in my mind: I'm terrified of losing her face. At least a photo is kissable, something to clench, something to pore over again and again. But in the hurly-burly of the airport, I'm struggling with a precise recall of my mother, my mind urgently flicking through an album of blank pages but finding nothing. How can it be so difficult to summon a vision of the woman who has cared for me from the womb onwards?

With the mass of strangers around me, I can remember only her picture as a young woman, posing with my father, my brothers and me in the last family photograph. It rests in our diminutive living room and always has done. Her face is an unforgettable portrait of calm wrath, but it's better than nothing. It's okay, Mum, I have you.

Second Incision

The plane roars down the runway and lurches upwards. My petite feet leave firm ground, my body departs the only place it's ever known: with each metre's climb, the plane is cleaving me from my mother like a second severing of the umbilical cord. For the first nine months of my life, mother and foetus were uninterrupted in our bond, my dependence total, until someone sliced through the cord on the day of my birth. I could do nothing about that. Death – hers or mine – was due to be the next bond-breaker. But today, it's *me* who makes a second incision: an extra unnecessary one, with help from Ethiopian Airlines flight 067. Congratulations, Meron, for putting impossible distance between yourself and the most important person in your life. The emergency exit doors are conveniently positioned and exceedingly well signposted. Maybe I should use one.

I inhale very deeply.

Instead of leaping from an emergency exit, I read about Lebanon. Henok printed off a page from the internet in preparation for my journey. It says: 'Lebanon is a small country lodged between Syria and Israel with a population of around four million. Beirut is the capital city of Lebanon. Life is pleasant in Beirut. Its nightlife is famous all over the world, providing entertainment both for the country's fun-loving, carefree inhabitants and for the visitors who, from the minute they step on Lebanese soil, feel the country's welcome.' Ah, soothing words! Whether true or not, I feel better already.

'Arabic is Lebanon's official language,' says my printout. I speak no Arabic but my English is very reasonable. Perhaps in my free time, I will attend evening classes in Arabic. I feel reassured by this prospect. 'Before the civil war (1975–1990), Beirut was known as the "Paris of the Middle East" due to its opulence and style. Indeed, Lebanon was under French Rule from 1926 to 1943, hence the continued use of French in some aspects of Lebanese life.' I want to learn French as well. Yes! Now I see it. I shall return to Addis fluent in Arabic and French, switching between four languages as effortlessly as taxi drivers changing lanes in Bole Road, without use of signs, mirrors or eyes. I'll be a multi-millionaire multi-linguist! I don't need to be a Hollywood movie star after all.

I'm passed a packet of nuts. Free nuts! I love *noise food*. Crunching and crackling: who's interested in sight, smell and taste when you can fill depressing silence with noise food?

I munch exuberantly as I deliberate over the climate notes for Lebanon: 'The weather is especially hot in the summer, with cool winters. A sea breeze can be expected to blow in from the Eastern Mediterranean Sea, cooling sunbathers on the capital's famous beaches.' Beirut has beaches! I will begin my new exercise regime by jogging along the sandy shoreline each morning before the sun is hot. My body will quickly sweat off the puppy fat, and the slender frame of an Ethiopian distance runner will step forward. I shall return to Addis and become a professional runner, probably an international track star within weeks. Haile Gebrselassie will leave unanswered messages on my voicemail. Derartu Tulu will copy my hairstyle and look ludicrous. Like Haile, I will have a major thoroughfare named after me in Addis, preferably one where nobody ever dies in road accidents.

'Lebanon is renowned as a centre of fashion.' I laugh out loud. It just gets better and better. I *love* fashionable things, even if I never wear them. How will that *not* touch me? I shall amaze Mum and my friends with head-turning dresses . . .

'What you reading, sister?' interrupts a voice from my left. She's Habesha but speaking in the familiar idiom of American English. To speak like this in Addis is seen either as excellent modern style, or as an outright betrayal of Ethiopia and all of its beautiful traditional mother tongues spoken for thousands of years. To me, it's a reasonable way to communicate but hardly a free pass into the State of Cool.

The woman is too large for her seat. Her stomach is sleeping on my elbow. The extra weight softens everything about her: she looks friendly solely on the basis that she is fat. She is so obviously a good person. I like that, my country likes that: Habesha people aspire to attain this weighty, friendly, floppy look. I should fatten up while in Lebanon: a rich country compared with Ethiopia and, according to my notes, 'endowed with a fertile soil for agriculture'. I shall return to Addis a contented curvy lady, quite obviously unworried by such issues as starvation and cramped aeroplane seats. I'll always have a kind word for my crushed fellow passengers.

But wait, there's a contradiction. I can't be a *fat* long-distance runner: it would upset all the generous donor countries. Skinny runners look better for Ethiopia's aid programme.

'Hello?' insists the voice to my left.

Maybe I'll take up shot putt.

'Sister?'

'Sorry,' I reply, 'just daydreaming about Lebanon. I'm reading about Lebanon. Do you know Lebanon?'

I really enjoy saying 'Lebanon'. I'll be a resident of Lebanon within hours.

'Yeah, I know Lebanon. You?'

'I live there.'

Lies tumble from my lips at times, often without malice or mischief, though I prefer not to call them 'lies'.

'Really? Your English is so good . . . you speak Arabic too?' she asks.

'Yes, I'm a multi-lingual . . .' I pause.

'What?'

'Er . . . shot putter.'

'You're kidding me,' she says with a flat tone suggesting total disbelief. 'You're gonna be a servant, right? First time, I imagine, by the looks of you. Why you gotta lie all the time?'

'Not really lying . . . more like projecting hope through my words, which is *not* in the Ten Commandments.'

'Ah! That must be why I smoke . . . not prohibited in the Bible. You just legitimised most of my sins, sister, thank you very much.'

'You don't look like a *major* sinner. What else do you do?' I ask.

'I shop, sister . . . I shop . . . always looking for the markdowns out there . . . can't rest till I got them all. Mostly in the States, when I visit my brothers.'

'Why are you going to Beirut? Are you a servant?'

'Third time. What does *that* tell you?'

And look at her! Positively full-figured off the servant life.

'But not everyone has a good experience, do they?' I ask tentatively.

'It's a question of luck . . . you get it or you don't. You won't know until it's too late. Not trying to scare you, but that's the way it works. What's your name?'

'Meron.'

'I'm Beti. Everyone knows me. I'm a success story.'

'I can see that . . .'

She laughs so loudly and intensely the plane seems to jerk forward suddenly.

'Don't worry, sister. If you use your head, you'll survive . . . with luck, you'll thrive,' continues Beti, unfazed by the turbulence. 'Two-year contract?'

'Yes, but only after three months' probationary . . . no pay till August. They get three months' free labour out of me.'

'That's tough, sister.'

A flight attendant passes me a tray. Her make-up is incredible. I want to be her, but without the plane trips.

'Free bread and butter! Fantastic!' I proclaim as I'm handed a dry roll with a plastic pod of butter. Beti grins at me: I am as fresh as they come.

The flight is fast. Beti chatters with many different girls like a celebrity. I sleep and dream about a pack of dogs chasing me through the streets of Cairo. I have never been to Cairo. But I have been there now and I don't like what I see. As I snap awake, the wheels smack onto the Beirut runway. We're beside the sea! I have never seen the sea. It's not quite the brilliant blue I expected, but filthy indigo is enough for *me*.

The time in Beirut International Airport is 5.45pm, 18th May 2004. That's 11.45 Habesha time, 10th September 1996. Eight years just flashed by in a single flight. I am now living in the third millennium, like most of the world. Welcome to the future, Meron!

Beirut Airport is brightly lit with white and grey stripes filling the voids between the aeroplane and an arrivals lounge. There are dozens of us; young Habesha girls, fiddling with our hair, manically chewing gum, waiting to greet our new families; to meet our destinies. How many of us will see Addis again?

We're herded like sheep into a quiet part of the arrivals area by a gruff Arab man with an achingly big stomach. He's the agency guy. He orders us to sit down on the hard white and grey floor. I'm next to Beti.

A few rows of Lebanese people gaze at us. They sit on chairs. When the agency guy speaks to us, his belly trembles as if nodding in agreement. None of us understand his Arabic, but he clutches our passports close to the belly. He shouts names, girls jump up, the Lebanese onlookers stride forward and escort the girls away, their fate decided. I'm trembling more than the belly. I don't want a hand-chopping, ledge-pushing type of sponsor family. I want a handholding, third-millennium family with a weakness for injera.

'Alem Getu!'

'Merry Demeka!'

'Hewot Beyene!'

'Meron Lemma!'

Ah!

I'm on my feet and turn to wave goodbye to Beti. Her face betrays concern for me.

'Call . . . soon as you have any problems, sister . . . and don't forget, we meet up on Sundays. Head for Badaro . . . you'll see the netelas . . .'

I can't stop to listen. People, my people, are waiting. Who's getting me? My new life begins *now*.

First Day in Lebanon
(820 days left)

I try to snatch my passport from the agency guy. As my fingers brush it, I feel the warmth of his belly on the passport, but it's quickly pulled away from me. He shakes his head at me as the passport goes to a dazzlingly attractive woman with dyed blonde hair, not a strand out of place.

She's my new mother! I feel instantly happy. Yes! Yes! *Yes!* I'm definitely smiling.

Around fifty years old, with a friendly well-proportioned face, she has the searing green eyes of a half-breed Siamese, the type of cat that occasionally skulks along our passageway in Addis. Her mouth is generous enough to engulf a large soup ladle, with shiny pretty teeth hanging from a bulwark of prominent pink gums. Faultless bone-chopstick fingers dance and draw my attention with fingernails filed into perfectly rounded daisy petals the shade of Ethiopian cotton bolls. I envy her slim body sporting today's fashion: tight black trousers, bright orange flowered top, sexy black boots with heels. I wanted a chic sponsor; it appears I've won the lottery. You see, Mum, I'm going to be fine.

She pretends to kiss my cheeks three times. Glossed lips hover above my face unable to land on Habesha flesh. This must be the Lebanese way, though there's nothing in my notes about that.

'Hello, Meron, I am pleased to meet you. My name is Rahima. But call me Madame. Welcome to Beirut,' she says slowly and carefully. 'Madame is French word. I speak French and English.'

Thank you, God!

'Hello, Madame,' I mumble. Shyness consumes me. A wide tree would be useful for hiding behind in these first few minutes. How about a baobab?

'You are beautiful, like your photo, Meron.'

'Thank you, Madame,' I giggle, suddenly a four-year-old.

'I choose you because the photo . . . you try to look good . . . others try to look ugly, maybe because they know Lebanese woman . . . we very jealous women,' she laughs. 'Not me . . . why I need to be jealous?'

Good point. I'm already jealous of her.

'Yes, Madame, I like to look good, but difficult in Addis.'

'I not like other mesdames, Meron. I want to see beauty . . . like young face in mornings . . . and my own face of course!' she chuckles.

She leads me outside, but doesn't offer to carry my suitcase. Madame points me into the cramped back seat of a waiting vehicle. A tall, tracksuited gentleman in his thirties handles my baggage as though it's as light as a letter.

He drives us away in an expensive blue Mercedes sports car, or some other type that makes a man of its driver. In Bole Road, a man is defined by his car: this guy in his Mercedes would instantly fill that yawning gap between mortal earthly man and our dear Lord God.

The way Madame and the driver joke and tease each other, I think he's her husband. The couple in front of me is a snapshot of joy. I feel relaxed. Madame doesn't seem like the ledge-pushing type.

'This is Mister Shafeek,' says Madame. 'He's international lawyer.'

'Have you been in a car like this before?' asks Shafeek in excellent English, glancing at me in his mirror.

'Not very often, Mister,' I answer. They chortle knowingly. Of course I haven't.

'Beautiful eyes,' he says to me, the glance stretching into a gaze. Madame cranes her neck from the front and checks my eyes.

'Mmm . . . you right,' she says encouragingly, 'certainly big.'

'Thank you,' I reply sheepishly, lowering my big eyes a little.

'I've been to Ethiopia twice,' he says. 'On business. I stayed in the Sheraton. Great hotel, so much better than the Hilton and Ghion. I've stayed in thirteen different Sheratons now. Can you believe that? I met a load of heads of state at the Addis one, all there for an African Union conference . . . really interesting . . . I saw Gaddafi . . . Mugabe . . .'

As Shafeek waffles, Madame caresses his schoolboy features with a light sweep. His black hair is greased back into a carefully groomed phalanx of curls at the back. Light stubble textures a face blessed without a single obvious flaw. Good teeth, delicate mouth, lovely boyish eyes, modest nose: he offers up an inviting image for Madame to stroke. In fact, he has some of Madame's attributes: searing green half-breed Siamese eyes, the bulwark of gums when he smiles . . . ah! He's the *son*, not the husband.

'And there's a huge square where everyone goes running, backwards and forwards . . . what's the name of it?' he goes on.

'Meskel Square,' I reply.

'Mister . . . you call me Mister.'

'Meskel Square, *Mister*. Sorry.'

'I used the Sheraton gym and the pool . . . yeah, not bad . . .'

Shafeek's body is compact, muscular and hard, unequivocally a product of gym workouts. I doubt he has acquired it by carrying goats on his shoulders like the Habesha farmers slogging into Addis, sweating and stinking of the animals they live with, their bodies sinewy from constant grappling with lively goats that would prefer not to be slayed. Instead, Shafeek's tanned contoured body has been pushing gleaming metallic weights and marinating in a sophisticated high-end aftershave. Adorable when deep in concentration, those emerald eyes dart mischievously into the rear-view mirror, checking me, checking the traffic, I'm not sure which.

'So cheap there. I could probably survive in Ethiopia for a year on a week's salary . . .'

Superficial yes, Mum, but Shafeek is the most handsome and most important man I have ever met. This is *exactly* the type of man we need in Ethiopia. How could Auntie Kidist settle for Desalegn when there are men like this in the world?

'The weather was good too, not oppressively hot. I didn't sweat like I do here . . .'

Madame snorts and says things in Arabic, some words familiar: Arabic and Amharic are both Semitic languages, but not close enough for immediate mutual understanding.

Urgh. I notice an incongruity in Shafeek's careful grooming. Like Henok, he houses something odorous within his shoes. A distinctive whiff has escaped and settled stubbornly in the car: nature's perfume unlocked. I'm homesick already.

Perhaps aware of his own emission, Shafeek activates the electric windows to purr open. I gaze out at Beirut, my new city. Impatient traffic crawls along hard asphalt streets. The air is heavy with exhaust fumes. A quick spurt of speed down narrow side roads and we're jammed up again. Shafeek pelts the car horn in the same instant as squeezing the brake. He manoeuvres us through such tight gaps that I instinctively draw in my breath each time. He's a superb driver, if a little irate.

I glance at men of all ages sitting on plastic seats along pavements, puffing away on elegant sheesha pipes, discussing 'vital' topics, staring back at me sneeringly: Lebanese men at leisure. I remember the Habesha men sitting on pavements chewing chat leaves, discussing 'vital' topics, staring back at me sneeringly. The life of a man.

Beirut's backdrop is immediately unremitting. Endless

rows of dirty yellow apartment blocks merge into a single many-eyed monster surging upwards from the ground to prod a fluffy blue sky struggling to be seen. Occasional decrepit, delicate houses with wooden window shutters and semicircular balconies punctuate the wall of concrete: these frail old French colonial homes are surrounded by the monster and their chances of survival seem slim.

Back at street level, swift young women with white-chalk skin and generous black eyeliner release flapping raven hair from ponytails and sweep along even pavements with such confidence that they have to be the happiest people alive on our planet. The staring men with the sheesha pipes watch them but stay *silent* when they pass by. Men may be men, but this is a civilised country.

It's all quite fabulous to my fresh Habesha eyes more accustomed to stumbling through mud, puddles and rubbish in streets where a single high-rise building would be regarded as a national landmark. Especially heartening is the lack of Habesha girls plummeting towards those hard pavements: Beirut looks harmless enough.

But the avenues are not a-flutter with banknotes dancing in the sea breeze. The streets are bone dry: they're not silted up with liquid-gold sludge gurgling from the drains. Money is not standing on the kerbside flagging a lift. Did I really expect to see a ticker-tape parade of free cash tumbling from the concrete towers? Many of my countrymen *would*. I think of Nati and smile.

'Meron,' starts Madame.

'Yes, Madame?'

'Maybe you want to know my job. Well, I am director of Lebanese bank. Name of bank not for you. But, important thing . . . me, I'm so, so busy and I have large luxury home. That's why *you* come here.'

'Yes, Madame.'

'We live floor thirteen. And here we are!'

'Yes, Madame.'

The block looks a little grubby.

'These marks you see on side of building . . . they from gunfire and mortar shells. We live on Green Line during Lebanese Civil War . . . they catch us between two sides. But this mean nothing to you, no?'

'No, Madame.'

She's right. My tourist notes on Lebanon are light on matters of heavy bombardment.

With the Mercedes safely resting in a basement car park, we enter through a door and I see the back of a black man. No, he can't be!

'Habesha!' I gasp excitedly.

He spins round to greet us. But he's Sudanese. Urgh! My heart sinks. Manning the door, 'Sudan' stands to attention for Madame and laughs disingenuously at something Shafeek says in Arabic. He's like the Sudanese I've seen in Addis. He glances at me without a flicker of interest. We're from the same continent, neighbours no less. This seems to count for nothing: African doorman meets African domestic with a welcome of such violent indifference I immediately despise him.

We shuffle into an antiquated lift that hauls us to the top floor. Shafeek is carrying my unappealing suitcase in his left hand. My mother beat left-handedness out of us as kids, and I have always been wary of left-handers since then.

'It goes down faster than it goes up,' says Shafeek.

'Be quiet, Shafeek,' says Madame.

'Elevators like gravity . . . maybe too much sometimes,' he cackles.

I'm not sure how to answer that, so don't. I'm content to stare at the scuffed floor as though it's the finest artwork in the Middle East.

'Just remember to use the elevator if you go outside . . . there is a quicker route but you might not like it,' he continues.

'Shafeek, that not funny . . . shut up!' snaps Madame as the door finally opens.

Madame's penthouse occupies the floor's entirety. The corridor from elevator to front door is decked in marble. The front door is wooden but grandiose. Sacks of money must be lying around within. I am certain now: I've been chosen for an extravagant royal paradise.

One of Madame's daughters answers the door. She is bearing a forced smile that reveals a fence of metallic braces clamped onto her upper teeth. This barely diverts my attention from her nose. It's gargantuan and completely dominates her head. With brutal hook and keen overhang, it's a beak designed for diving at small mammals and ripping them apart. I remember the lammergeyers effortlessly floating around on thermal jet streams above Addis, seeking out live prey and ready carrion.

'I'm Nazia,' she announces.

Unable to conceal my shock at her nose, my tongue is hanging out like a strip of flaccid injera. This is one of my less valuable traits. Seconds pass as I try unsuccessfully to haul it back inside.

'Hi, I'm Meron . . . nice to meet you,' I stammer.

'How old are you?' asks Nazia, allowing the forced smile to wane without the slightest effort at sustaining it.

'Nineteen.'

'Right. I'm twenty-one and I tell people I'm twenty-one. You look about nine . . . we don't need liars here,' she says pointedly and in frighteningly fluent English. My God, she's already ripping me apart. I am today's small mammal.

'Yes, Nazia,' I reply.

Had she been born Habesha, her mother would have massaged the nose into a faultless nasal passage from bridge to tip when she was yelling her way through the first few weeks of existence. My mother smoothed my nose every day with liquid butter to iron out the imperfections. It worked. Unfortunately, social status is not determined by nose profile. I am to serve this Lebanese lammergeyer unquestioningly.

'Mum, I assume soap and water will be making an appearance in the very near future,' says Nazia, waving a hand under her nose exaggeratedly.

'Of course, habibti.'

As Madame leads me through the hall, I flick a glimpse back at Nazia. I envy the long black hair spilling down the spine towards neat buttocks. She has a body like a coil of silk but breasts as flat as place mats. She might be angry about that. I would be.

I'm shown through the plush living quarters like a prospective buyer, Madame flaunting and flourishing as we hurry along, the apartment overwhelming me with its luxuries.

There are two spacious salons. In the first and largest salon, we are met by five burly white sofas implacably assembled around the room, all sporting lavish gold trim and attempting to mimic thrones where a king or queen might sit and spread out. They alternate with matching side tables, each offering a gold ashtray, family photo, quality cigarette lighter set in grey stone and a bone-china plate for sweet wrappers. My feet sink into thick Arabian rugs as they would into the loamy muck of Ethiopia's rainy season. Ostentatious chandeliers hang teasingly above us, their glistening crystals threatening to pour down in torrents upon my spinning crown. I barely notice the dark velvet curtains brooding in the back-ground: like the storm clouds over Addis and the Entoto Mountains, these curtains are dense enough to block out every chink of sunlight.

A second smaller salon is dominated by a mahogany cabinet with row upon row of displayed golden trinkets sparkling like diffused sunbeams. They seem to pinpoint their glows at the magnificent vases dotted around the room containing myriad dried flowers. I try not to focus too keenly on the burnished golden hoard: I feel guilty merely looking at it. Again, I see grand thrones where other people might put sofas. They look dangerously comfortable and try to lure my weary body towards them. But Madame is leading me through the apartment at a busy pace.

A third salon is not a salon, Madame insists. The 'TV lounge' is dominated by a low-slung auburn Arab sofa, clinging to three walls out of four. The sofa drips with blood-red cushions, encircling small polished wooden tables that crouch in the middle of the room like terrified kittens surrounded by hungry wolves. But the wolves are probably more interested in the TV screen large enough to enliven the entire fourth wall.

'We use tables for eating,' says Madame, 'while we watching television . . . is place we relax, like family.'

Madame's bedroom leaves me gasping with envy. She has two huge cupboards dedicated entirely to her shoes, and two walk-in wardrobes packed with hanging clothes. My fingers itch to lift them from their hangers. Breathtakingly high-altitude high heels point scornfully at my orange sea-level trainers. Long mirrors await my first appearance in Beirut. In Addis, these wardrobes would house families and I would happily live in one, provided the contents came too.

Dominating the room, Madame's double bed is an inviting lake of glistening silk, almost the size and azure of Lake Tana, Ethiopia's source of the Blue Nile. Imagine floating through that silk every night! Overlooking the lake is a bedside table bearing bottles of every conceivable hue and shape: brands of the world's leading perfumeries proliferate, the most exquisite fragrances on this planet only a single stride and squirt away.

We march through a modest but modern kitchen with plastic work surfaces and all the conveniences I'd expect in a developed country. I think of Piazza's fruit market in Addis, my vision consumed by oranges, bananas, grapes, onions and custard apples, while my nostrils inflate with the sensuousness of sweet garlic.

There are three bathrooms, four other bedrooms and a glorious balconied roof garden bustling with bushes and shrubs. The view from the balcony, across the crowded Beirut skyline towards a distant blue sea, is confirmation that the lucky residents in this penthouse occupy a position superior to all. And there's the Ethiopian flag waving at me only a single block away. My Consulate right on our doorstep: I can pop in for a natter in Amharic with my fellow nationals any time I please!

'You look like you've just won a TV game show,' chuckles Shafeek, watching me enraptured in wide-eyed wonder. I scarcely hear him.

In these few fleeting minutes, I glimpse a divine existence never previously imagined. I'm intoxicated on comfort, space, light and luxury: so unconfined and liberating. This Heaven-bound palace offers total relief from every snag and stress of our world. How could anyone ever be unhappy in here? A future of fine living is unfolding before me: a gift from God! If I am a great maid, perhaps Madame will consider adopting me? I hope to live here forever.

Arriving at a drab outside storeroom with a rolled-up mattress and a couple of hooks, Madame glances around for me.

'These things all for you, Meron,' she says, to nobody.

It's all been too much. The twinkle in her friendly eyes suddenly dulls as she finds me slumped on a particularly welcoming couch, my mind skimming and spinning down a silken cascade into a pool of bliss, my body curling into an unborn baby, slumbering contentedly, my umbilical cord in rapid repair. Am I unborn, born or reborn? Ah! New life!

As I lie in my bed, I snuggle into the warm gap left

by my mother. I hear chanting from an assortment of churches, a radio discussing English football, a rat scuttling across the roof, tuneless music blaring, Nati snoring, birds chirping, fists hammering on neighbours' doors, feet shuffling along the track outside, and inside, my mother bellowing into my ear . . .

'Me-ron! Me-ron!'

But that is not my mother's voice.

'Me-ron! What you doing?' shouts Madame sharply into my left ear. I jump perceptibly. Where am I? Ah, yes, the Kingdom of Heaven, somewhere in Beirut.

'Get off the couch! You not princess here! You not sit on *that* . . . you over there,' says Madame, pointing at a red plastic stool the height of a molehill. 'You sit on stool in *any* room only if we invite you.'

'But . . . thank you, Madame.'

An unforgiving plastic stool is slumming it even in Addis, where our handsomely carved wooden stools are planed down to offer two generous concave curves, adequate for most bony rear ends in Ethiopia. The plastic stool is good only for doorstops and performing dogs. There are not many of them in Addis.

'Where are the other servants, Madame?'

To service this palace, there has to be an army.

'Allah! Other? There *are* no others. Tu! You! *You* are the maid!' she proclaims.

'But . . .'

'Your English is great, but this word you delete it *now*.'

'But . . .'

'Yes! *This one*, it not helpful. Okay . . . open your suitcase on roof. All your clothes out! They have to go,' orders Madame.

'No!' I cry.

'And *this* word. Delete it. Don't worry, we put everything in big plastic bag until you return to Ethiopia.'

'But . . .'

Madame sighs loudly, garlic breath hitting my nose.

A black bin liner is held open for me to scoop in the contents of my suitcase, including my bag of kolo. It will have to wait two and a quarter years. Urgh! Madame ties up the bin liner as though trapping a rabid dog. The suitcase gets its own bin liner. This is not the Lebanese hospitality I expected. Of my original possessions, only a postcard and an Orthodox Christian prayer book survive. Madame seems to understand these two items are as important as my own limbs. The monochrome postcard shows a cherubic Maryam holding a crowned baby Jesus with the angels Gabriel and Mikael looking on. I could pray to Maryam's soft kind face forever.

'You keep this picture . . . like Mona Lisa . . . but not speak about Christian things in this apartment, or they out. *Delete them,*' says Madame. 'Okay, into bathroom and you strip.'

'Pardon?'

'Strip!'

What?

The bathroom door is closed behind us. Madame folds her arms and waits for me, coolly pushing the blonde hair off her face.

'Everything, Madame?'

'*Everything, Madame!*' comes the reply.

Oh God. What's this all about? I've just arrived. I still smell of Ethiopian Airlines. The ink is moist on my entry stamp. I've yet to use a Lebanese toilet.

I hurry into the shower and pull across the plastic curtain to obscure her view. I'm sure *that* will protect me. Madame immediately tugs it open.

'Not there, Meron. *You* don't use shower. For shower, you use bowl like in Ethiopia. The shower is for the family, not for you, the maid.'

I hadn't noticed a large plastic bowl of hot water. I am to sit on the toilet seat, apply soap to my body and sluice myself down with a large jug, the dirty water washing away in the floor's drain.

She leans her backside on the marble sink and watches me while I paw myself tentatively with soap. I want to look as unsexy as possible, but my breasts are annoyingly pert. I don't want to go near them in case it looks provocative. I dab the soap randomly. After a minute of dabbing, Madame sighs, rolls up her sleeves and marches towards me.

Please, God, no! It's my first day! This is not how I imagined my first sexual experience. Madame grabs the soap and a rough flannel: she works up a heavy lather before grinding it into every corner of my body.

'Not want extra passengers from Ethiopia,' she explains as she invades my personal interiors.

It's a businesslike incursion, rather than for pleasure. So that's okay, I reason to myself. I've been here less than twenty minutes out of two years: pointless negativity is not useful at this stage.

'We have soap . . . and water . . . in Addis . . . Madame!'
I yelp.

'Congratulations. Ethiopian people must be *so* happy
now. But they know how to *use* the soap? Look at your
colour . . .'

'What, Madame?'

'Your colour . . . almost *black*.'

Madame works the flannel over me for ten long minutes
like a professional. I feel like a well-sanded wooden stool
from Ethiopia, publicly displayed.

'And that thing must to go . . . no adornments,' insists
Madame, pointing at the black cotton maheteb around
my neck.

'Madame, I'm Orthodox Christian . . . if I die in Beirut,
I'll be flown back to Addis and buried in the grounds of
my church if I'm wearing this. Please, it's only a harmless
thread of black cotton, Madame.'

Madame isn't listening. She sprays an acidic substance
onto my head, followed by ferocious hair-brushing in
case my tangle of frizz provides free accommodation for
rogue insects. While I'm squealing, Madame snips off the
maheteb from my neck.

'So, Meron, now you must avoid *dying*.'

'Yes, Madame.'

'It not so difficult.'

'Can I call my mother to say I'm okay?' I ask, nursing
my burnt scalp, as she tosses a large white towel at me.

'Absolument pas! Non! Very expensive to call Ethiopia.
Later, you write letter. You not touching telephone. Allah!'

Madame hands me a pair of baggy white-and-pink-
striped cotton trousers and a matching buttoned smock. I

grin at their ugliness. Maybe they're pyjamas. That's okay.

'You wear this maid uniform every day for next two years . . . What you thinking is funny?' asks Madame.

'Nothing, Madame. I'm really happy.'

The flesh of my legs has to be banished from sight at all times. My hair must be covered with a white scarf: the knot is secured at the front, not the back because that might be misconstrued as attractive. I cannot wear knickers with a visible panty line: they have to be shapeless, voluminous and impossible to detect with the naked human eye. A bra is to be worn at all times, including at night in case I have to cook for anyone returning home late. Bra and knickers can be removed, however, for showers which must not be taken in the shower. There will be no miniskirts, heels, cleavages and lipstick for the domestic staff. Madame wants the domestic staff nullified into a nodding nobody, twenty-four hours a day. In my new uniform, I am to be ageless, sexless and stripped of all individuality, bar my name.

'Me-ron! Into kitchen *now*!' says Madame, yanking me away before I can glimpse my new persona in a mirror. She knows what she's doing. Madame corrals me along with her hands, now able to touch me, for I am cleansed.

As she prepares food, an elderly man limps past the door. Now at the level of toddler on my new plastic stool I look up at him.

'That Mister Abdul, my husband. He has bad walk because he crash car two years before. His fault . . . refuse to wear glasses . . . silly man,' says Madame bitterly.

I stand ready to meet the master of the house, but there's no introduction. Maybe she's embarrassed about the implausible age difference between them.

'Ab-di!' she shouts, with further instructions in Arabic. No answer.

'Ab-di! Ab-di!'

It's piercing but melodic. Madame holds onto the top notes and really sustains them. Abdul has to be deaf as well as blind if he can't hear this. Madame is irritated by his failure to respond.

'He get old . . . not hear me or not *want* to hear me. He have own supermarket.'

I'm desperate to know how old, but too timid for such a bold question. Nobody ever looks as old as this in Addis: everyone dies first. If I had a camera, I would take Abdul's photograph to show people at home.

Abdul shuffles past the doorway again, oblivious to his wife. He nurtures very white hair: a wispy cloud seems to have plopped onto his head, which wouldn't be surprising on this, the thirteenth floor. Tiny black eyes peep through gaps in craggy facial features. The size of Nazia's sharp beak owes much to Abdul's wilting bill, though the latter has a softer, rounder sweep: it droops benignly rather than points threateningly. We hear the front door slam shut behind him. I feel so relieved to see the master of the house hobbling very slowly: he will *not* be leaping astride me every time the weather warms up.

'How many people live here, Madame?' I ask quietly.

'Seven people live here. And you, of course. Me, Shafeek, Nazia, Abdul, Nuria my oldest daughter, her husband Hassan and son Mustafa. Nuria expecting another in three months. Eleven rooms plus roof garden to busy you.'

'I understand, Madame.'

Actually, I don't. Madame is rich enough to employ a team of professional cleaners but she chooses to hire a single Habesha maid to run through eleven rooms every day with a mop. I have a 'Gurage' madame. The Gurage people of Ethiopia are renowned for their miserliness.

There are three taps in the kitchen: two cold and one hot. I turn on a cold one but nothing appears. The other cold tap offers running water which I drink with my hand, as I do in Addis. The water tastes salty and revolting.

'Me-ron! Not drink that! Only for washing clothes and clean floor. Other provide drinking water for you, and cooking water for us. Come every three days . . . that when you fill up old plastic bottles. For us, family, we drink bottle water from Abdul's supermarket. You *serve* that but you not *drink* that. You understand?'

'Yes, Madame.'

'And other rules . . . after lunchtime, I not want to see you in salons or bedrooms . . . clean them in morning. In afternoon, your place right here in kitchen, or outside on roof. Evenings, maybe you watch TV with us, if we invite.'

'Yes, Madame.'

'Finally . . . yes, your eyes are big and beautiful, but you keep them *down*, you understand? We want maid service, not staring service . . . like you doing right now.'

'Yes, Madame . . . sorry,' I hurry.

Down go the eyes, but they instantly spring back into their natural ogling position. Like my countrymen, I stare: I can't help it.

'Seem to be Ethiopia thing . . . dangerous.'

'Can I write a letter to my mother now?'

'Ah, you are educated . . . not sure I like this. Yes, write letter.'

I write a brief note for my mother, kiss it and hand it to Madame with the Addis address. No other form of communication is available to me. It says: 'Hi Mum, everything is fine in Beirut, the house is good but big, family is kind, I think. Today, I saw the sea. Maybe tomorrow I will swim in the sea. Don't be sad. Ethiopian Consulate is very close to protect me. The flight was great. Free food but no injera! I feel happy to be here, but already miss you so much. Love, Meron.'

With luck, she might receive this note in around three weeks. There are computers in every bedroom, but I have never used one of these intelligent hunks of plastic and wires. They represent objects for dusting, not for communicating.

I meet the other daughter, the oldest of Madame's progeny: a pregnant Nuria and her husband Hassan, hospital administrator and cosmetic dentist respectively. Nuria's six-month bump suits her. She's stocky and dark, with a blatant line of hair resting above her upper lip. Black curls shoot out from her head, wilfully untamed. Her eyes are full of sleep and apathy, her mouth hasn't the appetite for a smile. The clothes – disagreeable dungarees – suggest she works underneath car engines. The bump is her one redeeming feature, albeit a different person.

'Hello, Madame Nuria,' I offer. My hand is outstretched.

'Call me Nuria, not *Madame* Nuria.'

A flabby hand is raised but not forwarded to meet mine. It looks scared of me. Doesn't it realise I've been purified?

77

Conversely, Hassan is smooth, smart and reassuringly tubby. Like Nuria, he's in his thirties. Unlike his wife, he's maintained personal standards in the face of marriage and offspring. Hassan's smile exposes glittering white cubes, his mouth resembling the entrance to a well-endowed salt mine. His playful eyes effuse energy and acumen, while the air around him smells of dried apricots.

Shaking my hand enthusiastically, he says: 'Nice to meet you, Meron.' This person I like.

I see their three-year-old son, Mustafa, asleep. Only Madame's solid hand on my shoulder prevents me from kissing his angelic features. In Addis, it is normal to kiss random strangers' babies and toddlers in the street. It would be odd *not* to.

As they continue into their two bedrooms, I notice Hassan's head. From the front, it's a polished shaven head, but the back view reveals a deep natural gash where the skull ends and the neck begins. This line both intrigues and frightens me. The groomed head of a Bole boy is usually a ball of loveliness to admire and stroke, but on Hassan it's a hairless knuckle with a disturbing slash at the join, like an extra grinning mouth. Hassan has two faces and one of them scares me.

'You only eat what we give you, Meron,' Madame states, as I'm passed a delicious spread of pitta bread and hummus. 'You not take food when you want it. That is thieves' thing . . . we punish thieves.'

No problem. With food like this, I'll be the new Beti, occupying two seats on my return to Addis. Mum won't recognise the balloon floating through her door in a couple of years' time. I will be the envy of Addis.

'By the way, you are fat girl.'

'Really, Madame?' I reply with a smile. It's a compliment, I'm sure, though also an exaggeration: I would describe my shape as 'comfortable'.

Madame busies herself around the kitchen.

'Before you serve food or drink, you wash and dry your hands always . . . every time. This important,' she continues. 'I check your fingernail too, every day.'

'Ishee, Mum.'

'Not start "ishee" thing! No Amharic! And I not your mum!' barks Madame.

I blush at the mistake. She turns my hands palm-upwards for a visual check. I pass.

'Okay, Meron, tomorrow I take day off work to teach you everything for your job. After this, I expect *service*. My standards are high, very high. You understand me?'

'Ish . . . yes, Madame.'

'Any question?'

'No, Mum . . . Madame. Sorry, I'm tired.'

But she *is* my mum now.

'Okay, go to bed,' she instructs. 'In small salon between display cabinet and sofa . . . you and mattress go in there.'

Madame is clever: if a burglar managed to break into her apartment at night, they would have to step on me first before they could raid the golden ornaments. As a human alarm, I would probably squeal very loudly indeed.

It's around 9.30pm, Universal Time, not Habesha time any more. Tonight, I sleep in a luxury apartment and it *is* a different universe. I am so many light years from Ethiopia, where our ramshackle home sits inconceivably beneath the same moon. Is Nati staring at it right now?

Falling onto my mattress, I say a prayer: 'Thank you, Lord, for delivering me to this extraordinary place. Tell Mum I am okay . . . much more than okay . . .'

I want to spend more time awake, thinking of Mum, Addis, Ethiopia.

Second Day in Lebanon
(819 days left)

The creak of an opening window wakes me. Madame is letting in some early morning air and breathing outwards with evident relief at the same moment.

'I not breathing your stale air,' she mutters to herself.

'Mum . . . Madame?'

'Meron, this is time you get up every day.'

'Ishee . . . that's fine, Madame.'

'I give you very very loud alarm clock tomorrow.'

We drink tea enlivened with freshly squeezed lemon juice. Madame sits on a high stool in the kitchen in tight blue shorts, her white T-shirt revealing the contours of her breasts. She looks amazing at 5.30am. I wear my new uniform which shows off the contours of a servant. As foolish as the baggy uniform looks, I feel proud. I'm a professional.

Madame is *the* professional. The way she sweeps, dusts, mops, wipes, scrubs, polishes and irons suggests Madame is wasting her time in the banking sector. It all looks so easy as she glides round the apartment, blonde hair flowing behind her, cleaning materials dispatched with precision and technique at such speed I have no time to think.

'Dusting is in circle. Look!' she shows me, stroking her cloth across a salon side table in an artistic sweeping motion.

Yes, easy, I encourage myself. I'm probably a third of her age.

'I hate dust . . . dust is *us*,' she sputters.

'Yes, Madame.'

'It's dead skin . . . floating around,' she explains with her hands feeling through the air dramatically. 'We breathe it into lungs, we breathe other people's dead skin. Common dust is . . . *yuk*!'

'Yes, Madame.'

'And in penthouse like this, we have dust from *all* Beirut. What means this? Means we get dead skin from all city . . . not only my family dead skin, but every man, woman, animal . . . their skin comes in here, on my furniture, on my food, on my lungs. Living things are *disgusting*.'

That sets my mind racing with worry. I could be creating dust as we speak. With luck, my dust will mingle unrecognisably with the rest, except that it's almost black and everyone else is white. Somehow, I must hang onto my skin for the next two years, though it's not obvious how I might do this.

'I have special checking system for dust, Meron.'

'Yes, Madame?'

'Oh yes, Madame. Some days, and I not tell you *what* days, but some days I wear white socks to walk around my apartment. I go all corners, all rooms, walking, walking . . . when finish, I look at bottom of white socks . . .

must be same colour as my husband hairs. If socks not white, you have problem . . . I need service from you, not problem.'

'Yes, Madame.'

Abdul is hobbling quickly away from the bathroom.

'You clean this bathroom every time he use it, Meron. I mean *every* time. I not go in there until you finish. Remember, I share same bathroom . . . I depend on *you* to clean it.'

'Yes, Madame. It's no trouble.'

'Okay, we see about that . . . not normal cleaning . . .'

Madame shoves me into the bathroom with a mop and bucket and waits outside. It's foul to all my senses. Breathing only through my mouth, I'm forced into skilful footwork. It would be too easy to slip up on the plops of sewage sprayed around without care or pattern. Either the lavatory's flush has an explosive tendency or Abdul is pirouetting through his morning motions. The latter is unlikely on a lame leg. But I see Madame's point: living creatures *are* disgusting. Half an hour of frantic scrubbing later, I emerge unscathed to find Madame chatting with Nazia. I have completed my first cleaning assignment and deserve a hero's reception.

'Good morning, Nazia,' I try cheerfully.

'Wash hands *now* . . . use Dettol,' says Madame earnestly.

Nazia ignores me. She's wearing a tight-fitting T-shirt as red as bright new blood. Her make-up is immaculate, the lipstick exactly matching the T-shirt. The nose glistens, more intimidating in the morning sunlight.

'Don't let her touch my clothes,' Nazia says to Madame in English.

'Pas de problème, habibti, I teach her everything today. She better than one before.'

'How *can* she be?'

'Give her chance, habibti.'

'Chances have to be earned,' says Nazia.

I wait for Madame in the kitchen. Abdul is in here, swishing around in loose-fitting blue silk pyjamas. The car accident left one leg longer than the other, noticeably longer. His shorter right leg has excess trouser: every four or five strides, he sighs loudly and stops abruptly as the silk unfurls from the waist downwards and flaps along the floor, requiring him to constantly gather up the extra material and tuck it back into the waist band. Nobody has ever thought to shorten the right trouser leg for him. Nobody cares enough.

'Can I help you with anything, Mister Abdul?' I offer in broken Arabic. I could sew up the trouser leg.

'Help? You think I need *help*? Yes, you can *help* me . . . keep out of the way in my kitchen, in my apartment, in my country . . . you shouldn't be coming here,' he gurgles in Arabic, or at least this is the gist I manage to extract.

Abdul's words fight their way out of a phlegmy whirl-pool, while he tries to juggle boiling coffee and a flapping pyjama leg. He seems determined to shield the preparation of Turkish coffee from me with his hunched body, but my eyes are too fast for Abdul.

Having filled up a long-handled silver pot with cold water, he adds a heap of sugar and two mounds of finely ground coffee from a packet that says 'Najjar'. Abdul then holds the pot over a gas flame, concentrating like a surgeon as the coffee begins to bubble. As soon as the foam rises up, he pulls the pot off the flame and lets it settle for a moment before stirring the coffee methodically with a spoon. He replaces the pot on the flame and repeats the procedure twice until eventually pouring the brown silty contents into a white demitasse cup. Coffee is in my blood, bones and soul: I have to witness this, even if I am not to drink the black nectar.

Madame gives me pitta bread and cheese before we continue with the cleaning tasks. Nuria and Hassan soon emerge from their two adjoining rooms, holding little Mustafa's hands between them. As Mustafa smiles at me, Madame peppers his head with kisses, repeating the word 'Habibi!' more than eight times. A final smothering cuddle that threatens to asphyxiate him makes the point emphatically. The moment Madame lets go, Mustafa runs towards me. Instinctively, I bend over and kiss him on the forehead, copying Madame but without the melodrama. Madame flinches.

'Not kiss her, Mustafa, or you be black too,' declares Madame.

Mustafa defies her and kisses me on the cheek: I hope this does not cause any upset for Madame or Nuria. Absurdly cute, Mustafa looks like a miniature version of Shafeek, but with a face held in constant surprise, the way life should be at that age. These Arab boys definitely *have* something.

Nuria is indifferent: she's not interested in who kisses who at 8.50am. This morning her dungarees are blue verging on black. I think of car engines: how would her bump fit underneath?

'How are you today, Meron?' asks Hassan, white enamel

glimmering proudly. His suit is cheap and dreary but with teeth like that nobody will see it.

'I'm fine, Mister, thank you . . . and you?' I smile.

'Hassan! We're going!' snaps Nuria.

Her words snatch Hassan away from me, but he glances back.

'That's good, that's good . . .' he says, his rear grin reinforcing the sentiment.

Ten minutes later, Shafeek appears in black button-up trunks, his hair tousled and face rugged from hard sleeping. I drink in the view of his great body. But the foot fungus is awake. Without *that*, he is a perfect man.

'I need my things . . . Allah, where are my things?' he mutters in our direction.

We go to Madame's bedroom. Inside a wardrobe sits Shafeek's underwear collection, mainly black briefs and black socks.

'Every morning, you help Mister Shafeek be ready for work. He is number one in this apartment. If he need you, you go to him.'

'Yes, Madame.'

'Always I check his underwear . . . but *you* take to him, after I check it.'

'Er, okay, Madame.'

'I buy his clothes. He finish with socks and pants faster than other people . . . I check them every day for hole, smell, elastic breaking . . .'

I want to laugh.

'And you warm-iron his underpants every day. This *really* important.'

'Yes, Madame,' I snigger.

'Not funny, Meron . . . he is international lawyer!'

Shafeek stumbles around in the kitchen, scrambling eggs for breakfast and glugging orange juice from the carton. He doesn't seem very sociable.

'Shafeek, can I eat some of your egg?' asks Madame in Arabic.

'Not enough to share,' he says grumpily.

What's his problem? You wake up in a palace like this and you still hate the world? I've always thought that wealth must bring with it a daily elation: that the rich leapt like shooting stars from their king-sized beds every morning and then spent their easy days rollicking around in knee-deep Persian rugs unable to contain their joy for this world. But some people seem a little dejected around here: perhaps Shafeek wants even more wealth.

Madame shows me how to lay out work clothes neatly on his bed, everything flawlessly ironed. His shiny pointed black shoes require no polishing, but I am to do it anyway, just in case a spot of dust has soiled them.

'In Beirut, how you look is *everything*,' Madame says. 'But not in Ethiopia . . . everyone look the same, yes?'

'Er . . . well, it . . .' I start, unsure of myself. She's not expecting an answer so I stop myself. It *is* everything.

Shafeek is leaving rapidly. He's wearing a dark blue double-breasted silk suit. I want to stroke my cheek on it. The red-striped tie is also silken. Gold cufflinks flash at me. Real gold? This man exudes quality and his face has settled down. The hair is gelled and neat. I can't imagine him committing murder now. He looks good and smells great. The polished shoes lock in his single odorous feature and reflect light like small black puddles attached to his feet. Nobody wears shoes like that in Addis. Instead, we stand in small black puddles.

'See you later,' announces Shafeek as he slams the door behind him, bulging briefcase in hand.

So this is an international lawyer. A tingle of pride dances down my spine. From tomorrow, that superb species of a man will be under *my* care, apart from the vital underwear checks.

Madame shows me the storeroom outside, next to the balcony. Paint on the battered door is lined with long grooves above the handle, like deep scratch marks, perhaps from an animal. It is the door of a grubby outhouse that seems out of place connected to such a plush penthouse. At least I don't have to sleep in here.

Inside, sacks of potatoes, sugar, salt, garlic, onions and flour fill the floor-space, while shelves are stacked with tins of tuna fish, sweetcorn and tomatoes. The idea of storing food is curious: there is no room for storing food in Addis. Besides, the Merkato and local shops stock everything we need and are always open. Stored food is never fresh food, and is an open invitation to vermin and insects.

Within seconds, I notice a small cockroach stretching its legs in Madame's storeroom, proving that Addis is right, Beirut is wrong.

'Madame, there's a cockroach,' I say, pointing at it crawling along the wall.

'I pay fumigator every three months but insect always they return,' she mutters, smashing her slipper down hard on the insect.

'Maybe he's escaped from Ethiopia,' I say. This is a particularly unwise comment.

Madame looks at me carefully, as if splattering the servant with the same cockroach-soiled slipper is now under consideration.

'I know you not nineteen, Meron . . . I not stupid. Really what age you have? Fifteen? Sixteen?'

'Sixteen, Madame.'

'Mmm, I think this. You still baby. Your head full up with dreams and idiocies.'

I'm not aware that it is, but I don't have a problem with dreams and idiocies. They're as good as anything else for filling up the head. I have to put *something* in there while I live.

The morning with Madame rushes past, rounding off with a chicken salad lunch. As I'm slicing onion, a sneeze gathers up inside my nose. Onions always do this.

'Aaa . . . aaa . . .'

Madame thrusts me across the room with a shoulder barge, the same way they play football in America.

'Aaa . . . choo!' I splutter wildly towards the floor.

'Next time, spit your germs away from our food . . . we not eating food with your germs, and I *hate* to throw food in bin.'

'Yes, Madame,' I say, rubbing my shoulder from the shove.

Madame makes some phone calls to her office. Bathrooms are left spotless. The balcony sparkles in the sunlight after we've sponge-mopped it. Madame points out Beirut's lighthouse and the famous Raouché Rock, but I can't see either of them: instead, the view is dominated by concrete roofs, satellite dishes, water cisterns and smog. Madame teaches me how to use the washing machine and the correct way to hang out the damp clothes. Her ironing technique is meticulous with lines as sharp as knives. I watch everything intently, absorbing the rules of the house.

Family members begin to drift home from mid-afternoon onwards.

'When Nazia and Shafeek arrive in home, you tell them what food is in fridge and ask if they like anything prepared.'

'What about Mister Abdul?'

'Not worry about him . . . he eat old chocolate and other expired food all day in supermarket. Nuria and Hassan eat rubbish also. I *let* them eat rubbish,' she says, waving her hand contemptuously.

Nazia returns home from university, dropping her bag on the floor for me to collect.

'Hello, Nazia!' I declare, picking it up behind her.

She passes her eyes over me, the way one does over decomposing meat. But, as instructed by Madame, I chase behind her, wittering as we go.

'Do you want to eat food now, Nazia? We have cooked rice, beans . . . and chicken salad . . . er, Mister brought fruit from the supermarket . . . there are grapes . . . red and white . . .'

Nazia continues into the bathroom without comment, while I gabble on.

'We have yoghurt and hummus from yesterday. Can I make the table for—'

Slam! The bathroom door is thrown shut in my face.

I'm not sure what to do.

'Can I make the table ready for you? There's fresh bread. Maybe you'd like some fruit juice . . .'

I hear the recognisable sound of trickling pee.

'Madame said there's also lentil soup left over from Tuesday. It should be fine . . . I can heat it up for you . . .' I go on.

Still nothing. Just the angry rip of toilet paper. It's difficult not to titter as I talk to a bathroom door.

'Er, Nazia . . . I'm in the kitchen if you need me,' I conclude. I hear the slosh of the flush. That was a sort of answer.

'Madame,' I ask later, 'what do I do if Shafeek or Nazia don't respond while I'm speaking?'

'What? They not have to answer to *you*. Your job is tell them everything . . . if they listening or not.'

'Yes, Madame, but I was talking to a closed door.'

'Not use this word again . . . *but! No!* Make friends with closed door.'

Nuria returns around 6.30pm with takeaway fried chicken. Mustafa is being reared on junk food. He smiles at my smile.

'Nuria, where's your husband?' asks Madame, reverting to comprehensible Arabic.

'Extra consulting,' says Nuria with a knowing tone.

'Again? Allah! What's this man doing to your marriage?' rages Madame.

'Well, I don't know, Mum . . . really I don't . . . why's the servant staring at me?'

'Sorry,' I hurry. It's a habit that will never be broken.

Shafeek is home around 8.30pm. I am to greet Shafeek at the front door each evening as he enters the apartment.

'Good evening, Mister,' I say, jogging up to him, sucking in his delicious Jean Paul Gaultier aftershave, potent enough to sit heavy in my sinuses for the rest of the evening, like my mother's snorted ginger root.

He's frazzled, with his face lined in new and extraordinary ways, his clothes hanging from his muscular frame like autumn leaves preparing to fall, the shoes tarnished and dulled, now clods of clay at the end of a weary body. He kicks them off regardless of the consequences. The aftershave is immediately suffocated by Shafeek's own sorry odour, a full working day in the making, probably nurtured by pacing sternly up and down Beirut's courtrooms.

'Hello, Meron,' he says, hurling the bulky briefcase in my direction.

Rocking back on my feet and almost toppling over, I catch it.

'Run the bath for me and put out my grey tracksuit,' he says, surging away from me.

'How was your day?' I ask.

He stops midstride without turning to look at me.

'Never ask me that again. Just do what I say.'

'Yes, Mister.'

Like an overheated hippo stomping towards a river, Shafeek requires a clear uninterrupted run at the bathroom, not the stultifying small talk of a lesser being fit only for trampling underfoot. I know my position.

As he rumbles along, sweat-sodden underwear is tossed

into the clothes basket while I try to brief him on the food situation. Madame interrupts me.

'You not leave these things in basket until next washing . . . maybe fermenting. They have to be out and hang to dry before they okay for washing machine.'

I rush to retrieve them. For at least an hour, I'm kept occupied by Shafeek's arrival and the related trail of duties. He's brought in expensive Italian pasta from outside. Shafeek doesn't need to care about calories or money.

'Tell Baba, there's extra for him,' he says to me. Shafeek sounds cute when he says 'Baba'. The Arabic word for 'Dad' was probably his very first utterance in this world.

'Hello, Mister!' I try as Abdul shuffles past a little later without even a glance. 'There's leftover pasta if you want it.'

'Baba,' I say quietly to fill the void where Abdul should have responded. It is wonderful to say 'Baba'.

Hassan is the last home, around 9pm. I see him creeping along the hall towards the kitchen.

'Where's Madame?' he whispers to me.

I point at her bedroom. He gives me a tab of chewing gum which I tuck away in my pocket.

'Hassan? Is that you?' shouts Madame.

'Allah,' mutters Hassan.

'Nuria!' screams Madame. 'He's back!'

By 9.30pm, Madame, Shafeek, Nazia and Abdul are sprawled on the long sofas in the TV lounge, watching an Egyptian movie. Nuria and Hassan shout at each other in their quarters. Madame surreptitiously turns down the volume on the television so we can hear the 'live' quarrel more clearly. Allowed to sit on my stool near the door, I am happy to listen to family salaciousness, but if I want more than the gist, I will need to improve my Arabic.

Nazia is agitated. She frowns at me repeatedly but this isn't solving her problem. Maybe I should be *doing* something.

'Je ne sais pas . . . I'm not sure if this is healthy, Mum,' says Nazia, during one of the rare lulls.

'What? Watching an Egyptian movie? Or you mean listen to the other two fighting?' replies Madame.

'Not that, or that. I mean letting the servant sit in the same room as us. It can't be healthy.'

'Ah, I agree, we are breathing the same air as her . . . maybe it's bad for our health.'

'Exactly, African air,' replies Nazia.

'But I'm not sure about leaving her in the kitchen . . . she has to sit in here, sorry, habibti,' explains Madame, as though I'm not in the room.

'Or she could go and clean something instead of sitting here and doing nothing . . .' suggests Nazia.

'Allah! What are you two talking about?' snaps Shafeek. 'She breathes the same as us . . . she's not sick! Leave her alone.'

Shafeek is racing up my list of favourite Arabs of all time, while Nazia has nowhere left to sink to.

'Of course . . . you *would* stick up for her!' says Nazia. 'If she wasn't a young woman, I doubt you'd bother speaking. Just like before . . . you're so transparent.'

'That's ridiculous, Nazia. *You* can't judge me. Who are *you*?'

'Just because you're a lawyer doesn't mean you can't be judged,' sneers Nazia.

'The servant is in here to serve us, in case we need serving . . . that's her job, Nazia. Don't talk nonsense about African air,' rebuffs Shafeek.

'The rational voice of a lawyer says I'm talking nonsense,' continues Nazia. 'Is that how you win your cases? What do you actually know about airborne infections in Ethiopia? Her lungs could be crammed full of deadly viral diseases looking to resettle in new lungs with low immunity. Let's hope those lungs are *yours*.'

I don't know what Nazia is studying at university, but I'm envious of her intelligence and shocked at her audacity. This girl is completely out of control. In Addis, no woman could ever speak like that to a man. Her father or husband or brother would probably beat her to death.

And Shafeek is on his feet! We now have live drama in two different rooms! The Egyptian movie is totally irrelevant, Shafeek is ready to fight for me like a protective father. My tongue hangs out in awe. He is my new Baba! A slender memory of paternal security flickers awake inside me.

'Hey, hey . . . you two! Stop it!' snaps Madame. 'Sit down, Shafeek! You're like kids! Don't worry, I'll buy a small television for Meron to watch in the small salon . . . then we can relax in here without her air . . .'

'You're buying a television especially for *her*?' exclaims Nazia. 'Mum! You can buy *me* one first.'

'Allah!' exclaims Madame, looking to the heavens. 'Fine, Nazia. I'll buy two. Voila! Pas de problème.'

The answers to difficult questions come fast for rich Muslims. I'm impressed.

95

Abdul says nothing. Nibbling away on nuts, or finger-nails, or fiddling with worry beads, he seems to be out of it.

'Meron, go to your bed,' Madame instructs.

'Yes, Madame. Goodnight, everybody,' I sing out.

Only Shafeek replies: 'Bonne nuit.'

It sounds like French again. Ha! Language number four begins here.

I'm laughing inside. The day has flashed by so easily. Madame gave me a duties roster for each day: it looks painless enough. I set the new alarm clock for 5am and say a prayer until my eyes water with weariness.

'God, thank you so much for what you've done for me . . . even more than David, the King of Israel. I can't believe what's happened . . . the great food, the beautiful apartment, a new television for *me*! It doesn't matter about Madame and Nazia . . . on every day of this new life, I will thank you. It's almost too much for me to express myself . . . thank you, God, thank you . . . at last, you have returned me to the world of good living!

'And bonne nuit, Meron!' I giggle.

For the second time in my life I have taken a plunge, and once again I can see the deep end should not be feared. I think of the Ghion pool and smile.

The Deep End

I was only six years old when Dad funded my first opportunity for an inglorious sinking. It involved a substance loosely related to water, stored in what the Ghion Hotel described as an 'outdoor swimming pool'. This rectangular body of liquid, where I would take my swimming lessons, was surrounded by verdant tropical plants sprouting gigantic dark green leaves that could fully encase a grown-up. Loaded with extra-strength chemicals, the deep end of the pool was exactly the same colour as the leaves: it lay viscous and still like a rich spinach soup.

The pool attendants assured us that chlorine was used to keep the water 'clean', but this cleanliness came at a high price: after one hour in the pool, normally caramel-tinted skin became a patchwork of blotchiness. Swimmers took on the appearance of burnt eucalyptus trees with rampant peeling bark. The day after my first lesson, I was neither white person nor black. This I found funny, such was my sense of humour in those days.

For the first two sessions, our young instructor Robel,

an athlete with a cavernous hollow where there ought to have been a stomach, allowed us to thrash around in the shallow end in what seemed like good practice for drowning. To be in warm – if skin-melting – water was thrilling for anybody in landlocked Ethiopia where the best of the swimming was usually restricted to Mr Hilton's flush guests. The Ghion Hotel pool was a distant but considerably cheaper second.

'Let's go, Meron . . . kick your legs and use your arms . . . same time! Together!' shouted Robel.

Down I went. But not very far. Only up to my waist. The shallow end was pleasantly non-threatening and only slightly green: more cabbage than spinach.

'It's the second week! Your legs are still five minutes behind the rest of you. Focus, Meron!'

'I can't control them, Robel. They don't get on with my arms. They want to be different.'

'Next week, it's the deep end. Tell your legs to get ready or you'll have to get a new pair that work properly.'

Robel didn't have the patience required of a teacher. At six, I knew I was stuck with whatever God had given me: legs *and* swimming instructor. How could I get a new pair of *legs*? Tuh! Robel was an idiot.

In the third week, panic set in as Robel marched us round to the deep end. It was dark enough to obscure the bottom of the pool. There were probably skeletons down there and a family of skulking creatures that sharpened their teeth on little girls like me. My fears barely subsided as Robel boomed out his lesson to us, a row of spindly children with splotchy skin.

'Today, we'll learn how to dive. Watch me dive into the pool. Watch how I hold my position through the air.'

We watched. He flew like a bullet into the green stuff. High on bravado, he repeated it twice. Robel was a great swimmer. We gasped and admired him. Nothing appeared to be dragging him down into the murk and Robel survived the deep end.

'Now, I want you to line up alongside the pool, equally spaced.'

We did this. Robel wandered down to the end of the line where I was quaking in my costume.

'Focus, Meron! Are you ready?' he shouted from behind me. He must have been five metres back, preparing himself to run at the water again, which was now becoming tiresome. Yes, Robel, we all know you're an expert diver. Bravo.

'Yes, ready . . . *again*!' I yelled.

I waited for a second. Nothing happened. Oh come on, Robel, stop wasting our money. Dad will be furious with this 'instructor'.

'I'm watching!' I shouted impatiently. Back then, I had confidence.

Come on, Robel!

He pushed me hard from behind. Argh! I was in the water before I knew anything, sinking deep into the emerald pond, the water becoming opaque as the sunlight dimmed, and then black as I sank further. For a second, I couldn't see anything. For a second, I thought maybe I would die.

Fortunately, my direction changed. Upwards! It seemed to take forever. My head emerging from the surface, I thrashed and flailed, but arms and legs somehow co-ordinated into a recognisable stroke, transporting me to the side of the pool, to the safety of dry land, panting furiously as I reached Robel's outstretched hands.

'You're not dead!' said Robel. 'You see, the water *doesn't* kill you. Be friendly with the water. It's not your enemy. Now you can swim!'

'Thank you, Robel.'

Everyone cheered and clapped. My anger turned to pride. It was a life-changing moment.

'You'd never have done it without a push from behind . . . I know you, and I know your legs.'

Robel was absolutely right. It would *not* have happened. But it did and I had amazed myself. I couldn't wait to sit on Dad's knee and recount my victory over the green liquid stuff.

Robel leant over to whisper in my ear.

'But by the way, Meron, don't *drink* the water . . . that *can* kill you.'

Third Day in Lebanon
(818 days to go)

I am sitting on God's knee. Or is it Dad's knee? Resolute
as volcanic rock beneath me, I feel sure God and Dad
have exactly the same kind of muscular thigh, both utterly
secure. Falling from this safe ledge would be impossible. I
look downwards at thousands of glowing Habesha faces,
many framed in white chiffon hoods: they all smile up at
me, every pair of eyes effusing joyfulness at my privileged
position. This must be the lap of God. I absorb the warmth
of their love and begin to swivel my head upwards to see
the Lord's face, to thank Him in person for delivering me
to Beirut and the good life. Meeting God at last! This will
be glorious! Except for an ugly repetitive sound, growing
more and more intense by the second.

The new digital alarm clock looks good, but at five
o'clock on Sunday morning the high-pitched beeps
plough deep destructive furrows across delicately balanced
dreams. Nobody likes to begin the day with an unfinished
dream: it affords disappointment from the opening second
of wakefulness. And what could be more disappointing

than having the face of God offered up and snatched away within the same final second of sleep? An incredible spiritual moment trashed by a cheap plastic timepiece. But if I can just close my eyes again, give me an extra second on His knee . . . please!

Reluctantly, as the Muslim call to prayer commences across the city, I get dressed. Breakfast is sweet tea and Hassan's chewing gum, 'fresh mint' flavour. I wait quietly for Madame.

I wait three hours.

Time elapses pleasantly and peacefully in Beirut, early Sunday morning. A slight saltiness in the air carries into my corner. I can almost hear the gentle sea stroking the beach, imperceptibly easing its way up the brown sand, the water warm and giving, my body relaxing into its soft supple hands. Take me, Mediterranean, take me to float on your great body of blue heaven. But where shall I drift to on my day off?

On Sundays in Beirut, Habesha maids attend an Ethiopian Orthodox Christian service outside a small convent church next to the Military Hospital, close to Badaro Street. Beti told me this on the plane. Afterwards, they eat injera and drink coffee. It should be a day for spiritual revitalisation, a day to rest and recover in good company. Combined with a swim in the sea, that will be perfect.

When she rises at 8am, Madame ambles bleary-eyed onto the balcony where I'm sitting in the sun, part-dozing, part-planning the start of my new exercise regime. I wonder how far it is to the beach. Maybe I will jog there, swim in the sea, and jog back to sup fresh orange juice in the sun.

'Meron? What you doing?'

'Waiting for you, Madame,' I reply dreamily. I feel a prickle of doubt as I speak. Something is not quite right.

'What you doing since you get up at five o'clock?'

'Waiting for you.'

Madame is torn between laughter and rage.

'Allah! You wait for me all this time? You joking . . .'

'No . . . Madame,' I reply slowly.

Disbelief lands with a juddering thump at this time of day.

'Three hours, sitting here? *What?* You waste time! You not wait for *me*. I not paid to clean this apartment . . . *you* are! This not holiday resort for Ethiopia! Your work start at five, prompt! On time! Cleaning bathrooms. Not three hours later! Allah!'

'Yes, Madame,' I gulp.

'What's the matter with you?' hisses Nazia who has picked up on the scent of a fraught conversation. 'You're here to *work*. She's totally useless, Mum . . . we're stuck with an imbecile.'

'Sorry,' I mutter wretchedly.

'Well, *move* it!' fires Madame. 'Guests coming! I pay you to get up early and work, not sit like Queen of Sheba.'

Guests are coming!

'Madame, can I have breakfast? I'm really hungry.'

She leans towards me.

'You chewing gum?'

Oh God. I forgot about that. I'm chomping away like an excited horse with a fresh bale of hay. No clever lying can extract me from this.

'Yes, Madame.'

'Where you get *that* from?' she asks, now annoyed.

'I found it . . . er, stuck to the bottom of a chair . . .'

'You do this in Ethiopia . . . eat old gum when you find it?'

'Yes, Madame . . . they leave it in a public place for someone else to enjoy . . . we like to share our food in Ethiopia, it's a cultural tradition . . . or traditional culture.'

Madame is taken aback, as am I. It's only the third day and my first convoluted story has spilled out without warning. Madame believes it.

'She's lying, Mum,' chirps Nazia.

'Of course she lie . . . they always do.'

Madame allows me a meagre breakfast of reheated two-day-old manoushe, Lebanese pizza sprinkled with a blend of thyme, sumac and sesame seeds called zaatar. Madame meanders back to her bedroom.

'Madame?' I whisper through her door.

'Allah . . . What you want? They come in six hour . . . apartment must be very very clean. Get on with it,' she replies from under her silk sheets.

My third day in Lebanon should be a little like my second day. I'm doing all the same things in the same apartment with the same utensils. But there's a vital difference: what Madame explained and demonstrated so succinctly and professionally yesterday was an optical illusion of minimal effort; a soapy sleight of hand no less. I have been tricked.

By midday, I've achieved exactly one third of yesterday's midday workload. The rooms are now three times larger, the dirt three layers deeper. My diminutive hands are barely moving, while the long hands of the kitchen clock are lithe, swift and inevitable. I've been pumping limbs continuously for four hours. The filth of this family is beating me. Time renders me empty with hunger. There's nothing left. *Already.*

A stunning bunch of bright yellow bananas is draped provocatively across a plate in the living room. Surely a single banana would not be missed. Abdul took two to work this morning. What about me? I'm slogging more than him. Just one will be enough. Off with the skin and it's gone.

I trudge to the balcony for more sweeping. Minutes later, Madame is at my side again.

'Who eating bananas today?' she demands.

'Mister Abdul took three this morning . . . I saw him,' I lie again, the words released involuntarily before I can censor them. Blinking is easier to stop than lying.

'Mmm . . . not sure about that.'

When Abdul returns half an hour later, Madame confronts and quizzes him immediately at the front door.

'Ab-di! Are you taking all the bananas again? Three are missing,' she says in Arabic.

Flustered by his wife's accusation, he tries to dodge past her, but the elderly Mister is too slow and unwieldy. Madame sticks her face into his.

'One . . . I took one!' he lies.

'Meron saw you take three,' asserts Madame, pointing me out on the sidelines.

Wonderful. He now hates me even more.

'Rahima! Who do you believe . . . your husband or a new servant straight off the boat from Africa?' rants Abdul.

During the rainy season, the drains in Bole Road gargle the way Abdul speaks.

'Exactly, she's new! She's not a thief only two days after arriving. Abdul, come on . . . tell me the truth.'

'Who cares about the bananas? If we got the bananas from my shop, they'd be free.'

'And black and useless,' Madame interrupts.

'We shouldn't have lost the last one,' says Abdul, limping away at last. 'Not like *that*!'

I'm confused. Bananas or maids?

'Ab-di! It happened!' Madame shouts after him. 'Allah! Don't keep on sulking about the past. And please take other fruit . . . like grapes, oranges, plums . . . not only bananas. You need variety, Ab-di.'

'Sharmuta . . .' utters Abdul from a safe distance, barely audible.

I know this means 'bitch'. I can't believe he said it, the strongest word in our language.

'Ab-di! What you say?'

Madame is shouting at empty space. She glances at me, unsure if I understand their Arabic. Me too: did he actually say 'sharmuta'?

At 1pm, Madame is preparing Lebanese dishes in the kitchen. Shafeek goes for a run. On his return, he sits on the balcony in only his dark blue Nike shorts, reading legal papers. I can't help loitering on the balcony. No words pass between us. Within a few metres of him, I can detect both body and foot odour. They are different. I already know his natural perfumes. Does he know mine? Can he detect my fascination? If I stand here long enough in his presence, will he eventually desire me? What would happen if I kissed him on the mouth, right now? Would I shortcut my way to wealth, or to death?

Shafeek's green eyes settle upon me. For a moment, I have his focus. What can I do with this? Wink? Grin? Lick my lips? Sit on his knee as though he's my Baba? No, none of these: I lack the confidence to unlock the treasure. He's too good for me. I jerk my gaze away.

We are immediately distracted. A truculent Nazia is shouting at Madame in a fracas over Abdul: he wasn't told about the party and has already left for his brother's house. Madame 'forgot' to tell him. Nazia slams the front door behind her. Excellent.

Shafeek stands and wanders away, completely unconcerned. Loose, dark blue shorts on gleaming, bronzed, strutting body: those colours work. Those body lines work. My eyes *work*.

By early afternoon, half a dozen middle-aged cohorts are arriving at the apartment, all clutching wrapped biscuits, sweets and flowers. I'm wiping surfaces clean in the kitchen after Madame's intense bout of cooking and I am clinging to an assumption of imminent afternoon release. Well-deserved, I'll be given the Sunday afternoon off. If Abdul and Nazia can go, it has to be a certainty for me. I'll visit the other girls at the Orthodox Christian service and speak with my God.

'Madame . . .' I start, unsure how to proceed with my request, as she tells Shafeek to prepare the sheesha pipe for a guest.

'What you want, Meron? Go and get more nuts from storeroom,' she snaps irritably.

'No, wait,' interrupts Shafeek, looking fabulous in a high-collared white shirt with silver buttons and cuffs. 'Get the charcoal from the storeroom while you're there.'

'But . . .' I start.

'But' is a banned word, and anyway nobody is listening.

Shafeek lounges decadently in the best chair of the salon, as if upon a throne surrounded by minions. He has a clear conception, encouraged by Madame, that *he* is the king of the house. Perhaps that means he is. The guests drink fruit juice and two of them puff on the sheesha pipe. The smoke is like sickly sweet strawberry. Madame gushes over a broad range of phenomena without discrimination. They speak in fast Arabic and I barely understand a syllable.

'Here's our maid, Meron from Ethiopia . . . a bit slow, but she folded the napkins . . . good technique, very nice,' says Madame at one point.

They glance at me for a second; one solitary second. On a good day in Addis, in pleasant company, I might tell an amusing anecdote, or sing a hymn, or perform a traditional dance, but here in Beirut, my single second of acknowledgement scuttles past like a cockroach on a wooden floor: I can't be sure that I've seen it.

For the lunch itself, the guests move onto the long sofa in the television lounge. This isn't just food I'm serving. A varied mezze of hummus, baba ghanoush (aubergine dip), warab enab bi-zayt (stuffed vine leaves), tabbouleh (parsley salad), labineh (thick yoghurt with garlic), fattoush (mixed salad topped with squares of flatbread), olives and different breads attacks my central nervous system, goading my senses from kitchen to salon; from toenails to fingertips, muscles twitching as if electrocution has gripped my body.

To eat the tiniest crumb of this mezze would be to confer sight on a blind man for a single moment: to taunt him with the briefest glimpse of visual ecstasy so that he sees exactly what he is missing in this world.

The main course will be fried fish or lamb kebab with roasted peppers and grilled halloumi cheese, followed by dessert of baklava and fruit plates of apples, grapes, apricots, dates, figs and pomegranates, concluding with Turkish coffee. There is enough rapture on these plates to satisfy the most repressed of appetites. As I lay newspaper across the table in advance of fish bones, I try to force my mind to shut down, or I shall never survive this impossible temptation. The Ethiopian hyena is a capricious beast and cannot be trusted. Perhaps it stirs inside me: my brother certainly accommodates it. Nati would not survive one minute in this job.

To distract my famished hyena, I track Shafeek's right hand while awaiting Madame's instructions. The hand is buried inside the front of his trousers. What is he *doing*? Touching, scratching, feeling, checking his vital machinery, unworried about the views of others, this is what he is doing. And suddenly the hand is outside, grabbing at kibbeh, using these meaty snacks to scoop up dollops of yoghurt, the latter plopping onto the fingers of the same well-travelled hand, which now aims for its final destination between Shafeek's upper lip and tongue, each finger and thumb sucked clean with a greedy relish. Shafeek's face seeps shameless sweat and pleasure. Other male hands follow similar unimaginable paths. Hyenas!

Madame offers me none of the food that I'm serving. A plate of rice and dry flatbread awaits me, suggesting that, despite first impressions, my Madame is odious. The dry flatbread looks like peeling mottled paint, and tastes marginally better. The rice is a dispiriting grey rubber that might be better employed as the grip on a cut-price training shoe. I'm finally learning the real meaning of hunger: I had to *leave* Ethiopia to experience this.

Recalling Proverbs 27:7, 'He who is sated loathes honey, but to one who is hungry everything bitter is sweet,' I have to disagree, Mum. Ethiopian honey is *never* loathed by anyone, and the bread and rice awaiting me in the kitchen are as sweet as a freshly mined slab of Afar salt. Can't the Bible offer me more than this?

'Me-ron! Stop staring . . . I told you about that before,' barks Madame. 'Come here!'

As the guests jabber away, I trudge through a spitting rain of olive oil, garlic, lemon and herbs – the four pillars of Lebanese cuisine – towards my Madame, while beneath my aching feet a resounding crunch of dry nuts and their kernels – pistachios, cashews, pine, almonds and pea-nuts – all crack away at me, each reconfirming the dreary cleaning duties to come. My Sunday is dissipating into unrefined drudgery. The spatter of guests' zeal upon my cheeks is the closest I'll get to swimming today.

'Me-ron! For fruit plates, we moving onto balcony . . . you serve us outside then clean this room. You doing so very well . . . excellent maid, really so excellent. I so happy with you . . .' continues Madame with encouraging sounds, the sounds one might whisper into the ear of a workhorse on its last legs, while oiling the shotgun behind its back.

Most infuriating are her suspended kisses of gratitude, hanging a full inch shy of my cheeks. I try to smile for the audience but it's a definite scowl. I am not the actress here.

Back in the kitchen, my hands full of soft fruit, I am confronted by a different madame.

'Me-ron, tidy your face!' shouts Madame sharply.

'What do you mean, Madame?'

'Wipe away angry eyes . . . we have company!'

'Madame, I'm sorry but I'm really tired . . . I have to rest . . .'

'Eh? Black people *never* get tired,' Madame begins. 'This important party. Your first party and we have so many more. Yes, I know it hard for you, but . . . why I am saying this? Get on with it!'

'I wanted a rest today, Madame . . . to go to church . . . it's *Sunday*.'

Her face reddens. Grapes are grabbed from me and tossed onto a tray. Her head comes at me, puts itself within a nose-length of mine, eye-to-eye, pupil-on-pupil. One hand clasps my hair from underneath the scarf and holds my head clamp-like in a painful tilt.

'Ow!' I peep.

'Meron, I had enough of this . . . change your atti-tude *now* or I deal with you,' she whispers with sufficient aggression to blast a gust of garlic into the roof of my gaping mouth.

'Yes, Madame,' I croak.

Mouth dry, eyes watering, my weary legs are going to buckle at any moment. Please give me space, I'm going down! My low blood pressure! Where's God's knee to sit on *now*?

But I am held steady, unwittingly by Madame, as she releases my hair and grasps my hands to check for dirt. I try to stop them from shaking but she must be able to feel the fresh sweat oozing from my palms.

'Fine. Do fruit plates.'

'Yes, Madame,' I manage, breathing outwards with relief as she stomps back to the guests.

Grim hours pass. Go away, people, please. Every additional minute they delay on the balcony is an extra minute on my legs: I doubt my legs will ever function properly again. I'll return to Addis in a wheelchair, hardly the long-distance running legend of my imagination.

'Me-ron . . . now we moving back into salon for coffee . . . you clean it already, yes?'

'Yes, Madame . . .'

And it will need cleaning again if you move back in there. God! Can't these people stop *speaking, spitting, dripping, dropping, dirtying, partying, peeling, breathing?* Can't you see what you are? You are not people: you are vacuum cleaners, garbage trucks, sewer ducts, cesspit suction pipes, all operating in reverse.

The guests are still here as a weakening sun finally suggests evening. Why has it taken so long today? In Addis, the sun used to charge headlong at dusk like a furious bull; in Beirut, it dawdles along like a listless grazing cow, lingering almost defiantly, hardly interested in sinking towards the ground within the usual daylight hours. This is not the sun I knew. The long march of the Lebanese luncheon service will finish me, if not today then a coming-soon tomorrow under this loathsome Beirut sun.

At last, these ever-shedding individuals eventually begin to leave maybe it has something to do with Shafeek. Publicly, he's lively and funny, yet by late afternoon, when he loosens his damp shoes a little, the atmosphere is instantly noxious from the foot fungus. Guests make their excuses for departure and I thank you, God, that there *is* a reason for everything.

Finally I rest, almost dead, slightly alive and certainly asleep.

Shafeek kicks my feet. It must be the middle of the night. What's he doing?

'Er, are you okay, Mister? Do you want any food prepared?'

'No, it's OK. Just checking you . . . or rather, checking *on* you.'

A whiff of alcohol and cigar breath blows into my face as he burps unashamedly. It revolts me. Public burping in Addis is taboo.

'Thank you, Mister,' I reply.

'So, how are you settling in?' he asks casually. 'I mean, are you comfortable?'

How I would love to tell him my body is in tatters after a single day of work. I feel fit to expire on each feeble beat of my heart and my mind is liquefying butter, melting even faster in his presence. How I would love him to hug me so tightly that I instantly dissolve into his warm protective mass and all fatigue is immediately irrelevant.

'I'm fine, Mister.'

'I'm sure you'll be a good worker . . . great eyes . . .' he slurs loudly.

'Thank—'

'Going to be sick now . . . clean up the bathroom afterwards, before Mum . . . Madame . . . whatever . . .'

He hurries away towards the bathroom. I immediately hear animal sounds, like a cow enduring a difficult labour. He repels and attracts at an intensity that exceeds all other men.

'Meron, it's ready!' he calls out proudly when the barfing stops.

Ready? Like a meal? Does he want me to set the table and call the others? Is this the final course of the Lebanese luncheon service?

It is difficult to believe, but within a single day, I have fallen from God's knee and landed in a pool of vomit, Shafeek's vomit no less. My father's words return to me: 'A life can change within a day.' If only I could remember what he told us to do, to make it change back.

A Repellent Visitor

My father was born with eyes intense enough to bore holes into the eyes of others. This forbidding pair of black drill bits assaulted strangers at great distances, long before gazes could be averted. But for people who *knew* my father, the initial pain of looking directly at him was quickly overwhelmed by the delight of his generosity, his evident enjoyment of company and his hunger for all that life had to offer. The eyes belied his words and actions, providing only a minor and temporary barrier to a city of friendships for the happiest angriest-looking man in the world.

Dad's clutch on happiness owed everything to his job as a train driver on the country's only railway service. Those ferociously focused eyes were invaluable for coaxing reluctant carriages along rickety moonlit lines eastwards from Addis Ababa to Djibouti, and back. Ethiopia depends on the small nation of Djibouti for its de facto port, the railway thus lugging freight and passengers of international significance.

Dad's post carried privilege, reverence and a spacious

villa, which in Addis meant a single-floored three-bedroomed house within its own compound, closed to the outside by a high white metal gate. The villa came with a short podgy maid – Almaze from Awasa – and a modest lawn with unkempt borders. When we scattered morsels of food in the garden, it became filled with shiny blue starlings that pushed and pecked so entertainingly I sometimes sacrificed my own dinner for the performance. By Addis standards, we were definitely rich and Dad made no effort to disguise this.

Conveniently for Dad's ever-expanding empire of companions, our residence lay just a few metres from the glorious La Gare terminus. This is where the Djibouti-bound train began its working day with my father at the helm. French-designed, this was less public railway station, more fairytale castle in its visual impression: eleven golden arches announced the entrance and this facade climbed ever upwards towards a double-decker red tin roof. Had it not been for the national flag waving from the upper ridge, I would have said the roof touched the top of the sky.

Inside La Gare, the platform boasted a straight line of sturdy wrought-iron palisades supporting a window-paned awning tilting upwards to allow a full view of symmetrical rails zigzagging into the horizon towards the distant Gulf of Aden. Not only was there shimmering symmetry and a glass roof, for a child La Gare was a playground populated by bands of jaded passengers, solemn whistle-blowing uniforms drunk on officiousness, piles of lost luggage – or soon would be – and silent carriages in sidings providing shade for resident goats munching on official 'Chemin de Fer' grass. Thank you, God, we had it all in La Gare.

I hardly noticed the slack trains. They moved too infrequently and sluggishly to offer any inherent danger to a scampering six-year-old who knew La Gare like a second home. Some days, the trains didn't move at all, or only very imperceptibly, from one siding to another. A happily endless cycle of mechanical failures helped to ensure permanent employment for many of my father's friends; some of them moving even less discernibly than the trains. We were part of a cosseted extended family of railway elite upon which the nation depended. I was nestled in contentment and I knew nothing else.

The iron knocker clanged against the white gate, as it did so often. Dad glanced downwards at me, cross-legged, playing the 'five stones' game with great skill and speed. His smile relieved the intensity of his usual glare. Mum sighed as she weaved dried grass into a colourful mesob for storing injera. Half a minute later, Almaze the maid clumped into the room.

'Tadelle to see Master,' she announced with a squeak.

'Yes, invite him in,' answered Dad without pause.

'Yes, Master,' replied Almaze and returned to the gate.

'Yet another one. Who's Tadelle?' asked Mum, sighing again.

'He's a fellow human, Werki-ye.'

'But which one?'

'The one who I've obviously forgotten, but will remember very, very soon.'

Mum began to shake her head. When Tadelle entered

the room, her shaking became more violent. But Dad refused to see it. Instead, he stood to greet the visitor with a generous grin. Slightly curious, I stood too, watching only my father's face.

'Ah, Tadelle! How are you?'

'Lemma! So sorry not to come sooner . . . it's been far too long. I've really missed you!'

Dad switched his eyes onto full beam for intense examination of this guest. My mother and I saw no spark of recognition. Mum sighed with sufficient force to signal the very last of the sighs.

'Yes, far too long . . . you should have come sooner,' said Dad as sincerely as possible.

I dared to stare at Tadelle. *Argh!* Somebody help me! The initial fright of his countenance caused my knees to give way and I slumped dramatically onto the floor.

'Meron? What are you doing?' asked Dad, looking down with an apparent glower.

He could see the fear in my face and smiled. In his eyes I saw an affection that would never diminish. Dad lifted me onto his knee and from this safe perch I was ready to regard Tadelle's full ghastliness.

He was wiry, stringy and knotty enough for my father to have employed him as a coupling link on his trains. Mum would have applauded this. On that first visit to our house, the lean face immediately told her everything she needed to know. Shining away like a worn table-tennis ball in his left cheek was a convex protrusion indicating the position of his chat cavity. This was the place in Tadelle's mouth where he rammed in as much of the toxic flora as he could manage: it retained its bulbous shape even when devoid of chat leaves. That day's mulch had left an emerald lipstick playing around the rim of his chew hole, while jumbled teeth wore an olive veneer that placed them within the skull of a thousand-year-old skeleton.

'Werki-ye, offer Tadelle some injera and wat,' ordered Dad.

'Eh? He's just a scrounger off the street. He doesn't know you and you don't know him . . . why would I offer this stranger our food?' replied Mum.

'The railways! We're old comrades on the *railways!*' declared Tadelle.

'There's only *one* railway in Ethiopia,' corrected Mum.

'It doesn't matter where, when, which, who . . . he's a guest in my house and we are all guests in God's kingdom. Let's share His banquet and share His love,' said Dad with absolute sincerity.

'I can see you are a good Christian,' said Tadelle.

'I can see you are a goat in man's clothing,' said Mum, referring to his leaf-chewing habit.

'Enough, my wife. Fetch fresh injera for this man . . . a blessed living being, breathing like us . . .'

'Yes, that's a pity,' interjected Mum.

'Sit down, Tadelle,' insisted Dad.

'Oh, I shall, I shall!'

Mum flinched as Tadelle rested his mucky rags on our most comfortable easy chair. Even to me, at the age of six, there was a clear difference between Tadelle's wardrobe and ours. We usually dressed in the trendiest jeans, trainers and T-shirts in town: modern attire for kids that nobody else in our road could yet acquire, while Dad wore striking flares that hugged his thighs and crotch. Honed muscles strained on the stitching of his huge-collared shirts: he offered the same soft bulges as our well-upholstered sofa. Dad picked up cheap imports from the Djibouti markets and brought them home as contraband. By the time the goods reached the Addis masses, we had moved onto the next fashion. Every man and child envied us. It was a sweet place to be. Compared with us, Tadelle was hardly in any place at all and quite possibly homeless.

'Why are you wasting our fresh injera on *him*?' argued Mum.

'Look at this poor man . . . he needs our injera more than we do. Tomorrow, it could be us knocking on *his* door for help—'

'He probably doesn't have a door. He's just some chat-eater off the street who heard you're rich . . . he's obviously here to rob us,' interrupted Mum.

'Wealth is a temporary illusion, my wife. Appreciate what we have today and share it . . . within a single day, you can lose it all.'

'Ah, within a day!' agreed Tadelle, nodding eagerly.

'He wouldn't need a day, he'd do it within an hour,' said Mum, rising to her feet at last to oblige the demands for food.

Mum's wardrobe became evident to Tadelle. Unlike us, she was allowed only the outfits of the traditional Habesha woman: long dresses that stopped just above the feet. Dad had bought a beautiful embroidered garment for her a week earlier, but with a slightly short fitting that unintentionally revealed her shapely calves to the world. It was this dress that Tadelle noticed as she left the room to fetch his injera. He made no effort to conceal his gaze. Dad caught it instantly but did not react.

Tadelle was a restless guest, unable to stay seated for more than a minute. He began to creep around on our floorboards in his dirty ten-birr trainers, unashamedly checking the possessions dotted about our room, stroking Mum's garish plastic flowers with his green-smudged fingers, weighing Dad's leather-bound Bible in the same gnarled hand, sniffing my worn white stones as though they carried an unlikely sea-salted fragrance, and insistently poking his stick-like index digit into our living-room wall, surprised at its firmness. Tadelle's age was unclear, though with only scraps of hair and a spaghetti dish of wrinkles carved out by the same repetitive jaw action, he seemed incomplete without walking stick and stoop. But there *was* a stoop. Towards *me,* perched on my father's knee.

'Hello, little one! You're a beauty . . .' he gushed, trying to touch my face with those green fingertips.

'I can swim!' I chirped as a form of defence.

I had spent the last two weeks reminding the world of my great achievement. For a landlocked nation without a public swimming pool, this was worth mentioning again and again. My confidence was soaring after Robel had performed his miracle shove.

'Well done, Meron!' Tadelle cheered, his green leaf ball clicking on the 'r' of my name.

He attempted to raise me from Dad's knee. Feeble bony hands grasped my ribcage, his arms like sodden cardboard flopping with the slightest pressure. He was so weak that my legs remained astride the lap of my father, who had the strength to lift up all three of his children in a single muscular swoop.

'You're very weak, Mister,' I observed as he gave up trying to lift me.

Tadelle laughed loudly and falsely, letting me plonk back onto Dad's knee.

'I'm not used to picking up such a plump healthy child . . . and I'm so weak from hunger . . . and . . .'

Mum returned with wat, injera and water. Tadelle stared at her legs again with an unmistakable leer. He devoured our food with the hand-speed of a hardened cotton-picker. It was all over within four minutes.

'Thank you, Lemma, your hospitality . . . and that of your lovely wife . . . is like a river of love spilling across the driest of Somali deserts, a glorious sight stretching into the horizon and never drying up . . . and . . .'

'What do you need, Tadelle?' asked Dad.

'Would a ten birr note float on that glorious river of love . . . for a fellow man?'

Without hesitation, Dad handed him the brown note. Mum was horrified but stayed quiet. With chat-money secured, Tadelle was quick to leave. Only his fusty musk lingered in the room.

'Lemma!' Mum started, gathering herself up for a clash.

'No! You listen to me,' fired Dad. 'I'm going to burn that dress straight away . . . it's disgusting. Poor Tadelle had to look at your legs while he was eating.'

Mum was Dad's and not for the gratification of others. Conversely, that did not mean he was *hers* and off-limits to others. Lemma had his share of weaknesses. Mum loved him too much to dwell on these.

'Ishee,' she said indignantly.

'Your mum doesn't understand *life* things,' he said to me, still balanced on his knee.

And, Dad, nor do I. Why didn't you write it all down for us? Now, ten years later, it is *Mum* who guides us through the 'life things'. But she is in Addis.

Now and the Foreseeable Future

Sixth day in Lebanon, 5am. New career as a downtrodden maid continues unabated. Only 815 days to go. No word from my mother yet. It feels like a year since I saw her.

This is the exact hour my mother rises. I think of her every morning as we awake together. Now, we share the hour but not the bed.

My mother is a vigorous riser. After washing and dressing, she crosses herself three times before covering her head with a white netela, made from the same linen as the constant white robe, the kemis. Common to all good Orthodox Christian women, Mum's concealed hair sees as much of the church's interior as her forever-hidden calves. Not a glug of water or morsel of bread is consumed before morning worship.

At that hour in Addis, the lighter grey tones of night's great black cloak are probably snagged on the Horn of Africa. As my mother hastens to the local Kirkos church, her vision is hampered by the drifting mist in unlit, unevenly cobbled streets, and also by her poor eyesight.

The coldness bites at her nose and fingers like a lively snake. Birds chirp hopefully, not entirely sure if they've mistimed the dawn. Once inside this church vibrant with huge doe-eyed murals of Christ and Maryam, my mother prays, chants, sings and performs prostrations, for four hours on an empty belly.

I wish she was here with me, comforting, cuddling or, at the very least, the residual warmth of her body and the smell of her skin lingering long inside our bed after she's risen, leaving me another four hours to slumber content-edly in her loving glow. Instead, I roll off my mattress and drag it outside to the balcony, to be aired in the crisp dawn, always loudly announced by the echoing minarets buried but not hushed amongst the high-rise concrete hulks of Beirut. While my mother performs prostrations on an empty stomach in Kirkos church, I similarly endure hard physical labour without nourishment. In the early morning blur, we share discomfort but not the cause. We've both made our choices and mine is a particularly questionable one.

Mum's remembered words move my body towards the bathroom: 'Be a good worker, show them your Habesha spirit . . .' Yes, Mum, I'm trying but this is not easy. Two hours of pre-breakfast mopping await me.

I breakfast at the same time as Abdul, 7am. For me: a small pitta bread, a lump of old cheese and a cup of tea, which sustain me through no more than five minutes. The moment I stand, I hear more echoes: from my stomach not from the minarets. Mum's breakfast genfo could blow me out for an entire day. Upon hearing an echo, she would stir up a second helping of the spicy buttery porridge, and another, until absolute silence came from within.

Occasionally, Nazia is in the kitchen before us, preparing the Turkish coffee for Abdul.

'Baba! Here! I made this coffee especially for *you*, with my own hands!' she proclaims.

I am intrigued by this statement. What does it mean? The coffee looks the same as always.

'Oh, Nazia! With your beautiful hands? Thank you, my daughter. How delicious!' gurgles Abdul, grabbing Nazia by the neck and kissing her passionately on the forehead.

This touching exchange always leaves me a little sadder as I imagine the delight of making coffee for my father, with the same result. What a wonderful way to begin the day.

If Nazia misses her alarm, I go into her bedroom and wake her.

'Nazia, it's seven-thirty . . . wake up, Nazia . . .'

'Thank you so much, *really* helpful,' she utters, barely out of her dreams and already dripping sarcasm.

I wait in case she needs anything.

'What are you looking at? *Go!*' she orders.

'Don't worry, Nazia, I'm always here if you need me,' I reply, unsure if I am being sarcastic or genuine. I am not well practised in sarcasm.

I slink off to the bathroom to tame Abdul's toilet treachery, before Madame's morning call. Abdul gets changed into his outdoor clothes: a tatty chequered shirt and wide black trousers pulled up to his ribcage. His old leather slip-on shoes are covered on the right side by excess trouser leg, while revealed in their entirety on the left. As a devout Muslim, he wants to expose his ankles but he's only fifty per cent successful. Madame frowns whenever she sees him like this, which is twice every day, except on Sundays when it's a prolonged once. Abdul only says goodbye to Nazia, Nuria and Mustafa in the mornings, plus a general 'Ma'a salama' to wish everyone a good day, which may not include me but I smile back anyway.

8am, I wash fruit and prepare breakfast drinks for Nazia (hot milky coffee) and Madame (fruit juice). In her bathroom, Nazia always sneezes violently three times in quick succession, leaving a fierce spray of toothpaste froth on her mirror for me to clean. I assume she is allergic to her own reflected image.

'Bonjour, Nazia!' I chant every morning. French words are ubiquitous here and Nazia is a particular fan.

But her studied avoidance of response is consistent and confrontational. A battle of wills has commenced: my silence would signal my defeat. I shall continue with the daily morning greetings until she replies, at which point I win.

Nuria and Hassan emerge from their quarters. I sneak an embrace with their adorable son, unless Madame is quick enough to intervene. Usually she isn't.

'Good morning, Nuria,' I attempt every morning.

'Mmmph,' she responds without eye contact.

'Hi, Meron, how are you doing? Good?' asks Hassan as constant as morning birdsong.

'Hello, Mister, I'm really really tired.'

'Right, right, good, good . . . don't forget to clean your teeth this morning,' says the cosmetic dentist, enthusiastically slurping a bottle of Pepsi Cola for breakfast.

Before leaving for work, Madame places a set of scales under my feet. The weight hardly changes.

'Fifty-eight kilo,' says Madame. 'You not work at efficient weight. I not like fat people, or people like you . . . going in wrong direction.'

'Yes, Madame,' I mumble.

'You see fat on me?' she asks.

'No, Madame,' I reply.

'We will keep eyes on you . . . this for your health.'

At 9am, Madame goes to work, elegant, fashionable, laden with designer-labelled accessories of affluence. Male colleagues probably fear her or fancy her, or both. How did Abdul acquire a wife like *this*?

'Look after my house like your life depend on this,' she says before locking the front door behind her.

'It probably does,' I say as the lock clicks, the prison gate secured as another day without outside contact looms.

On better days, I imagine I *am* Madame and the apartment is indeed mine. These are the days when I stand before her mirror and don her stretchy black dresses and matching heels, or a pair of baggy harem trousers coupled with glittered one-shoulder tops that would lure the purest of Beirut boys. The bedroom mirror flatters me and I can see that Madame's confidence is sourced from the exact point where I stand. I don't trust this mirror.

Shafeek is the last to rise and leave in the mornings. I make a cheese sandwich for him, lay out his work clothes and stand around waiting for a frantic volley of orders, usually involving underpants that are invariably wrong. He calls me into his bedroom, where he stands motionless and inadequate like a sweet young boy overwhelmed by the idea of dressing himself. He manages to pull on socks, vest and pants but lacks awareness of the fleshy bud poking out and catching the morning sun through the front opening of his loosely buttoned briefs. I am desperate to avert my eyes from this accidental exposure.

'My pants aren't ironed . . . look at them! Meron, what can you see? Look very carefully.'

'Erm . . . crinkles?'

'Are you one of those Africans that needs a hammer to the head before you understand something?'

'Sorry, Mister, I ironed them once already, but they have a natural inclination to crinkle, especially when worn by a person.'

'Not clever. Iron the pants again, Hammerhead!'

He disappears back into the bathroom, a second later charging out in towelling dressing gown, flinging crinkled briefs at my face.

'Empty or full?' he asks, as he knocks his fist against my skull with a dull thud.

'I don't know, Mister. Madame says full . . . full of dreams and idiocies.'

A little later as he moves towards the front door, I shout 'Goodbye, Mister!'

No response. I instinctively hurry behind him.

'Mister, Mister . . . Goodbye, Mister!'

'I heard you!'

Slam!

Once left alone, I have over four hours of hard labour ahead of me. Most days, bathroom cleaning, bedroom tidying, salon dusting and floor scrubbing predominate until Madame returns home for lunch at around 3pm. I aim for speed: I want to impress Madame. My mother has implanted a proud work ethic inside me, which I am fast coming to resent.

But three or four times a week, Shafeek returns home in the morning, a mere twenty minutes after he's rushed out, supposedly 'late'.

'I forgot my papers . . . Meron, what are you doing in here? In the kitchen! You're eating, aren't you? You're eating our food!'

A finger is pointing at me accusingly. I recall movies set in courtrooms, Shafeek's natural habitat.

'I needed a glass of water, Mister, sorry . . .'

He gazes intently at me. I have a glass in my hand. It looks plausible. Shafeek notices the cutlery drawer open. He walks across, yanks it right out. Nothing inside but cutlery.

'I know you've been eating something,' he says steadily.

Shafeek is under instruction from Madame to pull the 'forgotten papers' trick several times a week. He sits in his Mercedes downstairs, hoping I've started chewing on prime beef steaks before he bursts through the door. When genuinely late, Shafeek co-ordinates with Nazia. The Lammergeyer doesn't need excuses for her swoops. I am her carrion, but I make not a single false move. I eat nothing I should not: a victory for self-discipline but defeat for common sense.

Monday mornings, all bedlinen has to be changed. Wednesdays, I wash all non-whites. The washing machine is easy, but hanging the garments to dry on the balcony is bedevilled by complex rules. Clothes lines are each dedicated to one type of clothing, with a strict no-mixing rule: shirts on one line, skirts on another, and so on, until the trouser line, which must obscure the men's underwear. Even further back is women's underwear: Madame's lacy knickers are not for public presentation. Sundays, I tackle the whites, telling myself the same joke: 'Who is to be hung today? The whites or the non-whites? Sunday! It's the whites! Hang the whites!' It may not be funny but it kills a few seconds.

By 1pm, I'm waning. Two glasses of water are gulped down, often mixed with sugar. I douse my face. If I stop too long, momentum is lost. I have to keep the body working. Come on, Habesha professional, *push on*!

At 3pm sharp, Madame is home.

'Hello, Meron. How's everything?'

'Fine, Madame.'

But I am not fine. Please give me food. Let me rest. Instead, she goes straight to the Arabian sofa and pulls out a handful of pistachio husks from underneath the cushion, hidden earlier to test me.

'Obviously not finished!' she exclaims with a triumphant note.

'Big sorry, Madame, I thought I . . .'

'That not good enough. Now, clean all furniture again.'

And she walks away, her backside swinging behind her like kids scoffing from the back seat of a Bole bus that just soaked me with a kerbside puddle.

My hands are steady, but as I wash vegetables for lunch, the mind is panicking on behalf of the stomach. Bruised raw potato never looked better. I am not allowed to sit down for these chores. While Madame fries onions and peppers, olive oil spits from the cooker: I clean the cooker and its slippery environs at least four times a day but fresh fried food rarely makes it to my plate until three days afterwards, when it is practically ceasing to be food. When the lentils and rice come, I gobble them using a slice of stale bread and my right hand.

'Use your spoon!'

'Yes, Madame.'

I have my own battered spoon, more building implement than eating utensil. Nobody else touches it.

Nazia and Madame always eat lunch together, usually on the balcony. The conversations are prolonged and personal, as if every action or thought performed without the other has to be re-enacted in the presence of the other, or it lacks meaning. They are the closest I have ever seen two people who are not lovers. I am jealous of them, for myself and Mum.

Nuria's name is mentioned often, surrounded by words that mean 'lazy', 'dirty' and 'useless husband'. I wish I could participate on Hassan's behalf.

If Nazia can't finish her lunch, she blows her nose into a paper tissue and places the damp bundle upon her leftovers, or she coughs openly over the food. This ensures I am not tempted to fill myself up on her remnants, a spiteful ritual that never fails to astound me.

'Allah! Staring again! Go back to your place, Meron . . . in kitchen . . . and tidy up. Maybe white sock day today,' says Madame.

Madame lies down after lunch for exactly one hour. Nazia studies for her degree. I do more cleaning chores and play with Mustafa. Nuria wants the toddler positioned in front of a television screen for two hours, but I take the opportunity to frolic with him around the apartment. Let's give this little boy a childhood. I pretend to be a cross between wild dog and charging bull. Mustafa scampers and screams with delight.

'I love you, Meron! I love you!' he yells in front of Nuria, as she returns from work.

'No, no . . .' I begin, a little concerned at stealing the love of the family's cutest member.

'I love you, Meron!'

'Mustafa! What did you say? *I'm* your mother!' Nuria shouts. 'You tell *me*, not her. She's the servant. Remember what I said!'

'It's okay, Mum . . . not kissing her. She black and dirty . . . and she smell bad,' says Mustafa innocently.

'Good boy.'

Of course I'm dirty, of course I smell bad: I labour all day without a free moment for freshening up, without even a smear of deodorant at my disposal.

By 6pm, Madame is sliding along the shiny floor, kicking her white-sock-covered feet into random areas around the entire apartment: some of these are uncharted corners yet to be explored with the sponge-mop. She is soon wearing two-tone socks and screaming a high-tone 'Me-ron!'

'But I did this room, Madame,' I protest.

She stretches out her arm and yanks off a blob of chewing gum from the top of the door. How did the socks know about *that*? How would *I* know about *that*? The tops of doors have not been a major feature of my sixteen-year existence up to this moment. I was hardly aware that doors had 'tops' where small things might congregate. In Ethiopia, doors aren't thick enough to have 'tops'.

'Clean all this room again. And check all of door *tops*. Maybe tomorrow you get it right.'

She walks away, backside swinging. There are those grinning kids in the back seat of the bus again. I would love to slap them.

At 7.30pm, Madame often calls her mother. Similar to Nazia and Madame, the conversation is intimate and detailed. I gain a vague sense of delight from hearing Madame say 'Yes, Mum' repeatedly, as though it belittles her in front of me.

At 9pm, Hassan sprints out onto the balcony for a private conversation with a female client. The double-glazed balcony doors are locked shut behind him. As he natters secretly into the phone, Nuria stands the other side of the doors glaring at him. Madame positions herself a few metres behind Nuria. A couple of metres back from Madame finds me, watching with great interest. Beyond me, the Lammergeyer surveys all. Shafeek remains in the study reading his law books, rising above this charade. We take up these positions most evenings.

'Nuria! Who's that calling him?' Madame fumes at Nuria, in Arabic.

'Hassan! Who's that calling you?' Nuria rants at Hassan through the glass.

Hassan keeps his back turned.

'Doesn't he remember he's married?' rages Madame.

'Don't you remember you're married?' repeats Nuria at Hassan.

'When will he become a worthy husband?'

'When will you become a worthy husband?'

Hassan never answers the questions. I doubt there would be much interest in his answers.

I recollect Proverbs 27:15: 'A continual dripping on a rainy day and a contentious woman are alike.' I am tempted to shout this at Hassan, with additional advice: whoever chooses to sit beneath constant dripping is a fool. Hassan, get an umbrella or move.

I shout nothing. I know Nazia is there, but cannot stop myself from trailing Madame to the commotion. It's better than television.

'Do some work, Meron . . . this is none of your business,' Nazia hisses into my ear.

'Yes, Nazia . . .' And I walk very slowly from the scene, reluctant to miss a second of the drama as Madame's tirade gathers momentum.

'Nuria, I always said he was a waste of time. Look at you. Your life hasn't changed for the better since you married him . . . still wearing dungarees! You don't even take good holidays. You're still here, living in *my* house. And he's a player . . . look at him . . . a bad one, going nowhere, taking you there with him . . . have to change him . . . push him. Learn from *me*. Go to France for a break. Women your age go to France every year . . . you're not normal!'

'Allah! Mother! I'm trying to listen to him speaking to *her*. Will you please shut up?'

'Why does he waste all your money on takeaways? You're toppling backwards into the abyss . . .'

Only by grabbing my shoulders and forcibly guiding

me into the kitchen can Nazia pull me away from the brilliant furore.

By 9.30pm, Abdul is home. He changes immediately into the lopsided silk pyjamas and, oblivious to the plot, ploughs straight into the war zone. Nuria, positioned between cheating husband and chiding mother, receives the triple-kiss treatment from Abdul. And Nazia too. Why no kiss for Madame?

'Shall I prepare something for Mister Abdul?' I ask Madame, finding an excuse to ease my way back into the action.

'No . . . he fry egg or something. Why waste good food on *him*?' she responds in front of Abdul.

'Hey, Baba! Hassan's cheating on Nuria again,' announces Nazia in front of everyone.

Where there's a gaping bleeding wound, the Lammergeyer will swoop with precision. But Abdul is disinterested. He steers himself into the kitchen and pushes into his mouth whatever is lying around on the counter. Please, Abdul, it's not easy to read you. I would like to tap my fist on your mature prune of a head and see what's inside.

If Hassan is not the evening entertainment, I run between random shouts around the apartment: 'Meron! I want more food!', 'Meron! I need drink!', 'Meron! Change TV channel!', 'Meron! Come here!' I am learning to hate my name. They issue 'Meron!'s blithely, as though there are no implications, as though there is no limit to my dedication. Yes, I've arrived in Beirut with swollen tanks of goodwill and good faith, and yes, I leap to every call with a smile. But these are finite resources, vulnerable to ebbing.

These people are being irresponsible with something they do not understand.

'Meron, you need to understand something,' says Shafeek.

'Yes, Mister?'

'In Lebanon, families follow a strict running order of marriage and priority, from first-born to the last. Nuria is the oldest so she married first. Now, she's out of the family and should have left the apartment already. Any problems, she can ask Hassan for help, not you. I'm the next in line . . . it's *my* time now for maid service . . . until I marry and go . . . then Nazia has *her* time. Right now, you're here for Mum and me. Forget about the others.'

I wish I could.

At 11pm, most days, I have ten minutes for a body-wash using my plastic bowl. Madame performs her naivety act.

'You still up? Oh! I can't believe it. Why? Please not do *too much*, Meron. Take rest, go to bed. You like work-aholic . . .'

If I wasn't so tired, I would laugh at her false concern. Instead, hunger and exhaustion pull my body to Earth. I flop down on my narrow mattress and sleep immediately. Exhaustion beats hunger every time.

Ecclesiastes 5:12: 'Sweet is the sleep of a labourer, whether he eats little or much: but the surfeit of the rich will not let him sleep.' Occasionally, Mum, the Bible lapses into wishful thinking: show me a rich person who is too rich to sleep. *Mum?*

Another day ticked off. I count them all, the number

repeated inside my head throughout the day, each three-digit figure like a slow-digesting, overspiced Ethiopian wat outstaying its welcome in the gut.

Around 2am, Fridays and Saturdays, sleep is broken. Shafeek romps in late from a club, demanding chicken and chips. He reeks of liquor, aftershave, perfume, cigarettes and feet. Four of these are his, the perfume is not. The perfume is rarely the same. He has fun, I conclude.

I wait on my stool while he eats in front of the television in 'my' salon. I nod asleep every few seconds. But I have to wait: dirty plates don't wash themselves at three in the morning, and Shafeek likes using plates. He has more plates than food.

'Hungry, Meron?' he asks.

'Yes, Mister, very hungry.'

'Why? Don't you eat enough? We've got a fridge full of food.'

I stay silent. It's a statement not a question, and even if it is a question, I cannot answer it without implicating his mother's meanness.

'Chicken leg?' he asks.

'Yes, please.'

Shafeek tosses it across. I ravage the leg in seconds, then start on the bones. In Addis, many crack open sheep bones to scoff the soft marrow inside. Me? I'm a chicken-bone girl, breaking them open between my teeth to suck out the rich core. I do this without thinking. Shafeek stops watching television.

'Is that normal?' he asks on the first occasion.

'Yes, very normal for me, Mister,' I reply as splinters of thin bone tumble from my mouth.

'Your eyes look even bigger when you're chewing bones.'

I laugh. My body is emitting a joyous sound. I feel guilty.

'Thank you, Mister. I'm enjoying this . . . with you.'

'What are you doing?' Madame demands suddenly, in her scarlet silk gown.

'Mother, you aren't feeding her. She's eating chicken bones like a dog.'

I laugh again.

'Right. I'll see if I can find a collection of old bones for her tomorrow,' she mutters sarcastically.

'I think *you've* got a few, Mum,' slurs Shafeek, still a little drunk.

Madame pauses. I duck quickly onto my mattress with my own tired bones hanging together under a stocking of skin. As I drift back to sleep, I hear Madame scolding Shafeek in the hall.

'When will you get married and give me some rest? Your age is going fast . . . it'll be too late soon. It's your turn to find a woman, have a child and leave my house!'

Shafeek needs a wife and a baby. This cues my usual dream: I marry Shafeek and dine on his bones, leaving me unsure if I am pregnant, or bloated on his bone marrow, or my stomach is distended from hunger. I awake with the blanket in my mouth and an appetite that an entire carcass could not sate.

It is 5am, seventh day. My new career as a downtrodden maid continues unabated. Only 814 days to go. No word from my mother yet. It feels like a year since I saw her. She was right to mourn me early. But a second mourning might just kill her: the first was hard enough.

The Last Photograph

Only a month after my swimming success in the Ghion pool, it was Nati's fourth birthday. My father ordered a family photo to celebrate the day: we were rich enough to pay a professional photographer for such an event, but Dad's health could not be bought. Bedridden with a chest infection, he was racked with vicious chills, an escalating fever and an alarming difficulty in breathing. Each time he wheezed, I thought a locomotive was scraping through the station's points as it switched onto a corroded siding. His barrel of a chest pumped away like fire bellows and generated a thirst on him that demanded a large jug of water be filled every half an hour, the drinking followed by crippling bouts of hiccups.

The friendly doctor had visited us two hours earlier and said, 'He'll be fine.' Doctors in Addis never told their patients the bad news: it didn't help anyone to know the worst, and anticipated death had a negative effect on the demand for expensive medical treatment. Doctors had to earn a living.

My mother was dressing us in our best clothes when the iron knocker clanged on the back gate.

'Doctor's already been. Too early for the photographer,' she muttered.

'Almaze is going to the gate, Mum,' I said.

A minute later, she hurried back.

'Tadelle to see Master . . .'

'Why? What's he doing here again? He knows Lemma's sick,' said Mum.

'I don't know . . . he with a woman.'

'Woman? Okay, get on with your work, I'll see them.'

My mother sighed and headed for the gate. I ran behind her, the way I did when Dad's sleek grey diesel train pulled in, horn blasting, our gate flying open to cheer in its arrival, only fifty metres away.

'Hello? What do you want?' demanded Mum at the closed gates.

'How is he?' I heard from an effeminate male voice, or a masculine female voice, I couldn't be sure. 'He's a very good man . . . I hope he's not suffering. I can't forget what he did for me . . . never in my life, never . . .'

I looked up at the reedy voice as the gate opened.

Tadelle immediately leant towards me to stroke my freshly plaited head.

'Tadelle, don't touch her! Lemma's very ill. You can't see him.'

'I know I can't . . . I wouldn't be so insensitive . . . how could I. But this woman *is* anxious to see him . . . and with good good reason . . .' he gabbled slightly deliriously.

Beside Tadelle stood a typical countrywoman in a long beige dress, white shawl and purple front-knotted headscarf, all completely unco-ordinated in both colour and pattern. Her skin had the familiar glow of a field-hand, slow-cooked during countless harvests under the Oromo sun.

'Eh? Who? Who are you? Where are you from?' pressed Mum.

'I'm Kebebush from Woliso.'

My father was from Woliso, a country backwater town mainly concerned with the business of roses and other exportable flowers.

'Woliso! Why? What's the matter? Is his mother sick?'

'No, no, she's fine. I think he told you about me . . . I'm Lemma's ex-wife.'

'Eh? Ex-wife? What are *you* doing here? I haven't got time for talking to his ex-wife. He's a sick man, I have to care for him . . . and it's my son's fourth birthday. I've got two other young children . . . too busy for this . . . the photographer is coming. Just *go!*'

Tadelle seemed perturbed by her impatient manner. His chewing speed increased from a steady grind to an urgent gnaw. The egg-like side of his face convulsed faster than my eyes could follow.

'*Go?* Why? Why are you so angry? Please calm down. She's come a long way, Werknesh. Maybe you can give her food and drink . . . and me. We're all brothers and sisters in God's eyes, remember? Sharing the world's riches . . . our planet spinning on mutual kindnesses . . . fellow humans toiling . . .'

'Yes, yes, all nice words, but I'm not sure what you really want . . . or *her*.'

'Yes, it's such merciful coincidence,' continued Tadelle.

'She was sleeping on my floor for a modest rent, selling her chicken and kale and eggs in the Merkato . . . on her monthly visit . . . and mentioned Lemma . . . Lemma! I said I worked with him on the railways but he's sick, horribly sick, and here we are, delivered by the hand of the Lord, on urgent business . . .'

'It's really important I see him, before he's taken. Let me in,' stated Kebebush bluntly, a countrywoman speaking without Addis finesse.

Mum looked at both of them.

'Go . . . a . . . way,' she said in such a low steady voice that only an explosion could possibly follow.

Tadelle and Kebebush backed out quickly through our gate, Mum walloping it shut after them with a loud clunk.

'Where's the love of God in this house?' shouted Tadelle over the gate. 'She's your sister, not the Devil! Are you *mad*? I need nourishment . . . chicken . . . chat . . . *anything*. Do not forsake your fellow human . . . God is watching!'

Mum stormed back into the house. I trailed in behind, grinning at Tadelle's performance. With help from Auntie Kidist, she hurriedly prepared birthday popcorn, candles, bread and coffee ceremony around my father's bed.

'Now, my family . . . time for the special photograph,' panted my father as the photographer arrived.

Dad's hands were trembling. Mum was too angry to speak. Click, click, click went the camera. But bouncing on my father's mattress, I was oblivious to the grave nature of Dad's sickness and Mum's quiet rage; I thought the day was great fun. Life was becoming more brilliant by the minute. How fortuitous was I!

Three days later, Dad died of pneumonia. Mum told me he had been called away to Dire Dawa for work, and wouldn't return. Whatever the reason, God's illogicality baffled me. Why take my father away at *that* time? When we loved him so much? When things were so good? What was His reasoning? Why pick on us? *Why?*

But the logic of a six-year-old held fast. At least we had the photo, luckily snapped just in time. Happiness conserved forever within an image, reproduced and magnified countless times in my mind. Ten years later, I lie on a mattress in Beirut, clinging to that image.

In these strange surroundings, a new perspective occurs to me: if he hadn't died, I wouldn't be in Lebanon today. That is certain. I wouldn't be the person I am today. As always, God must have had His reasons, yet to be revealed.

True Nature of My Hosts
(730 days left)

I exchanged Addis for Beirut but I cannot say I am really *here*. It is a peculiar world, floating high above a land I expect never to enter or explore or enjoy. Sweeping the dust off the balcony every morning, I can see the city where the dust originates, but I cannot touch that place. Dirt accumulates beneath my fingernails quickly; the discarded dead cells of living beings, from a distant planet. We do not interact, Beirut and I; Beirut means nothing to me. I, in turn, mean nothing to Beirut. Within Beirut, I am an ant, if anything at all.

The third month in Beirut crawls past, ant-like, mostly on my hands and knees. Mum, you always talked about His reasons and His reasoning but I am overdue an explanation. What *am* I doing here?

After the first three probationary months, finishing tomorrow, I will be contractually bound without a let-out clause. At least the money will be accumulating. Yes, the money. Did I really come here just for *that*? Why did I have to see Selam that day? Did she go through *this* to

145

look like *that*? How many Habesha girls have made the same mistake? This is madness. It cannot be part of God's plan. I am confounded.

Beti said things might worsen the moment the contract is signed. 'They take advantage, sister, if you're not strong,' she said on the flight. And I'm not 'strong'. I've withered substantially. My head hangs naturally now. I look at people's shoes first and then the floor they are walking on. Those shoes need polishing and that floor wants mopping, before the vicious white socks come round again. The hanging head is reminiscent of my mother when she mourns: we have the same faulty hinge in our necks that works loose in the face of misery. But my hinge is threatening to give way altogether. If I hold out my hands, maybe I'll catch my own head. And Broken Neck has earned precisely *nothing* so far.

'Meron, come here now! Checking your weight.'

Go and weigh yourself.

'Fifty kilos . . . you lost eight kilos in three months. Must feel much better now.'

'I get really hungry . . .' I start weakly.

'I only thinking of you, Meron,' says Madame. I very much doubt she ever thinks of me.

'Thank you, Madame,' I say, watching her eat a bowl of rice and stale salad in the kitchen. When alone, she eats plain food that excites nobody, except possibly me.

'We only have fantastic food one or two times a week . . . Friday and Sunday, fish and lamb. Never waste money on fancy food for yourself, Meron,' she says. 'Just eat enough to keep going. You need stay thin so you can work well. Look at *me*! I eat same as you. My body good and very beautiful . . . no?'

'Yes, Madame, it is.'

It really is. She is a woman in her fifties with a pair of high-bouncing basketballs for buttocks. I can't deny that. Her body is much better than Mum's.

'Fancy food is like fancy clothes . . . bring out when have guests, not waste on yourself or your family. Show guests great food and great clothes, and they believing you always live like king and . . .' She pauses as Nazia enters the kitchen.

'Meron!' shouts Madame suddenly. 'Why you staring at me, *again*? Go and clean Mister Abdul's bathroom . . . he come home soon!'

Nazia looks at me until I slope away. This happens often now. Glints of Madame's humanity interrupted: she reverts back to the tyrant act, the act Nazia expects of her. What is this?

The phone rings. Nuria is in hospital for the birth of her second baby. It might be Hassan calling with news of the birth. Nazia runs to answer it in the small salon, but she *always* runs to the house phone. Is it possible that she has somebody special?

'Hello?' she says, followed by a stunned pause. 'You want to speak to *Meron*? Why? Who's calling? What do you want?'

She repeats everything slowly. It has to be from Ethiopia. I jog towards the salon. Three months since I left Addis and my mother must be desperate for contact by now, especially if the letters haven't arrived. Could it be her? My heart pounds against my ribcage as if trying to escape.

'How did you get this number?' demands Nazia into the phone.

I stand in front of her patiently. Nazia clutches the phone tightly. My right hand is suspended in mid-air the way beggars' hands stubbornly hang in the air for years and years outside Addis churches.

'Just tell me, why are you calling?' Nazia continues. 'She's not here anyway . . . Meron's gone.'

She smacks down the phone hard enough to shatter it.

'Who was *that*? Who's this guy trying to contact you?' she asks furiously.

I stay silent. Maybe Nati, but how would he get this number?

'I'm telling my mother about this,' she continues.

'You can,' I say, faking nonchalance.

I don't want Nazia glorying in my distress. But equally, I hate festering anger. I run immediately to confront Madame before Nazia can get to her.

'Madame, Nazia stopped me from speaking to an Ethiopian friend . . . she hung up! It's not fair!'

Madame tries hard to reconcile her environment. It is her kitchen in her apartment and her servant is speaking to her like an equal.

'What? Ta gueule!' she exclaims.

'You're not treating me like a person!' I continue, ignoring her order to shut up, and switching to Arabic.

Three months and I'm practically fluent. Nobody seems to have noticed. I speak to Madame in Arabic and she insists on replying in flawed English, as if unable to accept my mastery of her language.

'Allah! Why you think you here, Meron . . . for me to serve *you*? You not paid to sit and enjoy my apartment and use my telephone. You are servant! You forget this?'

'No, Madame.'

If only Shafeek was here to protect me.

'So clean bathroom, then you clean balcony again. There are coffee stains, as usual . . . they never seem to go.'

Spilt black coffee on the pink-hued stones leaves marks like the oil stains I used to see on La Gare's workshop floor. I remember those splashes of black tar like old friends: evidence of human endeavour. They *never* disappeared and nobody ever tried to clean them. But Madame hates *all* stains. For her, other people are stains waiting to happen. I roll my eyes unapologetically at her.

'And tidy your face . . . *now*!' she screeches.

Nazia grins; her braces glint. But I stand my ground. There are too many injustices being heaped on me.

'Madame, I've had no reply to my letters to Ethiopia . . . eight sent since I arrived . . . and nothing from my mother.'

All eight letters I have handwritten and passed to Madame. Admittedly, the Ethiopian postal system is run along the same lines as the lottery, with just a few lucky winners each week. But I can't help wondering if the eight letters didn't even reach the hands of the Beirut Post Office.

'Eh? Why you telling *me*? I not run postal service for you. Go and do some work or we sending you home like letters, before contract signing . . . *tomorrow*.'

I keep quiet. God, I need that money to provide some

flimsy rationale for all this. I cannot afford outrage. Things will get better, I'm sure. They have to. They *have* to.

Next day, the contract is signed and we are into a two-year term. I feel like it's an achievement: I have done hard labour for three months on zero pay. Today, the money flows in. At three dollars per day, it's more of a gradual moistening than a flash-flood, but nonetheless I want to share this news with *someone*.

I call Beti when the apartment is vacated. Her number is local: Madame can't detect the call.

'Beti? Is that you?'

'*Meron? Meron!* I been trying to contact you for three months, sister! Yesterday, a friend called your place, Habesha guy, said you'd gone. I been worrying so much! You didn't come to any Sunday services. I heard *nothing* from you. What's up, girl?'

'We signed the two-year contract today but, Beti, I think they're starving me to death. I'm hungry all the time, I get no rest, they scream at me . . .'

'I hear you, sister . . . that's our life in an Arab country. But if the men try to touch you, you gotta cry and wail till they're gone. They hate histrionics. You can act, can't you?'

'Yes, Beti, I can act and I can lie. But I'm weak. Beti, I need *food*.'

'You losing weight fast then?'

'I get their three-day-old food and rubbery rice. Bread is turning green or it's so hard I have to dunk it in tea to get my teeth into it. And fresh fruit? Forget about it. Madame has me on the scales every few days and now it's *dropping* off. I probably look like a mop . . . I'm too scared to look in the mirror.'

'Relax, sister, relax. Let me ask you something . . . the responsibility for your welfare rests upon whom?'

'My sponsor family . . . my Madame.'

'You got that right. So eat her food, sister.'

'Eat her food? That sounds dangerous.'

'Listen up . . . life or death? Simple choice . . . eat her food or starve to death, which is it?'

'I'd prefer not to slowly starve to death. It's not a good death. What can I eat? Madame checks the garbage every day.'

'Easy. Tomatoes, bananas, apples, cucumber, olives, carrot . . . fast, cheap, no skin except for bananas . . . you can chuck skins down the toilet. They won't miss them, no aroma. But don't touch oranges. They're dangerous . . . easy give-away.'

'Mmm . . . okay.'

'Cram olives into your mouth any time you can. Spit the pits through the window. And cook a potato . . . five minutes in the microwave, she's your baby.'

'But what about the potato skin?'

'Eat it! Just clean and cook and eat! But remember to open the window . . . potatoes have a smell. Don't bother with rice . . . takes too long. And forget about meat or fish. They're watching all that quality stuff.'

'So I can't boil up a pot of doro wat,' I say, beginning to salivate.

'That, my sweet sister, is completely out of the question,' Beti says, giggling.

I laugh. It feels good letting that go.

'Eat in the bathroom, lock the door. If anyone returns, you're taking a pee. They can't see you. Tomatoes are the best . . . with salt . . . no peel or core.'

'Oh, Beti, thank you . . .'

'Drink their milk. Just add water to top it up afterwards . . .'

I hear the key in the door.

'Got to go!' I whisper, hanging up.

Shafeek has 'forgotten his papers' again. He walks into the lounge and finds me on hands and knees, frantically shining a single floor tile for no particular reason.

'Meron, what are you doing?' he says, gazing at my lips. They are wet with saliva.

'Cleaning, Mister.'

'I forgot my papers again . . .' Shafeek trails off, his head spinning round as he seeks evidence of some illicit activity, as Madame demands of him.

'Can I get you anything, Mister?'

'Er . . . no . . .' he mutters, lifting up two cushions to check if I've stashed anything underneath them. He plays with them absent-mindedly, bashing them together and tossing one at my head, then the other.

'It's good to have a bit of fun sometimes . . . right, Hammerhead?' he sniggers.

Shafeek is not cute when he's pretending to laugh. I prefer him sad or asleep or speaking seriously to other lawyers on the phone. I love that.

'Er, yes, Mister.' I keep my Hammerhead down.

'I'm going now.'

'Bye, Mister . . . again.'

He's out. I sprint into the kitchen to prepare an 'illegal' snack. Two tomatoes are inside me while waiting for a small microwaved potato. Hot in my hand, I dunk it in cold water and rush towards the bathroom, but the brilliant yellowness of ripe bananas seduces me from a bowl in the small salon. I've been on my feet since 5am with only the breakfast of a humming bird to sustain me. Tomatoes, potato, banana . . . all in my hands and stomach. Ha!

Clickety-click, Shafeek! He's coming through the door *again*, and I'm suddenly sprinting. I dash into the bathroom.

'Meron! What are you doing?' he shouts gruffly at my back.

But he's too late. I'm inside, locking the door. I now have to swallow hard on potato and banana. Come on, gulp them down. The potato is too hot but I bundle it into my throat. A full stomach is worth the scorched mouth and the lip ulcers. In with the banana now. Ram it in!

'Meron!' he shouts again, smacking on the bathroom door, trying to open it.

Momentarily, I pull barely chewed food from my mouth and reply.

'I'm going to the toilet, Mister. I can't stop myself.'

I fling the banana skin down the pan, the banana now in my stomach, now untouchable. It's *my* banana. Ha! Ha! Ha! Ah, yes, sweet delirium on a stolen banana. The banana is so perfect: it couldn't be invented by man in a factory. It's so obvious that God makes them.

'Meron!' he shouts again. 'Come here, now! Or I'll kill you, wallahi!'

I believe him. I panic and flush the toilet hard. The last vestiges of potato leave my mouth. But the flush is too fierce, splashing the banana skin out of the bowl onto the floor, just the way Abdul tugs on it every morning. I toss the skin back in. Go down! Go down! I pull on the flush again: nothing happens. Come on, toilet, refill yourself! *Refill!*

'Meron!' he growls, thrashing the door handle pointlessly.

Shafeek is working himself into a frenzy, which is not very helpful. I try the flush again. This time gently. Please, please take my banana skin, otherwise I'll have to eat it. The innards of the toilet rumble and whoosh. Away it goes. Thank you, God! He makes them and He takes them.

I glance at myself in the mirror, checking for food around the mouth. I'm clean.

Outside, Shafeek looks at me hard. He's flustered, but I've seen worse in my sixteen years.

'I don't believe you,' he snorts, pushing past me into the bathroom.

I shrug my shoulders and continue back to the lounge for resumption of work while Shafeek noses around. He finds nothing.

'Oh, I forgot my papers again,' he declares belatedly, and heads off to work.

Nothing more is said. No evidence, no case. The banana is safely sitting and digesting away in my gut, secure from its rightful owners.

The same evening, Madame approaches me.

'Meron, you eat one banana today, yes?'

'No, Madame,' I gulp.

'I know you did.'

She seems certain. How can she be so certain? There were so many bananas this morning.

'I definitely did not,' I maintain, stony-faced.

Madame sighs irritably.

'I thought you will be good servant, but you are not. I see you took one . . . stalk is fresh and white . . . was *you* . . . admit it!'

'Not me, Madame,' I mumble, edging away from her as quickly as possible.

'You liar! And thief!' she yells at me, her face suddenly pink with rage.

I am not sure what to say or what to expect as Madame strides towards me.

A piercing shriek rings out through the apartment. It's Mustafa. He's fallen onto a metal drawer handle and cut his forehead. Blood is pouring out. Poor little Mustafa.

'Mama! Mama!' screams Nuria hysterically.

Madame is immediately distracted.

In the tumult, I walk.

Later, Mustafa has two stitches on his head. It is almost as though he took the fall for me.

Two days later, I'm entranced by those delicious vivid crescents once more. I break off another perfect banana: a comfortable fit between palm and fingers, as if designed specifically to sit in my hand. There are ten on the bunch – now less one – and two old stalks turned black with age. The fresh pale green stalk staring back at me is the issue.

I pick up Madame's superior lighter – polished heavy

grey stone with chrome striker – which is sitting just a short stretch away. I ignite it and hold the flame against the exposed stalk for a few seconds. It quickly blackens. Madame now has three black stalks to look at. But maybe she counts *them* every morning?

Later, she comes back to me on that very point.

'Meron, you stealing another banana.'

'Not me, Madame,' I lie.

'Why you lying? I know you did.'

'I didn't, Madame.'

'You come here.'

She leads me into the lounge and sits me down on the floor, in front of the television. Perhaps we will watch some TV together and relax a little. At last, some Madame–servant bonding, without Nazia butting in.

She flicks on the DVD player. Great, a movie! The vast screen is filled by a blurry black and white picture. All I can see is a skinny black girl in a revolting maid's uniform standing next to some bananas. She pulls one off and eats it. Seconds later, she holds a stone lighter to the stalk. Nice lighter. The girl is me. I'm a film star.

'Oh yes! You're right. I remember . . . I *did* eat a banana, Madame. I was so desperately hungry.'

She has left me very little room for fabrication.

'What you *doing* here, Meron? Where you learning things like that, burning a banana stalk to look black? Why you not stay in Addis Ababa and do good things with this *mind* you got? What you doing in my home, causing me problems, wasting my time, spending my money . . . Allah! Why you *here*?'

The volume has increased and the words are coming faster. Worse still, her left eyebrow is arched. A single arched eyebrow concerns me: it suggests imbalance within.

'I don't know . . . I'm just *here*, Madame.'

I don't have a considered answer at my fingertips. Does she want my entire life story?

Whichever muscle is tugging the eyebrow towards her fringe is certainly sure of itself. I fear the lever at the other end of that muscle: it is part of something unsettled, brooding, agitated, feverishly grabbing away at an eyebrow muscle as a precursor to some kind of unimaginable ire.

'No! I not believe you . . . you steal my fruit when you feel like . . . just because we signed contract!' gabbles Madame, now fully absorbing the atrocity that has occurred. 'You betray me *again*, Meron!'

'Er . . .'

'Why you eat my banana?' she screams. 'I know you bad before you come here. Agency tell me you look like bad girl in photo . . . I say "no, no, she got good taste, her hair look good", but now, yes, I see they completely right. You out of control! Like animal . . . why you eat my fruit? Bananas for my family, not for thief! Why? Why?'

The words don't come. Madame's trigger has been flicked, torrents of Arabic incoherence streaming from her lips. I don't understand a single word. Exaggerated gesticulations consume her flailing arms. I'm suddenly mesmerised by her hands flying off in all directions before my eyes. She could be batting mosquitoes buzzing around our heads, but I see no insects of any description. Madame's hair quivers in time with her body and hands. I've seen incredible choreography in Addis, but her wild movements *without* music are a triumph in the world of original dance.

Her hands are flying in too close to my head: I stand back a pace or two, but she closes up on me again.

'Talk to me! Talk! Why, Mcron? Why?'

My mind seizes up. Why? This is ridiculous. One banana and our world is on the brink of collapse! I start laughing. I can't help it.

Madame can't believe I'm laughing at her. She's momentarily stunned, before hard slaps land on my face. Ow! Ow! Madame's eyeballs are set to burst open like hot popcorn on the stove. She's singing out for Allah, the words strung together so rapidly it sounds like an exultant ululation sung at an Addis wedding. Ouch! Ouch! She's out of control, on another emotional plane, blabbering like the possessed. This woman is mad! Her hands fire in at my face, as though swatting a defiant fly that refuses to die: there's nothing I can do except duck and back away and shield my face from the attack.

'No, Madame, please, please!' I cry.

The Habesha 'sharing food' ethic seems so far away now. I've had my face slapped before in Addis, but never this torrent of blows for a miserable banana.

Madame's explosion detonates Shafeek, still in bed. Upon hearing her livid jabbering pitch, he comes bounding into the kitchen, teeth bared. I assume he's running to protect me.

Shafeek doesn't stop for explanation, charging straight at me in only his briefs.

'Shafeek! *No!*' screams Nazia, suddenly in the room with us.

He batters my skinny arms with his fists. I howl loudly: more from shock and disappointment than pain.

'Leave her, Shafeek!' urges Nazia again.

When Shafeek catches fire, the bubbly puppy turns apoplectic wolf: his stubbly cheeks purple with rage, skin instantly moist with angry sweat, voice unable to enunciate the streams of Arabic curses in a rabid wave of ranting. It's hard to reconcile this beast with the suave young lawyer who lobs chicken bones at me behind Madame's back. But when these Lebanese flip, they really fly. There's no middle setting.

'Stop, Shafeek! Control yourself! *Not this one!*' screams Nazia, but it doesn't work.

Shafeek pummels my arms again and again until a droplet of sweat hangs from his eyebrow. He brushes off the sweat, his wild green eyes so dilated the green is reduced to nothing.

Shafeek and Madame leave me in the kitchen, sobbing on the floor, nursing the bruises, my arms now textured like fried aubergine. Nazia slips away. Who in this house is sicker in the head? I want to shout obscenities at all of them but manage only feeble burbling in Amharic. I eventually trudge to the cupboard where I store my mattress, fall to my knees and kiss my carefully folded postcard of Maryam and baby Jesus.

'Yes, go and cry on your little picture!' shouts Madame at my back.

Later, I survey the apartment discreetly. Small devices mounted on the walls of the two salons have red flashing lights attached. Before today, I assumed they were smoke alarms or burglar alarms or something useful, but no, Madame has surveillance cameras. I am beginning to better comprehend the concept of paranoia.

I recall Psalms 39:5: 'Behold, thou hast made my days a few handbreaths, and my lifetime is as nothing in thy sight. Surely every man stands as a mere breath!'

If life is a mere breath, why would anyone blow it away on the obsessive and time-consuming details of mistrust and miserliness? Today, I envy Madame's life a little less. Any hint of human warmth is detected on a surveillance camera and instantly slapped out. Shafeek, the Little Boy, is simply following his mother's orders: I refuse to believe he would choose to viciously attack someone over a simple banana, but she . . . *she* deserves to lose *everything* within that mere breath. Surely that is God's will: reduce her, strip her, humble her, torment her until she can see death as the only possible escape.

I picture Madame in the place of my mother ten years ago. If only! Such imaginary delights are as good as perfectly ripe bananas snapped off, skinned and savoured, all undetected by surveillance cameras. Go on, God, put her there, *reduce* her.

Crossing the Bridge

For my first six years, I had taken God's loving presence for granted, and my mother's even more so. Most six year-olds do. In my mother, all I had observed was a ceaseless image of benevolence, radiance and sheer happiness. With my father's death, her face physically altered overnight, with tears streaming through all waking hours. The previous mould of constant joy had been remodelled into a permanent mask of tragedy with two ladybird wings fixed beneath the eyebrows, black blobs sat upon bright scarlet bulbs: her bloodshot eyeballs.

Three days after his death, when she checked our bank balance, tragedy embraced dread. Under Lemma's name, Mum found zero birr. Lemma's famous generosity was regrettable in a country where hardship breeds shamelessness. Acquaintances had sucked him dry through their bald requests: multifarious in excuse, uniform in motive. Many of these purported friends were not even poor, taking his money as a straight gift without obligation to repay. Thankfully, a small government pension for widows of railway workers would save us from total misery, while the villa had to be relinquished immediately.

The day we moved, my mother stood on the patio of our villa, surrounded by a throng of friends huffing and heaving with the furniture: I looked *hard* at her for the first time in my life. I saw someone yearning to be elsewhere, to be with Dad, in Dire Dawa 'on business', as Mum continued to maintain.

'Meron, hold your brothers' hands!' she shouted through the melee.

'Why?' I replied.

'We're walking to the new house . . . it's not far, but I have to watch everything. Be a good big sister, okay?'

I could see her point. A villa-full of quite reasonable possessions was to be transported by foot to the new home by around twenty helpers. They would be parading our best pieces to the many impoverished souls along the way, most of the destitute reclining on the old iron footbridge and the dusty tracks separating my idyllic childhood villa and a new slum home. My father's death meant we had to move half a kilometre to the other side of the tracks into a squalid straggle of a neighbourhood bearing no resemblance to our former residence. There was a high chance of theft along the route, or one of our 'friends' slipping away with whatever was in their hands. My mother kept those ladybird eyes on the essentials: beds, mattresses, cooking utensils, plates, coffee ceremony paraphernalia and us.

As I watched our furniture being marched across the bridge in full public view, subjected to a barrage of begging and ridicule, I was too young to see the procession for what it really meant for my mother: a profound public humiliation. Racked with endemic jealousy, the general public of Addis delighted in the degradation of those richer than themselves. Our downfall from villa to the wrong side of the tracks was a special day for them. My mother couldn't afford to pay for transportation or discretion. Her pride was taking a battering. *Yes, you deserve this, my Madame! I wish this for you!*

I held Henok's hand tightly. He was weak and controllable. Nati at four years old was already beyond handholding. He had barely surrendered a tear when first tasting Ethiopia's searing berbere spice as a one-year-old, cheered on by his proud father, and he had hardly cried since then. As soon as he could walk, he chased stray dogs from our entrance. He punched rats with his semi-formed fists. He tried to outsprint aeroplanes passing overhead. When Dad had beaten him as a three-year-old, Nati laughed into his father's face. And today, why would he want to walk with his sister? Nati made the fifteen-minute journey slouched on a sofa between two toiling gentlemen forced to stop every twenty metres to wipe the sweat from their brows. Nati travelled first class.

The iron footbridge from the station side to the slum side was a hundred metres across. Plumb in the middle, equidistant from old and new home, Henok pulled hard on my hand.

'I want the toilet!'

'Hold on, Henok . . . you go in our new house, okay?' I said, dragging him behind me. He wailed pitifully.

'I need poo!'

'Why didn't you go before we left?'

'I forget.'

'Mum, he needs a poo!' I called ahead to her. Onlookers guffawed. They lived for this.

My mother stopped dead in her tracks. She didn't even turn round. I thought she must be furious.

What halted her had nothing to do with Henok. Tadelle was standing there in Muslim clothes: full-length white galabiyya tunic and matching white hat. The same chat-chewing, egg-faced Tadelle who had escorted Kebebush to our house only two weeks earlier.

'Tadelle, what in God's name are you doing?' she asked.

'Ah, Werknesh! Going to the mesquita to pray. What does it look like?'

'I thought you were Orthodox Christian . . . you certainly were when we last saw you,' she said.

'Well, that was then. But now it's Ramadan so I'm Muslim. It's an important time of year for us . . . for me.'

'Do you eat with two knives?' asked my mother, invoking an analogy that I didn't understand.

'No, I usually use my hands, like most people in Ethiopia,' replied Tadelle, sniggering.

'Your neck must be tired,' continued my mother, undeterred.

'Not really . . . I raise the food to my mouth with my hands. Why would my neck be tired?' asked Tadelle.

'In the street, you're constantly turning your head . . . first to a Christian, then to Muslim, Christian, Muslim, Christian, Muslim . . .' she explained, twisting her head round from side to side. 'You change religion like other Habesha men switch between football teams when their side is losing. One minute Arsenal, next minute . . .'

My mother didn't know any other teams.

'Yes, Boiled Egg! What are you? Arsenal or Muslim?' I demanded of him at last, slightly confused by the conversation but sure that Tadelle needed confronting on this vital matter.

'Ha, ha, ha! I'm Arsenal, little Meron . . . but please don't call me Boiled— '

'Don't change the subject, Tadelle,' said my mother, irritated.

'Werknesh, relax! It's the same God. It just makes things easier economically, if I keep an open mind . . .'

'You get money from the Muslims at Ramadan if you happen to be Muslim.'

'Yes! They choose to give it to *me* . . . the poor. I am the poor. I can't *stop* them from doing that . . . it's the marvellous generosity of the Muslims. If the Orthodox Christians could compete with Ramadan, well . . . who knows? Of course, Christmas and Easter are monumental for the Orthodox Christians, and this helps to spread the goodwill throughout the calendar.'

Tadelle found original ways to make enough money for himself and his chat. No shame or embarrassment emerged from his words or manner: no sense of dignity ever sought to waylay him. Becoming a local politician would be a natural progression.

'Where's that woman?' asked my mother aggressively.

'What woman?'

'You know who I mean . . . the ex who came to the house. What did she want?'

'Ah! You should have been a little friendlier, Werknesh. Life is smoother that way.'

'Eh?'

'Nothing! I am called to prayer,' he announced piously.

'There's *something*, isn't there, Tadelle?'

'No!' he fired back too quickly.

'Come round to my new house . . . I've brewed some highly alcoholic tella . . . okay?' offered Mum, apparently forgetting Tadelle's two knives, his tired neck and his winning-football-team approach to religion.

'Okay. Why not? And in the meantime . . . could you lend an old friend a couple of birr?'

Surprisingly, Mum gave it to him.

'I shall pray for you ardently, Werknesh . . . your birr helps rush me to that cause.'

'And to chat-eating,' added my mother to his back.

Tadelle skipped along the footbridge with a bounce, white cap wobbling precariously on the side of his skull. I wished it would topple onto the tracks below but luck was running with the Boiled Egg. My mother, however, was deep in thought, unable to take a step forward. I tried to snap her out of it with distracting detail.

'Mum! Henok needs a poo!'

That would surely take her mind off *all* the problems. Henok bawled helpfully. She grabbed us and we rushed along the footbridge. As we veered right, into our new neighbourhood, we tripped and scrambled on the rugged track comprising a stew of awkward rocks lodged between ditches of greenish-black mire and slime-lined puddles. Local kids chuckled as we fell. Our new 'street' was not designed for rushing.

'Come on, Henok, we're nearly there, good boy . . . you can be the first to use the toilet in our new house!' I said encouragingly.

We followed the procession of furniture through a dark green corrugated-iron door into a tiny yard, leading without breath through another doorway into our new house.

It took a few seconds to adjust our eyes: it was like an instant nightfall.

'Mum, where's the house?' I asked.

'I think we're in it,' she said uncertainly.

Our possessions were dumped in the middle of a blackened hovel of walls made from railway sleepers, underneath a loose corrugated iron roof. Fortunately, strong winds rarely visited Addis.

'Isn't this just a shed to leave our things?' I asked hopefully. It couldn't actually be our house.

'This is the house,' said Mum, now certain.

'But there's no window.'

'It's fine, we'll leave the door open and use the electric light.'

'Where's the toilet, Mum?'

'Why?' she asked.

'Henok needs it, remember?'

'I don't know where the toilet is.'

She shuffled through the gloom towards the back of the house. This took no more than a moment. 'There's no toilet.'

Taken aback, I tried to look hard at Mum but I could barely see her.

'No toilet?' This was an alien concept to me. 'So what do we do?'

I began to panic. Maybe we could never go to the toilet again? We'd surely die in agonising convulsions. Hanging onto pee for an extra five minutes is painful enough but to do it *forever* . . .

'It's outside, round the corner,' said an uncle, picking up Henok under his arm.

'Outside . . . oh God, help this boy,' muttered Mum.

This would be a challenge for Henok, with his deep fear of outside public toilets. As my uncle carried him off, Henok began to scream. Warily, I looked at Mum again. She was weeping but I beamed at her excitedly, a moment of clarity suddenly upon me.

'Mum, it's okay . . . if we need money, we can change religion, like Tadelle. If we do that, we can buy a new house with a toilet. Easy! But don't forget to tell Dad so he knows where to find us, if he ever returns. What do you think, Mum?'

Her head dropped and her crying intensified. I changed my mind about really looking *hard* at her. I couldn't bear to lay eyes on such a miserable hunched-up creature. It was a shock. My mother's dignity was cruelly stranded in the lovely old villa on the other side of the bridge, together with Dad's charity, the stout maid and our blissful past as a complete family.

Familiar chairs and tables gradually ambled into the new shack like a reunion of childhood friends who had jumped into old age in the blink of a lifetime: all recognisable but suddenly depressingly ragged within the scenery of a slum. In the villa, nobody had noticed.

Within an hour, the new residence was almost too full with tatty furniture for anything else. When the sacred coffee stool finally arrived, space was cleared around it: my mother hastily sat down and arranged a coffee ceremony for the seven or eight cousins and friends hanging around, all young men hoping for some recompense for the furniture removal. Squatting on a grubby floor and supping freshly brewed coffee was the best we could offer.

My mother roasted some beans over the small charcoal fire, wafting the aroma into the faces of those gathered around her. This is customary. After a few minutes of light roasting, she energetically pounded the darkened sweet-smelling beans with the mortar and pestle, scooping them into the jubena, the clay coffee pot, along with hot water. We waited for it to boil up. At least three small cups would be consumed by each guest, some preferring to add butter and salt to the hot drink. Nobody could decline.

As difficult as everything was now, my mother seemed to be visibly relaxing as chatter and coffee warmed our new home. If God was preoccupied elsewhere, there would still be the coffee ceremony for solving problems and elevating moods.

A rattling knock on the dark green door took my mother outside.

'Ah! Tadelle . . .'

'Werknesh, sweet Werknesh! Welcome to my neighbourhood!' he cheered too loudly.

'Are you merkinyalo?' asked my mother, instantly recognising the signs of a chat high.

'I'm . . . oh, yes, good *good* chat . . . and I'm pushed for time . . . picking up new television . . . got to go . . .'

'New television? How can you afford that . . . ah yes, the fruits of Ramadan. Won't you stay for a swig of tella, Tadelle, and we can talk for a while?'

'Give me milk and I might find you some words,' he stuttered. Milk was the usual remedy for chat-induced frenzy.

'Milk? I don't have milk. So, tella then?'

'Tella . . . yes . . . close enough to milk.'

Tadelle slumped on the floor and swigged a mug of the heavy beer.

'Werknesh . . . how you manage now . . . no work, three kids, no money?'

'Lemma's railway pension . . . should be available after a few months . . . just waiting for the court to clear it, just a formality. Until then, we rely on help from family and friends.'

'But, Werknesh, maybe it's not coming . . . the pension. You got to be nice to the ex-wife . . . maybe she's not ex . . .'

'Eh? What are you talking about? Who *is* this woman?'

'Nothing! Nobody! But she's *poor* . . . from the country-side. Lemma left her there when he came to Addis . . . left her with family. She got a boy . . .'

'A boy? So what? I don't owe her anything. She and Lemma divorced, went their own ways. What was she doing back here before he died? That was hideous,' she said, glancing at me furtively. Did she say 'died'? Before Dad *died*?

'Werknesh . . .'

'Yes?'

'More tella . . .'

My mother obliged him. I could sense her unease.

'Listen, Werknesh,' he slurred, 'don't want to see you hurt . . . but . . . *but*!'

He laughed hysterically.

'But *what*?'

'But! Boy is Lemma's son. She need the pension for *him* . . . very *poor* . . . still got marriage certificate. She married him before you . . . she got the rights. But I don't know . . . the court will decide. I'm here to drink.'

'Hoh! I knew there was *something*. You can get out of my house now,' said Mum.

'See you after Ramadan . . . don't worry, I'll be Orthodox Christian again. You'll love me and vote for me like the rest of the sheep.'

Mum and I watched him meander a few metres along the track. He entered a particularly filthy-fronted house. I thought animals lived in there.

'I live *here*!' he shouted back victoriously at Mum, laughing stupidly but losing concentration on the jutting stones. He stumbled and bashed his head on a protruding corner next to his front door.

'Bye, Boiled Egg!' I shouted.

Mum slammed our door shut. I had a morbid curiosity to know what he had done to himself. I thought the 'egg' might have been broken.

'What about the ex-wife, Werknesh? You believe that?' someone asked.

'Lemma divorced her before marrying me so I can't see the problem. His mother witnessed the divorce. Why should the ex-wife get the pension?'

She left it hanging. Nobody spoke more. It was late: everyone shuffled out, the long day complete.

'Mum, why did you give Boiled Egg so much tella?' I asked, hoping to delay my bedtime in the new hovel.

'To get some truth out of him.'

'What's wrong with coffee, Mum? I thought coffee could do *everything* . . .'

'No, my baby, not true.'

That was a surprise. I thought coffee was second only to holy water.

'What happens if you don't like the truth?' I pressed.

'Well . . . it's usually good to know the truth . . .'

'And sometimes better to lie . . . yes, Mum? Like Tadelle pretending to be Muslim.'

'Wrong!'

She slapped me hard on the leg. That bitter slap was not enough to pre-empt a lifetime of lying.

'Lying is bad! It's in the Ten Commandments!' she shouted.

'But, Mummy . . . you lied about Dad. Said to *me* that he went to Dire Dawa for work, but said to Boiled Egg that he died,' I spluttered. 'You lied to one of us!'

'Hoh! You're too sharp. That was to *protect* you . . .'

How could I be too sharp? How was she protecting me when she had just smacked me? How could my father be *dead*? Who was this newly wretched woman? I hated Mum *then* as much as Madame *now*, but I see a clear difference: my mother's unattractiveness was elicited by poverty and grief, Madame's by wealth and greed. One had a better excuse than the other.

Ramadan (653 days left)

It's early October, on the International Calendar. This means Ramadan on this year's Muslim Calendar. My host family is Sunni Muslim but, with the exception of Abdul, the people residing in this apartment are not obvious with their religious devotion. Abdul prays five times a day, as expected, while the others are far more discreet with their worship. That is, until Ramadan, when I am at once surrounded by Islam's most dedicated of disciples for thirty days of undiminished commitment. If they want to do it this way, let them, but please do not drag *me* into it.

'Maybe you do fasting with us for Ramadan,' suggests Madame.

It starts tomorrow. I have no interest in being a Muslim. I'm hungry enough without extra fasting. Fasting for a month would probably kill me, completely.

'I'm not a Muslim, Madame, so how can I?' I reason, as I scrub Madame's fingers and toes clean of nail varnish, which must not be seen during Ramadan.

'Easy. You just eat when we eat . . . between sunset and

sunrise . . . food is plentiful. Be better if you on same schedule as us . . . many leftovers.'

Wait, this is interesting. A month of good leftover food beckons if I pretend to be a Muslim. But I risk becoming Tadelle, with his two knives. I'm sorry, Mum, but now I will do anything for leftovers.

'Do I have to pray, Madame?'

'You can if you want it, but not excuse for doing less work.'

So there's no point.

'I'll concentrate on the fasting, Madame, and eat all the leftovers.'

On the first day, everyone wakes early and worships at the dawn prayer, the women praying in their white hijab tunics and headscarves, and there is quiet contemplation. Before they leave the house, Madame and Nazia change into their regular outdoor clothes, though more downbeat than usual. Modern is exchanged for modest. They seem humbled and even nice. Shafeek is dressed in a typical stylish suit. I eat breakfast the moment Shafeek has gone, my fast immediately and purposely broken. I drink water regularly through the morning and take an early lunch. Nobody can expect me to fast *and* work.

But I have to labour harder than ever during the day, preparing the evening's iftar, the daily fast-breaking meal. By sunset, a banquet has to be ready for seven weakened disciples who have consumed not a drop of liquid or crumb of food since dawn. There will be seven courses, commencing with the traditional handful of dates to break the fast. It will last for two hours. They will sleep until half an hour before dawn. Those who need extra sustenance – Shafeek in particular – rise for suhoor, a final meal before fasting recommences with sight of the new day's sun. Food also has to be ready in advance for suhoor.

Shafeek is first through the front door, not quite the usual charging hippo. He creeps up to me, face drawn, lips dry. This dramatic transformation disorients me.

'Hello, Meron, how are you?' he whispers.

He's asking *me*?

'Erm . . . okay but tired, really tired . . .'

'Take a rest.'

'Thank you, Mister . . . but no time.'

He will not be so generous of spirit if his iftar is delayed by even a minute at sunset.

They take it in turns to pray in the lounge: there is only one prayer mat. Shafeek insists on praying at exactly the prescribed daily prayer times. The others follow after him.

When Madame and Nazia are home at their usual time – mid-afternoon – I am laying out cutlery and plates on the balcony. Seven courses for seven people: all other duties abandoned.

'How your fasting going, Meron?' asks Madame.

'It's hard, Madame . . . I'm parched . . . and so hungry,' I say, letting my tongue dangle for effect.

Nazia's dark eyes flash the strike of two lit matches.

'Mum, what are you doing? Meron isn't a Muslim. She's not eating iftar with us . . . this is *our* special time. How can she fast *and* work? It's not practical,' says Nazia, reading my mind with extra-large subtitles.

'It's okay.' I hasten to reassure her. 'I'm reducing the workload so I don't get too weak. Really, I'm very happy to fast during the day with you. It's a privil . . .'

'C'est fou! She *can't* do that! We need her strong to *prepare* the meals, not to *eat* the meals!'

'Er, Madame . . . please let me pretend to be a Muslim, please!' I beg to Madame.

Shafeek is on the balcony. I smile at him, hoping for more of that refreshing Ramadan benevolence.

'We don't like that . . . *pretending*. You either are or you aren't. Allah can see you are not a Muslim,' states Shafeek categorically. Madame, slumped on a sun-lounger, is hardly listening. This encourages me to speak more than usual. It might impress Shafeek.

'I know an Ethiopian guy called Tadelle, nicknamed Boiled Egg . . . yes, his name is a different story . . . anyway, he switched between religions, depending on the times of year and the festivals. He's now working for the government and prospering. I know it's not an ideal situation, but if he can do it, so can I . . . Mister.'

Ah! It feels great to banter away at last. I look up at Shafeek. He's gazing at me as though I have just set fire to his crinkled underwear.

'When Ramadan has finished, I'll hit you so hard,' he says weakly.

I start laughing. Surely he's joking? You don't *threaten* people during Ramadan, do you? I tap his arm playfully and giggle. I feel able to do this for the first time. He's so different and relaxed today. But Shafeek lets out a shout.

'Meron! Don't touch me! You've broken my wudu . . . I've got to do it all again! Get away from me!'

Starvation is not, after all, a recipe for making Shafeek pleasant.

'Sorry, Mister . . . I don't know about wudu.'

'Hammerhead, you don't know about *anything*.'

I later learn that wudu is the pre-prayer washing of face, hands and feet and that it can be invalidated in various ways.

The evening iftar is Heaven for them, and another place far removed for me. The idea of concentrated fasting for a month every year has great appeal: Orthodox Christians do it twice a week and during the build-up to Easter. But the way this family devours in the evening obliterates the privations of the day. I seem to be doing the Ramadan suffering for an entire family. They have subcontracted the pain to me. For two hours, I stand unfed outside the lounge, next to the half-open door, awaiting orders, listening to their gorging, sprinting to their service, wondering why my life has diverted into this particular dead end of Hell.

'We all have to work as usual, Meron . . . all day,' says Madame between spoonfuls of lentil soup, as I start to flag on serving the third course.

Work as usual? Right. She sits at a desk all day. No danger of her feet swelling up like a pair of dirty ripe yams. She's home at 3pm. I finish around 11pm. She takes snacks during the day: 'I'll make it up after Ramadan,' she says, whereas I have no chance of delaying *my* pain for another day. She has *me* to wait on her. I have *me* too, but '*me*' is too busy to manage even the basic necessities of her own life: I forget to pee for ten hours at a time; water only passes my lips in the wrong direction; my bowels shift twice a week if I'm lucky. In the kitchen, *she* snacks contentedly as *she* prepares delicious Middle Eastern dishes, while I become dwarfed by used plates stacking up faster than I can wash up: not just everyday plates, they are 'Ramadan Mubarak' (Happy Ramadan) plates, bought specially for the occasion with elegant patterns and requiring extra care in my *unhappy* Ramadan hands.

Plates, bowls, date stones, forks, blood, nutshells, mint, lather, tap water and tears, all sluice and slither around ten worn digits in the metal kitchen sink. The sink is my husband, the crockery and cutlery our children. The endless cycle of washing up perfectly encapsulates grinding eternity, in full grating practice. Is this marriage? I don't want a husband. The plates are pointless. The cutlery cuts me. Children will kill me. Oh God, I envy the dead.

Madame cocks her nose across the freshly washed bowls in search of a misplaced hint of Habesha, or other miscreant.

'Not good enough . . . do this pile again, Meron. This is *Ramadan*!'

And it's only the first day. From now until the final feast of Eid al-Fitr I am run ragged. There is barely time to rinse the sweat from my uniform. I stink like a menopausal donkey. Leftovers come my way so late at night can barely see the food for the falling eyelids. My head wants a pillow, my legs a level plane. Neither head nor legs care about the groaning emptiness between them. That can wait till tomorrow. Tomorrow is a blur lost to a congealed lump of yesterdays, a lump best left to rot in sealed plastic bag deep in the ground. That's where I'll be: Ramadan will put me there.

But time passes. Hard time. Hungry time. Grudging time. Rough time. Ramadan time.

'I wish Ramadan was the whole year round . . . the fasting, the giving to the poor, the prayers, the parties, the purification of the soul . . .' says Nazia on the last night.

'Oooh yes!' enthuses Madame.

I now understand that her largest gushes are saved for the greatest insincerities. From my records, I note that Madame has a full seventeen days of Ramadan to make up after her numerous fast-breaking indiscretions. Madame can't resist a handful of dates before the others get home. I've seen the stones in the garbage.

'It definitely makes us better people . . . you hear that, Meron? Watch and learn,' says Shafeek, stupidly seriously.

Excuse me! I appear to be starving to death: why not give food and money to *me*? My weight has dropped three kilos in the last four weeks. My body is a saggy bag of fatigue; my mind a fuzzy mush of anguish.

'Meron! Can you hear me?' shouts Shafeek.

I'm behind the door, awaiting instructions. But a sudden white light buzzes into my head. I think I'm going down. It's the low blood pressure again, scything away at my legs. I can't stay up, I'm toppling . . . thump!

'What's wrong with her?' I hear from Madame.

'I think she's having a fit,' says someone. Probably Nuria. She thinks she's a doctor just because she works in a hospital.

'If she's playing around . . .' says Shafeek, becoming outraged.

He's standing over me, pressing his oily hand to my forehead. Garlic rockets up my nostrils. Don't worry yourselves, I'm not dead. My head is full of flash bulbs, but I hear everything.

'I think she's fainted,' says Shafeek. 'This one is awful.'

'She could have waited till *after* Ramadan to start the dramatics . . .' starts Nuria.

'Let's just get rid of her,' suggests Shafeek.

'My son? No! Not this one as well. What are you saying?' says Abdul with a perturbed tone.

Not this one! I remember Nazia's urgent words during that first beating. The connotations are accumulating. But I can't believe Shafeek is capable of anything more than hot-tempered bluster and playground-punching. I don't *want* to believe it. He is essentially a good man: a handsome high-flying professional man, with occasional dips.

Shafeek pours water onto my head for no obvious reason. Hey, while you're there, shampoo and conditioner, please.

'Baba, maids are like cars. Good for convenience but if the brakes fail and the passengers are endangered, you're not going to keep it . . . it has to go . . . and quickly,' states Shafeek.

I am not aware that my brakes have failed. I can definitely stop if I want to, and I want to stop all the time in this place. Trying to open my eyes, I murmur a little.

'Meron! Wake up! Are you okay?' shouts Shafeek, revealing false concern.

'If she fainted, leave her on the floor,' orders Madame.

'Gets blood back into the head . . . better down there. Pull her away from the door so we can get to the kitchen without jumping over her like horses.'

Shafeek drags me a couple of metres along the floor. They leave me outside in a heap for an hour.

'Meron! Come and do washing up!' shouts Madame eventually, as though nothing has happened. Ah! The familiar call of Ramadan! And the last for this year.

After six more days of fasting in Shawwal, the month that follows Ramadan, I'm confronted by Madame and Nazia as they eat lunch on the balcony. They make an intimidating pair.

'We send you back to Ethiopia. You not good enough,' says Madame, Nazia nodding violently in agreement.

'But . . . *why*, Madame?'

'Too many problem. You quick, but you not have stamina. We not wanting servant fainting during Ramadan . . . not healthy.'

'You spend too much time just *watching* us,' adds Nazia, 'especially when Nuria and Hassan are fighting. That's not your business. You stand and ogle as though it's a TV show.'

'Shafeek think you not have respect and common sense. And my white socks still not white,' continues Madame.

This is devastating. After only four months, I have failed. I have earned almost nothing. And I thought Shafeek and I had a connection.

Argh! The ignominy of returning to Addis so soon, and having lost all my mother's savings. *No!*

'Please, Madame, let me work harder. I won't faint

181

again, I promise. I'll be the best servant in Beirut . . . *please*!'

'Go back to your poor country. When you learn how to work properly, you can try to return to Beirut, but with another family,' says Nazia.

'No, please! I'll do everything twice as hard . . . please, let me prove myself . . . one more chance, Madame . . .' I sob, falling to my knees.

They let me cry for at least two minutes in front of them. Madame sighs.

'I probably regret this . . . okay, one final chance. You got one month to show me you good maid,' says Madame.

'Thank you, Madame, thank you!' I yell, kissing her hand.

Nazia rapidly sits on her hands to pre-empt a similar fate. But why am I begging to clean this woman's dirt for the next two years? I have thrown myself into a black hole.

Where's Kidist?

I am beginning to understand how my mother felt at the outset of a long bereavement that would run into years. Now that every shaft of light in my life is closed off by a single solid curtain without hem, edge or end, I see only black.

I *love* black in clothes and men. But black is a night sky with invisible stars. Hopeful distant lights of the future are the stars imperceptible to eyes and telescopes: they are sitting out there somewhere, but overwhelmed by such blackness, they may as well be non-existent. If there is no light visible, they do not exist, although they do. That is the effect of black: blotting out all hope, when really it *is* there, indefinably somewhere.

'Mummy, why are you crying all the time?' I asked four months after we had moved from the villa. It was becoming a massive irritation: why couldn't this woman control herself?

'I miss your dad so much.'

'Can't we get a new one? Maybe with a big house . . . like before?'

'No, there won't be a new one, my baby,' she said bleakly. 'But one day, we'll get a new house, I'm sure of that.'

'Like Auntie Kidist's?'

'Auntie Kidist's house, yes, but I don't want a husband like hers.'

'When's Auntie Kidist coming to visit us?'

Kidist had shown her face on the day of moving and maybe three times since then but cameo performances only, each time a fraught second at the front door as if passing coincidentally. Conspicuously, suspiciously absent, she lived only minutes away on foot, with her husband, in a villa.

Kidist used to visit our old house several times each week, as one might expect of my mother's sister, and she never once refused a snack from our brimming larder. Kidist would potter around with my mother in the kitchen, unapologetically nibbling away, adding curves to her curves, never too keen to return home. She was almost a second mother, but younger and more inclined to chase us round the garden, screaming playfully.

'Why don't you phone her? I miss her, Mummy.'

'We don't have a phone. I miss her too,' replied my mother.

'Can't we visit her house? It's more fun there,' I implored.

'No, we can't. Her husband is . . . difficult to understand . . . different from nice people.'

'Like a pig?'

My mother smiled at last. Well done, Meron! But this was common knowledge. I was only six and I knew that.

We don't eat pigs in Addis. We don't *like* pigs in Addis. The Bible treats them with disgust. Kidist's husband, Desalegn, deserved such disgust. We felt dirty and soiled simply discussing him.

Another two weeks passed. Finally, she came to us and entered our home.

'Hi, Werknesh, Meron, Nati, Henok . . . how are you all?' Kidist said, perspiring lightly.

'Hello, Kidist, how are you? Where have you been?' beamed my mother.

'I'm fine, I've been working,' replied Kidist, smiling nervously. Kidist didn't work at this time. 'I just want to see if you're settled all right . . .'

If Kidist really *looked* at my mother, as I had, she would see new wrinkles etched into her tear-stained skin.

'Is that it?' doubted Mum. 'Why haven't you come before?'

'Busy with things.'

'What things? Kidist, you don't work . . .'

'Family things.'

'We are your family, aren't we?'

Kidist giggled. She looked around at our home, peering anxiously, nodding appreciatively, trying to maintain a face of casual interest rather than betraying her true feelings of fear, pity, horror and superiority.

What she saw was a cramped shack unsuitable for more than two portly people at any one time. It was meant for the manual railway workers: the men who laid the lines, repaired damaged rails, dug drainage ditches, shovelled coal, shifted sleepers, sweated and slogged so intensely that large body shapes were never an issue inside windowless living rooms the size of a coal shed.

Kidist saw that we had run into the buffers. There would be no domestic help, no garden, no bathroom, no privacy and, while Kebebush contested the marriage in the courts, no income. My brothers shared one bed, my mother and I the other. Our neighbourhood lay along a distant siding, well hidden from the prestige and pride of our French colonial palace, La Gare. From where I played in grubby puddles under criss-crossing lines of washing, not even the whine of the station's siren could be heard decreeing the beginning and ending of La Gare's work shifts.

Instead of the station's whines, whistles, clinks and clunks, other people's private conversations and quarrels provided a continuous loop of background noise, unavoidable in our quarters. Keen for entertainment, we peeped through the cracks in the sleepers that comprised our walls, watching our neighbours watching their television, our excited whispers quickly prompting them to block up the cracks with old chewing gum. We also heard loud rants and crashes from fights a few doors down, at which point neighbours raced in to separate husbands and wives before any real harm was done: domestic violence was summarily broken up without invitation to enter their home. Wives quickly learnt how to scream: this was the alarm system. Conversely, nagging and cuckolding was an eternal source of amusement for fellow residents while the sound of kids bawling was routine white noise, so ignored. Privacy and serenity had no place to put their feet up and relax in this block.

Our outside shower was a cold bucket of water over the head. I hated this and sympathised with cats.

'When will I take a normal hot shower, Mum?'

'You're not lucky. You're poor. A hot shower is not normal for you now. Nothing *good* is normal for you now.'

Fifty metres away, a row of four stinking toilets with rusty metal doors were raised above a gigantic cesspit on loose planks of wood where residents squatted. These provided relief for our neighbourhood: men, women and children alike. The cesspit was emptied every two months, more often if there was a public holiday. Public holidays always signified vast quantities of richly spiced meat wats, followed by buttock-clenching queues at the toilets the next day, women clutching jugs of water for cleaning themselves, men more usually with folded newspapers under their arms. The toilets were opened for three hours in the morning and four hours in the evening. Outside these times, we had to wander off and find a tree. A tree was forever preferable: once, a young woman fell through the cesspit planks and drowned.

Once a week, the neighbourhood women cleaned the tracks around our houses: garbage, sludge and excrement quickly accumulated, especially in the stagnant open drains running beside each path. Nobody else would do it. These women had a reasonable desire to avoid plagues of rats, legions of flies and a living environment that no self-respecting human would tolerate. The men were always 'working' when the weekly cleaning took place. It meant several hours of scooping muck into dirty sacks with small ineffective spades, a task that Mum had declined.

'I'm not doing such demeaning work. Three kids and

no husband . . . I have to work all the time,' she had said to the neighbours.

'You *must* do it. The kebelle says everyone's responsible . . . to avoid disease,' came the increasingly agitated reply each week.

But Mum had a point: our bellies would not be filled by voluntary sludge-shovelling tasks. Instead, she kept us alive by washing clothes for other families. The shame of such low-paid, menial work was too great for my mother to offer her services in the immediate vicinity: her customers were at least half an hour's walk away, the distance large enough for word not to get back that she scrubbed other people's rags for a living. Off she trudged each day, hoping to travel incognito, but as the embittered lady in permanent black, she was *not* invisible to our fellow residents.

At that age, I had no idea how long one should mourn for, or even what it meant. I didn't realise it yet, but for the next three years, my mother would sob daily, shave her head twice a week, wear the same black dress and netela, and assume a dour exterior designed to expel all traces of incoming friendliness. She had the same constancy as Tigray's sternest hermits living alone among the rock-hewn churches in the north. Indeed, she might have taken that path if it were not for us.

Kidist saw that the mourning permeated everything inside the new home, especially in the guise of neglect. In the villa, there had always been weary bodies hanging around on seats, settees, stools, and anything supporting the railway worker's rear: this dilapidated furniture now provided the *only* features of our new home. My mother refused to change the broken bed that she and my father had shared: now she and I endured it together. True horizontality became a distant memory.

Mum managed to feed us, but the quality was no higher than 'filler': the thin type of shiro wat made without oil and injera, comprising rice and barley in place of teff. If the plastic plates fell apart in our hands, lunch would be lost to the dirt-carpeted floor. Nobody else came to our house. You couldn't expect them to. To enter would have been to step into a cave of gloom, without television, strong light or comfort.

Kidist's eyes filled with tears as she took it in: her own sister in a place like this. The come-down was a vertiginous plummet through the social strata of Addis without a well-sprung horizontal bed conveniently placed at the bottom.

My mother brought out the best cure for Kidist's tears: fresh injera and shiro wat. We gathered as usual round the large plate, grabbing our strips of injera and scooping the wat into our mouths.

'Come on, Kidist, eat with us,' encouraged my mother.

Guests are *always* offered food if it is freshly cooked, and they are expected to eat it. Not to eat it, without robust excuse, is to invite war.

'No, no, it's okay, thanks.'

She loitered behind us, not joining in with the meal.

'Kidist, come here, don't be like an Eritrean . . . sit down with us, eat some injera, please!' insisted my mother.

'It's better than usual,' I tried. 'It's got butter!'

Mum frowned at me.

'I'm full,' said Kidist uncharacteristically.

'It's early, you can't have eaten yet, Kidist . . . please eat!'

Kidist duly pushed a mouthful of injera and wat onto her tongue. She grimaced. It wasn't the quality of old.

'I need to go,' she said.

'What can I say? You're obviously not happy here,' my mother blurted, now annoyed. 'You hardly ever come, and when you do, one foot remains planted outside, ready to hurry you away as quickly as possible.'

'I'm going, Werknesh, thank you . . .'

My mother looked up at her incredulously.

'I have hardly seen you for four months! And you look at my injera as though it is made from sand. What is *wrong* with you?' she asked fiercely.

'Sorry, my sister. It's . . . it's just a big shock for me . . . to see you like this. I can't take it in . . . you've let everything go. Desalegn said I shouldn't come any more. Maybe he's right . . . you need more time . . .'

'Of course we look poor! We're waiting for Lemma's pension to come through . . . there's no problem! The court's waiting for the kebelle to find the divorce certificate. Of course, they'll find it . . . his ex-wife is claiming a son by Lemma. She's claiming the pension for herself . . . but it's farcical! Just a matter of time!' gabbled Mum, with a worrying sense of overconfidence.

'I'm sorry, Werknesh . . . I'll let you eat without me. But I do want to help you, sister. Can I give you some birr?'

My mother remained seated. She lowered her head and mumbled into her chest.

'Just go, just go,' were the words I heard.

'But, Mummy, she's got birr for us,' I chirped, thinking she was being a little bit churlish to turn down money so offhandedly. 'Birr, Mummy, *birrrr*! What's wrong with you? *Mummy?*'

My mother raised her head to look hard at Kidist.

'I don't want her birr . . . I didn't ask for her help. I want the love of a sister!' she boomed at Kidist.

Urgh! Mum! This wouldn't happen if Dad were here. But Kidist was gone: properly, selfishly, unequivocally gone, before our dirt could stick to her shoes, before our blackness could engulf her. Kidist's departure confirmed our isolation as definite: such a slide into destitution thrust us into a solitary confinement without locks or bars, floating midpoint between living neighbours who looked through us and a dead father who looked over us. There was no certainty over which way God would nudge us.

Just a White Sheet? (618 days left)

Today is Wednesday, bedlinen day. Garments flap and thrash on the balcony washing lines as the cold November winds swirl around me. And immediately, right in front of my face, viciously tugged from its pegs, a single white sheet is snatched up by the wind. Too fast for my panicking hands, it is driven away by nature's invisible blows.

Madame's finest linen is going over, and maybe I will have to pay for that. I watch hopelessly as the fluttering sheet tries to fight the belligerent gusts like a fragile young woman clinging gamely to the balcony's chrome railings, delaying by sheer seconds what we all know to be inevitable. The sheet plummets towards Earth and I see, for an instant, a Habesha girl swathed in a white shawl, with matching petrified eyes quickly enlarging as her slender body speeds to a sudden fatal shattering on hard Lebanese cement.

My mouth drops open. What am I seeing, and what exactly am I believing?

I spot the sheet thirteen floors below, flailing on the ground as if in agony. It is definitely the sheet but . . . what was her name? Was she flown back to Addis in a box? Did she fall in love? Was that her mistake? Was it Shafeek? Did she take unborn life with her? Am I going the same way?

Like my family in our time of destitution, I am in a danger zone, lodged between life and death: there is no certainty over which way God, or my employers, will nudge me. Or is my imagination now running free and wild across windswept rooftops? Isn't this just a trouble-some bed sheet?

Occasionally, I have noticed a woman below, sweeping the ground-floor patio and watering flowers, always wearing a black body-length tunic, white headscarf and niqab revealing only her eyes. She's what I assume to be a 'strict' Muslim.

'Madame, I need to get the sheet from downstairs . . . the wind blew it down. I'll knock on the door of the apartment.'

'You not pegging it correct . . . too busy waving at servants in other apartments. I know you, Meron.'

'But I *never* do that, Madame.'

'Okay, but be fast, I watching you.'

'Yes, Madame.'

She pulls the door key from her handbag to release me outside.

Stepping beyond the front door for the first time in nearly six months stuns me. I can't believe I'm outside the apartment, outside the prison. I walk as slowly as I can, savouring every short stride along the corridor to the lift.

I inhale the stale air of the elevator as if inside a florist on St Valentine's Day. The notion of escape occurs to me: if I could somehow get through the main entrance, I'd finally arrive in Beirut! But escaping into the winter cold without money, passport, shelter or friend is hardly intelligent.

The wooden front door to the apartment thirteen floors below us is plain and unremarkable. A few seconds after a sharp electric buzz, the door swings open. A kind-faced middle-aged woman is standing before me, quickly securing her white headscarf, though without veil. I glimpse a strand of grey hair. Her ample body is clothed in her usual long black tunic.

'Hello, I live upstairs . . . how are you?' I start in hesitant Arabic.

'What do you want? What do you want?' she flusters.

'A bed sheet from upstairs flew down . . . onto your patio,' I fumble, and revert quickly to English. I'm afflicted by nerves, my confidence in shreds now that I am *outside*.

'No speak,' she replies bluntly.

I use body language to communicate the flight of a bed sheet, but possibly the lady thinks a sleeping pilot has crashed an aeroplane into her patio. Slightly alarmed, she beckons me to come in. I start to remove my shoes, but she shakes her head.

Through her apartment into the patio and I quickly find the lifeless sheet. Her face softening, the lady holds my hands in hers, squinting at the open sores around my fingers and knuckles. It hurts me to clench my fist now. The daily bare-handed scrubbing with Odex cleaning products is taking its toll. Her grimace tells me as much and the only way to deflect from the pain is to offer me a cup of tea. I would take a cup of Odex bleach from this woman. Her manner is genuine and her concern heartfelt.

The lady sits me down at her kitchen table. It's the largest table I have ever seen. Together we gaze out across the back of a handsomely carved timber monster. The apartment block must have been built round it: nobody could have squeezed this vast slab of varnished wood through her front door.

I glance round the room. There are no other occupants. No photos or signs of other human activity exist. There is a lady, a table, a prayer mat and a pot of tea. While the tea infuses inside a metal pot, 'Table Lady' – as I have already nicknamed her – coats my hands with Vaseline and encourages me to spread a finger-full across my chapped lips. She fetches a chipped but full-length mirror from another room and waves me over to it while she supports it in her hands. I am not sure if this is a good idea.

'Who's that?' I gasp.

It's a shock to see a sad scrawny waif blinking back at me in horror. What's happened? I'm suddenly an Addis street girl: a tatty old sack with feet. Table Lady is startled at my own shock. Madame's mirror has never revealed this: maybe some mirrors are better at telling the truth than others.

'Things very difficult for me . . .' I try in English. 'Do you know about another girl . . . er, falling?'

Table Lady is confused, pointing repeatedly at the sheet tucked under my arm.

'No, *not* this sheet . . . a servant girl . . .'

'You?'

'Not me . . . a person, a girl, like me landing on your patio? Please *understand*,' I implore.

'Another servant come now?'

Once more, I have to try my Arabic.

'Was a girl killed . . . here . . . yes? From upstairs? Do you remember?' I ask, pointing upwards.

Table Lady is careful not to react. I can see that. It's an unnatural response. Her gentle face is gripped by some unspecified fear. Or she has no idea what I am saying.

'Muslims always kind, helping people, do everything good,' she tries, somehow stringing English words together.

'But they're Muslims upstairs. My Madame is Muslim.'

'Yes, she Muslim.'

I know little of Islam but can see a world of difference between the woman in front of me and my Madame a tower block above us. I have never seen my Madame pray, except during Ramadan, and during Ramadan she was hardly . . . *My Madame!* I have completely forgotten her.

'I have to go!'

'Wait, wait!'

'What?' I ask expectantly.

Table Lady hastily wraps up a slice of sponge cake in a tissue. I feel like crying in the face of her kindness. Whatever 'type' of Muslim she is, it doesn't matter. This woman is essentially good, if cautious. In her, I see my mother.

I hide the cake inside the folded sheet retrieved from her patio and rush back. Madame answers the door. I trot in as nonchalantly as possible but there's a lift in my stride. I can't hold it down. I try to adjust my expression to the normal downtrodden indifference.

'Me-ron, where were you?' asks Madame.

'She was praying, Madame. I had to wait for her to finish, sorry.'

'But I watch you get the sheet. What happen . . . why you late?'

'Ah! The lift was busy. I had to wait.'

'Not busy . . . was silent . . . nobody using it.'

'It was busy, Madame!'

'Liar! Always some excuse. I know that woman. She have no child, she barren . . . not friendly woman. Always lie when she speak.'

'She didn't speak, Madame.'

'So why you look happy?'

I grip the folded napkin tight inside the sheet. My face will not settle. I have cake!

'I'm *not* happy!' I declare as angrily as I can manage.

'Give to me,' says Madame, wrenching the rogue sheet from my hands, cake included.

'I can wash it by hand, Madame . . . no need to waste water,' I try.

'Wash by hand? Like Ethiopia? That not cleaning it . . . no washing machine in poor country?'

'We do it outside, Madame . . . we do *all* washing out-side . . . us and clothes.'

'Oh. Not have bathrooms in Ethiopia?' she asks, genu-inely interested.

'No, Madame.'

'Yuk, no bathrooms . . . that not surprise me,' she spits, suddenly walking away.

But my cake!

The cake is lost. I am lost. And, judging from her tone, so is Ethiopia.

I make Turkish coffee for Abdul. Bubbled up and stirred three times, the coffee is a perfectly dense muddy slug of dark caffeine, thick enough to chew. I am proud of this.

'Merhaba, Mister! Here's your Turkish coffee . . . made by my own hands,' I rejoice, as he enters at 7am, overlong pyjama leg jumping and jerking along the floor like an elephant's trunk vacuuming for insects.

Abdul is taken aback. That's what I wanted. Shock. Shock him into being nice. Shock him into saying things he shouldn't. I have to know what happened.

'Turkish coffee made by my own hands,' I repeat. It's a winning line.

He focuses his tired eyes on me and raises both hands to the sky.

'Allah! It's not *Turkish* coffee. It's *Lebanese* coffee . . . we add cardamom for extra spice,' he says, grabbing several cardamom seeds for grinding.

'Sorry.'

'It's okay. Thank you. Make some for yourself.'

'Wow!' I cry. Those words caress my ears: someone has *thanked* me. And he is offering me real coffee! It's time to be friendly, and curious.

'Mister . . . er . . . how do I compare to . . .'

I can't concentrate: Abdul is standing behind the kitchen counter pouring olive oil from a jar into his hand.

'Aarrgh!' he pants. 'Aarrgh! Aarrgh!'

What the hell? It's the same pained outburst as when he burns his mouth with boiling coffee, which he does when late for work. I can't see what he's doing below the waist, but it's obvious where his hands are applying the oil. He is dabbing it on his penis.

What am I supposed to do? Does he need assistance? Or is this a preface to something malevolent? No! *Not Abdul?* Just because I made him some coffee? Should I scream hysterically?

I hold the packet of coffee and act as if reading it. I can't read Arabic. Nazia comes into the room. I'm truly pleased to see her. She pretends not to notice Abdul's odd procedure.

'Bonjour, Papa!'

'Bonjour, Nazia,' I reply, on his behalf.

Without a word of explanation, Abdul packs himself away and plonks the jar of olive oil back on the rack with the other condiments. I start making my own Lebanese coffee. Nazia's glacial stares ricochet off Abdul and me.

'Meron,' starts Abdul, now under duress, 'use the old grounds in the pot. You are not to use the new coffee . . . do you hear? I didn't give you permission to take that.'

'Yes, Mister.'

It is impossible to understand who runs things in this apartment. It should be Abdul, but he's barely hovering above *me* in the hierarchy. Nazia, Madame and Shafeek all have their moments of power but where's the consistency? To understand this family is like attempting to reconstruct one of the many collapsed cobwebs I find each day. There is an absence of regular, logical pattern. It is damaged beyond repair. And what happened to the previous Habesha ant entrapped within this confusing web?

Nuria returns from the hospital with her new baby, Medina. The apartment is warm with baby clamour and frantic cooing. Electrified by the arrival, Madame sashays

199

around with her first granddaughter, clasping the baby as if she's a delicate golden egg.

Countless guests come and go with baby clothes and assorted baby gifts. Nuria sleeps and feeds: Medina is more animated than her mother. Hassan is hailed as a hero, providing brief respite from his status as a pillaging dog. This is a temporary 'umbrella' from Madame's constant drip of consternation.

As she grapples with the baby, Nazia openly smiles for a few minutes, her metal braces causing instant screaming in Medina. I empathise with that baby. I want to wail like that too, all of the time, especially at Nazia's face. Meanwhile, Abdul's excited gurgling sets a high standard for Medina to follow. Shafeek barely acknowledges her: I'll assume he is not a lover of babies.

I feel as though we have entered a new era. These people cannot be murderers. Look at them drool over Medina: they're full of love. I love the baby too. She's a delight to hold in my arms. As soon as I see, smell, hear, feel her, I yearn for motherhood. Who will give me a baby? An Arab baby would be welcome.

'Meron! Nappy change! Come here . . . *now*!' shouts Nuria the following week. She has found her voice.

Before the birth, Nuria was surly but quiet, vast but mobile, lazy but capable. After the birth, permanently anchored to her bed, she soaks up food, depression, anger, sloth, boredom and neglect like a hungry frumpy sponge. I miss the old denim dungarees. At least they suggested an impetus towards physical activity, or, at the very least, a spot of car maintenance.

'Meron! Come here!' Nuria shouts again from her state of repose. Medina's yell is building up in intensity.

I'm standing beside a sprawling Shafeek who's called me to organise his day's clothes, though he is deliberating at a pace that might write off the entire Sunday. Only the punctuality required of Beirut's courts rouse him from bed with any speed from Monday to Saturday. On Sunday, he catches up with paperwork, and sleep. At this moment, 10.22am according to his bedside digital clock, he is fit only for dreaming. I have been standing here since 10.14am awaiting instructions. But sleepy-faced Shafeek has the charm of a dozy puppy: I'm content to ignore Nuria's request.

When she shouts again, Shafeek stirs.

'Er, Mister . . . Nuria is calling for me.'

'Why?'

'I don't know,' I lie.

'Go and see. If it's something quick, do it and hurry back . . . don't waste time with *that*.'

My duty is to Mister Shafeek, not to 'that'.

'Meron!' she bawls again.

I stomp along to her room. Nuria is half-lying, half-sitting in bed, with sheets and blankets strewn around haphazardly, pillows slumped on the floor, dirty cups and plates dotted about wherever there's space, and the occasional soiled nappy, happy to be kicked along the floor. There's enough dried food maturing away in here to make a meal: it does cross my mind. Nuria's legs are spread apart on the bed like a couple of lifeless blocks of timber, black hairs hanging off like splinters, reminding me of rough-edged railway sleepers. Her belly remains bulbous. What else is inside? She's *had* the baby. Have they left another four behind?

'You're too slow! I'm feeding her now . . . she couldn't wait for you to come and change the nappy,' Nuria grumbles.

'Sorry, *Medina*,' I say pointedly to the baby with a generous beam. 'I was helping your Uncle Shafeek.'

'Of course you were,' says Nuria bitterly. 'Ouch!'

Medina has clamped down hard on Nuria's left nipple. At the age of one week, Medina is already my best friend.

'Shall I wait?' I ask.

Nuria delays her answer. She won't be pushed into it.

'Mister Shafeek is waiting for me.' I press.

'And what about Medina? The nappy still needs changing. She can't do it herself.'

Hoh, Nuria! I take a deep breath.

'You probably don't have disposable nappies in Ethiopia,' she continues as Medina suckles noisily.

'Our babies eat so little that . . .' I start, tempted to feed Nuria a fib or two, but I take pity on her and shut up.

'Medina's been fed so she needs winding,' orders Nuria finally.

'You want me to do *that*? Winding the baby?' I ask, a little puzzled.

'Why do you think I just asked you to do it? Are you completely stupid?'

'No, not completely.'

Nuria's face is drawn, her hair lank, breath stale, clothes unwashed. It's difficult to recognise her as Madame's first daughter. I try to imagine Madame on her return from the maternity ward with baby Nuria in her arms, so impossibly pure and cute. Some people are probably at their very best in those first few days of life, before an inconceivable catalogue of personality defects and hygiene issues has been cultivated.

Nuria lifts the baby towards me, her breasts drooping either side of her body, brushing against her arms. Medina cries immediately.

'She's still hungry,' sighs Nuria and clamps the baby back onto her left breast. I watch, slightly awed. After a few seconds, Medina splutters.

'Nuria, I know what to do,' I say bravely. I've seen what mothers do in Addis when babies choke a little.

'Here . . .' Nuria says, more than happy to give her baby away.

Tapping Medina's back lightly, I blow steadily on the top of her head, puff, puff, puff and the splutters stop abruptly. Nuria looks on bemused. Madame enters at this moment and gasps with horror.

'Not a bad little trick,' says Nuria.

'Not do that! Hold baby's head away from your breath,' urges Madame. She's wearing her red gym gear. Madame is always tense before her Sunday morning workouts.

I try to hold Medina as far from my body as possible but she immediately vomits. I watch helplessly as her regurgitated milk shoots onto the bedclothes. I pass Medina back to a reluctant Nuria for more milk.

'Wait a moment and change the nappy, Meron.'

'Yes, Nuria.'

'You do know how to do that, don't you? Blowing on her head won't get you very far with a full nappy.'

Madame giggles and departs for the gym.

'Yes, Nuria.'

While I'm changing Medina, Nuria starts to grunt in her sleep. Medina is soon ready to return to her basket. But I can't let go of her. With the baby close to me, I'm aware of human warmth and a great tranquillity. Another being is responding with love towards *me*. I cry to myself: the first hug in seven months. It hurts to recognise the vacuum of love in my life. My mother hugged us through every age, dilemma, sickness, mischief and spare waking moment. Without hugs, I'm a shrivelled husk. I can't put Medina down again.

'Meron, what are you doing?' Shafeek shouts from his bed. I have completely forgotten him.

I place Medina back in her Moses basket and caress the marble-white skin of her cheeks.

'I hope my baby is like this,' I say out loud to myself.

Medina's eyes flicker open and shut as she struggles to fight sleep, her lovely black eyes mesmerising me: two beacons of innocence unspoilt by Lebanese bias.

'Argh!' I yelp as my left ear is grabbed, someone yanking my head away from Medina.

'*Why?* Are you pregnant?' Nuria whispers into the pained ear that she is grasping too tightly.

'Meron! Come here!' demands Shafeek down the hall, becoming rattier by the second.

'Are you pregnant?' hisses Nuria, using the ear to twist my face round to meet hers. 'Who was it?'

'Argh!' I gasp again.

The concern in her fraught face surprises me. Who is this violent Nuria, supposedly exhausted from childbirth but suddenly animated by a few harmless words? I want to step away but her grip is firm. I am forced into the path of oncoming panic.

'Are you pregnant?' demands Nuria again, but I don't hear her.

'I can't think . . . please let go . . .' I stutter.

'Tell me *now*!'

'I . . . I . . . don't know . . .'

I can see every scarlet capillary snaking around her eye-balls but the answer to her question completely evades me.

'You dismal little idiot. This will finish you! How long have you been pregnant?'

'Come here now, Meron, before I kill you!' shouts Shafeek from his room.

Pregnant? Kill me?

I can't move, speak or think. Of course he'll kill me. I feel a sickening drop into a much blacker place: odorous and ominous, overwhelmed by the hum of a million flies. There's no back door, no window or any way of escape. We're trapped, inert, finished. The worst of the world has arrived at our doorway.

Confidence Switches Tracks

The six hoary old women in their spattered sandals continued to up-end the sacks of muck onto our doorstep,
whooping like devilish monkeys, quite obviously enjoying
today's clean-up. They had shovelled up the grim waste
from the surrounding tracks with a rare vigour, intent
on inflicting a measure of revenge upon my mother for
constantly refusing to do her weekly duty with them.
They assumed her refusal to assist was rooted in snobbery
lugged across the bridge from our ex-life. In reality, she
was enduring hard labour to keep the rolls of daily injera
on our single platter.

'Where's your mother?' asked our next-door neighbour,
a sly elderly woman nicknamed 'Giraffe Tongue'. That
surly length of flesh flapping between her teeth had spread
hostility since the day we moved in.

'She's out,' I stuttered.

'And she'll stay out after we've dumped all this!' she
cackled. 'She shouldn't have left you here, a seven-year-old,

looking after the two little brothers . . . and you shouldn't have opened the door to us.'

The foul solid contents were slumped against our flimsy iron door. Nobody could get in or out without first clambering over a giant mound of muck. I couldn't run for Mum, or shout at the women, or even move my legs a single pace. My mouth was dry and my hands quivered with panic. For the first time in my life, I was exposed to the vileness of the real world. Maybe we would never have a home again, or we would have to sleep beside this pile for the rest of our lives, and scramble over it every morning. The blockade of human detritus was already attracting a sinister mist of flies, turning the sky a horrible deathly black. We would be rat food at dusk, bare bones by dawn. Tears dribbled down my face. My little brothers looked to me for guidance but I was watching my self-assurance leak away into the open drains. If only Dad was here. The girl who swam lengths in the Ghion was drowning and as I frantically gulped in the pungent air, I realised my mother was all I had and right now she was failing us. Where was she? And where was God?

We waited and waited. It was overcast and cold. More flies filled the air. Henok grizzled. Nati tried to leap over the filth, but instead his hands became caked in it. We had no water inside to wash them. Giraffe Tongue and the others celebrated with coffee next door. I prayed desperately for Mum's return, each extra second undermining my self-belief. Nati began to cry when he couldn't scrape the muck off his hands and it smeared across his face. If Nati was crying, things were desperate.

'Please, God, *make Mum come!*' I yelled, my tears adding to the quagmire of despair in our hut.

Eventually, she arrived, aghast at the scene. The women sniggered as they watched Mum's face change.

'Whose idea was this?' she bellowed.

There was silence.

'Come on. Be brave . . . who dumped this outside my house?' she demanded.

Giraffe Tongue stepped forward. Dressed in a dowdy long skirt, blouse and headscarf, she had just pulled on a smart black jacket to keep warm, the synthetic leather type that all self-respecting but insolvent Addis ladies would rent for a few birr the day before weddings and funerals.

'Me! You think you're too good for this work. This is what you get for that!' she screamed, the others hooting encouragingly.

Mum strode up to her and, without hesitation, grabbed the collar of her rented jacket. She tore it from the shocked woman's body, buttons popping into the air, stitches audibly ripping and Giraffe Tongue's arms almost wrenching off with the garment. It took a few seconds to completely separate the screaming creature from her sleeves. Mum's pent-up frustration spilled over, and there must have been so much of that: her husband's premature death, the loss of our beloved villa, the prospect of poverty, the desertion of her own sister, the daily degradation of laundry work, the delay in the widow's pension thanks to Kebebush, and now these terrorising hags. I gazed in admiration at the transformation of a woman: suddenly mad but supremely confident.

The others looked on, taken aback at my mother's

strength. I am not sure if any man could have done that. Mum tossed the torn jacket onto the garbage the way I had seen rich men throw cigarette butts in the street.

'Here . . . you can use *that* to clear up this mess. *Now!*'

Finally, I moved my legs and collected Dad's old baseball bat from our junk-filled cupboard. This was the implement he kept handy when travelling at night through Ethiopia's badlands near the Djibouti border. I tossed the bat to my mother outside. Now, in her hands, she wielded it in the faces of the muted women.

'If anyone has a problem with me, come forward. Come on! Let's decide this *now*. Step forward! Come on!'

I admit to uncertainty over this spirited approach, but the women began clearing up, in a submissive silence. Giraffe Tongue sobbed, but said nothing, the tongue finally stationary. My mother stood watching over them until the ground was clean again.

'Don't ever do that again,' she spat as they trundled away miserably with the sacks.

'Werk, Werk, Werk . . . I'm impressed by you.'

Tadelle dangled in the air like hung washing: it was difficult to see how his two-dimensional frame sustained the standing position for more than a second without crumpling in the light afternoon breeze.

'Don't be,' snapped my mother.

'That is the kind of woman I'm looking for. And now that you are single . . . what a tantalising thought.'

'I don't have any money, Boiled Egg. So why would you be interested in me? And to be honest, the sight of you fills me with nausea from my feet upwards,' said Mum.

'What about if I stay Orthodox Christian for a while?'

'Go away, scum.'

'I shall do that. But I might be able to help you first. Let me ask a question . . . why can't you be a good citizen like these wonderful women with their spades and sacks?' asked Tadelle.

'I haven't seen *you* doing much street cleaning, Boiled Egg . . . don't lecture *me*,' said Mum, walking away from him.

'Werknesh, *someone* needs to lecture you. You're poor now . . . and now that I work for the kebelle, I'm happy to be your guide.'

That stopped her.

'Work for the kebelle? You? How did *that* happen?' she asked, astonished.

'Come on, Werknesh, think about who you're speaking to,' he said, following Mum into our house uninvited.

'I am. Like an unwelcome fly, you buzz around every birth, death and marriage ceremony in the neighbourhood for the free food and whatever else is going. And now in the kebelle! My God, you will defecate on this neighbourhood.'

'Exactly! I'm a *known* person. I am Boiled Egg . . what a great name! I cause no real harm. How can I with that nickname? Eggs are trustworthy. People voted for me because they *know* me. My name is my passport to political glories.'

'We live in a strange country,' she replied, shaking her head in disgust.

Tadelle sat himself down on our old sofa. Mum flinched.

'And we have a strange blockage in the courts of this strange country,' continued Tadelle. 'Your husband' divorce certificate . . . we can't locate it at the moment. And you probably need that pension to feed your children. So, as a man who likes to eliminate suffering, in the name of the Lord, I put myself at your disposal for negotiating an arrangement with Kebebush. I think she'd disappear back to the rose bushes of Woliso with that thorny, dubious son if you were to offer some reasonable incentive . . . Werknesh?'

'What can I offer? I'm poor. Look at us! I have nothing, Tadelle. I need the kebelle to *help me* . . . please find the divorce certificate!'

'Werknesh, you're a good woman. It would be a shame if you couldn't be reconnected to men in some way . . . you offer so much. I would be happy to . . .'

'Impossible! Do your job! Why does everything need a price?'

'Okay, okay, we'll do our best for you with this peculiarly evasive document, and of course, the kebelle can help with free barley, free sugar, free T-shirts, schoolbooks for the kids . . . all this for twenty birr.'

'I pay twenty birr to get *free* things from the kebelle? Tadelle! Find the certificate or I'll *break* that boiled egg of yours,' said Mum, waving the baseball bat around like a professional.

'Werknesh, let's see a little humility in your new-found poverty. Now that you're one of us, learn the language of *peace*. Or your family will waste away in horrendous discomfort.'

'What's happened to this country? And the politicians?' said Mum, raising the baseball bat high above her head as if to attack Tadelle. He looked up, terrified.

I tried to shout at her. Nothing came out but a weak croak as Mum laughed insanely.

'I *am* this country!' shouted Tadelle, suddenly dashing for the door, screaming as he went. 'Twenty birr . . . only twenty birr for free things! I can *help* you, Werknesh!'

And he was out. Mum glanced at me with a wide grin. I saw the confidence of Dad in that grin. Thank you, God, at last.

Shafeek's smirk reminds me of that confident grin. But I am looking at Shafeek in Beirut, who is looking at Nuria clutching my ear, and he clearly knows she has crossed the line. He relishes his sisters' mistakes.

'How long have you been pregnant?' demands Nuria, unaware of Shafeek behind her.

Focus, Meron! This is Beirut. This is Nuria, *Nuria*, asking a question. *Just answer it!*

'What? Pregnant . . . *no*! No, Nuria, I'm not pregnant! I was just saying . . . when I have a baby, I hope it's something like this . . .'

'Leave her, Nuria! You're wasting my time!' snaps Shafeek with an air of absolute authority. 'Let her do the duties she is paid to do, for me, which do not involve you and your family.'

The lock on my ear is released.

'Yeah, yeah . . . leave Medina alone and just go,' she says to me flatly, her body lunging back onto the sheets, her face immediately reverting to apathy as though Shafeek is not even in the room.

I should be grateful for Shafeek. But, I don't know.

Hariri and Medina (549 days left)

Today is Monday. It is St Valentine's Day, 14th February 2005. Nine months have passed in Beirut. I count every single day but hope to remember none of them. Red roses and a romantic candlelit dinner will not mark this day out, I assure myself as I prepare Abdul's coffee to a fanfare of Medina's morning bawling. Nuria and Hassan's parental responsibilities obviously finished with Medina's lift home from the maternity ward two months ago, as it is me who services the baby every two hours throughout the night with milk, hugs and nappies. Only the anticipation of Abdul's coffee and friendly chatter carries me through.

'How are you, Mister?' I say in Arabic, now impressively fluent but still unacknowledged by my unwitting teachers.

'Be careful of love . . . it can cost you your life.'

'Really?'

'It's killed me.'

'In what sense, Mister?'

'In every sense. She's taken what she wants. I'm the coffee grounds, good for nothing . . . except fertiliser on the plants.'

'Oh! Mister, can I have fresh coffee today?' I ask, sensing my chance.

'Yeah, okay, but if Nazia or Rahima come, forget it.'

And I need the coffee more than ever. My period is coming and back pain is the usual forerunner. They have been getting more painful by the month, if they come at all. I'm not resting or eating as I used to in Addis. I have no Panadol and Madame hates wasting it on me. I don't like asking her: she instantly converts me into the leper of Lebanon.

Shafeek has a huge carton of Panadols in his bathroom: he munches them like crisps. I love crisps. Noise food! I could steal one but he might notice and batter my arms again.

'Do you have any Panadol, Mister?' I ask Abdul.

'What? Aarrgh!'

He's dabbing the olive oil again.

'Why are you doing that, Mister?'

'It's sore and dry from the cold. When you get to my age, you'll understand . . . Aarrgh!'

I doubt that.

'Why do you have to do it in the kitchen?'

'Aarrgh! What? The olive oil's *here*, in the kitchen.'

That same jar of olive oil is constantly used by all members of the family, usually on bread or salads or hummus rather than genitalia.

'Ah, I see, Mister.'

'Aarrgh! Mulu, what did you say you need?'

'I'm not Mulu. I'm Meron. Who's Mulu?'

'Previous maid. I'm confused . . . old age,' he says, shaking his head.

At last, we have a name.

'What happened to Mulu, Mister?'

He stares at me, forgetting for a second the serious business of olive oil application.

'My girl, what did you say you needed?' he asks steadily.

'I need Panadol, Mister,' I say carefully back into his ravine-grooved face.

'Mmm . . . why?'

'Back pain from my period.'

'Ah, okay . . . I see. I thought . . . *Aaarrrgh!*' he says, resuming the dabbing.

'Thought what, Mister?'

'Nothing, nothing. Dabbing isn't enough . . . it needs pickling during these winter months. Yes, I'll give you some Panadol if it shuts you up.'

I slurp the fresh coffee while Abdul rifles through Shafeek's cabinet of pills. He gives me a row of ten sealed tablets. I swallow one for now.

'How do I compare with the previous maid, Mister?' I try.

'Now . . . shut up,' he growls at the floor. 'Forget about the last maid. It is not the will of Allah that I ever speak of this matter . . . it is done, it is in the past and must *stay* in the past.'

'Thank you, Mister. And sorry for asking about Mulu . . .' I offer, but he's away.

I conceal the tablets in a golden sugar bowl living three shelves above my sleeping spot in the small salon. Nobody ever touches these trinkets. When I polish the bowl once a week, there's not a single fingerprint on the gleaming veneer: it is seen every day but handled never.

Mid-morning, everybody is out, except Medina who is still screaming. Panadol can't help her. A four-month-old baby doesn't understand the common cold: she's trying to breathe through a stubborn bung of mucus blocking up her little nose, oblivious to the joys of an open, oxygen-swallowing mouth. Understandably, she's upset when air doesn't arrive in her lungs. 'Crying is good for loosening the blockage,' said Nuria on her way out. She is a rubbish mother. I can do better than that.

In Addis, I have seen mothers suck out the nostril jam with their own mouths and spit it away. I'll do that for Medina and give everybody some peace. She's not even my daughter.

I hold her head steady, and one, two, three . . . slurp! And spit!

One hour later, Medina is rested and content. I'm an unsung hero.

Like young mothers in Addis, the only way to combine cleaning and baby-caring duties is by wearing Medina on my back inside a large shawl: she burbles happily as I jig about, singing traditional Ethiopian music and allowing rhythmic shoulder jerks to shake us around the kitchen, my favourite dance partner clinging to my skinny frame. For an hour or two each day, I feel like a real Habesha mother.

A sudden boom sounds in the distance. It might be an accident, perhaps. I think nothing of it and continue with the chores. We have another two hours before Madame returns for lunch. I'm frying fish left over from Friday. A drop of my saliva rolls onto the silver scales. Two hours is a long time to salivate over fish which I cannot hope to eat.

Two hours. That leaves time to bathe and change Medina, to bottle-feed her and then put her down for a sleep. With luck, I will steal a few minutes watching the Fashion Channel on television, always in Madame's bedroom, lolling on her lake of a bed, remembering to change the channel back to CNN or she will stumble upon my secret. I have already sneaked five minutes this morning.

Bathing Medina is generally a moment of fun. Today is no different. She's still kicking her legs and remembering those not-so-distant days as a permanently submerged foetus doing lengths inside Nuria's vast interior. I smile at the thought. For the first time, though, I use bubble bath. This is even more entertaining than usual, until I lift her from the enamel bath. Just for a second, I remember the moment when Nuria grabbed my ear and quizzed me about being pregnant: the urgency in her tone, the Addis flashback and the horrors of childhood entrapment still haunt me.

I am holding Medina safely away from my breath, but she sneezes violently and my mind is not focused on this baby. I feel her soapy body slipping from my grasp. No! No!

Smack!

That's her head hitting the side of the bath, the sound walloping into my stomach. Medina lets off such a raucous scream that all my mental faculties are disabled. Grabbing Medina out from the bath, I clutch her tightly to my bosom and within seconds my own tears are dripping onto her forehead. Is she all right? Is she hurt? *I don't know!* I'm not a doctor, I'm a domestic. All I can see is a baby's bright red tonsils rattling with the pitch of a thousand dying cats.

I see no blood anywhere, but blood clots on the brain are not usually visible. If she dies, I die. This is the direction of my thoughts: the window ledge is already beckoning me, without even the precursor of sexual assault. In this household, accidentally killing Medina would definitely be enough to send me over.

No!

Wrapping Medina in blankets, I carry her quickly to the bedroom: put her in the cot and let's see what happens. She immediately falls silent and closes her eyes. At least screaming means living. But silence? Dead people are silent.

'Medina! Medina! Medina!' I try. No reaction. God, help us! Should I be whacking her on the chest as hard as possible? Or inflating her like a party balloon? *I don't know!*

I hear the front door fly open. No! Not Shafeek surely! His time has passed. I nervously shout out: 'Forgot your papers, Mister?'

No reply. Someone's bashing around in the hallway. Perhaps it's Nazia. She won't acknowledge me. I leap into the hallway to check. It's Madame.

She stares back at me, her wilting body a dying tree, her face whiter than the moon, her mouth and eyes wearing the fright of a hunted creature cowering in the shadows. She carries the aura of death. How could she know? It was only a minute ago that I dropped the baby.

'Hariri is dead!' she wails.

This means absolutely nothing to me. Some person has died. Probably not a good moment to mention Medina's little accident.

'Sorry, Madame. Er, Medina is asleep in bed.'

'A bomb! Killed him in cold blood!' she despairs, hands clasping the side of her head.

'Terrible,' I say as dramatically as possible, shaking my head, not wishing to admit to total ignorance.

'Suicide bombers . . . but why? Why?'

I remain silent, unsure how to proceed without incriminating myself in some way.

'Help me!' Madame cries as she drops all her belongings on the floor and staggers into her bedroom, collapsing onto the bed with unrestrained sobbing. This is *not* one of her acts. She grabs the TV remote control. The Fashion Channel flashes onto the screen. Oops.

'Me-ron! You watching this again, on my television?' she snuffles.

'Sometimes, Madame, I press the buttons on the control by mistake while I'm cleaning. Sorry, Madame. By the way, Medina is a bit quiet this morning,' I blather, but Madame is hardly listening. CNN is on the screen. It shows smoking carnage 'Live from Beirut'.

Rafik Hariri, the revered ex-Prime Minister of Lebanon, has been assassinated by a massive roadside bomb, leaving twenty others dead. He was a national hero adored by Sunni Muslims for his reconstruction projects in Beirut and for his stance against Syria – whose forces still occupy Lebanon – while reviled in equal measure by the hard-line Shia Muslim movement Hezbollah. I hear that much.

'Syria did it! They jealous . . . we have money, we have tourists . . . now, *nothing*!' she shouts at the television with real venom.

'Do you need anything, Madame?' I ask timidly.

'Yes, I need so much . . . I need safe, free, prosperous Lebanon without Assad and the Syrian dogs feeding off us.'

I chew my bottom lip. I am probably the last person on Earth who can provide such a thing for Madame.

'Can I check on Medina?' I ask, edging into the hall.

But Shafeek comes charging through the front door, his head like an overripe boil.

'Mum!' he shouts as he enters Madame's bedroom. 'It's Hezbollah!'

Madame gazes at him in horror before embracing him and crying hard into his shoulder.

'No, my son! Syria! We all know that . . . CNN says so!' she blurts as Shafeek pats her on the back soothingly.

'No, Mum, Hezbollah . . . it has to be. Meron! Come here!' Shafeek storms out without waiting for Madame to reply. I follow him to the television in the small salon. He punches the remote control repeatedly until he finds Al-Jazeera News.

'Do you need anything, Mister? There's hummus in the fridge from yesterday, or baba ghanoush . . . fried fish for lunch . . . Mister?'

'Yes, find the killers and hang them up by their balls with piano wire.'

It feels appropriate to remain silent again. I can respond to requests for food, drink, clothes or bathroom accessories, but not to missions best left to the Lebanese Armed Forces. I shrug at Shafeek. Maybe he is also a killer and should be hung up with piano wire. Has he considered that?

'Our self-determination begins *today*, but *you* don't care about Lebanon. Why would you?' he asks, puzzled at his own question. 'If this happened in Ethiopia, I wouldn't give a shit. I really wouldn't.'

'Thank you, Mister. Oh! Medina is sleeping a lot this morning . . . maybe too much.'

I feel compelled to draw someone's attention to Medina's possible plight. Perhaps it's not too late.

'Fantastic! You've made a baby go to sleep . . . you want an Olympic medal? Just shut up about *her*. Hariri is *dead*! Al-Jazeera says Israel . . . Mossad . . . to destabilise us and drive out Syria. Could be right. Tell Mum . . . now!'

'Pardon?'

'Allah! I'm not repeating it!' he spits in my face. Shafeek throws the remote control at me. Fortunately, it misses and clatters into the wall, probably broken.

'Erm, okay, Mister.'

I trot along to Madame.

'Mister Shafeek says it's Israel or Moss . . . Syria . . . or Hez-Jazeera or I don't know. Medina.'

'What? No! Tell him definitely Syria . . . I'm on BBC now. Jumblatt talking.'

I dart back to Shafeek.

'She's on the BBC now. I think she said Syria . . . according to Jumblatt?'

'What? *That* jerk? Are you *crazy*?' He blows up at me, frantically trying to stick the remote control back together.

I hear the front door open again.

Abdul is home, extremely early: he seems disoriented within his own home and unsure on his feet. He sees me gaping.

'Mulu . . . I need help,' he falters.

Yes, but so does Medina. Anxiously, I run to help him. Maybe this is it. Three down inside the hour: Hariri, Medina and now Abdul. And then four, when I am given the quick shove.

He slumps onto the sofa in the TV lounge.

'Oh . . . so pleased you're here . . . are you feeling better with the Panadol?'

'Yes, thank you. What is it, Mister?' I ask urgently.

'I need you to put on the television and find a news channel that knows what it's talking about, preferably a Lebanese channel.'

'Oh, okay,' I say, a little deflated. He's lost the ability to turn on the television.

I flick through the channels for him. They are all full of the same thing. We settle with LBC News. The Lebanese Broadcasting Corporation should be Lebanese enough.

'It was Hezbollah, you know, the Shias. They're jealous! Hariri was a great man . . . he made Beirut what it is today,' Abdul moans.

His face is suddenly twitching and ready to burst: hands go to his eyes, crying seems a distinct possibility. No man ever cries in front of a woman in Addis. It's almost illegal. I place a comforting hand on his shoulder. He retains his composure.

'What does Shafeek say?' he gurgles.

'Jumblatt's a jerk . . . and I think he said Israel did it, but I'm not sure.'

'Tell him it's Hezbollah,' he says, as though this is absolute *fact*.

I am returning to Shafeek, but Nuria and Hassan enter the apartment. I can't believe it. Hassan is still grinning. How will he react if his daughter is declared a vegetable?

'Hello, Meron, how are you? Good, good? Clean your—'

'Meron, where's Medina?' interrupts Nuria.

'Very asleep . . . I wouldn't bother her for a few hours.'

'Oh, fine,' replies Nuria.

'You cleaned your teeth today?' asks Hassan, slurping a can of Pepsi.

'Yes, Mister . . .'

'Why are your teeth so *white*?' he asks.

'Ah, well, in Addis, we use mafaqiya, a natural tooth-brush carved from wooden twigs to make teeth gleam,' I explain patiently as Nuria disappears into her bedroom.

'Really? What about your, er, gum colour? Why are your gums bluey-green?'

'They were tattooed when I was a baby . . . again, to enhance the gleam of the teeth,' I answer affably. Why are we talking about gum tattoos right now?

'Now *that's* what I call cheap cosmetic dentistry, but I won't be offering it to my customers,' laughs Hassan.

'Sorry, Mister, I have to go . . . Hariri's dead!'

'Yes, of course!' he retorts, snapping into instant seriousness. He passes me a lump of chocolate. Hassan is not of the same world as other Lebanese: there's a defective gene on the loose, but it's an agreeable one.

I swallow the chocolate hard before rushing back to Shafeek. He's still standing in front of the television, hands stuck to the back of his head.

'Mister! Mister Abdul says it's Hezbollah. Do you want to check on Medina?'

Hairline cracks on a baby's skull would be compelling courtroom evidence. He's an international lawyer. It's his arena, not mine. Do something useful, Shafeek.

'Mister? Can you check Medina?' I repeat.

'Allah! No, I can't! Hammerhead, why would I do *that*? It's Nuria's . . . Hezbollah? No, no way . . . who says that?'

'Er, Mister Abdul . . .'

Shafeek hurls the broken remote control to the ground, sending shards of plastic across the floor, ensuring it has switched to its last ever channel.

'It's broken! I can't change the channel, Meron,' he whines at me pathetically.

There is no point in trying to respond.

'What does the BBC say?' he asks.

'I don't know.'

I don't care. I'll be smashed into shards too if Medina has gone. Just like Mulu.

'Meron!' yells Madame.

'Coming!'

She's holding a tissue to her eyes.

'Get more tissues from cupboard. What say Abdul?'

'I think he said . . . er, I don't know. I'll ask him again. Medina's really quiet.'

'Ah! Medina . . . the future of Lebanon. For her generation we will find Hariri's murderers . . . country must be *perfect* for her.'

'And for the other four million people, Madame . . . she's just one person.'

Not listening, Madame nods sagely.

'Meron!' yells Abdul.

I jog back to him in the lounge.

'How do I find Al-Jazeera on here?'

'Sorry, Mister, I'm—'

'Meron!' shouts Shafeek from my right.

I drop the remote on Abdul's lap and sprint back to Shafeek down the hallway. I remember the avid table football games in the Addis streets played by Nati, Henok and so many young men, whacking the little plastic ball from one end to the other. In this apartment, I am the ball.

At this moment, Nazia returns.

'Morning, Nazia. There's hummus and grapes and bread and . . .' I manage, skidding to a halt in front of her.

Ignoring me, she throws herself onto her bed and switches on the television immediately. No tears from the Lammergeyer.

'Coke with ice,' she replies finally, without looking at me.

She begins tapping into her new mobile phone: Nazia is more preoccupied with Valentine texts to her unofficial boyfriend than some national emergency.

'Me-ron!' demands Madame from behind me. 'Tell Abdul, it's Syria!'

'No, it's not!' screams Nazia. 'Meron, tell him it's Israel.'

'Meron! Where are you?' shouts Shafeek.

'Where's Al-Jazeera?' gurgles Abdul.

I am now caught in the hallway between four different people and four televisions, all spouting high emotion. It's Middle East cross-fire. But who *is* the enemy? Who are the teams? I would really like to know before the football is booted out of the arena.

And I remember Mum, suddenly mad but supremely confident against Giraffe Tongue and the others. I inhale deeply. One, two, three . . .

'*Medina is asleep!*' I scream from the bottom of my lungs.

Silence. For the briefest of seconds, we have peace in this Lebanese home. It works!

A shrill baby's yell rings out. It's Medina! Very much alive. I sprint to Medina's cot and lift her to my bosom. Ah! Simplicity, purity, humanity! Lebanon's future alive in my arms. Medina smiles back. This is *not* a sick baby.

'Come here, Meron!' snaps Shafeek.

I rush into Shafeek's room, Medina now screaming for milk at maximum volume.

'Go outside with it! I've got a headache. Too loud, can't hear the television . . .' he orders. The same happens in the other rooms. We're ejected by the entire grieving family.

Yes! Together, we amble back into the kitchen. Nobody else is hungry: I eat two large portions of fish. Ha! The salty smack of sea meat on my tongue brings tears of joy to my eyes. We're *all* crying today!

And then I remember Proverbs 14:13: 'Even in laughter the heart is sad, and the end of joy is grief.'

'You stole my Panadol . . . at least ten are gone,' whinges Shafeek at me, mid-afternoon, in the hallway.

'Not me, Mister,' I splutter.

Madame is with us in a flash.

'Me-ron! I said *no pills*! What you doing? Is it your period coming . . . is it usual back pain?'

'I didn't take the Panadol, Madame . . . my period already came and went, don't worry.'

I hate talking about this in front of Shafeek.

'*Already?* You not tell us? No! Can't have done . . . date is wrong,' replies Madame indignantly.

'Yeah! How did you get better so fast, Meron? Periods don't just come and go like that . . . we'd have *known*,' butts in Shafeek, international lawyer with specialism in the menstrual cycle.

'Sorry . . .'

'*Sorry?*' Shafeek and Madame seem to say simultaneously.

I grab a broom and sweep hard. Maybe they will disappear. I keep sweeping. I want no part in this conversation. Mum would know what to say to them: she would comprehensively repel them. How, Mum, *how*?

'You can't just steal my tablets! That's *not* how we function here, Hammerhead . . . you've got to *learn*!' rants Shafeek.

'We getting tired of this,' continues Madame.

Sweeping, sweeping, sweeping, before the beating comes. Think of Mum again. If you touch me, I'll laugh so hard into your contorted faces. She always told me angry people age fast: at the current rate, Madame and Shafeek won't make the next Ramadan.

'Allah! It was *me*,' says Abdul.

You sweet old man, if only I could kiss you plumb on those chapped, chipped lips on that huge wrinkled olive of a head.

227

'I gave her the Panadol . . . she was suffering in pain and wanting to work . . . a few cheap pills. So what? Leave her to *work*! There are bigger things happening today. Hariri's dead!'

Madame and Shafeek cannot reply. I look at Abdul to smile, but he's already hobbling off.

I have only ever known two old people, including Abdul. He partially restores my faith in this strange race known as 'the elderly', a faith formerly devastated by my grandmother, Mama.

As for Hariri, he will never be old and Shafeek is right: I'm not in a position to care.

Lemma's Mama

Eighteen months after my father's death, there was still no decision from the Addis courts on my mother's pension rights. Disastrously, Tadelle's kebelle office had failed to locate the necessary divorce certificate. Mum had refused to liaise with Tadelle in any way. But Kebebush had found a letter from her own kebelle in Woliso, stating she had been with Lemma up to his death: apparently, she had nursed him in his final days, as if my mother had not existed. The onus was now on my mother to prove the divorce had taken place. Justice was fading fast: Mum had to act.

There were three witnesses to the divorce: Lemma's two best friends in Woliso and his mother, Mama, who lived on her Woliso farm. The two friends had no interest in travelling to Addis to support us, and not being acquainted with Mum, why would they? Instead, my mother had to persuade Mama to return to Addis for a court hearing. This was probably the last chance. Without her word as evidence, the pension rights would be passed to Kebebush and the implausible son, unfairly condemning us to a life-time of poverty.

Mum phoned her mother-in-law countless times. At first, nobody answered. After a few weeks, the line was dead. Only a single option remained.

Dad used to visit Mama every month. The last time I saw her was two years previously just before Dad's passing. I was remembering those happy days as the bus finally arrived in Woliso, depositing Mum, Nati, Henok and me in the dusty bus lot. Fooling around in the road, a small boy had been caught under the wheels about halfway through the journey: the mortified bus driver was arrested – before the villagers lynched him – and quickly replaced. This was a standard delay.

We set off along the rutted, potholed road towards her farm, all of us in worn shoes that managed to locate every excruciatingly sharp pebble ever exposed to tender foot flesh. Two years earlier, we had scampered barefooted and carefree around her lush, well-tended yard and across the barley fields. We had climbed the banana trees, milked the cows in the sheds and fattened up on the richest genfo and soft cheese imaginable, all from fresh cows' milk. Mama had managed the land and her dairy business with the dis-cipline of a ferenji – like the French or British – everything done very correctly and with great skill. I did not recall a single sharp pebble from those days.

This time, hopefully, all would be the same, though our clothing was visibly declining into ragtag garments, not renewed since Dad had gone. I wore my black school shoes out of necessity: one bore an expanding hole in the upper leather, concealed to onlookers by colouring in my bare skin with black ink. We were the same as other street kids now.

'What's happened, Mum?' I asked as we arrived at a gate hanging from its hinges.

'This doesn't look good. The road was never like this before. And the gate! Stay close to me, all of you!'

We crept towards the farmhouse. The greenery of the front garden had turned into a barren dirt-yard with not a plant to be seen. One ailing old banana tree remained, barely alive with a decaying brown trunk. It lacked the enormous bunches of ripening bananas, and where were all the handsome broad green leaves that had provided us with natural shelter and doubled as nature's own disposable plates? All other trees had been unceremoniously hacked down, leaving an ugly profusion of scruffy stumps and pared branches.

'Where are the ploughed fields full of cereal?' I asked.

We used to eat handfuls of the soft barley straight from the harvest. Now all we saw were thorn bushes.

'Where are the cows?' asked Nati, already nosing around. 'The sheds are empty, Mum!'

'I don't know . . . I don't know.'

As we approached the front door of Mama's large dark-timbered farmhouse, we could see the old curtains, ripped and thin, hanging in the stained windows. Peering through, we could see only gloom inside.

'Hello!' shouted Mum into the house.

Slowly, we entered. Mum reached for the light switch. Click, click, click. Nothing. No electric light. Instead, the embers of a fire glowed in the middle of the sitting room. Where we once wrestled with Dad on a lovely thick carpet sat a dying fire with smoke drifting towards discoloured brown walls. Old newspapers had been stuck onto a third of the walls to keep them clean, until someone had run out of newspaper. The smoke made us splutter, but the smell of cow manure quickly overpowered it.

'It's horrible in here! And there's no furniture, Mum,' I whispered.

Mama used to have a full set of chairs, tables, book-shelves and so on. Now, only a fire with a black pot hanging above it.

'I expect the fire ate it all,' replied Mum.

It was a disorderly continuous fire, the type that guzzled burnable objects ad infinitum, never to be put out. Things were added and added, the ash accumulating, the smoke staining, the pot blackening and nothing else to show for it.

The moo of a cow sounded from a side room.

'Mum . . . the cows . . . we've found them!' declared Nati, running towards Mama's bedroom.

Four of the scraggy cows were tied up, out of the fifty or so we had seen before. They looked malnourished and glum. Flies buzzed round the dollops of muck on the floor. And Mama, asleep on a bank of earth next to the window, her wooden bed gone the same way as the other furniture, only a tatty pink blanket covering her stirring frame.

'Mama! It's us! We're here!' we shouted.

'Oh. Let me kiss these children,' her pale face said unsmilingly, eyes half-shut, with only the faintest hint of real interest.

As she raised her head to greet us, ripples of wrinkles seemed to cascade from her cheeks. On her hunched bony body, she wore a loose flowery dress and brown plastic shoes. A gnarled, untamed stick sat next to the bed awaiting its duties: it was the type of walking stick picked up from the ground and put into immediate service without refinement. As Mama used it to raise herself into a standing position, we were watching a woman who had been shunted into old age without the fond hands of others to soften the arrival.

'You bring meat?' she asked, squinting at Mum.

'No, Mama . . . how are you?'

'I don't eat meat now . . . only kale . . . not since you killed him.'

This was not the conversation anticipated by my mother.

'What's happened to this place?' asked Mum, hoping to avoid difficult topics.

'Sold the cows, burnt the furniture, neglected the farm . . . I'm waiting to die, Werknesh. I want to die in great pain.'

'Shall we make the fire and cook some kale? I think the children are hungry. The bus took five hours . . . someone was run down by the bus . . . had to wait for police . . .' said Mum.

'We're all guilty in the death of Lemma . . . you, me, Addis . . . I let him go, you married him and kept him there. In the countryside, he was strong. In Addis, with *you*, he lost it.'

'Mama, where can we sleep tonight? We'll stay one night and go in the morning . . .' continued Mum.

Mama began to move her body, supported by the stick.

'Okay. Sleep on the floor, on the old curtains, under the animal skins. Cook what you like, but not meat . . . since he died, I stopped meat.'

'Yes, you told me. It's okay. We brought bread and coffee and sugar.'

'I eat kale and potatoes.'

Mama was no longer Mama. Not in my eyes.

On the walls were the only remaining features from before: photos of Dad as a young man and boy. Mama had worshipped him religiously and, it seemed, ruinously.

'Ah!' cried Mum, seeing the pictures. 'There's Lemma! May he rest in peace. May the Lord be with him.'

Mama swivelled towards my mother with a face of spite.

'Werknesh! Save your scanty little clichés. We can't rest in peace. *We* need hurting . . . hurt us, Lord, hurt us! Make us suffer for *him*!'

The cows seemed to moo in agreement. They didn't have long for this world and they knew it. My mother hustled us out of the intoxicating fly-blown bedroom.

'Let's go outside and get some fresh air . . . you can play outside, Nati. Come outside, Mama, with us,' tried Mum.

'That won't save us.'

Ah, relief! In the sunshine and fresh air, we relaxed and drank coffee on Mama's steps. She sat with her back to us.

'Mama, what's wrong? Join us, please . . .' pleaded Mum.

'I never look towards Addis . . . when I sleep, I give it my feet. It killed my boy.'

'Mum, I need the toilet,' whispered Henok.

Mama heard him.

'If you need a shit, go over there somewhere, and cover it with dust afterwards. We don't have the old enclosure. . . burnt it. Go over there where I can't see you,' she said, waving into the distance.

It used to be a comfortable cubicle surrounded by banana leaf partitions, the two servants always maintaining the hole in a healthy state and using the dried accumulation as fertiliser on the fields. There was little point in asking about the two servants: they probably scarpered the day Lemma died and Mama's life turned to ash.

Henok declined the invitation to shit 'somewhere over there'. One night and we would be back on the bus, grateful for that cramped perilous murderous vehicle, speeding us once more to the relative luxuries of Addis.

'Er, Mama . . . I need to ask you a favour,' began Mum.

'There's no milk. They've dried up. They'll be dead in a month.'

'No, Mama, not milk. It's about the pension . . . Lemma's railway pension from the government, which I need for feeding these children.'

'Lemma?'

The word itself as precious as fresh-cut beef steak: I hoped Mum knew what she was doing with it.

'What about it?' demanded Mama.

'The problem is the divorce certificate. You know, the divorce from Kebebush . . . that you witnessed. the certificate has disappeared and the court still thinks his inheritance should all go to Kebebush and to the boy who's supposed to be his son. The only way I can prove I was his legal wife is by bringing the divorce witnesses to the court. Lemma's old friends won't come to Addis to help me. That leaves you . . .'

'I don't know what you're talking about. I eat kale, potato and beetroot. Good enough for me. I deserve no more than that.'

'Will you come to Addis to help me, Mama? I mean, for the children, not for me . . .'

'Go to Addis? How can I? Addis murdered my son. I can't even *face* Addis . . . how would I *travel* to Addis? Are you *mad*?'

'In the name of Lemma, *please*, Mama!'

No answer. The old lady began to thump her chest repeatedly with her fists, hitting herself as hard as possible. My mother covered her own eyes, and then Henok's, but the sickening thuds of her blows could not be silenced, until she was too exhausted for more, falling backwards onto the dust at the point of collapse.

It was too late for the last bus back. I didn't sleep that night. None of us did, on that filthy ground underneath insect-teeming animal skins. I wanted to kiss our little house when we returned. I loved Addis. I told myself never to leave Addis again, or I might regret it.

Hot Summer (432 days left)

In Addis, the temperature never exceeds twenty-eight degrees Celsius. When thirty degrees came to Beirut two months ago, I believed my sweat would run dry. Now as we nudge forty degrees in mid-summer, standing, breathing, walking, washing the grapes, grinding the garlic, preparing the olives, squeezing the lemons all require careful concentration, or down I shall clatter like a fatally wounded elephant, unlikely to stand again. Headaches cling to and tear at the inside of my head like cats on quality sofas. My heart pounds like a tribal drum if I blink. This would never happen in Addis. Every heavy second here is a second of regret: every bead of sweat is moisture grudgingly lost to Beirut.

It's like Dad's railway, a single-gauge line, but it's not Addis to Djibouti. A single-gauge line of thought forges towards a single destination. I see only two letters on the station platform sign: A and C. There's no B, just AC, as in 'Air Con'. As in Air Conditioning. I'm headed only in that direction, on a continual circuit, towards the only possible destination in the Beirut summer. I have to get to AC before I derail. AC, AC, AC . . .

'Don't touch this, Meron, we not wasting air conditioning on Ethiopia person. Maybe you have accident and freeze to death . . . this is possible,' says Madame.

As soon as I believe Shafeek has not forgotten his papers, I kneel in front of the AC unit in Madame's bedroom until the goosepimply chicken skin arrives and it's time to snatch twenty minutes of work. Without the AC, nothing can happen. I extinguish the chilled air only minutes before Madame arrives home.

On one of these turgid days, Madame arrives home particularly relieved that her room is already cool. She's a little pink with heat and short of breath as she falls into her bedside chair with a loud sigh. I notice an expression quite different from anything I have seen before. Madame is affected in some way.

'Meron, get me cold water now . . . before I boil,' she slurs. I detect no alcohol on her breath.

'Yes, Madame. Are you okay?'

'I need water and . . . get water.'

I return with water. She gulps it down vigorously and pats remaining droplets onto her face.

'You from Ethiopia. I suppose heat not affecting you?' she asks, as I wait with her, happy to be in the coolest room in the apartment.

'I get hot, Madame, in the heat,' I say. That seems obvious. I'm not even trying to be funny.

'Yes, Meron, but in other ways. Hot in other ways. I mean . . . urges . . . urges to get physical relief,' she says.

'No, Madame, I hardly ever need the toilet when I'm too hot,' I reply.

'Not that. I mean activity . . . you know, Meron, *enjoyable* activity,' she says, winking at me.

'In this heat, yes . . . swimming.'

'Swimming? You go swimming in Addis Ababa? What? You only know the *word*. You not *swim* in Addis.'

'Yes, you're right. It feels good just saying the word, Madame. We say a lot of words in Addis. Swimming is one of my favourite words.'

Madame creases her face and looks at me densely.

'Anyway, Meron, doorman coming up here to help me with . . . something. When he comes, do not disturb us. You stay on balcony. You come inside and I kill you. I mean really *kill* you.'

That familiar word again.

The intercom buzzes three times. Within two minutes, the Sudanese doorman is at our front door. I let him in. We exchange stares. I remember his contemptible glance on the first day. He has not aged well since then: cheeks, nose, lips, eyes, chin, forehead, warts, they all charge outwards from his charcoal-black face like rainforest trees fighting for sunlight. After he retires from door-manning, he could become a cartoon character. I think I'm staring at him. My tongue is out. Madame shoos me away as though I'm a curious goat.

I seek the afternoon breeze on the balcony. After about forty minutes, I hear the front door slam. Madame calls me in. She seems distant and doused.

'I go to have sleep now. Why don't you . . . I don't know . . .'

She disappears back into her bedroom and closes the door. It's not like her to leave instructions hanging in the air. But I like it.

This minor event happens about once a fortnight during summer, especially on the sweltering days. I make no effort to discover the secret. I simply crave any spare draught drifting across the Eastern Mediterranean towards the Levant. It seems unfeasible to function in such heat. Almost everything is unfeasible, except whatever Madame is doing.

Shafeek is unable to wander from bedroom to kitchen in his briefs without a light film racing across his forehead. His wooden back-scratcher has to be replaced every month because the teeth turn black and mouldy. Within a single day of use, the collars on his expensive French-tailored shirts become the skid marks of juggernauts. I have lost many hours, probably days, of my life to his stained collars. He appears to sweat burnt rubber.

To relax in the summer, Shafeek reads legal papers, except late at night when he unwinds over half an hour of soft-core pornography. Unfortunately barefooted, he uses 'my' television tucked away in the small salon for that act. It is of no importance to him that I am lying a miserable metre from where he slavers and stinks.

To me, Shafeek's television sex looks like a very strange affair requiring two people, sometimes more. They must have vast amounts of energy to thrust flesh into each other, hour after hour, apparently never actually finishing what they have started. Most of his movies seem harmless and almost educational, but I can't sleep through them:

the grunts and groans of sex are pitched at an alarming level, not dissimilar to the deathbed throes of malaria victims. People say that 'sex sells', but if it were by sound alone, it wouldn't turn a profit for anyone. And do these people not have other things to do, especially the women who might want to tidy up their beds occasionally? It must be 'linen washing day' every single day in their clammy world.

'Really, it's natural, it's mechanical, it's personal, it's boring . . . yet, I can't pull myself away,' says Shafeek tonight, and he tends to say every night like a weak 'forgotten papers' excuse. 'I am literally unable to move away from this television, Meron . . . maybe you want to sleep but I'm stuck right here, watching sex.'

'Yes, Mister,' I mutter from my mattress.

'You do *like* sex, don't you?'

I can't answer that for fear of implicating myself. Presumably, everyone is programmed to *like* sex? There has to be some incentive for making new people. Possibly Shafeek's question is less abstract than it sounds: what would sex be like with Shafeek? Is Shafeek propositioning me? Or is that ludicrous? I can't stop wondering. The heat is affecting me. Every intelligent cell in my head yells 'No!' at the potential danger of sex with Shafeek, but the non-intelligent ones turn me into a screaming hot kettle, boiling over within seconds in his presence. What *is* this?

I close my eyes and feign sleep.

'Hammerhead, I know you can hear me . . . do you like sex?' he repeats.

I can't risk a reaction. Mum! What's the correct answer?

'Mister, I don't know,' I try.

'Ah! I understand . . .' he chuckles, like a boy with a trapped wasp.

He understands what?

'Are you okay? Do you want a Pepsi?' Shafeek whispers at me, waking me up abruptly.

'Mister? What's the time? What do you want?' I mumble warily.

I peer through the night's semi-darkness at him. I can't read the expression on his face. What *does* he want?

'It's past one . . . want a Pepsi?' he murmurs.

He sits down on the end of my mattress in the small salon. I'm awake now.

'Yes, please,' I whisper. Speaking too loudly will touch Madame's hairpin trigger of a hearing system and, thanks to me, there's no cushion of dust to absorb the rustle of sedition.

'First, tell me what you think of me . . . honestly,' he says.

Shafeek is within grasp. I'm playing with fire. And some demented element inside me is heating up. I don't know how to switch it off. But I am sure I don't want sex with Shafeek. Or do I? *Need time to think!*

'I'd be more honest, Mister, with a Pepsi in my hand . . .'

Shafeek creeps away and brings the Pepsi. Buying a few seconds of thinking time achieves nothing but his heightened anticipation of my answer. Nerves zip around in my guts like fireflies as he eases back onto my mattress, expectantly.

'Here's your drink, Meron. You see, I look after you . . . I'm like your father.'

'Yes, Mister, thanks, but I don't have a father now.'

'In Beirut, you do. if you need any help with *anything* . . . I am right here, your Baba. What do you think?' he asks, leaning on his elbow closer to me.

'Er . . .'

I am becoming confused. Is he seducing me? Or is he really a new Baba for me? Wasn't I hoping for true love before I surrendered my virginity? Do I need to employ Beti's advice: the hysterical wailing?

But Shafeek is an international lawyer. This could change my life! And anyway, it *could* be true love, if I can just forget the defect-heavy personality that's so obviously the fault of his work and family and upbringing and genes . . .

'Yes?' he says slowly.

'Wait a second,' I reply, gulping from the cold can, the first soft drink in sixteen months. Ah! Straight up my nostrils, eyes water, instant rush! Build a monument to the elation of sweet fizz! I can't believe *anything* is better than *this*. And here comes . . . oh God . . . *Baaarp!*

I emit a massive burp completely involuntarily. It resonates through the apartment like the horn blast on my father's train, enough to alert the entire city of Addis to his arrival. In this case, it's Beirut that gets the news.

Shafeek winces as I catch my breath.

'Shhh, Hammerhead!' he whispers.

'Sorry, Mister, I couldn't control myself . . . first time for months.'

Shafeek is just staring at me. I'm not sure where to put my watery eyes. He's already halfway up my bed. It would be so easy just to succumb. Is this how Dad conquered

Mum at the beginning? Through simple force of presence? And it *did* result in true love!

'Answer my question.'

'Erm . . . I think . . .'

When is the correct moment for histrionics, Beti? *Now?*

'What is happening here?' booms Madame.

Thank God for my wind. Shafeek jumps to his feet.

'Nothing, Mum . . . Meron is drinking Pepsi . . . I don't know why . . .'

Thanks, Shafeek.

'You gave it to her. Obvious! Listen, Shafeek . . . she's stretching tentacles towards the weak point of the family . . . *you*. She'll exploit you and bring all the family down. Like the last one. Shafeek, no more mistakes! Go to bed!' demands Madame, who still assumes her Arabic is unintelligible to me.

'Yes, Mum,' replies an eleven-year-old boy.

That is that. The Pepsi is out of my hand. He's gone. My chance to be impregnated by a rich Arab and tossed like a ragdoll from a Beirut balcony: all lost to a single belch. I should be grateful. But there was something raw gnawing away inside me, purposely pushing me towards blatant danger. Does that mean I *did* want sex with him? Or was that the shove of true love sending me hurtling towards childhood's end? I hope not to find out.

After the doorman's second visit to Madame's bedroom, I feel pensive with Abdul the next morning. We now share his Lebanese coffee regularly.

'Merhaba, Mister . . . how are you today?' I ask, as I do every day.

'Hello, Meron,' he sighs.

It's only 7am and we are already warm in Beirut.

'Too hot for you, Mister?'

'I'm fine . . . but I don't have anything else to say about the world.'

'Ah,' I reply. I'm not accustomed to this type of conversation. Habesha people always have something to say about the world.

'I've lived through civil war and so much bloodshed in Lebanon.' He pauses. 'I'm still living but life has dumped me somewhere else . . . I don't have anything I want to say today or any day. We've fought for so much, but now look at us. The country is independent at last, thanks to the Cedar Revolution, but honestly . . . we're a disgraceful collection of people. And Hariri is . . . *was* . . . the most corrupt of the lot.'

I nod my head. I'm really stuck for clever dialogue. Abdul stares at the floor and mumbles on.

'The modern world means nothing to me . . . nothing. The obsession with money and appearance . . . the old values have long gone. I can't even talk to my own family . . . it's all meaningless . . . I can relate to nothing. The world is a tragedy in progress.'

The foamy coffee has bubbled up three times. I pour it out. Maybe it's better to let old people bubble up and burble on too, as much as they like, without constraint. Something interesting should dribble out by the end.

'It's not that I'm giving up with life . . . it's just that I know I can't change anything in any way even though I see so much that's wrong around me. Whatever I do or say is pointless.'

'You helped me with the Panadol. *That* was good, Mister. And perhaps you could help me not make the same mistakes as Mulu. I think I'm drifting in that direction . . . and I can't stop myself . . .'

'At least, we have Allah with us . . . Allah knows best,' he continues, as if not hearing me.

He downs the coffee in one gulp and mutters to himself as he limps away. I'm still unsure if I want to be old or not. It is good to be wily and wise, but what if you know *too* much, like Abdul? To *know* you can't make any impact on the world sounds like a terrible curse.

'I know about it . . .' says Abdul suddenly back in front of me.

'Pardon, Mister?'

'Just because I'm old doesn't mean I don't *see* things. I see more than she thinks . . . *sharmuta* . . .'

'The previous maid or the other bad thing?' I ask urgently.

'What other bad thing?'

I have strayed into an alligator swamp. Abdul is a Muslim. I absolutely cannot say anything about the Sudanese doorman's visits, or people will die. Or at least one person will die . . . the big-mouthed maid. Think, Meron!

'Tell me, child. What *other* bad thing?' he presses.

'The . . . er . . . the . . . Hez-Jazeera.'

'What? It's Hezbollah . . . you really *are* a Hammerhead! Shafeek is right,' laughs Abdul, hobbling away.

'Mister?'

Abdul! What about Mulu? And me? *I need help.* My head is so muddled. I have to get out.

*

The disappearing bedlinen has become a weekly event. A strong breeze arrives promptly every Wednesday morning, hastening first the sheet and then my own descent to the ground floor, where my friend offers cake and comfort.

'Can you help me escape?' I ask Table Lady in reasonable Arabic.

'I feel very sorry for you. I really want to help you so much, but it could be difficult for me,' she explains, genuinely apologetic. We drink sweet tea at the table.

'Okay,' I say, flattened. She was my best hope.

'I have to live here. They are my neighbours. I mustn't upset them. I'm sorry, so, so sorry.'

'It's okay, I understand.'

'I really would like to help you because they're bad people . . . yes, you *should* escape, but . . . I'm really sorry.'

'Yes.'

'Why don't you come for lunch with me on Sunday? I don't have anyone to share it with. Can you come . . . please?'

I need help with a daring escape plan, not Sunday lunch.

'Madame won't let me come. I shouldn't be here right now.'

'You are so beautiful, things will be good eventually for you, but please don't do anything you might regret.'

'I'll try not to,' I lie. Of course I will. 'Just tell me one thing . . . when you go out through the side-door where the Sudanese doorman sits, what happens if he's not there to buzz you through?'

'At night, it's a different man . . . Egyptian, I think. A little unfriendly.'

'No, not at night. I mean, during the day when the Sudan man should be there but isn't, for whatever reason.'

'Ah! If he's gone to get lunch?'

'Yes, if he's gone to . . . get lunch . . .'

'In that case, the intercom goes through to the other entrance. You just have to shout "Open the door, please!" and the unfriendly Turk will let you through. But at night, it's a Syrian . . . extremely unfriendly, or extremely asleep. The black man is my favourite. I'm sorry!' she giggles.

'Interesting. Thank you.'

'But I don't need to speak to anyone . . . I have a key,' she says quietly.

'Pardon? A key? Can I borrow it?' I try, my heart beating a little faster.

'Not really . . . no. I need it. I'm so, so sorry.'

Me too, more sorry than she can imagine.

Madame almost jumps on me when I return to the apartment. I have been downstairs for half an hour.

'But she was praying, Madame!' I plead, this excuse long overdue for a replacement, but mindlessly neglected.

'Liar! You lie again and again! Until you came, we never had problem of sheets disappearing every week. Now, Wednesday, every Wednesday, gust of wind has programme to blow in from Mediterranean to remove one of my sheets . . . you think I believe this *forever*?'

'I suggest we change the linen hanging day to avoid the Wednesday morning winds, Madame.'

'No. We change position of washing lines and we punish servant when she lies.'

Medina is beginning to stir.

'I'd better go to Medina,' I say, seeking my usual means of legitimate escape.

'If you not hanging around downstairs with barren woman, you squeezing my granddaughter. I think that will stop as well. I not wanting her in contact with liar.'

'But I keep my mouth closed, Madame.'

'And I know you use air conditioning during day . . . electricity bill increase 4.6 per cent.'

'Maybe from Shafeek watching loud television all night.'

Up goes her left eyebrow. And in comes the palm of her right hand. *Slap!*

That was inevitable. It stings for a few seconds. I shrug at Madame, as if to say 'so what?' Madame is about to sling another hand at me when Nazia appears.

'If you're disturbed by him, you can sleep outside on the balcony,' she suggests.

Madame beams at the idea.

'Yes, good idea, Nazia. Now it so hot and all doors are open . . . we breathing your air, and how dare you forget *Mister* . . . he is *Mister* Shafeek!'

With nights on the balcony, things change for the worse. It may be less exposed to Shafeek's night-time soliciting, but out here the winds whistle around my ears, while sirens and car beeps sail up randomly from the streets below, keeping me from deep sleep. Napping outside like an Addis street kid, I'm grabbing at snippets of sleep that shave my dreams into slideshows.

I'm becoming dogged by drowsiness. There are long spells of daytime unaccounted for: I'm asleep but acting awake. For the perfunctory tasks this is easy, but when people speak to me, their words prod me like beeping alarm clocks. Every new request is a 5am wake-up jolt. Each one reminds me of the heat, the hunger, the hard labour, the lack of humanity and now the sleeplessness, all strapped to my wings like lead weights, firmly shoring me to this concrete column of incarceration.

God, what have I done to deserve this?

I lied. I lied to Madame about the sheets. I lie to her a lot. I lied before I came to Beirut, a lot. The age on my birth certificate is a lie. I would not be here without that lie. I'm a wicked barefaced liar. And *that's* why I'm here: punishment for all my lying. The Bible is not sympathetic towards lying. Proverbs 30:8 says: 'Remove far from me falsehood and lying.'

So I have been punished. Fine. Now let me go home and be a better person. Come on, God, intervene like you did before. A deserving sinner is reaching out to you. *Please*. A viable escape plan would be a really useful miracle.

When He Intervened

Auntie Kidist worked as a secretary for an international freight delivery company in Bole Road, near the airport. Desalegn had always been fiercely against it. He detested his wife enjoying her own income and the associated independence. He loathed the idea that she worked for another man, her boss. He reviled the fact that every minute she spent in the job was a minute not attending to his needs. To him, it was intrinsically evil.

Eighteen months after our trip to see Mama in Woliso, his thundering voice thumped its way into my head.

'It's almost midnight!' Desalegn started, as I put the phone to my ear. 'So she must be with another man. I'll *kill* her when I see her . . . without even listening to her lies. This is what happens when you let the wife take a job. She gets a new boss . . . the boss is a man, men *need* things. She forgets her boss is *here*, in the house! I need my dinner!'

'Wait . . .' I said, passing the neighbour's phone to Mum, just behind me. 'An animal needs feeding . . .'

'Hello? We don't know where Kidist is. Leave us alone.'

'You liar, you're cruel. How's my young son to sleep on an empty stomach?'

'Cook him some food.'

'Eh? I should kill you too. And I *will*, if you don't find her.'

He hung up.

'Poor kid . . . gets a beating every night, but tonight on an empty stomach. What kind of man will *he* be?' said Mum.

As we all lay in bed that night, unable to sleep, uncertain if Desalegn would storm into the house at any second, Kidist's disappearance was unmentioned. We hadn't seen her for three years and anyway, who would blame her for deserting that ogre? My mother still had a scar where once she had come between Desalegn's belt buckle and his son. This perhaps explained why Mum had just deposited a machete under her pillow.

Two days later, on my ninth birthday, there had been no word from Desalegn, and the machete lay undisturbed.

To celebrate my birthday, Mum bought five gorgeous oranges and nothing more. These were the dark days when she washed laundry by day and ran a very minor cotton-spinning industry by night. The workers were us, her three children, sat cross-legged beside Mum's feet on the floor of the poorly lit room, eagerly plucking at the freshly picked clumps of cotton to remove stones, insects and dirt. We used our fingers like combs to flatten and straighten the cotton bolls for Mum's spindle, where it was skilfully spun into a continuous yarn. Mum sold the yarn to keep us clothed and fed.

It was three years after my father had died. Mum *still* donned the attire of a heartbroken mourner and assumed the demeanour of a battle-weary soldier. The court had reached no decision on her disputed pension. Our home was completely unchanged. Nobody visited us for coffee. Even worse, we had no television. Mum devised her own entertainment. The five gorgeous oranges.

'Please, Mum, no!' I squealed as she tore off the peel and hurled it hard at my head. 'Ow!'

My brothers and I learnt to instinctively duck and shield our faces whenever the aroma of fresh orange smacked our young nostrils. How a lump of orange peel could hurt so much amazed me. But the secret lay in Mum's arm action: she whipped the peel at us the way stones would be flung at a marauding pack of stray dogs. We tried to take shelter under bedclothes, but she ripped them off the bed and bombarded us with hard peel, laughing manically as she did it. Orange peel was her fun time.

'Happy Birthday, Meron!' she shrieked as a clump hit me squarely on the forehead.

'No, Mum, no!'

'Orange peel never killed anyone,' she declared. But nobody had ever thrown orange peel like she had.

Yet oranges were better than sweetcorn, her other diversion. My mother always bought five cobs of sweetcorn, a habit rooted in the days of my father. But there were only four of us now. When we had finished chewing off the toasted kernels from our cobs, Mum announced the fifth cob would be eaten by whoever was strongest in a fighting contest. We threw ourselves into a wrestling ruckus on the hard floor while Mum rocked back and forth chortling so hard it distracted us from the strangle holds, karate kicks and arm twists. Nati or I always won; never Henok. He stayed close to Mum, occasionally daring to prod one of us in the back with his gnawed cob before scurrying to the safety of Mum's lap. It didn't occur to us that she might be insane: a very reasonable way to cope with a prolonged and painful mourning.

'Who wants another orange?' she asked as we tried to find the scattered bits of peel inside the beds. The lost lumps usually appeared as a maddening tickle in the middle of the night.

'Me! Me! Me!' we all chanted.

'Well, we'll fight for it,' she declared.

'No, Mum! Not the oranges as well!'

Why couldn't she tear the orange into equal segments for sharing? Oranges were surely designed for easy sharing. Nonetheless, we were throwing ourselves forward into battle, when a sudden clatter at the door startled us. Kidist crashed into the room. After a three-year desertion, she was amongst us. We looked at her, then at Mum, back at her, back at Mum. What were we to do now? Carry on fighting for an orange?

'What do you want?' mumbled Mum.

'Werknesh, my sister, big big sorry . . .' she began quietly, baubles of sweat clustered upon her forehead and threatening to trickle down her misshapen face.

'What are you doing?' asked my mother, perplexed.

'Help me, Werknesh! I think Desalegn's going to kill me!'

My mother shrugged indifferently, unaffected by the urgency in her sister's pitch.

'*Your* husband is *your* problem—' she started.

'I know but he's out of control!'

'Three years?' Mum said as though not hearing Kidist.

'Werknesh . . . I've really missed you.'

'Get out, Kidist.'

'He said he'd kill me—'

'Yes, we know. He called us two days ago and sounded upset about your absence . . . angry about your job as a secretary in Bole . . .'

'I know.'

'He thinks the job comes with . . . requirements. Does it?'

'Werknesh, I've got no qualifications, I'm not a trained secretary . . . of course there are requirements. But that's not the reason I was away for two days—'

'Just leave my house.'

'What?' gasped Kidist. It surprised me too. I thought Mum would be pleased to welcome her sister back. I would be, if I had a sister.

Kidist fell to the floor in front of my mother and kissed her feet frantically.

'Please, Werknesh! He stopped me from coming! All these years, I really wanted to see you and the children. Please, my sister . . . my sister . . . I love you!'

'Get up!' snapped my mother, yanking back her feet as quickly as possible. 'Stop it!'

Kidist had forgotten that her sister hated having her feet touched.

'Leave us alone, Kidist!' shouted Nati, asserting himself as the man of the house at the age of seven.

Kidist glanced round in the half-light.

'Who's that? Nati? Is that you? And Henok? Meron? Look at you all!'

Real tears splashed down Kidist's cheeks. She tried to hug all of us, but Nati pulled away fast. I had missed her. Kidist, Henok and I cried in a tight huddle, our grip passionate and firm.

Nati went outside. Mum sat with her head bowed, unable to look at us. Eventually, she raised her eyes from the ground.

'So . . . is he coming after you?' she mumbled.

'Yes and I'm really sorry to involve you . . . the last forty-eight hours have been horrific beyond your imagination. But I did realise how much you mean to me. Please believe me!' said Kidist, wiping her damp cheeks.

'I can't . . .' began Mum, shaking her head. 'You walked out on us, abandoned us. We've been through Hell since then . . . we're still fighting Kebebush for Lemma's pension . . . the final court decision is next week. That's three years of surviving on what I can scrape together from cotton spinning and laundry work. Look at us, Kidist . . . *look*!'

Kidist hardly dared. Only two things had changed in those three years: the height of us children and the weight of worry bloating the bags beneath my mother's eyes. Everything else was identical: black, shabby and broken. Kidist drew breath.

'Oh God! Werknesh, please forgive me. God forgive me. I did a terrible thing. I can *see* that! Oh dear Lord . . .'

Kidist was on her knees again, praying. Nati had left the door open, allowing a shaft of moonlight into the room. It fell precisely where my aunt knelt. With palms pressed together, she whispered a spontaneous prayer of forgiveness, the moonlight illuminating her with a soft silvery glow. For a few intense seconds, I was enraptured. Despite her age, Kidist had the appearance of a sweet young girl oblivious to all sin: almost cherubic. I wondered if it was a glimpse of God or, at the very least, something to do with His work. Even if it was only a trick of the light, I was still impressed. The light from the moon came from the reflected light of the sun, and the sun must have come from *somewhere*. I know mankind did not make the sun. This inexplicable beauty had to be the work of God. At last, He was in our house!

'Where's my wife?' came Desalegn's gruff voice from outside, piercing the silence with the brutality of a gunshot.

Kidist leapt into the air, petrified. I admit to also leaving the ground for a second. Kidist held a hand to her mouth to prevent involuntary screaming.

'Not here!' shouted Nati, still outside.

'Sharmuta!'

Mum crept over to the bed to pick up something. The machete! Gleaming in her firm hand, it had until this moment only been used for the slaying of animals, mainly sheep and goats. Now I understood the logic: Desalegn was an animal and I didn't doubt Mum's capacity to use it.

Seeing the machete, Kidist gripped her mouth even harder. Enhanced by the moonlight, I watched her eyes enlarging until they appeared to completely fill the top half of her head.

'Have you seen her?' Desalegn was asking Nati.

'Yeah.'

'When?'

'Three years ago . . . we all *hate* her. We hate you too.'

Desalegn grunted.

'You're a pig,' said Nati.

Smack! Smack!

Flesh-on-flesh sounds were audible: somebody slapping somebody else. But no shouting or crying. Instead, Nati was guffawing, an aggressive mocking sound, followed by the quick footsteps of Desalegn chasing Nati.

That seemed to do it. Desalegn disappeared back into the night. Kidist looked at my mother.

'My sister, sorry . . . I want us to be real sisters again.'

Nothing came back from my mother, sitting down again, resolutely staring at the floor. Wisely, Kidist stayed silent. We all did, waiting for Mum to speak. Something had to come out, one way or the other. A long minute passed. I tried to guess what Mum was thinking. Her face told me nothing. How do you hastily sew up a broken heart? Cotton yarn can't do it. Kidist wanted instant reconciliation. I didn't think my mother could manage it.

Instinctively, I put my hand over her mouth.

'Don't speak, Mum, it's too difficult for you,' I whispered, easing the machete out of her hand.

She kissed the palm of my hand and looked at the ceiling.

'Thank you, Lord, for delivering my sister safely back into our arms . . . we've missed her so much. This is a gift from the Lord Himself . . . I see that,' she said finally, standing, opening her arms, inviting Kidist into her embrace. Uncharacteristically, Mum sobbed vociferously and violently for a solid ten minutes. Kidist supported her, as my mother weakened at the knees, three years' worth of bottled-up emotion spewing out.

Eventually, out of boredom, Henok and I went outside to find Nati. In doing so, we missed Kidist's story: where *had* she been for two days? But that would come later.

Nati told us how he laughed right into Desalegn's face after being struck twice by the pig. To Nati, that was funny.

As birthdays go, it was a memorable one, but I don't remember who got the fifth orange. Ah! It must have been Nati. *That's* why he went outside: for the love of God's spectacular ball of juice.

A week after Kidist's angelic moment in the moonlight, the court finally recognised my mother's legal right to her late husband's pension. After three years, the judge lost patience with Tadelle's kebelle for misplacing the divorce certificate: he threatened to send in the police and arrest anyone they didn't like, which ruled out nobody. This put Tadelle in such jeopardy that he disappeared as successfully as the divorce certificate. The 'lost' divorce certificate was located behind a filing cabinet within a swift thirty minutes and Tadelle was later fired for absenteeism.

Kebebush's fraudulent claim was demolished, despite a last-ditch attempt to sway the court by presenting her dubious son, in person. With an inability to look anyone straight in the eye and the sullenness of a lame bull, he held not a single Lemma quality and was duly herded out of the courtroom. Bizarrely, some months later, a teenage *daughter*, the physical double of Henok, emerged from the

Kebebush camp. Ethiopia's rural backwaters were characterised by their shambling education system and Kebebush was a product of this: we shall always be thankful for such a system.

So God intervenes. That is obviously what He does. I am quite certain He will offer me an escape plan. It's definitely coming. *It is.*

One Chicken Short (388 days left)

Nuria, Hassan, Mustafa and Medina moved out of the apartment a week ago. I will miss the children and Hassan. The lumps of chocolate, the morning greetings and the fixed smiles on *both* sides of his head: Hassan's absence leaves tiny but sweet gaps in my day. Lucky man, he escaped. Can't I just disappear too?

Madame returns home after having expensive cosmetic surgery on her face. In tackling the forces of nature, she is trying to control every aspect of her life, but this particular tactic happily restricts her movements for a few days. While she recuperates, I am temporarily entrusted with the family cooking. Madame's Arabic cookery book is where I begin: she sends out orders from her bed – 'Page fifty-four, Me-ron!' – but I can't read Arabic. Even the pictures are difficult to understand. Maybe I don't want to understand them. Maybe if I am incompetent, Madame will send me home early and escape will be simply achieved.

Today, something about rice, but page fifty-four to my eyes is potato. When she expects fish, I deliver chicken. Cooked vegetables prompt salad. Requests for dinner plates yield soup bowls. Portions specified as 'large' come 'petite'. Delicately flavoured is overspiced. Daily variety turns weekly. The pleasure of the palate becomes painful.

'This is ridiculous . . . you deciding what we eat!' Madame declares disbelievingly after a fortnight of my nonsense.

'The Arabic recipes are so difficult to understand, Madame . . . I'm doing what I can.'

'I give you one last chance. My best friends coming for dinner tomorrow to celebrate my new face. You cook chicken breasts, I know you can . . . one per guest. Only enough for one breast each person so not mess it up, Meron.'

'Yes, Madame.'

Abdul and Nazia are away, Shafeek very much present. Chicken breasts are in the oven, Madame and I are fussing over other dishes. She should be in bed relaxing her face, before the strains of false delight tug on her newly sutured tucks. Instead, she's been at my side all day, scooping fingers thick with yoghurt, snacking on random salads, pinching and patting her paunch every hour with the words 'You're next'.

'I getting changed, Meron. Get chicken breasts out to cool in five minutes. We serving dinner in one hour. Lay table and do usual artistic thing with napkins. Eat *anything* and I murder you.'

'Yes, Madame.'

At last, she's gone. A dollop of hummus whets my appetite. Nobody will miss that.

I ease the chicken breasts out of the oven: they ignite my senses. I remember crafty Tadelle's face that day he thought a chicken was juddering away under Henok's metal bowl. Fervent and predatory, like me, now . . . my right hand is stretching towards a golden fizzling fist of breast. I have no control!

Madame's shadow is at the doorway and I pull back my hand.

'Meron, do table . . . chicken has to cool.'

She's right. How would I eat a breast straight from the oven? In ten minutes, one of the breasts will be mine, and I already know which one. It's slightly deformed and should be removed before the anomaly upsets the guests.

I sprint into the dining room, fiddle with napkins, lay mats, count out cutlery and puff on dusty glasses. I think only of a cooling cooked bird. Back into the kitchen . . .

Shafeek is here with the same idea: I can see him thinking about it, his hand ready to snatch.

'Mister!' I exclaim.

Shafeek stares at me indignantly.

'There's only one . . . only one chicken per person,' I declare.

'You don't tell *me* what to do,' he snaps.

But Shafeek is not about to jeopardise Madame's cooking. He slouches out of the kitchen.

Before I realise what's happening, I am eating the breast! White succulence is dervishing between tongue and teeth, saliva blending with oozing fleshy juice, mouth gobbling and gulping, all within a handful of heavenly seconds. She can catch me in the act, but it's too late. We are officially one breast down.

I sling the bone underneath the oven. I might come back for that later.

Madame returns to the kitchen, glowing with the occasion: her new face emitting rare warmth and humanity. This is her night to be youthful again. The surgeon did a good job, pulling taut the lines of dread. I toy with the idea that each wrinkle represented a moment of meanness in her life, but there were not enough lines to validate that theory. Now, she has an open, pure face. Her eyes have a generous sparkle. Her cheeks shine. It is difficult to imagine an atom of nastiness sticking to her. I hope the surgeon's cut went soul-deep.

'When we eat, you sit in the kitchen, keep quiet and eat your rice. Come when I shout,' she instructs, helping me to carry the dishes.

Half an hour later, guests are seated, dinner is served. The chicken breasts are dished out by Madame. I'm called to the table.

'One chicken missing. Where is it, Meron?' Madame enquires, in front of seven Lebanese diners, their faces fixed expectantly on me as though I am the evening performance.

'I ate it, Madame.'

Slight gasps are audible. Madame is smiling falsely. Her stretched face is no longer designed for this. Her grin suggests the blind fear of a woman facing down a charging elephant. The surgery is straining at the seams, threatening to unravel. This is a nightmare for Madame.

'What I say? Eat chicken or cook chicken?' she tries, in a sarcastic tone, which sparks off giggles amongst the women.

I stay silent.

'Meron, you forget . . . you have to eat *rice* because you fat, *not* chicken,' she continues, still playing to the audience. Again, there is muted laughter, but definitely muted. She's fatter than me now.

I remain silent. I have already told her the truth. There's nothing more to say.

'So, Meron, where *is* other chicken? Shafeek waiting for his chicken,' Madame says forcefully, now irritated. She thinks I have stored it away for later consumption.

'It's in my stomach.'

'No, not true . . . you not do that to us! This servant is mad!'

I shrug my shoulders. What can I do? The chicken is gone.

'I've still got the bone . . . if he wants . . .' I mumble.

'Meron, if you not give me chicken right now—'

'What, Madame? You'll kill me, like the previous maid?'

This interjection creates a room-full of astonishment. What have I said? This isn't God intervening: it's *me* intervening with all the madness I can gather.

'Meron, you make horrible mistake. Mulu died from cleaning accident . . . slipping from the balcony, trying to clean windows . . . this type of accident. Very sad for everyone, especially me.'

Madame looks set to sob, while the others nod solemnly to confirm what she said.

Shafeek leaps up and flies into the kitchen, his stony

courtroom face serious enough for the grimmest of murder cases. For ten minutes, he silently and rigorously ransacks every drawer, cupboard, container, box and sack populating my work area. He finds no chicken, not even the bone. Surely there is insufficient evidence to sentence me, except that I admitted it.

'Actually, I *will* kill you,' declares Shafeek in front of the others. They murmur in his support.

Dinner is resumed, the atmosphere a little hushed now. I return to my stool and eat rice. So, what happens now?

After only two hours, the guests leave in a subdued mood. I stand awaiting cleaning instructions in the kitchen. Shafeek comes at me like a tiger. He grabs my neck and tosses me to the ground. I think he might ravage me.

'Meron, what do you want?' he shouts down at me.

'I'm a person . . . I want to eat *normal* food,' I sob into the plastic floor. 'All I've had today is rice.'

'What? Not again!'

He marches into Madame's room. I can hear him: 'Why aren't you feeding her? Of course she steals food if you're going to starve her . . . and today it was *my* chicken. Are you mad?'

'Allah! She is servant! Nothing more!'

'Mum, you have to give her proper food!'

'After today? She ruin my party. She talk about dead maid. She steal your chicken. I give her punishment, not food.'

'Everyone has to eat! If servants don't eat, they get sick, you lose money . . . be sensible!'

They shout for a good five minutes, a really *good* five

minutes. Shafeek is doing this for me! I am revived, but I fear Madame may do something violent in the night. A humiliated Madame can't be trusted during sleeping hours.

'Me-ron, boil up the water!' she demands from her bedroom as Shafeek stomps down the hall.

I am reluctant to boil up the water. Some maids are painfully scalded, permanently scarred: it's a known punishment. Beti mentioned it on that very first day: 'Never go near boiling water after a row with your Madame.'

'Meron, water!'

I run to her.

'Madame . . . can I prepare you a snack, or a drink . . . or maybe you would like me to clean the bathroom again.'

Anything but boiling water.

'Boil the water, Meron!' she screams at me from her bed, her pretty pink tongue appearing to stab quickly at the air, new wrinkles instantly blossoming around her eyes. The way she looks now, the cosmetic surgery fees were utterly wasted.

'But, Madame—'

'No *but* . . . just do what I tell you. You have to learn . . . you are *servant*!'

I stumble back to the kitchen to boil up some water, as instructed. Maybe I should lock myself outside on the balcony? Maybe. But the kitchen floor is suddenly beneath me again, for the second time in ten minutes. I am crouching with my head tucked into my abdomen, nose pressed up against my kneecaps, arms wrapped around my head as if under attack from Mum's orange peel.

'Me-ron! What you doing?' shouts Madame down the hall.

She's coming! I wrap myself tighter into an unassailable human ball.

'Mum!'

Shafeek is speaking to Madame outside the kitchen door.

'Take these, Mum, and relax for the night . . . please . . .'

'Yes, okay, habibi . . . you're right, I need sleep.'

Shafeek's sweet sleeping tablets!

Half an hour later, I'm still here, on the kitchen floor, keeping my head down. Madame's snoring is perfectly audible. I avoided the fury, thanks to Shafeek.

'Meron, come here . . . check the water for me!' Shafeek shouts from the bathroom. He's filling the bath tub, unable to determine whether the temperature of the water is correct. Not the remit of an international lawyer. After his support tonight, I am happy to indulge his ego.

I reach the door of the bathroom. He's standing naked before me, arms folded. His face has an arrogant intensity, hardened by a sly smile saying 'Behold me in all my glory'. I stare at his penis, throbbing ominously towards the stars. Perhaps he wants to take me there. My eyes smart and fill with water. Madame's deep snoring provides background noise. Shafeek has me completely to himself.

'Meron, come here, check the water,' he repeats, the water only a short stretch from where he's standing. 'You stole my chicken, so you can do me this favour, in return.'

I edge forward slowly, unsure if the water really wants checking or not. Perhaps it does? I really hope it does. I remember Kidist and Mum, reunited. God intervened! He intervenes at moments like this. That's what He does, unless there's some sort of oblique reasoning that nobody will see in their lifetime, which is the type of intervention I hate.

'Can't *you* check the water, Mister? My back strain has suddenly returned,' I try, flinching unconvincingly.

'Come here and check the water. You can at least do *that* for me,' he says slowly and clearly.

He's right. The back strain does not warrant a second of delay. In fact, there is no back strain. My body is moving closer without any conscious effort, as if reaching for the golden fizzling chicken breast, as if running instinctively towards my father's open arms. My protective hug awaits me. I am within an arm's length of him. The whiff of his feet hits my nostrils. He points at the water. Is it cold or hot? I'll need to bend over the bath tub with my backside high in the air. The water needs checking. I would do *anything* for my father. My Baba.

But I pause. This is not right. Focus, Meron!

Shafeek is not my father: I am not touching that water. Where's God? Where's the intervention? *It's not coming.*

'I've got an idea for your feet!' I shout into his rough stubble.

'Eh? What?'

'Your feet . . . they smell bad.'

'What did you say?' he stutters, unable to believe it, eyes bulging, arms dropping to his sides.

'Everyone can smell them, all the time. You have a problem, Mister, a really *bad* problem, like my brother . . . but I can help you with this.'

Shafeek attempts to focus on me. He's been thrown off-course by a verbal bullet. His thoughts recover and collect themselves up fast: the agile mind of a lawyer, reckoning, reasoning, rationalising, racing through the options to present an eloquent intellectual solution.

He wallops me hard in the face with his fist. It sends me flying to the floor.

I let out a wail that a woman would only reveal in childbirth, or a child's death. Tears spring from my eyes immediately.

'Do you know who you're speaking to? I could do *any-thing* to you . . . kill you, rape you . . . torture you. How dare you talk about my feet!' he blabbers, nursing his hitting hand.

I sob and scream. Like a newborn foal, I try to get to my feet. Shafeek pushes me back down with a sharp thrust and kicks me hard in the stomach. Ooof! I'm pawing at the floor pathetically below him.

I cry at the top of my voice from the bathroom floor. Come on! Somebody must hear me. Even a shambling, shuffling Abdul would be a welcome sight. Alas, nobody's here except Madame, who's comatose on sleeping tablets. I'm wasting my efforts.

Shafeek just stares at me. As the seconds pass and I continue to howl, his penis withers. It points at his rank feet, accusingly.

'What's the idea?' he says finally.

'Scrub lemon juice onto your feet every day . . . it works for my brother,' I snuffle.

'Get out.'

I grip the side of the bath to clamber to my feet and dip my hand into the water dutifully.

'The water's cold, Mister.'

Locking myself outside on the balcony and crying myself hoarse, it's a long night ahead but sleep and sunlight eventually come, if only in quick succession.

The following day, I bear a black eye. Shafeek avoids eye contact with me. Nobody mentions it.

It's a normal day, until evening when Shafeek comes home late and stands near my mattress.

'Meron,' he whispers, as my stomach suddenly tightens with tension.

'Yes, Mister?'

'*Next* time . . .' and he wanders away, a little unsteadily, to vomit in the bathroom.

Two days later, Nazia and Madame are loafing on the sofa, about to eat. Shafeek wanders in barefooted, his feet aromatically silent from where I'm perched on the plastic stool. The others notice something amiss, but are not sure what. Madame's nose is raised in the air, readied for any suggestion of the usual pungency. None is forthcoming.

'We need to buy more lemons,' pronounces Shafeek. 'They're good for the health.'

Yes, mine.

Kidist's Bid – Part One

Mum related the story to me when I was fourteen: the story of Kidist's disappearance before the reunion with my mother on that life-changing night of oranges and moonlight. Now in Beirut, three years later, I take comfort from the story: the idea that escape can suddenly present itself, with only the nerve of an opportunist needed to make it happen. Kidist needed escape from Desalegn: I need it now from Shafeek. While I await God's helping hand, I will take any inspiration you can offer me, Auntie.

Kidist and her colleague, Adi, usually finished work at eleven o'clock (5pm) and caught the free bus service for company workers, heading up Bole Road. On this occasion, they worked four hours' overtime and missed the bus. Unperturbed, Adi and Kidist started walking along Bole Road, hoping to catch a public minibus. They were all full. Instead of squandering money on a private taxi, the women drank tea together until the rush-hour eased. It was close to 10pm when they sauntered past the conspicuous London Café, with its protruding fuselage of a real airliner. Adi was chatting interminably about her 'great' brother studying at Addis Ababa University. Kidist had known Adi for two years and never connected with her: Kidist loved the titillation of gossip, not the open competition of boasting. She had little to boast about and had run out of gossip half an hour earlier. All office scandal had been dissected beyond the point of fun.

In her late twenties, Adi was ten years younger than Kidist and, with a slender waif-like body, her waist had the circumference of her neck. Adi must have weighed the same as one of Kidist's legs, without the shoe.

A smart black car stopped abruptly beside them, possibly a Mercedes Benz, but probably not. Kidist was unable to identify car makes.

'Hey, ladies, need a lift?' enquired a beaming gentleman in his mid-thirties, leaning from the driver's window. His eyebrows were untamed bushes, forming a hanging garden of hair above his eyes. Every wrinkle, twinkle and hairy strand suggested a kindness that Kidist craved in a decent Habesha man. Look at this guy with his open face and untended features: he put other people before his own preening. He was evidently successful but selfless. How had she got it so wrong with Desalegn?

This happened frequently in Addis. Complete strangers offering lifts to other strangers. Kidist and Adi exchanged shrugs. Why not? Neither would usually have accepted a lift from a stranger, but what could possibly go wrong? The car was respectable and expensive enough: the driver obviously had money and seemed unlikely to commit violent robbery or something similarly malicious.

'There are no more buses . . . which way are you going, ladies?' he said with a smile.

His clothes suggested office worker, maybe bank or insurance. This fellow with his affable unfussy countenance was difficult to fault.

Kidist thought of Desalegn, increasingly fraught as the minutes of her lateness ticked by. He could eat out for once, let him be fractious, let him stew in his own juices. Or maybe she would never see him again. Temptation was tripping over itself as Kidist's imagination quickened into a gallop.

'Near Mexico Square,' said Kidist, at last.

'Perhaps not . . .' began Adi, suddenly coy.

'You and me together . . . we're fine,' replied Kidist, now very keen to converse with the kind gentleman.

He skipped out and opened the back door for them, like a professional chauffeur. This pleased Kidist. With her figure, she didn't expect too much attention, but Adi was younger and more attractive: in the back seat, both could relax without the risk of wandering hands. It was like travelling in a VIP taxi, but free!

'Mmm, okay,' said Adi, slipping into the back with Kidist.

A wire mesh separated front seats from back. Perhaps formerly an upmarket taxi of some description for diplomats or presidents, mused Kidist: one of those black limousines blazing along Bole Road to and from the African Union, but only after other road-users had been swept aside like street rubbish. It added to her sense of ease in this pleasant stranger's car.

'Work at the airport, ladies?'

'No, nearby, but we missed the service bus. So thank you very much for this . . . our families are probably worried because it's getting late now,' said Kidist, happy to mention the 'families'. She didn't want the chauffeur, however benign, forming a misunderstanding of the current situation. Presumably, if he wanted a business girl, he would cruise Chichinya Street. Quite obviously, Kidist and Adi were *not* business girls, in their work blouses, knee-length skirts and flat black shoes. Kidist relaxed a little more.

'Ah! You have families. Wonderful!' he said. 'I love kids. I have five children, oldest seventeen and youngest four. Of course, we have our problems sometimes, but the house is always lively, two girls, four boys. How many do you have?'

'I've got two, one of each, and Adi has just one boy so far,' said Kidist.

'Did you say you have five children . . . two girls and four boys?' asked Adi, checking the figures. She was studying accountancy in evening classes.

'Yes, we lost one.'

'Ah! Sorry. Really sorry,' they both replied in tones of sincerity.

'Thanks. She died of a complication.'

'A complication? How terrible,' said Kidist as compassionately as possible.

'So, you must find it hard to balance work and home lives with your jobs?' he said.

'Yes, really difficult sometimes,' replied Kidist, warming to him by the second.

'How do you find time for all the cleaning and washing and cooking?'

'You just have to get on with it, as fast as possible . . . with time and practice you get better and better at it.'

'I really admire you . . . all housewives should be celebrated, given medals of honour.'

Kidist liked that. This gentleman was commending her efforts in the home. No *man* had ever done that before. In Addis, it was amazing to hear such words.

'Thank you so much!'

'Perhaps you even enjoy it?' he continued.

'Not really, but we do it for our families.'

'Of course, of course . . . wonderful.'

The pleasure of speaking to a charming wealthy gentleman forced Kidist to look hard at her own beast of a husband. He could never replicate this man's genuineness. There had to be a way to divorce the undivorceable, decided Kidist: a legitimate escape from the captor masquerading as husband. It was time she probed a little into this fellow's married life. What if there are cracks? Her heart beat a little faster.

'Does your wife work?' asked Kidist.

'Not really,' he replied abruptly.

'Oh . . . but I am sure she's a really happy wife with a husband as appreciative as you,' said Kidist, sensing a way into this potential new partner.

'No, she isn't.'

'Oh! Sorry to hear that . . . you deserve better . . . me too. I'm Kidist, by the way . . . er, what's your name? Can we meet up again?' she gabbled excitedly, the idea of escape now embedded within every living cell liberally coating every heavy bone.

'Pardon?'

My Escape (365 days left)

'Pardon?'

'Could I go back to Addis early, Madame?' I ask again. 'I've finished exactly one year of the contract.'

To me, this would seem like an opportune moment to accept our differences and go our separate ways. Or at the very least, allow me to slip back to Addis intact with at least *something* in my pocket. Madame could find a new maid: one who's less interested in eating food, retaining her virginity and generally surviving beyond the age of eighteen.

'No.'

Madame is reading financial reports on her bed.

'Why not, Madame?' I persist.

'Go away. Go find new dust. White socks day today.'

'I will. But I'm owed a year's salary now, today. Could I have that? Please . . . Madame?'

'Don't worry, I keep it safe . . . I am director of bank, remember?'

'Sorry, Madame, but I want it now. It's *my* money. Give me my money, please.'

'Different ways to say "go away" in Arabic, some with words and some you not imagine with your small brain. Ask me one more time and we see about *them*,' she replies.

Today, I expect to see money falling into my hands. At $100 per month for one year, I'm due $1,200. Even with that paltry amount for fifteen months' hard labour, I will go home in blissful disgrace.

'Make sure you collect your money each year,' I remember Beti saying on the flight out, 'or they might decide it's easier to send you over the balcony than pay a couple of thousand bucks.' But my Madame is not paying me. I have to speak to Beti about this.

'Beti . . . it's me, Meron! How are you?' I say later.

'Hey, sister! I'm wonderful! How you doing? Eating enough now?'

'Not really, but surviving day to day. I don't like the people here, Beti, they turn crazy over nothing.'

'They paying your wages, sister . . . we all got our problems. Or has the master *done* something?'

'Yes . . . no . . . but it was very close. I need to get out before it happens . . .'

A moment of silence.

'I don't know, sister. You survived a year . . . escaping could be more dangerous than staying. Girls caught escaping got *big* problems. Why not do one more year and collect the money? Can't you do that, sugar?'

'No, Beti, I *can't* do that. He's closing in, and besides, I can't spend another year missing my family, another year starving and miserable, another year of beatings. I'm going home! But how, Beti, *how*?'

More silence.

'I recommend you jump from the ledge.'

'Eh?'

'They catch you, they gonna push you anyways.'

'Beti, *please* . . . I need passport and money, right?'

'Not essential. You a pretty girl. With sex, you could get money on the street, easy . . . Arab guys fall for us real fast. And you need a fake passport . . . but I don't want this getting back to *me* . . .'

'Sex? Like a business girl? How much do I have to do?'

'Depend on how good you are.'

'I'm a virgin.'

'Ha, ha, ha! If you're *really* a virgin, you can forget about it! You need experience. You can't just go out into the streets and make money like that.'

'Oh.'

'You *really* a virgin?'

'Yes.'

'Er, okay, so . . . what about the guy in your apartment . . . probably *very* interested if he knows you're a virgin. You get him, maybe he'll help you escape . . . understand?'

'Eh? Shafeek?'

'If he's the master, yeah . . . get real close to him, might open doors. But careful, sister, these Arab guys don't like condoms. Pregnancy is also gonna give you problems.'

'I'd prefer to sidestep that scenario . . . he's the one I'm escaping from. If I steal money and passport from my Madame, I just need to get outside and run, don't I?'

'Where you running, sister? Think your ass can run home from here?'

'To the Ethiopian Consulate. It's just round the corner. I see the flag every day. They'll help me.'

'You can try that, or try the ledge . . .'

'Come on, Beti, it's our Consulate . . . Habesha helps Habesha, right?'

'Good luck with that thing you got.'

'What thing?'

'The sweet innocence thing.'

Madame doesn't watch her back when opening and closing the bedroom 'safe' where cash is deposited. I have spied her through the crack in the door a hundred times. It is not a safe with a combination: more of a locked cupboard. Madame keeps the key on the same bunch as her door key and car keys. The bunch lives inside her handbag. When she's not at home, the keys aren't either. I have no escape plan. I'll at least try for the money and passport: with these in my hands, I'll bide my time until an opportune moment arrives. Like Kidist, the idea of escape is now embedded in every living cell dotted about my scrawny frame and probably in the dead ones too.

These are my thoughts as I wipe away the daily grime in Madame's shower unit. It's 2pm, two days since speaking to Beti. My head is dizzy from lack of nourishment. Earlier, I foraged through the kitchen garbage and found a half-rotten apple. Yes, Abush, free food! Addis street kids are better fed than me: Abush said the stomach adapts to eating trash and, anyway, all the germs are in Germany. Not funny any more. Half-rotten means half-edible, but half-brain-dead is what I am. My spinning mind turns to hairpins.

I have seen hairpins successfully used in movies. I have a hairpin in my hand, extracted from my hidden bushel of hair. I am at once in Madame's bedroom. Unable to restrain myself, the hairpin is being twiddled around inside the lock of the money cupboard to see what happens. Within a few seconds, it clicks. The little wooden door floats open. I gasp at it. So simple! I laugh quietly.

Inside are piles of cash and documents. Ha! Got you! Neat wads of American dollars and Lebanese pounds rest within Madame's secret bank. And passports! But only Lebanese. My passport isn't here.

I carefully remove only the money I am owed, leaving behind handsome sums that could function well outside, my moral compass holding true. I will buy a new passport: why not from the Ethiopian Consulate? Isn't that their job, to replace lost passports for Ethiopian nationals? Why do I need to prostitute myself in the streets for a pompous little book of blank pages?

One thing I've *never* seen in movies is the re-locking of doors with the same hairpin. Madame's cupboard door obstinately hangs open, the hairpin now good only for pinning back my hair. I have the money but the threadbare plan is already blown apart. If only I had gum, or glue, or anything sticky to hold the door closed, to buy me time. There isn't very much of that. It's 2.35pm. Madame will be home in twenty-five minutes.

I rapidly sew two pairs of baggy knickers together, inserting the stolen cash between them, completely invisible to the most observant of Mesdames. I wear the knickers, now worth a fraction over $1,200. At last, the shapeless garments of oppression have some use and value. Hard-earned cash presses into the crack of my backside. This is probably symbolic in some way but I don't have the time to deliberate why.

Madame returns from work promptly. I have failed to stick the cupboard door back into its closed position.

'Hello, Madame! I took my first year's salary from your bedroom cupboard, thank you very much,' I sing out the moment her eyes meet mine.

I have never seen this in movies either: immediately confessing the crime to the authorities. Without proteinous food or mental stimulation, my mind has decomposed into the pure green mulch that Tadelle used to munch all day.

Madame pauses as she focuses on me. Her brain reorients itself to deal with the maid claiming some outrageous theft. She giggles, thinking it a tremendous joke. Incidentally, it's nice to see her genuinely happy for a few seconds, with a rare face of jollity.

'Meron . . . I swear, you crazy! Very funny. You make me laugh. Yoghurt for you tonight.'

For the love of God, yoghurt! I *love* yoghurt. If a Habesha maid taking cash from the bedroom of a senior Lebanese bank director with a mere hairpin can be interpreted as funny enough for yoghurt, then let her laugh. Except that it's not a joke and she doesn't know it.

'Doorman coming in five minutes. Go to balcony when he calls up.'

Still tittering, she doesn't wait for my answer, but gently pushes the front door closed. The catch of the lock doesn't clunk shut with the usual solid click. The front door is not closed. I don't think she has done that on purpose. Madame is usually so careful with locks, doors and so on. But she's having a bad day, without even realising it.

Madame hurries into her bedroom, door keys still in her hand. Surely now she will see the cupboard door unlocked. Nerves gather themselves up in my abdomen. I could just run out of here but Sudan is downstairs. I hold myself in check for the abrupt buzz of the intercom. I hear the spurts of perfume spray. Why waste it on Sudan?

The buzz comes. Madame has changed into a lacy nightie. Sudan is on his way. I have money in my knickers, an open front door and the Ethiopian Consulate only a block away. Look, Kidist! An opportune moment for escape has arrived! My pulse races. I have to make a decision. Come on, Meron! *Escape!*

Nothing. I'm frozen to the spot. Confidence eludes me. Meron Lemma is going nowhere.

'Me-ron! He coming. Go on balcony!' shouts Madame at me. 'Still daydreaming about your break-in? Ha! Ha! Ha! You really are . . .'

Madame has wandered back into her bedroom. She screams. At last, she's noticed the hairpin's masterstroke. *Now!*

'*Me-ron!*'

My hand is already on the front door handle. And I'm out! I glance at the lift indicator. The red light says it's coming up, now on floor six. That's good enough.

I fly down the stairs, jumping alternate steps for greater speed. I hear Madame's flusters above me, but she's going nowhere in that nightie. Lebanon is Muslim. No one runs around like that!

Down and down I leap. Finally, I arrive at Sudan's vacated exit. I stab the buzzer by the door with my index finger, preparing my Arabic for a quick 'Open the door!' but all I hear is a furious Arabic voice coming back at me, and not really good Arabic: it's the Turk. Madame has alerted him from upstairs. What now? I'm finished. I *am* completely stupid. Nuria was right.

After a few moments, just standing, awaiting my inevitable crucifixion, Table Lady appears at the door. She has a key. The door is open!

'Meron! What are you doing?' she muffles through her niqab, slightly alarmed.

'Escaping! Sorry!'

I slip round her. I hear a few spluttered utterances from her, but they have a positive ring. She has no intention of stopping me.

Within a second, I'm outside. Outside! Cars, people, shops, freedom! I have arrived in Beirut!

My vision is immediately filled with the pale grey of concrete, smearing itself over every building: roads and people seem to be wedged in between the vast skyward slabs. But at least these lucky souls are free!

Behind me I hear the door crashing open. Sudan is right behind me. I start sprinting along the street. I'll outrun a Sudanese doorman. All he does is read the newspaper all day. I'm Ethiopian. We outrun everyone. Except I'm almost immediately breathless and Sudan is yelling at my back.

'Stop her! Stop her! Thief!'

What do you mean, *thief*? What's all *that* about? What does Sudan know? He's charging after me as though this is personal. I've never hurt him. Sudan and Ethiopia are not at war! Not yet anyway.

The plastic sandals feel like huge sofa cushions attached to my feet. People are staring at me. If I don't speed up, someone will grab me.

Focus! I think of our great Olympians. Derartu, Tirunesh, Haile, Kenenisa, Abebe Bikila, Miruts Yifter: come on, Habesha heroes, *shift her*!

Sudan can't get me. I'm round the corner and into a busier street now, but ther are too many pedestrians to run smoothly. I drop into the gutter. It's going well. But where am I going?

I look upwards for the Ethiopian flag. Nothing. I have no idea where to run. The view from the apartment made it seem easy. It was a simple hundred metre jog 'home'. But down at ground level, I'm blind. Help me, God! Intervene!

'Excuse me . . .' I start to say to a swarthy man in sunglasses.

A car screeches behind me, then toots again and again.

'Stop her!' screams Madame from the car window.

I don't even look round, just sprint again, Madame's Porsche almost at my side, traffic cop ahead in a dark blue uniform. His swift eyes catch me.

'Stop her . . . she's a thief!' shouts Madame. I try to dodge round the thick-set cop, but his hands are as fast as his eyes. The cop holds my wrists until Madame pulls up beside us.

'I want to go to my Consulate!' I scream.

'I want to take you there!' Madame snaps back at me, wrapped up in a patterned shawl to cover herself. 'Get in!'

I am bundled in. The police guy wanders away, smiling at Madame's flirty wave. Inside the car, she says nothing to me.

We're outside the elusive Consulate within seconds. From the outside, it looks like a pleasant residential block, apart from a plastic strip across the front saying 'Consulate General of the Federal Democratic Republic of Ethiopia'. Beneath this are our flag's three colours: the horizontal green, yellow and red bands. It's a welcome sight.

'Get out!'

Holding my hair, she hauls me inside the building and up a single flight of steps. Stuck to a reddish-brown door I see a poster of our Prime Minister, Meles Zenawi, smiling benignly. Again, this encourages me. Friendly Ethiopia, my country, is behind this door.

The reception is a small room with chairs that seat two Habesha girls and a single Lebanese soldier. He seems surprised to see us: maybe we need an appointment. Impulsive escape wasn't on my mind this morning, sorry. The two Habesha girls prefer not to look at us.

Another Habesha girl pops out from one of the offices leading off the reception.

'Yes?'

'I want her out of Lebanon!' demands Madame.

'Yeah, me too . . . I want to go!' I add with equal force.

'Sit down, please,' says the Habesha girl, leading us into a cramped office. She speaks good Arabic, but her young face is twisted up like the warped rails they used to bring back from the Dire Dawa stretch. The heat did that. Maybe she blames the heat as well.

'She's stealing my money!' declares Madame.

'They treat me like dirt!' I retort.

'She's so lazy, insolent—'

'They don't feed me enough!'

'Today, I offered her yoghurt and she stole from me! Please lose her!'

'Her son wants to get me . . . like he did with the last one . . . I'm very frightened . . .'

'Enough!' shouts the girl. 'We're closed.'

'You close at five . . . now three-fifteen,' says Madame.

'No problem for me. I'll sleep *here* in my Consulate,' I try.

The Habesha girl is quick with the contempt, sighing like someone who's found a dead rat in her wat, the customer service very much in the Addis style. I feel at home. A tart aroma hangs in the cluttered room. It's late lunchtime injera. I glance around in case there's a handy plateful nearby. I am home!

'You're not sleeping here. This is a Consulate not a hotel. Where's your passport?'

'I have that,' says Madame. 'Well hidden.'

'Okay, are you sure she's Ethiopian, not Sri Lankan or Bangladeshi or . . .?' asks the Habesha girl ridiculously.

'I am *sure*. Listen, this girl . . . I don't know what she's doing here. I feel like she only came into my house to cause problems. Her housework is bad, she lies so much, steals, talks back at me . . . they're not usually like this!'

'Please,' says the Habesha girl, 'what do you think *we* can do?'

'You've got the contract . . . send her back!'

'With what? The Consulate doesn't have money for *that*. You'll have to pay her air fare.'

'What? I already lost money taking her into my house. She stole my money today!'

'Did you?' asks the Habesha girl.

'Yes, but they've treated me very badly . . . bad food, too much work, no day off, beat me if I make a mistake, no outside contact—'

'Wallahi, she lying!'

The Habesha girl's face twists a little more as she looks me up and down.

'Yes, I can see you're not a good worker. That doesn't actually surprise me.'

'Eh? I can't believe what I'm hearing. We're the *same* nationality. You're paid to *help* people like me, not to agree with the Lebanese,' I say, finally switching to Amharic.

'When you come here, you have to be a donkey,' she replies back in stubborn Arabic. 'Ethiopian girls can't clean well . . . we all know that. The day you leave Ethiopia, you have to do exactly what they want. If they want a donkey, be a donkey, if they want a horse, be a horse, cow, be a cow . . . doing whatever they tell you.'

'But I'm a person, not a farmyard animal!'

'No! The moment you leave Ethiopia, forget about being a person.'

Madame nods in agreement.

I launch into a stream of Arabic curses. I don't know what they mean but the way I spit them out creates a sudden hush in the Consulate. Where's the support from my government? The Consulate is of no use to *anyone* in

Beirut, except for those who draw a salary from it and for the Lebanese with errant servants.

'Excuse me! That's enough! Where did you learn such language?' asks the Habesha girl, visibly shocked.

'From her!' I declare, pointing accusingly at Madame.

'How many years have you been here?' asks the Habesha girl.

'Fifteen months.'

'But your Arabic is so good.'

'You see!' declares Madame. 'Too intelligent to be a maid. I can't handle her.'

'The only choice you have is to send her back with *your* money or continue with the contract for another year, but with some reassurances—'

'She can pay for the flight. Where's my money, Meron? *L'argent!*' demands Madame, putting her hands into my pockets and finding nothing but damp paper tissues from recent weeping episodes.

'The contract probably says you have to pay salary *and* airfare if you decide to break it,' the Habesha girl says to Madame, finally offering me something helpful.

'Show me the contract,' demands Madame.

The Habesha girl reluctantly rises to find the contract, revealing a bottom like the head of a huge mushroom, swaying in the wind.

'I not losing money over you . . . you staying, Meron,' whispers Madame aggressively. 'If you demand to go home, Shafeek will get you in courts and we put you in prison for theft. And same if you say any more about dead maid. You not see your family for years and years, maybe never. We do anything we like to you. *Anything*.'

I nod without looking at her. There's no reason to doubt her.

The Habesha girl returns with the contract. I see my photo from fifteen months earlier stapled to the top of the page. My face was so fat!

'Look at me. Look what they've done to me!' I gasp.

'Meron!' hisses Madame.

'I'll stay here but I want better conditions . . .' I stutter.

'But where's my money?' asks Madame.

'Give back the money,' says the Habesha girl.

Madame has been richly humiliated by a servant girl with a hairpin in her own bedroom. I don't have any more tricks to progress this bid for freedom.

'I'll get it out. Where's the toilet?'

The toilets are authentic re-creations of Addis lavatories. I rip open the knickers and my hard-earned dollars are back in the wrong hands.

Madame agrees to better treatment for me: eating what they are eating, getting enough rest, no more beatings, working only for Madame and not the entire family. Madame agrees to check the problem with post from Addis, now remembering she forgot to mention the new postbox address and 'very sorry for that'. She signs a document to say so. I promise not to steal again, or to escape, or to lie, or to moan. It's all there in black ink: reasonable words, but words without power as soon as we're back in that apartment again.

The Habesha girl in front of us buckles under the strain of it all. The time is now 5.45pm. The Consulate is empty. A question pops into my head.

'So who cleans this place? Ethiopia, Sri Lanka, Bangladesh, Philippines? They all clean for Arabs in Beirut, and we're at the very bottom . . . so who cleans for the Ethiopians in Beirut? Who's lower life than us?'

'Nobody. *We* have to clean it,' she replies resentfully.

That makes sense.

As we walk outside, the Ethiopian flag flutters proudly above us at the end of another ineffectual day of helping not a single Ethiopian in need in Beirut. Five minutes later, the same flag waves at me when I arrive 'home' again. I shrug back at it and turn away bitterly, not an iota of hope in my own state.

For a few months, Madame and the others treat me with a degree of respect and try to smile a lot. It's painful, especially for Nazia. But Madame lets me use flour to make my breakfast genfo, just like Mum does.

'Allah! Where's flour gone to? Strong wind take it like sheet on Wednesdays? You use one month of flour in two weeks. You not doing *that* again.'

And we instantly revert to the pre-escape state, exactly where we were a few months ago when I took succour from remembering Kidist's hopeful escape bid. That failed too.

Kidist's Bid – Part Two

Kidist's mind was trampolining with the possibilities of leaving Desalegn. This suave driver had already demonstrated more appeal than Desalegn had managed in five years.

'I'm Kidist . . . what's your name?' she repeated through the wire mesh.

'Don't worry,' he replied a little offhandedly.

Don't worry? Kidist expected an elaboration, but nothing was forthcoming. She glanced outside. Bole Road was empty, and they were moving fast. She hesitated in re-initiating the small talk. Perhaps he had lost his wife. He might be lonely, shy, looking for a new partner. Kidist's mind picked up speed. This is fate! Or maybe he didn't want to talk any more.

As they rolled into Meskel Square, he suddenly veered hard over to the right and pressed down on the accelerator, heading up towards the Hilton.

'Excuse me, sir, we need Mexico Square . . . we should have gone straight on,' said Kidist. Perhaps he was tired, not thinking straight, this poor guy with five kids, or was it six?

No answer. He tightened his grip on the steering wheel as they sped up the long hill.

'Excuse me!' shouted Kidist.

He flicked down the central locking, securing the passengers in the back. Kidist tried to open the door, pointlessly. The windows lacked winding handles: they were resolutely closed. The chicken-wire partition was firm as they tugged at it, both now sensing danger.

'What do you want?' Kidist shouted.

Nothing. No response. The women were quickly becoming petrified. Adi grappled with her mobile, desperately prodding the numbers. Her husband wasn't answering. Again and again, she tried.

'You can take our money, Mister!' yelled Kidist.

'We're not rich, but you can have what we've got . . . please, Mister!' whimpered Adi.

'We have families, children, husbands . . . just leave us here!' continued Kidist.

Adi started screaming. Kidist sobbed. The guy concentrated on driving fast, reacting to nothing inside the car. Kidist used the modest heel of her shoe to try smashing the window, to no avail. They shrieked at the occasional pedestrian, but it was a Monday night: only business girls and the homeless were out now. Shouting was futile.

Adi's husband finally answered his mobile, but she couldn't accurately describe where they were: somewhere beyond the shops of Kasanchis, but dark, unrecognisable lanes without landmarks. She gabbled, almost hysterically. The husband might not have understood her. Kidist's mobile wasn't working at this time: she had let the battery run down to stop Desalegn harassing her at work.

The car entered through a high gateway and rumbled into the drive of a medium-sized villa within its own compound. If this was his house, he certainly had money, but was not within the elite of Addis. A younger man closed the gate behind them and dashed across to the front door of the house, inside a veranda. He was standing to attention like a willowy soldier on the parade ground, shoulders bending in towards a chest area where no chest existed. His face was keen and bony. Kidist didn't like the look of him: she thought he was concealing something in his right hand, maybe a blade.

Their chauffeur unlocked the car doors. He turned to face the two shaking ladies in the back.

'We're here, my home,' he said comfortingly. Kidist drew no comfort.

'I'm not young, sir . . . I'm a mother of two . . . in the name of God, look at me, I'm too old for you, my breasts are wilting, my skin has stretch marks. Under these clothes I'm a tiger . . . I mean, I *look* like a tiger—'

'Don't take her!' interrupted Adi. 'She's right! You want a younger woman. I beg you . . . she's too old . Her heart's weak, maybe she'll die. Do you want the death of an old woman on your hands?'

'You'd *hate* to see my body . . . it would make you sick to the stomach. Let me go and I promise not a word to anyone,' pleaded Kidist, beginning to unbutton her blouse. One glimpse of her drooping breasts would be enough to buy her freedom, she decided.

'I'll give you a good time, a really good time, but let *her* go, for mercy's sake,' cried Adi.

'Look at me . . . I've fed two babies with these,' implored Kidist, her breasts appearing to slop out of their bra cups without assistance. 'You were a baby once, you grew up on these! In the name of your mother, let me go . . .'

'I don't have a mother,' he muttered.

'In the name of your sister!'

'I don't have a sister. I don't have *any* family!'

'In the name of God! And Maryam! In the name . . .'

'Shut up, both of you!' he snapped. 'I don't want sex with you. Don't be so crude. What do you see on my veranda?'

The women peered through the dark towards the house.

'A young man?' said Kidist, unsure of what she was looking at. 'He wants . . . you know . . . the sex?'

'No! He's my servant. Behind him.'

'Ah! Broom, mop, buckets . . . er . . . a pile of clothes?'

'You will clean my house tonight and wash all my clothes by hand. And you will make a good job of it, or I *will* have sex with you. Do you understand?'

Kidist stared incredulously.

'You picked us up to do your housework?'

'Yes, I do it once a month. My servant isn't much good at it, so we use this free system. Get out of the car!'

'We'll do it! We'll do it!' cried Kidist, the relief visible on her face. Adi hugged her tightly. Extra housework, not robbery, not rape and not murder! They were joyous.

Adi's mobile was ringing. The servant grabbed it roughly from her hand.

'Get going! You've got all night if you want. I'll be here, just watching,' said the master of the house.

Kidist and Adi started on their tasks, sweeping and mopping a three-bedroom house crawling with a month of dirt, dust and bugs. Kidist's housework speed defied her plumpness: all that energy stored up within the corpulence was unleashed on the captor's grime. Meanwhile, he drank coffee, smoked, watched some television and inspected their work. The servant retired to bed after an hour, apparently a little weary. All he had done was open and close the front gate, nothing else. Kidist couldn't help wondering what kind of servant that was.

After three hours, they commenced the laundry, all by hand. There wasn't a single female or child's garment: only the clothing of two males, one a moderately rich businessman, the other a standard scraggy Addis lad. This was not a family home, thought Kidist. Without family, this man had become a dangerous freak: family protected society from being overrun by this type of warped individual. Family protected society from itself. This was the beginning of Kidist's enlightenment, as she squeezed the guy's fetid underwear between her powerful chubby fingers.

'We've finished . . . can we go? Please?' begged Kidist after two more hours.

'Good work! You must be hungry.'

'Well, yes . . .' she began. They were both famished and shattered.

'Me too! Cook us some wat, and then we'll have some more coffee,' he ordered.

The women plodded into the kitchen and cooked dinner.

'Mmm, that was pretty good,' he declared an hour later, having gorged on good food with his female companions. 'Maybe next time, we'll have doro wat . . .'

'What? Next time?' squeaked Kidist, her face crumbling in dismay.

'Only joking, though if I see you in Bole Road, I might just stop for you and invite you over again. It's been a good one. Now then, what time do you start work today?' he asked, the light of the new day peeping through the windows.

'One o'clock,' said Adi, meaning 7am international time, her eyes puffed up and bloodshot.

'Good timing. I'll run you down there to make sure you're punctual.'

'Thank you,' gasped Kidist.

What a daft thing to say, she said to herself.

'By the way, big lady, you've got a good friend there,' he said, glancing at Adi. 'She really loves you. You two are great together, like close sisters. Actually, I *am* going to look for you again. The two sisters!'

Kidist felt a spear of guilt lancing through her heart. Adi wasn't her sister. She already had a sister, who loved her far more than Adi. Her *real* sister, Werknesh, three years spurned by Kidist and here was God's punishment, a night in this freak house. Kidist felt desperately sick at herself. Werknesh would have given her *life* to protect her younger sister.

Family protected society. What did *family* really mean to Kidist? Everything or nothing? She had to go to Werknesh and attempt to repair everything. Her sister needed her. Kidist sensed this very strongly. Almost as though this freak had been sent to find her, to rescue the relationship: God had a reason for everything and everyone.

The kidnapper covered their eyes with scarves and drove them down Bole Road to work. Kidist and Adi struggled through a full day of work before returning to Adi's home in the evening. Exhausted and unable to face her husband yet, Kidist spent the night there, convalescing. The next day, Desalegn refused to believe her story and hit her around the head with his fist. Kidist's kidnapping experience lasted a single night, yet marriage to Desalegn would continue her captivity in a different guise for as long as she, or he, lived. They'd had a full Orthodox Christian church wedding: divorce was therefore impossible.

That evening, the evening of orange peel entertainment in our home, Kidist trudged over to see us, her face swollen, her pride swallowed. After unsuccessfully beseeching my mother to forgive her, God made an appearance, via the moonlight, the sisters were reunited and everything changed for the better, for us.

Auntie Kidist is probably still with the ogre today. The 'freak' is probably still using his free housework system. I spin it around in my head and wring it dry for meaning, especially the way good can emanate from bad. Kidist's story and the positive consequences confirm my suspicion that events lead to events lead to events and this unbroken chain is overseen by God to ensure the world is a better place: at least indirectly, incrementally and eventually.

He doesn't always intervene in the most dramatic of ways – sadly – but there *is* a grand plan, much too intricate for mortals to understand. And my Beirut predicament is in there somewhere, presumably just sitting below the 'Urgent Action' list, about to slip into the latter any day now . . .

Death Impending (42 days left)

Only six weeks from freedom! *Six weeks!* It's really nothing. I'm laughing at Lebanon. Beirut is beaten. No need for escape! No need for faint optimism! No need for divine interventions! I sing as I work. Look at me *now*, Auntie. Your story and the other memories from Addis have inspired me through to the end. And don't worry, Auntie, I remain untouched.

Madame makes an observation.

'Look at you . . . happy. Maybe because almost white now . . . because you stay with us for so long and you wash every day . . . true?'

Taken in by the certainty in her voice, I check myself in the bathroom mirror. I really scrutinise myself hard. No change. My skin remains the same insipid milky coffee as when I saw myself in Table Lady's mirror so long ago. Is Madame not aware of Jeremiah 13:23? 'Can the Ethiopian change the colour of his skin or the leopard change its spots?'

'Maybe with extra year, you get like Michael Jackson,' she quips.

'Extra year? But I'm on a two-year contract.'

'We buy extra year,' she says smugly.

'But I was expecting to see my mum in six weeks . . . Madame, *please*!'

'Oh! You remember to call me Madame again . . . when you need something. That is you, Meron . . . manipulator. But I not pay airfare for another one like you, so you stay. Anyway, what is difference at your age? Another year, and so what? Time not have value for *you* . . . and you make more money if stay.'

This is bleak, bitter news. Madame has persuaded the agency to extend my contract. I have no say in the matter. I sob secretly for two days and nights: during prayer times, I yearn to wail across the Beirut skyline, dovetailing my moans with the chants of multiple Imams rising out of the concrete. Howling at the sky is all I can do. I have hit the buffers again. I make the adjustment: from 42 days remaining to 407 days, from bright star of hope to deep-space black.

Three days ago, Nazia's graduation ceremony was difficult for the princess. Madame went with Shafeek, but without Abdul.

'Sorry, habibti,' she explained to Nazia afterwards. 'I couldn't go to your big event with your father. People would have *seen me*. Baba is an embarrassment. He looks like a refugee-camp person.'

Nazia hasn't spoken to Madame since then. Abdul is also effusing a silent fury: I hate to see him like this.

'Mister . . . maybe I can help you with, er, your clothes . . . make you look even better,' I suggest one morning.

'No! I wear the clothes I feel comfortable in . . . from my era . . . from the time when I met a beautiful young woman with no professional qualifications who said she loved me, in these *same* clothes . . . and then accepted marriage with me and accepted my help with tuition and my money to get her through the bankers' exams . . . happy to live off the supermarket profits and raise a family. All that time, I was still wearing the *same* clothes . . . until one day, she makes it to the top of the tree and her salary outstrips mine by several noughts . . . my clothes aren't good enough any more. I compromise at home and wear those clown pyjamas . . . just so I can share a bed with her . . . *sharmuta* . . . apart from forty years of life and the clown uniform, I'm completely *unchanged* in every way . . . the man she originally adored. But she . . . *sharmuta* . . . why am I telling you all this?'

'I don't know,' I shrug. 'You have to say it to *someone*, Mister.'

'Don't touch my clothes . . . sharmuta,' he mutters.

Later, when I find time, I sew up that overlong silken trouser leg but he rarely crosses my path now. Spending all his free time at Nuria's house with the grandchildren, Abdul is out of the apartment by 7am and returns around 11pm every night, just in time to forage for food and change into his altered pyjamas. He's barely living here.

Poor Abdul. I try to speak to him in the mornings, but not even a 'thank you' for the pyjamas. I miss our morning conversation.

*

303

My head is getting thick with conversations I haven't had. In Addis, personal problems dissipate over coffee ceremony and chatter. We are a sociable people: we open up the shutters, invite in the light, change the air and shake out the dust from the lungs. If we don't discuss problems, we become Henok, addled with silent brooding and internal bleeding, our brains literally beating themselves up until the blood pours forth. But here, unseen and unheard, I'm left with the company of only myself. I have to speak. A muttered soliloquy is beginning to spill out of my existence.

'Have you forgotten me now, Mum? Or do you still cry for me every day, like you did for Dad? At least he was put in the ground . . . you knew he wouldn't return. But me? You don't *know*. Maybe you think I'm dead but you can't be sure . . . and well, Mum, I *am* dead . . . that's how I feel . . . like a dead person. Do you mourn for me with the shaved head and the same black clothes? Have my brothers finished playing football yet and noticed I've gone? Would death be better than this existence? You always said time would pass if I kept my head down and worked, but it doesn't. One day is one year . . . we don't move forward . . .' I continue in Amharic.

Shafeek is staring at me. I have failed to notice him reading documents on a sun-lounger.

'Who are you talking to?'

I don't respond.

'You're going mad . . . hey, Meron! Meron! Stop wasting time. You can't do that *here* . . . it's disturbing me.'

'Listen to him with everything. I've got nothing . . . he's alive, I'm dead . . .' I persist in Amharic.

'Meron!' shouts Shafeek. 'Shut up! Shut the fuck up!'

I hear him.

'Sorry, Mister . . . forgot myself,' I stutter, traipsing back to the kitchen.

Forgot myself? What's happening to me? I'm Meron Lemma from Ethiopia, how would I forget *me*? Every day I see me, cleaning Nazia's froth-sprayed bathroom mirror, I am forced into a daily exchange of self, and it is an unpleasant encounter. My eyes used to be major assets, but are now two sunken squelched olives, good only for pizza topping and pavement garnish.

And my lips! I remember the Addis street kids in slack, washed-out Manchester United shirts from the 1990s, passed down a hundred times, the torn shirts at the end of their lives: from the bright dynamic Reds to a drab lip-skin pink. My lips need colour.

As if defying the logic of the mind, my hand reaches for a lump of beetroot from the fridge and rubs it along my lips repeatedly until they boast a reddish-purple stain. It's not a film starlet's scarlet rouge but it *is* an open act of rebellion. Next, tilting a glass horizontally, I hold a lit match inside, allowing smoke to blacken the inside of the beaker. Once extinguished, I use the match to scrape through the carbon residue and smear this onto the contours of my eyes, like black eyeliner. Where's the bathroom mirror? I have to see this.

'Wow!' I say, pouting absurdly. 'Meron Lemma, you beauty! *There* you are.'

'Meron!' shouts Shafeek.

I look again at myself. What am I doing? Shafeek is

precisely the *worst* person to have a free front-row seat for this sudden show of unannounced beauty.

As rapidly as possible, I scrub and scratch at my ridiculous make-up with soap and water before dashing towards the TV lounge.

'Meron!'

Shafeek is sprawling in baggy shorts.

'What nuts have we got?'

'Pistachios, Mister.'

'Get them and take a handful for yourself.'

'Thanks, Mister!' I grin.

Noise food!

Shafeek has noticed my smile.

'Mmm . . . you've definitely *got* something,' he smirks knowingly.

I back my way out of the lounge as quickly as possible, trying to erase the smile as I go.

Later, I'm back on the balcony. We're higher than most high-rise blocks. I can look down onto other roofs and see distant people, and their washing lines, their pot plants, kids' toys, empty bottles, rusty furniture and all the other paraphernalia of a passing life.

'Can any of these people be as despondent as me?' I ask myself. 'I'm eighteen and all I can do is attract the attention of a murdering rapist lawyer. And with Abdul never here, the murdering rapist lawyer is the nicest person in the apartment. Can I get any lower?'

I wave at somebody on a neighbouring tower. I think he's an older guy, like Abdul, puffing away on a cigarette. He sees me and looks away. He's not engendering happiness. In fact, who is? I don't know *anybody* in this apartment outwardly joyful.

'I've got my excuses for being miserable . . . but the rest of them? We should all join hands and leap off this concrete diving board together, a simultaneous escape. Not many ways to escape this prison . . . but jumping is as obvious and convenient as the emergency exit on the flight from Addis. Would anyone notice *that*, a splattered ant in a Beirut street?'

'My landing will be an asphalt thud, not a Ghion splash. I dare you to push me, Robel. Where are you? Shove me, while I'm not concentrating . . . *please*. But is this how Mulu died? Driven to insanity and then to suicide?'

Mum's mad-but-confident tactic suddenly seems ruinous. I sense a piece of Mama inside me: I want to beat my chest and scream. I want to *run* at that drop. Hurt me, Lord, for putting myself *here*, for effectively killing myself without actual death. Standing here or splattered down there: what's the difference?

A violent thunderstorm seems to be gathering in the distance.

I'll never find out how my death is reported. Or even if it *is* reported. I don't even have *that* to look forward to. Why has praying not delivered me from this abyss? *God?*

I peer over the balcony. My head swims, my stomach drops.

'Where's my last-minute reprieve? *Something, please, God.*'

There's another smack of thunder. I look around for lightning. Maybe I'll go the same way as Tadelle's wife: a pure Old Testament death at the end of God's fuming finger. That would at least tell me He's circulating around these parts, whereas if I kill myself, I cannot be buried in sacred ground, risking an infinity in Hell. So what? I'm already there.

But there's no lightning. Big distant bangs, sudden flashes on the ground, drifting smoke, wailing sirens . . . what does it all mean? And do I care? Hariri, Beirut, bombs . . . no, Shafeek, I don't care about this place or you or . . . maybe it's the Ethiopian Army . . . invading Lebanon to rescue me.

No army, no deity, no body is rescuing me. I amble inside instead and switch on the TV. No one is home except me.

My God! Israeli bombs are raining down on Beirut, the television tells me. Allah! Just for a second, I'm excited by this: the simple burst of news into my dire life. It's outside on the balcony, I can see it . . . I can see the news in front of my eyes. I am part of this world after all!

But it sinks in. A random bomb might just wipe me out. Yes, I'll consider jumping from a high-rise building, but needless victim of a war I could never possibly understand is not a death to be contemplated. It must be the worst possible way to go.

Life is sweet again. I want *more* of it. This is God's work!

I sit tight for Madame. She'll know what to do.

'Mum, we have to leave *now*!' implores Nazia.

'Yeah, she's right about that. It's too close, Mum!' barks Shafeek with real fear in his eyes. He's home early today, sharing a meal with the other two.

'I'm right about most things . . .' says Nazia dryly, blinking at me.

'You're wrong about *that*.'

Madame tears off some bread and chews it steadily. Madame loves her acts. She turns her head dramatically to look hard at Shafeek and Nazia. Abdul is not here, as usual.

'Not yet. Bombs are still on the outskirts, in the south, Hezbollah is the target. Running from the city in panic is *not* the correct thing to do, especially now . . . everyone else is doing it. We've seen all this before. Stay calm, check the situation, we go to Jabal when I say we go. Okay?'

Shafeek and Nazia lower their heads to slurp soup solemnly, nobody questioning Madame's orders. Occasional bomb blasts can be heard but they are distant. Once more, a flutter of adrenalin within me, I'm thoroughly absorbed by their growing trepidation. I'm seeing new behaviour: my masters quaking. I perch on the very edge of my stool in the corner, all thoughts of kissing asphalt lost in the ether of embattlement. Maybe we *are* all going down together! Rich, poor, lawyer, lammergeyer, servant, all equally dead. Ha! Ha! Ha!

All except for Madame. She's the cool lady. Maybe the coolest I've known. Yet, if I were to march into the kitchen and openly munch an apple, she would forget the long-range missile flying in towards her balcony. Is this the secret to success? Rage and rail at the trivial, but float through cut-throat decisions like you're making toast.

'Something is different about the servant,' says Nazia.

'Meron!' Madam barks. 'What you wearing on your

face? Lipstick? Eye-liner? Wash your face now before I scrape off with brush! Très très grotesque.'

The anger rushes into her face, proving my point with perfection.

I call Beti discreetly.

'Beti, habibti, what's happening? Are we going to die in a war?'

'Hey, sister! Time to go home! Ethiopia is taking you home.'

'Why? What do you mean?'

'Our government. They're providing a free plane trip home for all Habesha in Beirut, including those without passports . . . it's amazing!'

'Free?'

'Free.'

'Allah! So we get our freedom, for free. Mother Ethiopia! At last! Are you going, Beti?'

'I don't know . . . probably stay in the family's basement in the countryside. It's safe there.'

'I want to go home.'

'Just get yourself to the Consulate, sister.'

'Yeah, I know where that is.'

'And get your wages from Madame.'

'Mmm.'

Later, I explain the situation to Madame.

'. . . and so there's no airfare and all I need are my wages and I'll walk to the Consulate. Think I remember where –'

'I never see selfish person like you before. Meron, you incredible. When your host family has problem, Israel attacking with bombs, you want to leave us. What about family? We need your support now, but you forget us.'

'So can I go, Madame?'

'You are really low life. No, you not going! Be professional, do duty . . . you stay here with us. You part of family . . . we share so much together. You like my daughter. How you leave your mother in middle of war? Are you *crazy*?'

Madame goes about her business as usual for two days until the bombs edge closer. Mid-afternoon, with Nuria and her family also arriving, everyone is packing furiously to leave.

'What's happening, Madame?' I ask.

'Time to go. I got special visa papers for roadblocks and out to Jabal, our country house. We got basement there. All rich have basements in Lebanon,' she tells me, as she gathers up her best jewellery and heads for the front door. 'We come back after bombs stop.'

'Yes, Madame . . .' I turn to get my own meagre possessions.

Within five minutes, everyone has marched out of the apartment and I duly follow Madame to the front door with my plastic bag of spare clothes and toothbrush. Madame veers round suddenly.

'Meron, what you doing?'

'Following you, Madame.'

'What? *You?*' she chuckles. 'We not have space for servant in Jabal. You can eat food from fridge.'

'Pardon, Madame?'

'Eat anything you like, but not waste electricity . . . if we have it. Bye.'

As the key locks the door from the outside and her high heels click down the marble hallway outside, I can only stand and stare at the closed front door. I can't believe this.

'But I am family . . .' I whimper to nobody. 'How can you *do* that?'

They have abandoned me. Death is definitely coming. I hold my face and cry.

I have to speak to Mum. I try to call her on the phone, but the line is dead, like I will be. To be buried in the rubble of a luxury apartment will be as cold as any other tomb. All I have is Maryam and my prayer book and my faith in God. Everything else in here is worthless. Golden sugar bowls and silk sheets and Persian rugs, they won't save me.

For three days, heavy bombs drop on our neighbourhood, usually at night. Sleeping is impossible. Again and again, each cracking boom leaves me winded and shrieking the eyeballs out of my head as the building is smacked from side to side, each shudder making me want to retch up the insistent nausea from the pit of my stomach. If only I could rip out the frayed nerve-ends from my juddering flesh and burrow behind my scarlet eyes until I get hold of that horrible pounding throb and crush it between my thumbs. But screams and sirens from streets below tell of much worse suffering wreaked on others.

I can't stop thinking about God's reasoning: why is this city a war zone? Why are thousands of highly skilled professional men and women, mostly good people, probably being paid decent salaries simply to obliterate feeble cleaners like me? I'm a good person too.

'Please leave me alone, I'm Habesha . . . I'm no threat to you,' I mumble uselessly from time to time.

During the daytime, there is some calm. I watch the news and doze fitfully on Madame's bed. I peer over our balcony every hour or so, checking: is this apartment block the last remaining building in Beirut? All I see is a grim mist hanging heavily upon rooftops. Thick dust wafts into the apartment. I imagine Table Lady downstairs, cowering beneath her table: no cosy basement in a country house for her. We shall be buried together.

With shops closed for the previous few days, the only food left in the apartment is rice, potatoes, onions and rotting fruit. For me, it's the usual fare. At night, though, I go hungry. With missiles randomly crashing into surrounding blocks, my stomach is too tightly knotted to accept food of any description. Every time my body begins to relax, another brutal crack shatters the peace and another ribbon of stomach lining loops around itself and pulls the whole convulsing shebang into a taut ball of pain. If the bombs don't destroy me, my stomach will.

'Israel, the Lord's own land! What have I done to *you*? This can't be God's plan.'

I am utterly certain I will see you, Dad, very soon. I clasp and kiss my prayer book as though it is God's extended hand. I feel that death is closing in now. If it is my time, what can I do? Nothing, *nothing*! *God, I am reduced to nothing! Why am I abandoned to this lonely death?*

I remember Tadelle.

Tadelle's Angel

After the Kebebush pension fiasco was resolved, we were not suddenly rocketed back into the upper echelons of Addis society. The widow's pension for railway workers was no gold mine, but we did have a few birr available for new furniture and crockery, and life for my mother mellowed a little.

Inspired by Kidist's return and that single divine illumination, Mum commenced a rigorous routine of daily worship – in place of work – while continuing to raise three moderately intelligent children. Discarding at last the tatty black gown of mourning, she took up the traditional white cotton shema. All white, always white from now on. Religion extracted her from the black days and provided the solace for which she yearned.

By the time I was sixteen, my mother had gone beyond white and found true radiance. The Bible's wisdom pulsed through her every voluntary action, as she actively assisted all those around her. She openly cried for the deaths of complete strangers, she invited the neediest in the neighbourhood into our house for coffee and injera, she patiently advised the uneducated and generally behaved like an earthly angel effusing the love of God.

For Mum and fellow Orthodox Christian worshippers, Jesus Christ was the new draw in town and word was just beginning to spread *today*. The news had to be diffused until every living being was abuzz with the deeds of the Lord, as though *today* was the very first day of Christianity, every turned page of the Bible laden with fresh insight, every verse more worthy of keen discussion than the country's current news stories and scandals. The coming of Christ continued to reverberate in Ethiopia with happy surprise, regardless of the two passing millennia with all their scientific ideas, industrial progress and the many ephemeral acts of men. Today was the day the Lord had made and *today* the angel would be tested.

'Have you heard about Tadelle?' asked Alem.

'No, what happened?' replied Tsigereda.

'Yes, he doesn't look good . . .' said Elsa.

'In what sense?' asked Helen.

'His hair is thinning,' said Alem.

'Ah! It must be the usual thing,' replied Mebratt, as the others gasped with varying degrees of shock.

Six middle-aged women in white netelas and myself were squashed into our snug living room like white feathers packed into a pillow. Their faces were kindly and benign but sometimes their words could be too jagged for a pillow's padding, and I sensed my mother's extreme discomfort in the midst of this regular gathering. She tried to keep her head down, preparing coffee, but occasional remarks would spike her.

'Tadelle's skin is dry.'

'That means it's dropping off . . . '

'Oh! He's obviously got it.'

'And he's refusing alcohol. I offered him a glass of tella, and he refused it.'

'Ah! So, he's started taking the tablets . . .'

'He had the flu . . .'

'Of course, he did . . . that's normal.'

'When he walks outside, he discreetly carries a reused Highland bottle of water.'

'That says everything . . . definitely HIV!'

'Why is a Highland bottle definitely HIV?' asked Mum, like me, trying to follow the quick-fire chatter. At times, I wasn't sure who said what, and today, the excited prattle defeated me.

'He needs the water to swallow his hourly HIV tablets.'

'Ah.'

Mum poured coffee into six white demitasse cups and passed them round. There were usually at least three coffee ceremonies in our house every day and my mother *always* had money for good coffee, however expensive the beans. Whenever the question of financial priorities arose, she reminded us that life came from God, but without nature's caffeine coursing through our capillaries, we couldn't possibly do all He expected of us in our exquisitely short appearances on His planet. Mum thus neatly married the demands of the Bible with the rituals of coffee consumption.

'It's just so obvious . . . the hair, the skin, the tablets, the Highland . . .'

'Another one lost to HIV.'

'It's no loss. There are no tears for that one.'

'He'll be gone within months.'

'Enough of this rumour-mongering!' snapped Mum, her face darkening. 'This is a religious house! My coffee is not being provided to fuel the exaggeration of scandal.'

Mum was eager to avoid the pitfalls of inane chatter, so her coffee came only with passionate religious debate. In a million other homes, however, the coffee ceremony was the factory floor of Ethiopia's gossip-production line and, once an item was on the conveyor belt, it could not be withdrawn – however untrue it might be – until it finally emerged as fabricated 'truth' ready for mass consumption. 'Truths' in Addis were rarely true.

'Just drink up and gossip outside,' added Mum.

'But Werknesh, it's Tadelle. What can we do for him?' asked Tsigereda, trying to bend the subject in a slightly more compassionate direction.

'He lost his job at the kebelle . . . hiding official certificates,' said Helen.

'And lost his wife . . .' said Elsa.

'To a bolt of lightning and there's nobody to support him . . . he's got four kids,' said Alem.

'So, he's lying down only two doors from where we sit and we are Christian women . . . it's logical that we should help him,' said Mum.

'What? *Tadelle?* Why do I want to die from *his* HIV?' asked Elsa aggressively.

'It doesn't matter if he dies *today* . . . I'm not helping that parasite,' added Mebratt.

'Yes, let him die,' said someone quietly, probably Tsigereda who originally asked the question about what we could do for him.

'Dying? That's God's work, not yours . . . don't meddle in His work,' interrupted Mum. 'I don't care if it is Tadelle. He's a living, breathing man, a creation of God. We are taught to respect and care for everyone, not rumi-nate on their *unproven* cause of death.'

'Even Tadelle?'

'Him more than anyone.'

'After everything he did to you?'

'Enemies and traitors need even more love than the rest . . . they're always the unhappy ones. Matthew 5:44: love thy enemy.'

This seemed to halt the conveyor belt of 'truth'. Muted muttering and hard glances towards Mum filled the void for a few seconds.

'In fact,' started Mum, 'doctors say this type of mass persecution of sick people is a major accelerator of death in Addis. The sick are abandoned at the exact moment they need support . . . it's death-by-gossip.'

'So, you'll go to his house and care for him?'

'Of course? Won't you?' replied Mum.

Everyone laughed. To visit an 'HIV house', if only declared as such by rumour, was to openly invite one's own tortuous demise: people knew as much about HIV as they did about genetic engineering. HIV had become the new leprosy.

'It's just like when Lemma died ten years ago and I was

suddenly poor . . . everyone abandoned us, including my own sister,' said Mum bitterly.

'So, go and care for him.'

'I shall!'

I accompanied Mum with a large chrome tray of injera to his messy shed the next day. As I poked my head into his drab living room, the stench of stale urine made my eyes water. I hardly dared imagine what pestilence was scuttling through the deep shadows. Mum immediately threw open a small window and collected up plates lying on the floor, while I stood perfectly still, trying to make out Tadelle's features under a pile of blankets. After half a minute or so, I finally glimpsed a single peering eye, blinking at me.

'Mum, he's there.'

'Yes, I know. Tadelle?'

He groaned half-heartedly.

'Ah, good, you feel much better today!' Mum sang out.

I felt like laughing. Anyone could see Tadelle was a considerable distance from 'better'. Even his famous egg-like protrusion – the chat disfigurement – had subsided.

'Werknesh?' he mumbled. 'Have you come to finish me?'

'Don't be silly! I'm here to help . . . the past is past. Today you're in God's hands. You have nothing to fear,' said Mum, tidying away dirty cups and plates.

Tadelle's head sprang upwards with the speed of a catapult.

'No! Leave me . . . after all I did to you! I can't face the guilt . . . let me die in the agony that I deserve!'

Tadelle was truly sick. I couldn't believe he was saying

this. The old Tadelle never refused anything offered to him for free and was even less likely to request agony. I remembered Mama begging God for the same. What is His stance on requested agony?

'Shut up, Tadelle,' snapped Mum. 'You look good, you have to stand up. Let's get you outside in the sun, try to eat, drink some coffee. You have to make yourself strong for your children. Come on, Tadelle! Be a man!'

I giggled. Tadelle, a man! Mum shushed me abruptly.

After feeding him a thick broth made from boiled bones and vegetables, Mum prepared coffee for Tadelle and gave him traditional medicine prepared with the herbs damakesse and feto. He clambered to his feet and managed to stand outside in the sun for ten minutes.

'Werknesh . . . your name is totally accurate,' said Tadelle. Werknesh in Amharic means 'gold'.

Mum made daily visits to Tadelle's filthy shed for a fortnight. She aimed to cook, clean and prepare at least one coffee ceremony for him and his children each day. But Tadelle made little progress until finally she insisted that he went to the hospital to check for HIV. The result was negative.

'So what *is* wrong with you?' she asked him outside Black Lion Hospital in Bole Road.

'Apparently nothing. I had a bit of flu and then people began to talk.'

'Yes, they said your hair was thinning . . .'

'I'm getting old.'

'And you refused a glass of tella . . .'

'Elsa's tella is revolting and undrinkable.'

'So you were abandoned and left to die.'

'Until my angel came along. Really, Werknesh, it's the loneliness that hastens sickness, not the sickness.'

Heavy-hanging time was never a welcome guest in the poorer neighbourhoods: melancholia was dangerous enough to kill a grown man. An animated coffee ceremony, though, could slide time along like a well-oiled locomotive, dropping us off in mid-afternoon, when we thought it was still late morning. For the 'non-infected' of our neighbourhood, many years would pass in the protective cocoon of friendly chatter, mutual support and daily certainty, helping to evade the one vital question: 'Should my life not add up to more than *this*?' As soon as the forces of gossip attacked, social abandonment struck hard and this dire question swiftly followed one into bed, a bed that might not be left.

Tadelle, however, soon recovered under the superior daily care provided by my mother.

A few weeks later, Mum played host to the same five women. As they nattered about the neighbourhood's most recent 'victims' of HIV, Tadelle himself entered our house.

'Good morning, all!' he cheered.

Tadelle had gained weight, his skin glowed and he clutched a Highland bottle containing tella beer. But these features had negligible impact on the other visitors. The five ladies immediately forgot their line of gossip and, like synchronised rabbits, baulked with fright at the guest. If only they could scamper into the protective undergrowth, but Habesha etiquette demanded that they greet him with at least a reluctant salutation. Inaudible murmurs followed.

'Oh no! I forgot the cooking . . . my onions are burning!' babbled Tsigereda, rushing out of the front door.

Elsa picked up a coffee and hesitated to sip it, before putting it back down again.

'I've drunk too much coffee already this morning . . . I really shouldn't have come. Better go before I'm addicted,' she laughed nervously, tripping towards the exit.

This left three: Helen, Alem and Mebratt. They changed positions, without any subtlety, to maximise their distance from Tadelle. But that wasn't enough. Conversation was stiff and stilted. They wanted a quick escape.

'Yes, I'm coming!' Helen suddenly shouted at the door, supposedly in response to a yell from outside. But I'd heard nothing. Mum and Tadelle were equally mystified. Helen sprinted for the door, her pretext unquestioned.

Alem desperately glanced around at us.

'What happened? It must be an emergency! I'd better go to her aid.'

And she was out.

Now solitary, Mebratt held a hand across her mouth, pretending to rub her nostrils, as if this would somehow block the hypothetical virus from entering her air passages.

'I'm very worried . . . they haven't come back . . . I'd better check,' stuttered Mebratt, before diving for the exit.

Mum and Tadelle laughed heartily together. It is at this precise moment that Tadelle noticed the metal bowl resting beside the front door. He licked his lips and thought of the perishing chicken squirming beneath the bowl at supper time. Talking endlessly about the Old Testament, and the irrelevance of the New, seemed to Tadelle like a splendid way to gain romantic attachment to Werknesh and, more importantly, to fatten himself on her daily chicken feast. Several weeks later, he made the mistake of lifting the lid on Henok's rancid trainers and creating the funniest moment in my family's history, prompting my mistimed Lebanon announcement, Mum's reluctant agreement and finally to here, Beirut, Madame, Shafeek, bombs and the battle of Meron Lemma.

Nothing Beats Nothing
(401 days left)

If Tadelle can survive a lonely death-by-gossip in Addis, I can *easily* survive a lonely death-by-bombs in Beirut. Yes!

No. My thoughts are turning to gibberish. I can't stop the bombs: I could be dead a single second from now.

But after three days of Israeli torment, Madame returns in a quiet spell. As the key turns in the door, I contemplate grabbing a knife and charging at her. After everything I have done for this family, *why did you leave me?*

I'm too beleaguered to attack a person, my hand trembling too much to hold a knife.

'Oh, you alive, Me-ron!' she declares jubilantly. 'You so lucky!'

I'm standing in the exact spot she left me. I doubt my facade has improved since three days ago. Why come back? To check I'm properly terrified? To check I've cleaned up the new layers of dust? Is today a white sock day?

I think again about that knife. I could plunge it into her and run free. But look at me, look at Beirut: I'm not running anywhere.

'We spend three days in basement and now need cleaning. We want you, Meron.'

Ah. My ticket out of Israel's target zone. Squeeze mop, sponge and Dettol. I willingly accept.

Madame and I slip through the army roadblocks around Beirut like olive oil through tissue paper. Her documents seem to contain magic words that transform edgy surly youths in green, red or blue berets into charming young men prepared to remove any obstacle before us. I think the car – a purple Porsche – exerts some influence. Madame's extra high heels and very tight jeans may also have some effect.

On the way, I see the devastation wrought by Israeli bombs and bite my fingers with fear. The ride in a Porsche is forgotten when I see distressed locals fighting in the streets over depleted food stocks remaining in semi-shuttered shops. Welcome to the world of hunger, I want to shout through the window. Openly flirting with the troops, Madame seems oblivious to the mayhem.

Once out of the city, Madame can dispense with the act and relax.

'If we have good neighbours, not Israel and Syria, we can have fantastic country. We got everything . . . skiing, beaches, trekking, nightlife, cuisine, history . . . and friendliest people in Middle East,' she says as if I am a naive tourist.

But from where I'm sitting, the Lebanese are mentally disturbed. I can't find a single word to participate in this conversation. I am seething.

'Biggest problem is not the neighbours . . . it's the men. What you know about men, Meron?'

'My father was a man, and my two brothers are also men—'

'Is your humour playing with me again?'

'I know a lot about men, Madame, a lot. We have them in Addis . . . yes, it is a big problem.'

'*What?*' she chortles.

'But no man could ever get me . . . I've seen it all, Madame.'

'What *you* know? What man chased *you*? You young and single and just girl, Meron. Look at me, look at my age . . . I *know* men. Listen to me, learn from me, copy me . . . before they get you, you have to do preparation. No glamour, no fun in married life, nothing *at all*.'

'Really?' I say, a little shocked.

'Meron, marriage has different rules, everything change. When they get you, men change. Can be difficult if you not adjusting to your husband, because he not adjusting to you. Wife has to find path around him, path not cut *across* him, or upset him. For example, if he come home and say he too sick to eat dinner at home, it because he eat outside. Husbands decide to eat outside sometimes without telling you: just accept it. Food can wait for another day. Not waste money on fancy food for him. Keep for guests. Save money for yourself, so not dependent on him. Not asking him questions to try and get information. This irritate men too much. He has secrets, so you can have yours. Never reveal secrets to him; never show him all your heart; always hold something back as insurance. Be self-confident, not overreact, not be sad about his behaviour, not . . .' She stops and looks at me. I'm captivated. She should be an apostle for the innocent young women of the world. Madame giggles endearingly.

I want to ask about her incongruous relationship with Abdul and her unfulfilled expectations for Shafeek, but I can't. I nod in awe, my mouth sucking up dust again. At last, this is the Madame I have always dreamed of meeting.

'Babies, children . . . they easy . . . just give them food, but adults, adult men . . . très difficile. You have to be smart with them . . . très intelligent,' she continues.

Madame is confiding personal details to me. I am now *special*. Madame trusts me with intimacy. She likes me. I have a foothold. I'm edging my way up from the very low-liest of entities in the apartment to something, I assume, that has to be better. I envy her bedroom, her mental agility and the way she's in control of every aspect of her life: finances, fitness, family, fashion, occupation, copula-tion, Madame stuns me in the sheer mastery of all around her. One day, Madame and I might be friends, equals, companions, like her and Nazia . . .

For a few minutes in her snug low-slung passenger seat, whizzing up the side of Lebanese mountains as the sky turns pink, I'm fooled by Madame's veneer. But I remember Proverbs 26:23: 'Like the glaze covering an earthen vessel are smooth lips with an evil heart.'

She *should* be an apostle, but for the one glaring omission: geniality. The ability to be genuinely nice was sacrificed the moment she sniffed Abdul's money all those years ago. Can she ever like or be liked by *anyone*? With so much controlling to be done, 'like' has no place in her lexicon.

But does it have to be that way? Do confidence and money automatically breed control? And does this always evolve into cold-heartedness? Or is it all a cover for her fear of poverty? As Mum says, the rich live in dread of losing it. Ha! And what happens if Madame does lose it and on the same day, her fading beauty is beyond her control and she is forced to fall back on a personality as small and sharp as a pin prick? Without the geniality, people will queue up to draw her blood.

No. I prefer to be me: so utterly reduced to nothing that I fear nothing and no one. I am an unbeatable zero. In maths, you can multiply nothing by a million and it will still be nothing, impervious to other numbers. Most of Ethiopia has always had nothing, yet our culture has somehow defied and survived the influence of foreign powers. A 'nothing' is round like a ball: try to throw it away and it bounces back in your face. And that's me now, an impervious invincible nothing, ready to fly back into the face of those who manipulate me.

By the time we reach their farmhouse in Jabal, I'm asleep. As the car door opens, I find myself in some kind of rustic paradise. The sweet aroma of endless pine trees elicits a cough of joy from me. Out of Beirut! Out of my prison! The dust of bomb damage sputters out of my lungs.

An elderly woman whose black shoulder-length hair is probably a wig approaches us gingerly. Emaciated, she's unsteady on her feet but attempts a thin smile at me.

'This my mother, Meron.'

'Merhaba . . . Madame's mother,' I stutter.

'Come this way, child,' she rasps. 'Rahima, get her working fast . . . she can do the house as well.'

'Yes, Mum.'

'She looks healthy enough . . .'

We follow her into the basement of a farmhouse. It's piled high with tins of food. Abdul restocks the basement every six months from his supermarket. Madame is always ready for Israel, Syria, or whoever else might attack her.

The entire family is inside the basement, sitting around, looking tetchy. Nobody is pleased to see me except Mustafa and Medina, the kids. Now I can see the problem with sharing oxygen and food in a bomb shelter with your Habesha servant. They would prefer me *outside* the shelter until the cleaning is needed.

Cleaning takes two hours. Afterwards, I enjoy tinned peaches. Madame's mother is unhappy about this, but I have to eat.

The Israeli bombing ceases the same night. We're back at the apartment in the early hours as though nothing has happened. But they left me in a war zone. I have changed. I am *nothing* to them, and that will be my advantage.

The memory of my initial 'pride' when I first came to the apartment is almost funny. I lie awake grinning at my own innocence and obedience in the early days. Back then, I didn't realise I was living with a race devoid of heart.

Today, I have one year left on the contract, again. The Israeli battering has calmed down. Normal life has resumed for most people. They are lucky. I have been on a war footing for more than two years now, unsure who will attack me for the most trivial of reasons. That is the way I see it. War.

It's them or me: Madame, Nazia and, sadly, Shafeek. They drew the lines and we've been in a private war of attrition ever since. The first year was theirs, and the second too, but the third, beginning today, that will be mine. The raw little Habesha girl is banished forever.

I am Mum in her baseball-bat phase, and now making things happen. This morning, as I handled Madame's fitness manual, it fell open on a well-thumbed page: her daily exercise regime revealed! The very same that keeps Madame's buttocks in such spectacular shape. Madame's body is worth having. I memorised the regime and at 5am sharp tomorrow, I plan to perform a thirty-minute session on the balcony in total secrecy. Sit-ups, stretching and jogging round the perimeter of the roof garden are the main components. Self-determination begins here. Confidence will ooze from every pore. In one year's time, I'll be standing in Addis looking fabulous, or I take down my oppressors with me. I am not Mulu.

The early morning air is fresh and light when I roll out a mat on the balcony's concrete. It feels as though Beirut is mine. Apart from those in prayer, nobody else is awake and active. If some major question is asked of the city's citizens at this time of day, few will be as sharp as me: I'll fling back an answer before the rest can lift their eyelids.

By 5.30am, my body is gleaming, I'm so far ahead of the rest of the city, it inspires me to go harder: four million, olive-oil-soaked, paunchy Arab bodies paralysed in dull slumber, and me, feisty and fighting fit on the roof of Beirut: above and beyond their blinkered dreams about real estate, nightclubbing and skewered lamb.

My withered eighteen-year-old body aches at first, but within only three days the daily routine has visible effects: feminine form returns to my hitherto shapeless, wasted frame. Clear thinking is replacing the heavy fog inside my head. Housework has become a series of easy gliding movements, just as Madame demonstrated on the very first day. Life is enhanced.

In my third week of exercise, a full hour races by before tiredness tickles my muscles. Rich trickles of sweat dribble out of me. The bathroom mirror is beginning to love me, and vice versa. My loose servant togs caress my curves after two years of disinterest. In Madame's fancy clothes, I stand agog at myself. Now, I'm getting gorgeous!

The next morning, mid-session, I hear Madame speaking on the phone.

'Yes, she trusts me,' I hear from the balcony.

The kitchen window is wide open and my ears are unable to stop listening.

'Eighteen . . . healthy . . . what choice do we have?' Madame continues. 'Maybe six months or a year before another comes through. Too much waiting for us . . . especially at a thousand dollars a week.'

Madame begins to sob. It's not often I hear this sound.

'It's better if she doesn't know anything . . . okay, I'll start it,' she says, finishing the call.

It is an odd moment.

These days, the kitchen is properly mine. The street kids in Bole Road with their pickpocket skills were slick. But me, now, on my battleground, I've made thieving food my daily bread. It *is* my daily bread. Thieving is not encouraged by the Bible, but like soldiers in war I have my excuses: God can see that I'm stealing to survive.

Strictly off-limits, the fridge buzzes at me as chickens cluck at foxes: inevitability stalks our relationship. The low hum alone activates my saliva glands. Once inside, I ram food and liquid into my diminutive mouth. Spreadable substances (hummus, baba ghanoush, butter) are spread further: nobody notices reduced depth. Drinks in cartons (milk, fruit juice) lose concentration: water is such a good mixer. Malleable products (falafel, soft cheese) are reshaped to hide loss, using a spoon to smooth over incriminating finger prints. But sealed goods (ice cream, chocolate) I have not yet cracked.

'You went in fridge again . . . I know you have, Me-ron!' Madame says once a week or so.

'No, Madame, not me . . . must have been Abdul, or Shafeek in the night, or . . .'

'Enough! I know was you, but I not sure what you steal.'

I shrug my shoulders. Before leaving for work, Madame traps a light slither of tissue paper in the fridge door as she closes it. When I open the door, the slither slips out and she knows I have been inside. The tissue is as light and indiscernible as a patch of human skin. Sometimes, I locate it and reinsert it. Sometimes I do not. Those are the days I plunder little or nothing.

Beyond the fridge lies a similarly lush world of devious consumption. Wrapping one of my long black hairs round a chicken leg ensures it is noticed by whoever tries to eat it: the cry of revulsion from the dining room means the chicken leg is mine ('Urgh! Meron! Take it away!'). Stale bread earmarked for the servant is swapped for the fresh new loaf meant for the family: after some time, the latter forgets the taste of good bread, while the taste buds of the servant become ever more refined. Dried milk powder is stirred daily into hot water and consumed for protein: if hot water cannot be obtained, a handful of dried milk powder is thrown into my mouth, followed with a glass of cold water. Let the stomach be the liquidiser.

When placing a new batch of eggs inside the refrigerator, I poke an outstretched finger into the shell of a single egg.

'Whoops! Madame, an egg's broken,' I say, licking my moist finger.

'Again! You throw that one away. But be more careful!'

'I think it was already broken.'

'Oh really?' she says, knowingly. 'You have good ears and your eyes like lasers, but your hands are useless lettuce leaves . . .'

'If only they were edible, Madame.'

'What? You not funny, Meron. I sure you getting bigger . . . maybe we check your weight again.'

'Just a little constipated, Madame.'

The contents of the broken egg find their way into a sugared mug a little later. Three eggs a week are consumed with this ruse.

Bottled mineral water from Abdul's supermarket, meant only for the family, is consumed by the servant. The family unknowingly swigs a blend of both bottled and tap water, sometimes only tap but they seem to live. Similarly, I am a little remiss with fruit-washing, but they survive: why would I wash fruit that I'm not allowed to eat? I often bash an ugly brown bruise into a perfectly good pear, then carefully wash it and place it with the others.

'Give that bruised one to Meron,' they say.

'Thank you very much,' I reply, munching the cleanest pear in the bowl.

Madame always checks my lips after kitchen work: undue dampness indicates something improper – food or drink – has entered my mouth and triggered the seepage of saliva. I'm constantly scraping at my lips to give the pretence of dryness. Madame is happy only when I appear to be fresh in from a gruelling trek across the Sahara. My eyes also give me away. She says they become bigger and more 'innocent-looking' when a transgression has been committed. Instead, I concentrate on the guilty hangdog look with lips splitting open like overripe tomatoes and eyes squinting like a pair of brown apple pips, as if hoping to glimpse a distant oasis.

'Meron, you look terrible today,' she says.

'Oh, okay,' I reply, rather pleased with myself, and letting it show.

'No, really. You look terrible. Guests coming today . . . your face not good for appetite of corporate bankers.'

'Sorry about that, Madame,' I reply.

'Not be sorry. Is good for *me*, good for my diet to see your revolting face,' she says.

A chink of wit from Madame. I'm tempted to engage with it, but I can't be sure of her limit. Her patience is as friable as the Sahara earth I have just theoretically trampled across for the last few weeks.

'Me too,' I try. 'When I'm hungry, I just look at myself in the mirror . . .'

Madame shoots a look at me. Her limit is already reached. Sahara earth turns to dust.

After a month of good exercise, I am ahead. I feel better than at any time since arriving and nothing they can do will upset me. I know how to play the servant game. I am winning it.

'You not okay,' Madame says to me as I chop onion.

'I'm fine, Madame . . . just the onion makes my eyes water.'

'No, you very sick . . . look terrible again,' she insists.

'Don't worry, I feel absolutely fine,' I insist back at her. I remember looking at myself this morning: brilliance shone back.

'Listen, Meron,' she starts, emptying a packet of white tablets into her hand, 'you take tablet.'

'No, no, no. I don't need a tablet. Thank you, Madame, I'm really fine.'

'If you not take tablet, you not get food. I want to make you better . . . I care about you.'

I raise my eyes to the sky. Maybe I've overdone the Sahara look recently, but this is ridiculous. I hate taking drugs of any kind, especially those of an unknown variety for a phantom sickness that an unstable banker – not doctor, pharmacist or nurse – has diagnosed for me. What is this inscrutable lump of white powder being pushed into my face?

'Madame, it's okay, I'll drink some coffee,' I try.

'I not offering coffee. I giving you this tablet. Take this and you can have coffee . . . sound good?' She beams encouragingly and unconvincingly.

'What is this tablet, Madame?' I ask.

'Tablet to make you feel better. This what tablets do. Me too, I take these . . . and look at me.'

True, Madame looks great for her age. My hand goes out slowly. The pill is dropped into it. She passes me a glass of water, conveniently handy. I tuck the tablet under my tongue and gulp down the water. Madame seems content. The moment she's away, I spit the pill out and push it inside my headscarf.

'We started it . . . should be in time,' she mutters on the phone.

Again, I'm outside the kitchen, exercising hard, listening hard. Ten minutes later, I see Madame crying. An hour later, over breakfast, she notices my rude health and administers another mystery tablet.

The same routine occurs each day for four days. Madame makes an emotional early morning phone call, later studies me carefully with evident disappointment and then reaches for the tablets. I make no fuss. No pill touches my gullet.

Nobody tells me anything. Shafeek and Nazia are sombre and untalkative. Abdul is hardly ever here: he's staying with Nuria, Hassan and the children. But on the fifth day, I catch it as Madame's voice chokes with emotion.

'Mum can't wait longer. She's critical . . . insisting we do it now . . . but nothing is happening to the girl. I can't see anything in her . . . not changing, just getting fatter on *my* food. Yes, of course she's taking them . . . yes, Sofia! You're right! Maybe it's protecting her.'

I understand her mother is seriously ill. Sofia is Madame's sister, caring for the sick mother in Jabal.

Madame checks my whereabouts, glances at me out-side and strides purposefully towards my cupboard. She rummages through my possessions until the folded post-card of Maryam is located. Madame rips it apart, carefully and coldly. No apology or explanation follows. I'm utterly distraught.

The white capsule continues to be distributed, same time, every day. Madame stares at me suspiciously as it goes into my mouth, but my tongue provides effective cover. I'm good at this. After eight days, I have an accumula-tion of eight pills. It would be easier to toss them out of a window, but I'm curious: if I ever get out of Beirut, I shall test the pills on a street dog in Addis. It might drop dead in front of me, or gleefully bound down Bole Road, barking dementedly at the taxis. I might even take legal action.

I store the tablets loose in Madame's golden sugar bowl, side by side with the supply of Panadols from Abdul, still safely sealed in their plastic container. There will be no contamination.

'Hammerhead, what are you doing?' asks Shafeek, sweat dripping from his brow.

He's only walked from car to elevator and from elevator to front door. At around 11.30am, it must be Shafeek's 'forgotten papers' check on the maid, except that this excuse has long been forgotten. Nobody else is in the apartment.

'I'm cleaning, Mister,' I answer dutifully.

Only a second earlier, I was on a stool, placing pills in the golden sugar pot several shelves above us. It was close.

'You can put the TV on if you like . . . listen to some music,' he suggests.

Without waiting for my answer, he turns it on. A weak-voiced, raven-haired, full-figured beauty in a stunning gold lamé dress consumes the television screen. Shafeek is immediately engrossed. It's Haifa Wehbe.

I continue dusting, pretending not to watch. But I'm dusting air. She holds both of us in her doe-eyed awe. Her act is surprisingly sexy: side-profile body-jerks, hypnotic finger-pointing at the camera and seductive facial expressions from little-girl innocence to devious diva within a single toss of the head. Every man in Lebanon might be licking his television screen at this particular moment. Before I realise it, my own hips are gently gyrating. Shafeek notices immediately. At this exact moment, I understand the disadvantages of improving my body.

'Hey! You're just like Haifa. You *are* Haifa! You look so good now!' he rejoices.

'Really?' I say, half-flattered, half-petrified.

Please don't decide you want sex with me just because I danced for a couple of seconds. Please don't be that shallow, Shafeek.

'Yeah . . . Haifa Wehbe . . . I can't believe it, she's working here in my house!' He laughs. 'Do some more dancing, Haifa, please!'

'Sorry, Mister, I have to do some washing up now . . .'

I scuttle away like a timid mouse.

Ten minutes later, Shafeek wanders into the kitchen in only a pair of black briefs. My eyes linger on them. They are plainly too tight.

'Do you want some lunch, Mister?' I stutter.

Shafeek should be in work by now.

'Yeah, maybe I'll make pizza,' he says, staring at me staring at him.

I hand him some flour. It might be easier to walk out of the kitchen, but he's blocking my exit.

'Can you teach me how to make pizza, Mister?' I ask, turning my back on him to wash a few items in the sink.

Shafeek reaches for a chopping board next to the sink, brushing against me. It's an obvious reach. I quickly move sideways to avoid stray hands.

'What's your problem?' he says.

'Nothing, Mister . . . I'm just giving you space to work.'

He makes a play for the cutlery drawer, which happens to be next to me. Again, I dart to one side.

'You look like you're dancing again, Meron,' he comments, edging towards me. I'm cornered between oven and fridge. 'I can't resist Haifa in my *own house*.'

Comparisons with Haifa are ludicrous. Yet I want to hear it. I deserve recognition for my physical transformation. But I don't want to hear it from Shafeek.

'I'd better go, Mister, before I get blood on the kitchen floor . . . my period is really heavy today. I can't hold it back,' I lie, clutching my stomach in pain.

'Wait!'

Shafeek puts his hands on his hips and studies me intently for long seconds.

'Where's the blood? Nothing is coming out. It's not your time. I *know* it's not your time. This is evidently a fabrication . . . you've stood before me and lied,' he states, for a moment back in his law courts.

He's right. I sense a difficult moment is upon us. We

watch each other intently. He folds a newspaper in his hand, steps forward and runs it along my breasts playfully, backwards and forwards, as though sweeping frivolously along the keys of a piano.

'Nothing wrong with you today, Meron.'

I quickly turn my back on him, but I'm at the sink with nowhere else to go. I start to rinse some dirty cups.

'What's the problem, Meron?'

'Nothing,' I croak.

Where's the new Meron? I am back in the shack with my brothers, barricaded in by a heap of muck and slime that reeks strong enough to attract a black mist of flies. I'm a little girl who needs her daddy, too useless to defend myself. What was Beti's advice? Focus!

'I'm just playing.'

'I'm not in the mood for playing at the moment, Mister.'

'I know you like me,' he says, his breath hitting my left ear as he moves closer. 'We never finished our evening together, the night you ate my chicken. And now, I ask you to repay me for the chicken.'

'How?' I tremble.

I am sandwiched between kitchen sink and slime, with nowhere to go. It could have been so simple to give in to him, Mum.

Mum's Intervention

Two weeks before I was due to leave for Beirut to become a downtrodden maid, Kidist had to be told of my new life abroad. With her susceptibility to extreme jealousy, such an announcement required careful presentation. If Mum was in the room, Kidist might feel humiliated in front of her sister, knowing the bounty from Beirut could leapfrog our family over hers. This would risk another sisterhood feud that might last years and years. God had limited patience and we could not assume He would intervene again. I needed to employ considerable tact in how I broke the news to her.

When my aunt called round, Mum stepped outside into our little yard on the pretext of squatting over a washing-up bowl full of cooking utensils.

'Auntie, what do you think about these girls who go to Lebanon and make a lot of money?' I asked softly.

Slumped on our broken sofa, Kidist was perspiring from the mid-afternoon heat caught beneath our corrugated iron roof. With no windows or fans providing draught, my family was effectively baked alive every afternoon in that oven of a hut. But it was a slow cook: after ten years, we were still not 'done'. Kidist wiped her forehead and winced.

'Lebanon? That's suicide! And if you're thinking of doing it, I'll do everything I can to stop you. And anyway, your mother would kill you before you even got on the plane,' she bristled without checking the volume.

'Just a question. I'm not saying I'm interested, but it seems like a reasonable way to make good money,' I continued, undeterred.

Pots and pans jangling in her ears, Mum made a good show of being too busy to hear us.

'It's also a reasonable way to lose your life, Meron, and your virginity. Arabs *never* use condoms. *Never*. And they expect you to work like a donkey. All this just for money . . . I agree your family needs money, but having lots of money won't make you *happy*.'

Kidist was patently terrified that we might once again be richer than her. And happier. In fact, we were already happier.

'Mmm . . .' I mulled.

'And enforced captivity is an awful thing,' she continued. True, Kidist did know something about that.

'Mmm.'

'Why don't you take evening classes in something useful, like computing or accounting? You've totally wasted school. In these evening classes, you can meet a good man for marriage. You won't find anyone in Bole Road . . . Meron, you're wasting your life.'

For an aunt, Kidist was viciously over-opinionated and riddled with paranoia. I was even *more* determined to go.

'Why would I be interested in computing or accounting? Why would anyone?'

Still outside, Mum pulled the front door closed. This meant she was relieving herself in our minuscule yard, on the same patch where running water flowed from a tap and we did all the washing up. A small drain struggled to carry our various liquids away. This was the usual protocol for the lucky ones with taps, but with the door closed, Kidist and I were now feeling like fresh loaves, with crusts hardening and both still on the rise.

'Meron, they are not just boring courses. The intelligent men attend the classes . . . they'll be fighting over you.'

'Right, intelligent men like Desalegn? Auntie, the girls who come back from Lebanon have real money and confidence, not a certificate in accounting and a man like Desalegn. They *choose* the man they want, not vice versa. Not like you and Mum . . . happy to accept whoever came along and agreed to marry you, regardless of the man's character.'

The temperature inside was racing upwards.

'*What?*' hissed Kidist, her head visibly pounding with blood and ire. 'I had confidence! I chose my husband!'

'Auntie, you did not. You were poor and ageing and desperate . . . we *all* know that . . . you would take anyone with the faintest of prospects. But *Desalegn*? The morning after your wedding night, you were hospitalised. I'm not going down that route. I'll do the choosing.'

I had accidentally checkmated Kidist. To protest that she had picked her beast of a husband through her own free will was to admit to pan-frying her own brain. The subtle approach had been ditched.

'I wasn't desperate!' she cried, flinching uncontrollably, sweat streaming down her forehead, cheeks vibrating so hard they threatened to work loose from the face. 'I chose *him*! Desalegn was cute in those days . . . *really*! And I wasn't that old, *really*! He was kind and good-looking and . . . and . . .'

Mum reopened the door at last, allowing a blast of cooler air to hit our faces.

'And . . . intelligent. *Really!*'

Really? It was time for me to shut up and watch Auntie Kidist grease her pan. I refused to follow her treacherous path into a marriage of Hell. Without Selam's money and confidence, I was unlikely to unearth any of those rare gemstones of the male species able to sustain a serious, meaningful, loving relationship. *Why shouldn't I choose the man I am to love and marry for the rest of my life?* Why should I be left with a hefty rump of leering leaf-eaters and countryside wife-beaters queuing up to harass, marry and flatten the reticent virgins of Ethiopia?

'You can't let her go!' Kidist blurted at Mum through the doorway. 'She's talking about Lebanon . . . it's suicide!'

Mum looked up slowly, still wary of her sister after she had abandoned us in our poverty some ten years' earlier, despite the subsequent reunion. Whatever her motives, Kidist was evidently passionate that I should not go. I tried hard to assume it was borne out of genuine concern for my welfare but jealousy clung to Kidist like the fat on her hips. Neither could be shaken off.

'And where's your wedding ring?' asked Kidist, stepping into the yard with me close behind, keen for the cool air.

'Stay inside, Meron,' said Mum.

'It's too hot!' I protested.

She closed the door anyway, forcing me to slump back onto the sofa. But metal doors are not favourable to confidential conversation.

'She's determined to go, my sister. I don't like it, but let her discover the real world,' reasoned Mum.

'No, Werknesh!'

'Yes,' said Mum firmly.

There was a pause while Kidist huffed.

'So, if she really *must* go, she should take the contraceptive injection . . . two-year protection against those Arab boys who don't care about condoms. A pregnant maid is a dead maid!'

'A definite *no*, Kidist. If Meron wants to remain pure, she needs an incentive *not* to have sex . . . these injections are like special visas for casual sex. She's only *sixteen*!'

'But Werknesh, they're an insurance policy against pregnancy and murder.'

'Hoh! Not true . . . they're an open invitation.'

'But, she's a virgin . . . the virgins are the *most vulnerable*.'

'She won't be advertising her virginity to the men of Lebanon.'

The conversation continued for over an hour in this way. Mum eventually got her way at the same moment as Tadelle turned up for his daily religious debate. No more was said. I remained unprotected but 'pure' and still do until this moment.

Destiny Arrives (302 days left)

Shafeek presses his bulges into me. Only the fabric of our clothes protect me from his unashamed awakening. Is my virginity to be stolen over a sink of coffee grounds and crockery? Will I forever associate the sweet pungency of my national drink with the bitterest moment of my life?

'Mister, I really have to do this washing up, very urgently,' I say, trying to control the quaver in my voice.

Why, Mum, why did you have to be so *good*? Urgh! You meant well, but I'm not an angel that can just flutter away from danger. Here I am, pinned down, with no choice in my destiny. Kidist was horrendously correct.

'Madame will be back soon, really soon, Mister.'

'I don't think so . . .'

I feel his hands grabbing my waist.

'No, please! Waahh! Allah! Allah! No, please! Waahh!' I wail, slinging my arms around hysterically, sinking to my knees as Shafeek steps away with surprise. Letting my entire body slump to the floor, I emit multiple cries of 'Allah!' in the direst, most heart-wrenching moan I can manage, my hands grasping for the heavens as though I am drowning in acid. My acting is so dramatic that within seconds I believe it myself and feel genuinely moved to violent sobbing.

'Okay, okay! What's the matter with you? I didn't touch you!' shouts Shafeek, watching my vigorous performance with confusion, standing in front of me for at least a minute, apparently checking its validity.

Please go away! Crying like a fresh young widow is completely unsustainable, though I remember Mum managed it for three years. Finally, he walks away. It worked, Beti! They *do* hate histrionics.

An indeterminate period of time later, the front door clicks open. I breathe outwards. Madame finds me in the kitchen standing motionless in a corner. I am wiping tears from my face.

'Me-ron! What you doing? You miss your family, or maybe your country?'

'Yes, Madame.'

'Why would you miss your country?' she sneers.

Madame thinks Ethiopia is nothing but sand, people and holes, the people living in holes in the sand: sub-Saharan, sub-human, a wasteland of wasters, a country of scrub, with the people fit only for scrubbing and whatever Shafeek has on his mind.

'I don't remember, Madame,' I mutter wretchedly at the floor.

'Anyway, today, I check your mouth. I think you not swallowing tablets. You still sick, so *sick!*'

I glare back at her. I can't take this foolishness any longer.

347

'I'm *not* sick. I took the tablets, Madame . . . that's enough! No more! Thank you. I'm better now. Look at me! I feel fantastic!' I gabble at her, skipping round the kitchen in a rare display of youthful vigour.

Perhaps I have lost my mind, and at the very least Madame will have to catch me if she's to force a pill down my throat.

It works. Madame watches in dismay as I hop around, chasing invisible butterflies.

'Enough, Me-ron! Enough, Me-ron! Take tablet! You sick! Now you sick in the head!'

Eventually, she storms out of the kitchen, face in hands, almost certainly crying. *Good!*

Two days later the phone call comes. Nazia runs to the phone in case it is Mohammed, her banned boyfriend.

'Leave it, Nazia!' shouts Madame.

'Hello?' answers Nazia anyway.

'What's the point in an expensive education if you're going to waste your time with a slow-moving Sidon boy . . . what is he? Pro- or anti-Syria? What does his father do?' asks Madame, not expecting an answer.

'It's for you, Mum,' says Nazia, handing the phone to Madame with evident trepidation.

'Hello? Yes . . . no . . . *No!*

'What is it, Mama?' asks Nazia as Madame carefully puts the phone receiver down and her body begins to crumple into the spot where she stands.

'Habibti . . . my Mama . . . she's dead,' Madame gasps from her knees, hands clutching her head as it rocks back and forth. 'We didn't get a donor . . . renal failure.'

Madame glances at me, her eyes filling with fury. I walk away before there's trouble. The supposition is simple: Madame wanted a kidney for her mother and the tablets would in some way enable a timely theft from my abdomen, perhaps without my knowledge, probably without my permission and certainly without my recompense. I should be grateful that my Madame was humane enough to use tablets: the bodies of dissected dead maids – pushed first, raided second – often arrived in Addis, the organ removal undisguised upon the mangled corpses.

This is what Mum called meddling in His work and, quite rightly, everything has failed for Madame.

I have the same dream twice, or almost the same. The first time, I am checking the bath water again, but I plod naively towards Shafeek as if ignorant of the danger. The second time, it's obvious he's aroused, but I walk on towards him, unable to check myself.

In both dreams, his hand flies out and grabs my arm. He twists me round sharply so that my face is square with his. A hand claws on the back of my head and thrusts me towards his face. My headscarf is ripped off. An overpowering garlic tongue pushes hard into my mouth. He clutches my hair so I can't back off. A hard object prods at my belly button.

Something wild is triggered within me. Catching him by surprise – and myself – with a surge of passion from my own tongue, I press myself into *his* mouth and grasp the back of *his* head. I drill my kiss into his face. His squashed nose damp with sweat, I feel his head shaking with panic.

I have lost control.

I catch sight of my right eye in the bathroom mirror behind Shafeek's head. I tilt my head to see both eyes reflected over his hairy shoulder. But I am looking at my mother's eyes. Her eyes seem at the point of dripping tears for eternity: her face is so open and hopeful, so generous in unquestioning love for me. How could I disappoint that face? A few fateful seconds of sex with this man could finish me, and her.

I blink and the eyes on the mirror are not hers. They are Madame's. I am Madame. And Shafeek's hair is suddenly an Afro.

Irritatingly, I awake at this exact moment, on both occasions. But I spend the day pondering the meaning. The dream has to be a warning. Or a bleak statement on my mental confusion. Or just a dream.

Shafeek has finished circling me: it all seems so predictable now. I always thought I would save my virginity for the one I truly love. But I make a decision. I shall *not* lose myself to Shafeek, whatever happens. This is a matter of principle. A small but perfectly functional kitchen knife will rest in my smock pocket from now on. Next time, I will use it and we will *both* go down. The new Meron will not dither.

A few months later, Madame makes her pronouncement to Abdul, Nazia and Shafeek over evening kibbeh. I stand beside the table, waiting on them.

'It is really important to travel abroad every year to expensive places with your friends. I make money for this reason. But this year, we are *all* going to France for two weeks . . . all the family together. Meron will remain here, as usual.'

'Not me,' starts Shafeek. 'I'm too busy. Sorry, Mum.'

'Oh, Shafeek, mon cher! We all want you there. You deserve a break, please! For me . . .'

'No, Mum . . . it's crazy at the moment.'

Nazia stares at him relentlessly.

'I thought you were always *quiet* at this time of year?' she says.

'Yeah, usually, but this year we've got three major cases looming. Why are you so keen for me to go?'

Nazia doesn't answer him. I am not certain that she really wants to leave Beirut either. Mohammed, the unacceptable boyfriend, is affecting Nazia's usual tight alliance with her mother. He is not bourgeoisie enough for Madame; the Paris trip might help Nazia to forget him and realign her priorities.

'And what about Baba?' asks Shafeek.

Baba is pretending not to listen.

'*He's* not coming,' replies Madame, aghast. 'He stays with Nuria. You think I want my husband shopping with me in Paris? Allah! Too slow.'

'Sharmuta,' mutters Abdul to himself.

'All the family' means Nazia and Madame. Abdul shoots her a glance, but he knows his place. Shafeek shoots *me* a glance. Nazia follows its course. I don't react. I know *my* place.

My mind swims with apprehension. This is it, the deep end. Destiny has arrived. Shafeek and I will be alone together for two weeks of . . . what?

*

Next morning, Abdul makes a rare appearance in the kitchen. If only he could return to us for two weeks. He would be an unwitting guardian. Yes!

'Nuria did it for me,' he explains, half-heartedly pointing at his newly dyed black hair.

'It's better than white, Mister,' I say encouragingly. But I thought he was sporting a black beret.

'Not really . . . Rahima says it keeps me in my fifties . . . tuh! But at the cost of wearing a Jew's kippah on my head . . . whatever I do, I lose.'

'I know how you feel, Mister.'

'Well, that's *something*.'

'It *is* something, Mister, really something special.'

Empathy for the plight of a fellow human is undervalued: now I see that. It's an unglamorous emotion without the dramatic punch of love, hate, envy et al., but when two souls come together and spontaneously empathise with *each other*, it's surely the foundation of friendship.

Abdul pauses and looks hard at me.

'Mulu, you do a great job here . . . we appreciate that.'

This astonishes me, my eyes filling up with tears in a second. It's like another gulp of Pepsi. He may not be the master of the house but those few words mean more than anything that anyone else has said. Calling me the wrong name is immaterial. I have stopped correcting him.

'Thank you, Mister, that's so kind of you. Can't you move back here, Mister? Just for a few weeks while Madame is gone?'

'*This* windy fortress? Allah! How can I? I'm too old for such a bleak place. My friends are in Hamra and Ras at ground level . . . same as Nuria and Hassan and the supermarket. I'll be in Heaven soon enough without having to live up here in the miserable suburbs.'

'But I'm worried about things while Madame is away . . .'

'Shafeek's here.'

'Yes, Mister, and I'm very scared . . .'

I pause, hoping to elicit some unease within Abdul.

'You may be scared, child, but it comes to everyone . . .'

'Eh?'

'Old age . . . it cannot be avoided except by the tragic young ones.'

'And I don't want to be one of *them*, Mister . . . especially here, in the next two weeks, with Shafeek,' I try again. How plain do I have to be?

'So, keep your body healthy. Eat plenty of garlic, lentils, onions, carrots . . .'

Why am I left with this old man as my only hope? *Why*, God?

'How old *are* you, Mister?'

He grins at my impudence. But that's as far as it goes.

My theory on elderly people who won't disclose their age is quite simple. They're *frightened* to say their age: God might hear them and realise He's forgotten to remove the battery from these particular individuals. It's best to keep quiet, hoping God doesn't notice the oversight. I will not press Abdul into an answer. Better to let him run down of his own accord, and without lumbering him with my problems.

With a swift twist of his wrist, Abdul knocks back his Lebanese coffee and limps away into the safety of a fantastical ground-level world where there is nowhere to fall to.

*

353

Nazia is more uptight than usual.

'If you even think about wearing my clothes when I'm away, I'll finish you,' she says to me as I wipe round the bathroom basin. 'And I'll *know* if you do.'

'It's okay, Nazia, your style is not really to my taste.'

'No, but my Mum's *is*,' she snarls. 'I've seen you.'

Nazia slips out of the bathroom. I feel compelled to track her through the apartment. An alarm bell is ringing inside me. She disappears into Madame's bedroom suite and closes the door. I push my ear as far as possible into the door's crack. Madame's shrill pitch easily penetrates the wooden door.

'Quel problème, habibti?' she says.

'We can't leave Shafeek with the servant . . . it'll be a disaster.'

'You think?'

'Haven't you noticed them . . . the eye contact . . . and smiles . . . the touches . . . I'm sick of it,' continues Nazia.

'You're right! That night . . . remember? When I caught them sharing a Pepsi,' adds Madame.

'Mum, we're looking at a repeat of last time. I'm *convinced.*'

'Allah! No! Not that! We're not going through *that* again.'

'I'm worried about Shafeek . . . that girl will leech off him if she gets a chance.'

'Who, *Meron*? She's never had a relationship,' says Madame contemptuously.

'Mum, I *know* her. She's changed so much. There's nothing innocent about her. Look at the way she flaunts around, trying to catch his eye. Around him, she's like a snake.'

Hoh, Nazia! *Me* like a snake?

'Maybe we shouldn't go, Mum?' she says hopefully.

Madame is quiet for a while. The subtext involves Nazia and her unsuitable boyfriend. This could save me.

'Oh habibti, yes, she *has* changed. Too confident and cheeky. Shafeek needs protection from himself. So, what are we doing? Taking Meron to France with us?'

'Allah no, Mum! She'll come back having learnt French . . . why should she have *that* for free?'

'Mmm . . . what then? Maybe get Nuria over here for two weeks . . . she can enjoy the food with the kids . . . help them save money.'

Nuria? That would be awful.

'Yes, Mum, that's it,' accepts Nazia with false enthusiasm.

Shafeek is furious, though he manages to act his way through the conversation with Madame before returning to his bedroom to punch a computer screen while shouting: 'Allah! Why am I living with these imbeciles?' It is the first time he has used his computer for anything useful.

On the day of Madame and Nazia's departure, Nuria is back with her squat body forever lost to flab and dungarees, and a face long enough to fit beneath an entire truck. Hassan has stayed at home with Mustafa, while the toddler Medina accompanies her mother. I want to hug Medina tightly: I have missed her so much.

'Don't touch her!' shouts Nuria.

Unsure who she is addressing, Medina and I look round at Nuria, both of us accustomed to simplistic commands thickened with needless impatience. Regardless, Medina toddles towards me, unhindered, unaffected. I plop a kiss upon her raven hair. Nuria grabs Medina away before I can squeeze her with affection. Nuria glances up and down at me.

'You've changed.'

'Thanks,' I reply.

Within two hours of Madame leaving for France, Nuria and Shafeek are at war.

'I need her for toilet-training Medina,' says Nuria, referring to me.

'No, you can't. Meron works for *me*, not you. Why haven't you toilet-trained the baby yet? It's too late.'

I want to chuckle. Shafeek lecturing about babies!

'Medina is not a baby. What do you know about that, Shafeek? What do you know about anything in the real world? You haven't even got married yet. Mum is tired of you hanging around. Your time is up. Nazia is waiting for you to go . . . there's a serious boyfriend.'

Shafeek blushes. Embarrassment or fury, I don't know, but Nuria has hit a raw nerve. Shafeek is not good with raw nerves.

'I've got a career. I don't have time for wives. I work, Nuria, *work*! I don't lie on my bed all day and fart like a warm corpse, bloated on cake, dressed like a kibbutz muck-raker . . . what happened to you, Nuria? You were a beautiful sister. Now look at yourself, you've lost it all. You epitomise shame and failure. Even Mum says that.'

I'm taken aback. Nuria is unable to speak. She marches out. The front door slams behind her. The humiliation is a hundred times worse because I'm standing here ogling like a keen spectator.

I look at Shafeek. He throws his hands towards the ceiling in despair. Sibling disappointment seems a major issue. I hope never to confront it.

Nuria raps on the front door urgently. I open it. She has forgotten her daughter. She pushes past me to get the toddler, who has wandered through to the TV lounge and found one of Shafeek's moccasins. She is now lifting it to her nose in front of us.

'No, Medina! Yuk! Don't touch that!' screams Nuria, racing at Medina to pull the shoe from her face.

I can hardly control my laughter. Medina waves at me as Nuria hauls her out of the apartment. I wave back enthusiastically. The ramifications of this hasty and highly enjoyable exit are slow to hit me.

Shafeek is livid. His head looks poached.

'Meron, I'm going to the gym to work off some aggression. What have I done to deserve a sister like *that*?'

'I don't know,' I reply. He's obviously done *something*.

I have about two hours to decide how I will survive the next two weeks without being raped, losing my virginity, getting pregnant, committing murder, being murdered or whatever else might befall me, or us. All scenarios lead to the same high ledge, Mulu's ledge. Whatever I do, I lose. If only we had listened to Kidist. *Mum!*

There are no more memories from Addis to sustain me. The bank is empty: I have to use what I've got here, *now*, every last snippet of wisdom, every buoyant word of prayer and every inflated puff of Habesha spirit.

Deliver Me (176 days left)

I bow my head and say the Lord's Prayer with the pieces of my ripped Maryam postcard cupped in my hands: ' but deliver us from evil . . .'

I frantically try to call Beti. We haven't spoken for at least a year. I need help. A strange female voice answers the phone. I carefully replace the receiver on the telephone to hang up.

I sit in the kitchen and fiddle with my knife. Is there a 'safe' way to stab a person? I'm not a trained surgeon or a knife-fighter. I'm a maid. *Preventing* Shafeek is the aim, not *killing* him.

I begin to cry. What choice is there? I have to let him do the deed as painlessly as possible. I hope that like Arabic writing, his sperm swims and squiggles in the wrong direction. It doesn't have to be violent. We could just make love nicely, without all the unnecessary right hooks, left jabs and upper cuts. The words 'making love' have a positive tone. Why am I visualising a vicious affray? Can I not simply *reason* with him to be gentle? I might enjoy it! We might be a loving couple. We might be husband and wife! He might use a condom.

Gentle? Enjoy? Loving? Couple? Condom? Listen to myself! I'm deluded. He will do what he's programmed to do. My words will be nothing but flurries of drifting dandelion snow in halting nature's stampede towards sweet release. Nazia will spot the bump after three months, Madame soon afterwards. Or they might not. If they do, Mum will have the grim rectangular box within four months, maybe two months before I am due back in my living state. Mum will then have an additional three years of mourning, six years in total. It will kill her. And who will get my wages?

Mum . . . and *Tadelle*? No! Mum's missing wedding ring means Tadelle, in lurking leeching courtship with Mum: by now, probably married! Urgh, no! *Mum!* What a revolting thought to have in these last few moments of purity.

The key turns in the front door. My time is out. I swallow hard and wipe my eyes. Time to accept my fate as a condemned Habesha maid in Beirut.

'Hi, Mister!' I shout dutifully from the kitchen.

In this second, I know what I have to do. I hurl my knife back into the kitchen drawer.

'Mister?' I try again and rush into the hall to confront my master.

He's sitting on a chair by the door, his scarlet face dotted with new plops of perspiration. The towel in his hand is wet with the stuff. He mops his head again, ignoring me.

'Mister . . . can I wash your things for you? Would you like some baba ghanoush and flatbread?' I whisper nervously, trying to weigh up the risk of pregnancy as I speak.

'Yeah, yeah, not hungry, get me Panadol . . . my head's on the point of exploding. Too hot for gyms.'

I rifle through his medicine box, but no Panadol. And no condoms either. I have never seen a condom in Lebanon.

'There's none left, Mister.'

'So give me the tablets Baba took for you . . . those were *mine*.'

'You want *my* Panadol?' I ask, a little nonplussed at losing the precious pills Abdul had given me on the day of Hariri's death.

'Just get the tablets, Hammerhead. I don't have the energy for it.'

The golden sugar bowl gleams at me. It has served me well. I open the lid and find the two sets of tablets: six remaining Panadols encased in their plastic tray and eight loose mystery pills. An interesting proposition sweeps into view. The Panadols will stop Shafeek's headache, allowing him to do unspeakable things to me which could lead to my own demise. But the mystery pills? They will have unknown effects on Shafeek that only Madame would know about. For a few seconds, I juggle with the notion. Ha! Poisoned by his own mother, via my hand! These little powdery tablets could offer swift, single-handed justice for *everything*. Maybe, *this* is God's will. He is guiding me towards finishing Shafeek: retaliation for Mulu's murder, for Madame's tablets and for all other suffering endured in this upper-class penitentiary. At last! Maybe I am to be the angel of death.

'Mercy not murder . . .' go the imagined words of my mother. 'We all have our vital moments of decision. Mine was the forgiveness of Kidist and caring for Tadelle . . . I showed mercy for their mistakes. Your decision is *now* . . . as an Orthodox Christian, you'll be judged by this decision . . . especially by God and by your future self.'

But, Mum, does Shafeek deserve mercy for what he's done, or is about to do? You and Dad were *too good*. Where does it get us?

'Meron!' he booms suddenly. 'Move it with the Panadol!'

I sigh and push out a pair of Panadol caplets through the silver film. This is the will of God.

No, it isn't. Shafeek, you're the test dog. Let's see what happens. Just the one tablet, I promise. Okay, two, to slow him down a little. I wrap them in a paper tissue to maintain the illusion of hygiene. Returning to Shafeek, he swallows one with a glass of water and keeps the other wrapped up for later.

'I'm going to bed,' he grunts, and trudges down the hall to his bedroom.

I am safe for today. You see, Mum, there is a middle path.

I gorge on lamb that Madame left in the fridge for Shafeek, and I retire to bed early, unsure of tomorrow. Thirteen days until Madame and Nazia return from Paris.

Next day, Shafeek is due to get up for work. Nothing happens. I check on him at around 11am. He's already extremely late and not responding to phone calls: the phone seems to be ringing itself into a frenzy today.

'Mister?'

He rolls over and gazes at me, his face drawn and wretched.

'I feel like . . . some . . . thing.'

He's surprisingly inarticulate. I give him water.

'Do you want breakfast?'

'Yeah, no . . . I don't . . . no. Bread, tea.'

'More Panadol?'

'No, already taken it.'

I prepare his breakfast and return to some gentle dusting. There will be no back-breaking chores with Madame gone, though I will at least appear to be doing something should Shafeek appear.

An hour later, I glimpse Shafeek staggering back to his room.

'Can I help you, Mister?' I ask.

'No.'

I doze my way through the afternoon after a tuna salad lunch. I'm eating well but my stomach is tight with tension. I wish the phone would go to sleep. Around 5pm, as I come out of the bathroom, there's Shafeek again, still in his pyjamas, looking as though he has gained about fifty years. In fact, I see Abdul in Shafeek at this moment: an incomprehensibly old man.

'Mister, how do you feel?'

'Eoorgh . . .'

'Can I get you another Panadol?'

'No. Took six already.'

'Six?'

'I took four more of yours . . . still not working.'

My body goes limp. My legs might buckle. Cold sweat breaks out on my upper lip.

I wait a couple of seconds while Shafeek continues into his bedroom and slams the door shut.

My heartbeat drums in my ears. I race over to the golden sugar bowl. Oh God, what's he done? Inside are six sealed Panadols and two loose mystery pills. Six mystery pills down! Shafeek is possibly, probably, killing himself. But how did he know about the stash? I swivel my head round and see the surveillance camera. Shafeek, you idiot! He watched me doing that ridiculous Haifa Wehbe dancing and caught me hiding the mystery tablet only seconds earlier, thinking it was a Panadol.

By now, I'm sweating profusely. If Shafeek dies, I am definitely dead. This was not the plan.

I remove the two mystery pills from the pot and empty them into the toilet. It takes two flushes to drown them. But what *are* they?

It occurs to me. If Shafeek has to be rushed to hospital, they might need the pills for analysis, diagnosis, whatever they do with sick people. And now the pills are swilling around in the Beirut sewers. Well done, you Hammer-head! You *are* completely stupid. I look down hopefully into the toilet bowl. Nothing. For once, I'm devastated to see the bowl sparkling clean.

I run into Shafeek's bedroom. He has collapsed onto the bed.

'Mister! Are you okay?' I squeal.

His head jerks up, annoyed.

'I told you. I'm a sick man. If I need you, I'll shout . . . Go!'

'I'll give you another Panadol,' I mumble.

'Don't want . . . don't work. Call a doctor,' he mutters.

'Yes, Mister,' I say calmly.

A doctor would declare me a murderer, of a murderer. I'm not calling a doctor.

Shafeek falls asleep quickly. I have to nurse him back to life: this is what I *must* do. I sit with him while he sleeps, watching in case there's a change for the worse. The doctor's phone number lies next to me as a last resort. I pour trickles of cold water into Shafeek's mouth. I can't touch his head for too long: it is like a desert boulder absorbing the heat of the midday sun. Bed sheets are drenched. I drape wet flannels on his forehead. He murmurs back at me deliriously. Keep on murmuring, Shafeek, keep on murmuring. But he gets hotter. Random words are thrown out. Food is thrown up. His breathing is long, deep, loud: like a dying dog trying to bark again and again. I remember Dad in his last few days. I'm becoming scared. The doctor's phone number screams at me. The telephone continues to ring as though alarmed at unfolding events. Shafeek is almost silent now. Please wake up!

I make one last effort. The ripped pieces of the Maryam postcard are scattered onto his heaving frame. I pray to God while bits of card rise and fall, rise and fall, rise and fall, with his huge gulps of air.

'Come on, God, help him! I made a big mistake. I didn't mean to meddle with life and death . . . sorry.'

I sit here for three hours, talking to God like this, mostly incessant pleading, shameless reasoning: corralling Him into saving both our skins.

I hear the clickety-click of the front door. No! I throw myself under Shafeek's bed.

Nuria? Or, who?

Abdul limps past the door, rummages around in the

kitchen for ten minutes, chews on things noisily, belches unapologetically and hobbles back with an enormous bottle of fresh olive oil. He glimpses me under the bed and stops dead. God! He *does* see everything! I wave frenetically at him to move on. Abdul's eyes are glassy and useless but he gets the message and shifts onwards and out of the place without a word. Ah, thank you! Preparing his Lebanese coffee every morning and listening to his ceaseless burbling have finally paid off.

Poor Shafeek, almost dead, lying here without realising his father has crept past. Poor Abdul, thinking his son is pleasantly slumbering when he's actually warming up his own deathbed. Why didn't I ask Abdul to help? He would have known what to do. *Another* mistake! I have effectively killed his son. I *deserve* to die.

Minutes tick by. How will I explain this to Madame?

No! Why should it be anything to do with me? He simply got sick and died. These things happen. It's *her* fault and of course those poisonous tablets. But how will I explain it to God?

There's a clickety-click at the front door again. Abdul! Yes, he'll call the doctor and everything will be fine!

I run into the hallway.

'Mister, Mister! Shafeek is . . .'

Madame and Nazia stare back at me, suitcases in hand.

I am a White Sheet (174 days left)

'Good afternoon, Madame. Good afternoon, Nazia,' I say as dutifully as possible without a note of emotion in my voice. I gulp hard to prevent my tonsils shrieking across the room.

'Meron . . . oh,' says Nazia, my squalid existence suddenly dawning upon her once more. It is not a greeting, but a statement of lament.

'There's tuna salad, kibbeh . . . er, a little lamb . . . Shafeek ate it . . . I could heat up some pizza . . .'

'Bonjour, Meron,' starts Madame. 'What you doing? You look terrible. How is Shafeek? Where is Nuria? Why no reply when I call again and again? We very worried about silence, come back immédiatement. Meron . . . where is everyone?'

'Mister Shafeek is . . . having a sleep. Nuria? Sorry, Madame, I don't know about her. I feel a little sick.'

'Nazia, you see? I told you there's nothing wrong . . . all this way back for *nothing*. Okay, Meron, carry our luggage into bedrooms and unpack everything and wash dirty laundry and help me prepare dinner and . . .'

I smile. The old routine sounds so reassuring. Nazia's scowl only adds to the sense of normality.

'No smiling, Meron, it annoy Nazia.'

'Sorry, Madame.'

Madame doesn't hear me. She's striding into Shafeek's bedroom.

Madame races out of the room, absolute panic wrought in her eyes. The eyes catch me.

'Meron! What's happened? What you do to him? *Meron!*'

I can't speak. I can't think. It's the same moment as when she first beat me. The raised eyebrow is launched, arms are flying out, words are fired at me, there's a sense that my entire body has been rammed into a giant microwave and someone has just pressed the 'Start' button. It can only be seconds before my skin is stinging, blistered and burning.

'Nazia! Call Doctor Ali, *now!*'

'Yes, Mum! I knew she'd do something.'

'Meron! Meron! What you do? What he eat? Allah! Why he nearly dead? What's happening . . . tell me before *I kill you!*'

'Madame . . . shut up just for a second!'

Stunned by my outburst, Madame manages to hold herself in check for a few seconds.

'I will tell you what happened . . . not through loyalty to you, but because my mother taught me the value of human life. I can't stand here while Shafeek dies, as much as I despise him. If everyone in the world valued every other person's life, all war would be history, including

Lebanon's wars against Syria, Israel . . . itself. God created us, God should take us . . . nobody has the right to take another person's life. I show mercy towards Shafeek, towards you . . . '

'Meron, tell me *now*, or you are dead!'

She grabs my hair through the headscarf and drags me towards the TV lounge. Argh!

'Please, Madame!'

The balcony doors are inside the TV lounge. I can't get her hands off my head.

'Argh! The tablets, Madame! The tablets that you gave me . . . to get a kidney for your mother! It was a mistake!'

Just for a second, she stops to consider what I've said, then continues the painful haul towards the balcony. I try to throw my body to the floor but she's strong enough to yank me back onto my feet with my hair. Her grip on my scalp is rigid and unbearable: I am howling with the intensity of a hysterical hungry baby. Madame is too tough to resist. She's going to kill me. Outside, as the sun briefly floods my vision, she swerves suddenly left towards the storeroom and shoves me in roughly, before slamming the door shut and locking it from the outside. I hear her feet jog back into the apartment and I sink to my knees in the semi-darkness, bawling.

'I tried to do the right thing! I tried to be a good person . . . don't let her kill me! Mum, where are you?' I wail, undefeated memories of abandonment marching back into view.

Please, not again: not the trauma of the stinking blocked doorway. *Focus, Meron!* I breathe hard for a few seconds, the way I did in my morning workouts. It clears my mind, relaxes me. After a while, I calm down a little and reach through the small window opening in the storeroom door and try to stretch towards the outside key, my fingernails falling short by the length of a hand. I feel them scratch at the door's paint and remember the marks I'd noticed before. Poor Mulu! She was in here too!

'Mulu?' I say out loud in Amharic. 'Is this what happened? Were you as lonely and depressed as me? Did Shafeek take you, and Madame push you? Were you Orthodox Christian? Did they return you to the dust of Ethiopia . . . to be made fertile by your mother's river of tears? Oh, Mulu . . .'

I must concentrate on the coming storm. I am not Mulu. The moment Madame opens the door, I have maybe a single second to make some kind of attacking move, enough to flatten her and let me dart inside the TV lounge towards the safety of a bathroom with a lock.

If I can lift this sack of onions and hurl it straight at her chest, this would knock her down. And I'd be outside, sprinting for refuge. The sack is incredibly heavy, almost too much to lift. I quickly pluck out the juicy red onions, one by one, until it is about half-full. I drag the sack up onto my shoulder, ready to chuck like a shot putter in the Olympics. I have never done this event but I am absolutely certain I can emulate the monsters who flick a tiny metal ball a few metres to earn themselves money and medals. I wait near the door with the sack in launch position.

Minutes plod by. I am waiting too long in the ready position. The throwing arm wants to hang limply at my side. The onions are bobbing about restlessly. I am at the point of just letting the sack crash to the floor.

The door swings open. *Now, Meron!* I struggle frantically with the sack: if I can just toss it hard at the silhouetted figure in the doorway. But instead, the onions clatter onto my feet. I try to move my feet but this unbalances me and I slump backwards onto sacks of potatoes. Madame charges in and grabs me by the hair before I can clamber to my feet. Yelping like a street dog pelted with stones, I'm being dragged hair-first into the hard-hitting sunlight. We edge towards the chrome balcony. I'm trying to dig my feet into the smooth paving stones that offer no useful ruts or bumps. I can't do anything but slide and struggle and scream manically, my hands thrashing around my head to stop her firm clasp. I don't want to die!

I shout out anything that comes into my head to stall her progress.

'Look at you! Your own family hates you! Especially your husband . . . about the Sudanese! Maybe he'll kill you for that! You're a tragedy in progress!'

'You are little bitch! Try to kill my son!' she squeals at me and seems to grow in strength at my provocation.

I can't stop the inevitable. We're at the balcony and she's snatching at my ankles to lift me over, feet up, head-first. I kick out desperately but she doesn't care. She's got them and my feet are off the ground, my stomach riding hard over the chrome digging into my ribcage, my head tilting upside down, I manage to grip the balcony rail with my right hand . . . I'm not going! *Please, God! I'm not Mulu!*

But my feet are higher and higher in the air and this is it. I try to tighten my hold on the railing, but it's only one hand . . . that one hand won't save me. And this shiny chrome railing was polished yesterday by the same hand.

Today, there's not a speck of dust to delay my palm's slip.

'I love you! Madame, I love you!' I scream in a final effort at reaching into her hidden humanity. Anything to stop her. I feel my stomach coming back up my throat, my eyes bulge . . . I see the street so sickening below me, people, cars . . . *Oh God, no!*

'Nooo—'

'No, Mum!' screams somebody else.

Madame yells and her clench on me is released.

Someone is rapidly pulling my legs back onto the balcony and holding my head to stop it crashing onto the hard stone floor. But I still fall heavily and sprawl for a second, confused, unable to understand anything. I look round and see Madame sitting on the floor a few metres away, rubbing her leg. On seeing her, I scramble as far from the balcony railings as possible and keep going until I am firmly adhered to the balcony door. I clutch the handle, panting huge gulps of air into my lungs, my legs ready to run further and deeper into the relative safety of the apartment, but I pause for a second to check what has happened.

It's Nazia.

Madame gets up and charges for me again, but Nazia swings her arm round Madame's waist to throw her off in the wrong direction, both slumping onto the floor together, neither really hurt.

'Mum! Leave her!' screams Nazia.

'She nearly killed Shafeek . . . she has to go. Get off me!'

'Don't touch her! Not this one!'

I can't believe it. Nazia is a decent human after all. Maybe there was an emotional connection with Mulu?

Perhaps she wanted to keep her distance while secretly trying to protect me?

'But, Nazia . . . she's just a servant . . . like the last one, it doesn't matter . . . she has to go!' sobs Madame, tears now streaming down her face.

'It matters, Mum! Kill her and who will clean our toilets? We won't get another maid if a *second* one goes over. I hate this one more than you, but she does all the things you and I weren't born to do . . . and we'll get a new one soon enough. Just a few more months, Mum, be logical!'

'Thank you, Nazia,' I mutter bitterly.

'Shut up, you!' Nazia fires at me.

'Murderers,' I spit.

'You see? She knows everything . . .' starts Madame.

'Mum, I don't want to stay here with you if there's no maid. Just *leave* it.'

'What? You only want to be with your mother if there's maid service included?' gasps Madame, visibly shaken by Nazia's statement of intent.

'And we *can* have maid service if you don't discard this one,' replies Nazia, hardly answering the question.

'Nazia, my daughter . . . you are not going anywhere until Shafeek is married. Then, when you find a suitable man to marry, yes, you can go, but not *before*.'

'Yes, I know the system, but, Mum, I will not be waiting around long.'

'You are *not* marrying Mohammed!' shouts Madame. 'Allah! You've really changed since Hariri and the Revolution.'

'Eh? Mohammed and I have been together longer than *that*.'

'What? *No!*'

I can't believe these two. They have almost forgotten I am standing here accusing them of murder. I begin to walk inside.

'Hey, we not finished with *you!*' Madame shouts at my back.

I could just ignore it and continue on inside. But here I am, intervening again without meaning to.

'A life was taken here,' I begin. 'A Habesha maid . . . so what if she wasn't as important as Hariri? It's still the same thing . . . murder. You are murderers.'

'How dare you compare Hariri with a maid from Ethiopia!' spits Madame.

'Meron, if you want to live, go inside and clean toilets,' says Nazia. 'That's your life.'

There it is again, inside my head, Mum's voice. Ecclesiastes 3:19–20: 'For the fate of the sons of men and the fate of beasts is the same: as one dies, so dies the other. They all have the same breath, and man has no advantage over the beasts: for all is vanity. All go to one place: all are from the dust, and all turn to dust again.' I feel my cheeks redden with rage. Who do these people think they are? They are biding time between nothing and dust, just like the rest of us, yet they behave as if blessed with some special status, way above us mortals. I can't believe their arrogance. I have to speak.

'If that's your only reason for keeping me alive, Nazia, then you can flush it down your precious toilets. Come on, push me, kill me . . . I wasn't born to be your slave. I'd rather *die* than continue here under you. Come on, *do it.*'

I walk back into the glare of the sun. Madame and

Nazia don't move, not sure what I'm doing. Maybe I'm not sure either, but instinct has taken over, a ruinous fighting instinct.

'If *you* can't do it then I'll go over anyway. No other Habesha maid will get stuck here . . . and I love the idea of you two scrubbing bathrooms for the rest of your lives. You'll join the human race at last.'

Meanwhile, I'm going to *leave* the human race. I stride towards the balcony, furious enough to do this. I'm Habesha. Stubbornness until foolishness encroaches. Madness as confidence. And I don't expect your intervention, God: I'm dealing with this. Everything is under control. I can jump into the deep end without help. I am Meron Lemma, strong, confident, daughter of my mother . . . about to see my father again and sit on his rock-solid knee, ready to retire from the long march of the Lebanese luncheon service and be scraped into a box and sent back to the dust of Ethiopia and buried without a blessing.

God can see what's happening: I don't *need* the blessing. There'll be one less Madame to exploit us. At last, I know why I'm here. A reason for everything, and the money is the very least of it. *Come on, Meron, show them!*

'No, Meron!' they both scream.

It makes me hesitate.

'Why shouldn't I?' I shrug.

'Habibti, stop her!' shouts Madame at Nazia.

'*You* stop her! It's your fault. Say something to make her stay, Mum. Allah!'

Nazia looks genuinely startled at the thought of cleaning an apartment she cannot yet leave, almost a prisoner like me. That harsh front she adopts is stripped away.

Vulnerable at last, Nazia has the look of hunted prey while Madame seems flummoxed. She either wants me dead or she doesn't. A minute ago, I was almost victim number two, but now the consequences of losing this particular life are pinching at Madame's murderous imperative. She swallows hard on that overused throat.

'You've got nothing to say . . . so I'm going,' I say, starting on my last few metres of life, once more towards the gleaming chrome balcony.

No tight little window ledge for me. I can really spread my wings from this diving board, and if I can imagine I'm a white sheet, maybe it will hurt less. No dithering. I'm a white sheet. Gravity is in command, I'm a white sheet, time to go . . . Focus, Meron, this is for Mulu and the others. I am running at it . . . *I'll be free!*

'But your mother!' yells Madame.

That word catches me. Mother.

'For her, you do anything . . . won't you? We all do anything for mothers . . . me included. But I make bad mistake for my mother . . . so sorry, Meron!'

'Me too,' I say, both hands gripping the railing. 'I'll do *anything* for her. If only I'd thought about that three years ago . . . I wouldn't be standing here about to finish myself in front of you two . . . sharmutas.'

I have just called my Madame a bitch. She and Nazia pretend not to hear it, as they do when Abdul makes the same accurate assessment.

'Your mum, she want to see you so bad, Meron . . . when you have children, you understand this. You are her baby. Me? I really want to see Nazia every day, and Shafeek and my grandchildren. I do anything for them . . . it all starts and ends with family.'

Poor Nuria. The dungarees haven't made the cut.

'And Nuria, of course,' continues Madame belatedly.

'But family doesn't explain your cruelty . . . and your murder. That's explained by . . . I don't know, I can't find the words to describe something so terrible.'

'Yes! Much better to look for words than kill yourself, Meron . . . much healthier,' says Madame, with an unlikely smile.

I shake my head and want to smile back. Sometimes, she is so farcical. But this must be another of her acts. I'm not sure if I believe her or not. But I *am* desperate to see my mother's face again, and to imagine it streaked with tears because I'm in a box from Beirut appals me. It blocks my path to oblivion. After everything she's been through. This ghastly prospect is enough for self-preservation. *Mum, I have to see you again. I am not dead.*

Sorry, Dad, no reunion today.

I turn round and return to work, glancing back to see Nazia lightly embracing her mother. False as it seems, I am warmed by it, though nothing about those two should warm me in any way at all. It warms me because my mother deserves this kind of embrace from the daughter who left her in mourning at the airport three years ago. I owe her so much.

At least I do not have the death of a man on my conscience. For two days, Shafeek staggers around, shouts my name, uses the bathroom, eats an egg or a banana, mumbles into his mobile, vomits the food, watches TV until his eyes close with fatigue and sleeps an inordinate sleep. We leave recovery to Doctor Ali's medicine case and my own absolute dedication.

After a week, Shafeek is eating solid food and it's staying down. Yes! His face is still grey and lifeless but I sense the patient has turned a corner. I do my chores with relish.

'Meron . . . thank you,' he mumbles once.

'Mister, it's a pleasure. I'm pleased you're getting better. It's a relief.'

'But why didn't you call the doctor when I was sick?'

'I'm not allowed to use the telephone, Mister. Don't you remember?'

He knocks his fist on my skull.

'Hammerhead . . . next time, I'll make you *eat* the telephone. You are really, really stupid.'

Shafeek soon ambles around tentatively on the balcony, soaking up sunshine, slurping orange juice, flicking through the newspaper. Nearly there! He makes calls to his office, his voice lucid and confident again.

Around this time, Madame finally talks to me as serenity descends on this troubled home.

'Meron, you really something special. If all Ethiopia like you, it become strongest country in world.'

'Thank you, Madame.'

'You nearly killed my son . . . but . . . I can't be angry with you. Maybe there was reason. It's okay, we very close now.'

'Thank you, Madame. There was a reason.'

'Mmm . . . but listen to me. You not to say single

word to Shafeek about tablets, or us fighting, or Mulu, or anything . . .'

'Yes, Madame.'

We must not upset an international lawyer's delicate sensibilities.

'He know nothing about Mulu, not even pregnancy. I protect my son from bad information, so keep your mouth closed.'

'But he had a relationship with her, Madame . . . and one thing usually leads to another . . .'

'Yes, Meron, usually. But not Shafeek make her pregnant.'

'Uh? Abdul?'

'Don't be crazy girl.'

'Hassan?'

Madame shrugs: the eyebrow lurches upwards to suggest an irritated 'Yes' without saying it.

'Everyone think Shafeek, but not him. If police interested again . . . not Shafeek have the problem. He is good son.'

'Of course he is, Madame.'

Maybe it suits Madame to believe this. I will never be sure about Mulu's philanderer but there is no question about who pushed her off the balcony. The Lebanese police chose to believe the account of the 'window-cleaning accident', as they always do. Lebanese windows and balconies are notoriously dangerous, even when nobody is cleaning them, and there would be no point in attempting to persuade the police, or the Ethiopian government, otherwise. This is common knowledge in Beirut. The Mesdames of this city will never face justice.

Leaving Lebanon (27 days left)

'Meron, you come back to us, yes . . . we all want you here again,' starts Madame as I commence my kitchen cleaning duties.

'Mmm . . . I don't know about that,' I reply, a little taken aback.

It is bizarre but I am the celebrity of the apartment. Shafeek thinks I nursed him through a raging fever, while Madame is anxious to avoid the fees of hiring a new maid, with all the additional problems of induction and familiarisation. After three years, I'm regarded as good enough to stay, and Madame is comfortable with me knowing about the past. Uncoincidentally, she's dining me on chicken shawarma and kibbch every day. It is almost as though attempted murder has brought us together.

'Me-ron . . . please come back! We *need* you . . . be better next time, I promise,' Madame pleads.

'Let's see how it goes in Addis, Madame.'

'I have suggestion. Why you not leave your money here

and come back to work after few weeks' holiday in Addis?' she says, deadly serious.

'No, Madame, I need my money with me in Addis, all of it . . . for my family,' I respond.

I'm due to return with $3,600 and not a dollar less. Madame will jump on the slightest pretext for docking those hard-earned wages. Beti warned me about this.

'Me-ron, you might lose it . . . your money safer here in my bedroom,' Madame continues.

It is difficult not to scoff. She is quite insane.

'I'll be careful, Madame, but thanks for your concern.'

'Why you not come back, Me-ron?' she implores. 'We looked after you so well . . . remember your birthday?'

'Of course . . . wonderful.'

They bought me a cheap card and some popcorn. I hate birthday cards, especially when they depict a delicious birthday cake the size of a train's wheel, when in reality there is *no* birthday cake. In Addis, we eat popcorn every day at every coffee ceremony. It's noise food! Does she think annual popcorn is enough to lure me back to Beirut? Annual popcorn and multiple attempts at murder are not obvious in their attraction.

'Oh, Me-ron! Not lose yourself to *man*. You too young to marry. If you marry fast, you be old fast. Why you not make good money with us, then you start business in Addis in few years?' Madame soldiers on.

'I'll think about it, Madame,' I say, careful not to jeopardise my earnings. 'I'm not sure what business I could run in Addis.'

'Three more years with us give you plenty of time to think and plan, and you have capital for something at the end. You still only be twenty-two . . . young business-woman!'

With the body of a grandmother and the brain of a cabbage.

'But,' continues Madame, 'you probably want little time with your family, especially your mother . . .'

Unless she received any of the letters that I entrusted to you, my mother will assume I'm dead. My appearance might kill her with the shock. Or maybe *she's* dead? Anything can happen in 1,200 days and nights of separation.

'I'll call you from Addis if I decide to return . . . which I might . . . I probably will,' I mumble, hoping to appease her.

'You have *two* mothers now! You not learn as much from other mother as from me.'

'Yes, I've learnt so much from you, much more than school,' I add.

'Yes, you have.'

'I'll miss you, Madame,' I manage with the most unblinkingly honest face I can muster.

'I miss you so much, Me-ron!' she gushes, stroking my left cheek affectionately.

She's a better actress than me.

'Mustafa and Medina miss you so much . . . and Nazia,' she continues.

I choke as though a noose has been tightened round my neck. *Nazia?*

'Sorry, Madame . . . I'm overwhelmed.'

'So, you come back?' she tries again.

'We'll see . . . I'll definitely call you, Madame, I *promise.*'

'Okay, I trust you, Meron,' she says as Nazia walks into the room.

Madame kisses me three times on the cheeks, French-style. It's real flesh-on-flesh contact. There's warmth in those lips. Now, I see it. Madame is trapped within her own viciously controlled world where true happiness never has a chance: I actually pity her.

'Allah! Mum? What are you doing?' asks Nazia, dazed.

'It doesn't matter, habibti! She's one of *us* now!'

'What?'

'Sorry, habibti.'

And when she tries to break out of this world, her daughter is there to prod her back in, and vice versa. Madame and Nazia should separate for their own good.

Nazia has refused to speak to her mother since the triple-kiss incident two weeks ago. Madame is considerably subdued but continues in her unflagging quest to tempt me back.

It's difficult to imagine Madame and me strutting around the downtown boutiques in our shades: a couple of leisurely Lebanese Mesdames popping down from our high society in the clouds, to see the little 'street people' up close and to peruse the latest trends. But here we are and, as barefaced bribery goes, it's not a bad idea. Madame is also using her time with me to blatantly foster Nazia's jealousy: this might help to restore their relationship.

My head swivels and spins. Madame clutches my arm to guide me through the throng of other shoppers. I have forgotten how many individuals meander around in city centres and fill up the space like hundreds of snapping piranhas in a stagnant pond. It is truly frightening. I have seen all four million Lebanese citizens in this single outing. Madame attempts conversation with me but I cannot reply intelligently. Other people are a novelty.

I point at things hopefully, especially glittering clothes in alluring shop windows. Thanks to the Fashion Channel, I know what is stylish, but my Madame's intentions of bribery waver in the face of price tags, her predilection for Gurage miserliness undiminished. After three hours, we return home almost empty-handed. Madame bought a single item: a lock for her fridge, 'ready for next Meron'. This is not the best incentive for me to return to Beirut.

'Before you go, I've got a special gift for you, Hammer-head,' says Shafeek. 'I'm on a business trip for a week . . . interview . . . so maybe won't see you again. I might be working abroad from now on . . . out of this place at last.'

'Really? I'm leaving in two days, Mister.'

'Yeah, I've got you something you've always wanted. Something you'll do *anything* to get. Something that's deserving of three years' service. Something only a Hammerhead will appreciate.'

I am now excited. Obviously, I deserve *something* for reviving the sick fool back to life.

'What is it, Mister? Gold?'

Maybe an ornament. Maybe the golden sugar bowl!

'Similar colour,' he chortles.

'Can I have it *now*?' I beg. 'A gift for *me*!'

'I'll just check if we've got it . . .'

He walks into the living room.

'Yes. It's here! Come here, Meron! Good girl! Come, fetch!'

I race out of the kitchen.

'Here it is, Hammerhead!'

He hands me a banana, freshly torn off from today's bunch. I look down at the lifeless piece of fruit and back up at Shafeek's face of ridicule.

'Oh. Thank you, Mister,' I say tersely.

'Enjoy it, Hammerhead!'

I toss the banana out of the window with all the disdain at my disposal. He stops laughing, the face darkens.

'Go fetch, *yourself*,' I offer.

'I'll kill you for that.'

'Easily achieved, Mister . . . if you just remove your shoes for a second . . .'

Shafeek cannot believe my audacity, which delays his march towards me by a split second, in turn allowing Nuria's visiting children to run into the salon to see us.

'Come here, Mustafa and Medina, my babies!'

I embrace them together. Shafeek stomps out of the room. He's lost it. The moment has gone. I shall never see him again. I am safe from him.

On the morning of my flight, I appeal to Madame for one – just *one* – phone call to Ethiopia.

'If I call my mother quickly, she could meet me at the airport. Please, Madame, very quick.'

'Not from here, no way. You call her in airport with *your* money.'

She insists I clean the apartment as usual before we head to the airport.

'If you not finish in time, you miss flight. And it *is* white sock day.'

I'm not sure if she's joking and decide not to risk it. I thrash the apartment with bleach and polish. It might sustain them for a few days, until the next victim is ensnared. Thinking of her, I locate the scrap of my Maryam postcard bearing the gentle eyes that gaze down on the baby Jesus. On the back of the scrap I write these words in tiny Amharic letters: 'Madame murderer. Escape!' I sew the scrap into a pair of freshly washed trousers confident that nobody else will be wearing them until the next maid arrives. She will feel it immediately rubbing against her waist and will ask, I hope, to leave before the contract is signed. That will at least save another Habesha sister from the beasts. I also sew a pair of Madame's oppressive white socks into the interior of mine: they will be my souvenir from Beirut.

I throw on my old Addis clothes and tidy up the minimal possessions. Madame stands beside me in her white ankle socks for the last time.

'Here, Meron, a gift from me . . . to replace your Jesus postcard.'

She hands me a photograph. It is of her, my Madame, without a single wrinkle.

'Thank you. That will help me remember everything you did for me.'

'Exactly, Meron. Thanks to me, you changed.'

She tramps around the place in her white socks for a few minutes. They stay white.

'Good luck, Mulu!' gurgles Abdul, as we leave the apartment.

'Thanks for your friendship, Mister. I'll miss you!' I exclaim. Friendship doesn't have to mean remembering names.

'Me too! You're a real friend. You listened to me . . . you made a difference to my life,' he replies.

'What?' retorts Madame, visibly surprised. 'She's Meron, not Mulu . . . you're confused. Just when the maid is leaving us, you get dementia . . . *wonderful.*'

As we head for the door, Nazia shrugs at me: her parting gesture.

'Au revoir, Nazia!' I rejoice. 'Good luck with all your personal difficulties. I'll pray for you . . . beaucoup.'

'*What?* You speak French?' she asks indignantly.

'Oui, oui!' I sing out for maximum provocation.

'Allah!'

I am about to cross the apartment's threshold into the outside corridor when Madame puts out a hand to stop me.

'Airport baggage checks start here, Meron.'

'What do you mean?'

'I mean this . . .'

Unable to resist a final bout of distrust, Madame laboriously checks every item in my possession in case I have slipped in something illicit. Does she take me for a common thief?

Madame is methodical but unimaginative: she is un-initiated in the art of sewing garments into the interior of others and fails to locate the white socks.

Inside Beirut International Airport, Madame counts out $3,600 in notes. Wrapped inside a white handkerchief, she pushes the wad into my cleavage.

'It is safe there, Meron.'

She hugs me tightly and kisses my cheeks three times. I feel her lips on my face again, the second time since she returned from Paris. Maybe *she's* changed. I hope so for the sake of the next maid.

'Look at your hair now, Meron,' she says. 'See what happens when you use shampoo and conditioner! Maybe in Ethiopia, your hair would *never* grow.'

It has not been cut or tended for three years. Naturally, it has grown.

'Yes, that's right, Madame, all the women have very short hair, just like the men,' I lie, for the last time.

'I know you not phone me, Meron.'

'I'll try.'

'Think of me here . . . alone. Shafeek is moving to different country, Nazia wants to get husband fast and move out. Nobody left . . . only the maid for company, like daughter. Why can't it be you?' she implores.

It's no act. I see a tear, maybe two.

'I'm not sure, it's possible, Madame . . . depends on so many things,' I bumble.

'Goodbye, Meron.'

Madame kisses me once on my forehead, hands me the elusive Ethiopian passport and leaves me standing in the departures lounge, a disoriented little girl left in an airport. As I watch her backside sway into the distance, I want to call after her, which is absurd.

'Madame . . .' I say weakly. 'Madame.'

She can't hear me.

I stand, inanimate for long seconds, unsure what I am. Eventually, I make it to the toilets and find a mirror. It's like Table Lady's mirror, a truth mirror. My hair resembles a thick, ugly sprout: in Addis, people would think I slept with sheep and was raised by them too. I'm wearing tatty old jeans and a loose sweater. My shoes are plastic sandals open at the toes. I will not be phoning Mum: she must *not* see me like this. A black plastic bin liner full of my original possessions rests by my feet. Where's my original suitcase? Argh! Madame must have burnt it. I don't belong in an airport. I belong in a field. In a field, I would only attract attention from grazing animals. In here, I *am* the grazing animal. Madame has dumped a decimated sub-being onto the concourse, not the ordinary everyday person that she used to be.

I Return (0 days left)

On the plane, I have two hours of interrogation from other Habesha passengers: 'Why do you look like this?' 'What's the problem, my sister?' 'You look awful . . . how has this happened?' 'Are you sick?' 'Do you need money?'

I cry a lot and snivel out incoherent answers mainly in Arabic and English. I have almost forgotten Amharic. But it drifts back as I'm forced to answer these strangers: slowly, slowly until its familiarity warms me like an old friend. Each new sentence returns colour to my character. The words of my language are me remembered. Multiple neon lights are fizzing into action upstairs and the old Meron is stirring from her monotone trudge.

The Yemeni Airlines flight transits in Sana'a, Yemen. A woman stares at me as I stagger around with my bin liner in an airless waiting room.

'My sister, do you know what you look like?' she asks. I could take the question as an insult, but I've seen myself in a mirror and I know what she means. I'm a wandering anomaly, a lost soul, a poor humble miskin.

'It depends on the mirror . . .' I start. It feels weird to speak to someone who's not my master or madame. These people are my *equals*. I can say whatever I like and they won't hit me. 'Actually, why don't you tell me what I look like? I don't trust these Yemeni mirrors.'

She laughs.

'Okay, I'll tell you. You look like I did a few years ago after I broke up with my husband. And broke is the word. He *broke* me. Physically and mentally. After three years with this guy, I looked like you.'

'My God, I must look terrible!'

'You do, sister, you do. Working as a maid in Beirut?'

'Yes . . . and it was three years. But I'm not broken.'

'Mmm. Let's get you into the Ladies' toilet and tidy your hair up . . . what do you think?'

'Yes, Madame . . . sorry, yes . . . yes, my sister.'

Blen is a successful Habesha businesswoman in her thirties. On the Addis flight, she sits next to me and soothes me with jokes about Habesha men. She has seen everything the Habesha man can throw at a woman and channelled the negativity into fierce motivation and drive. Blen has definitely got the confidence. Within half an hour of meeting her, she is my hero.

But the anxiety is building inside me. Every mention of Addis churns my stomach. I can't eat on the flight.

'I need that,' I say to her.

'Need what?'

'Your confidence . . . it's a *good* confidence. I thought I had it all back, until today in the airport. When my Madame walked away it just seemed to drain out of me again.'

'Don't worry, we'll get you looking good and then it'll surge into you. Trust me.'

'I trust you, Blen.'

I already trust this woman like my mother. My mother!

We arrive in Addis two hours later. My hands are trembling as we march into the arrivals lounge. Instinctively, I fall to my knees and kiss the floor of the airport. People around us laugh: they're happy for me. As my lips brush the shiny floor, I see dust. I expect to hear Madame's voice in my ears: 'Why haven't you cleaned this floor, Me-ron? Why haven't you cleaned the entire airport? Afterwards, you can sweep the runway . . . white sock day . . . Me-ron!'

As I kneel there, my backside in the air, the emotion pours out of me, tears splashing onto the Addis dust, my legs refusing to raise me from the floor. Blen rushes to help me up before I attract too much attention.

As we approach the exit, I see numerous little black balls in the distance, bobbing around as if they have a life of their own. And, of course, they do: they are people's heads waiting at the barrier. I stare at them and gasp. So many black people! Blen grabs my hand and drags me outside like my mother.

Overlooking the car park, I feel the Ethiopian sun embrace me. The Beirut sun was a harsh glow with stabbing dagger-rays: in Addis, it is perfectly warming and bright, with welcoming beams like tender caresses. It has the touch of God.

'You and me, sister . . . we'll stay one night in the Wanza Hotel so you can get yourself together. In the morning, we go to Merkato and buy you some clothes, then the beauty salon. By dinner time, you'll be ready to meet your family. How about it?'

'Why don't you have any children, Blen? You'd be a great mother.'

'I'll take that as a yes.'

Her smile is born of the Addis sun. I can feel it. A day with Blen would be a pleasure. I'm not ready to meet my family. After three years of no contact, I want it to be a successful 'return', not a pitiful creeping into the house like a sorry prodigal daughter hauling a worthless bag of tat behind her. My pride is intact. No need to inflict more shock on my mother than is necessary. Let her see prosperity, joy and occasion, not hair like a wild thorn bush: I've jetted in from glamorous Beirut, not tramped in from war-torn Mogadishu.

Next day, Blen fulfils her promise. In Merkato, we buy a large suitcase and a pile of new clothes for my family. Let them believe I lugged these trendy togs all the way from Lebanon. In the beauty salon, the hair is finally beaten back and pummelled into a recognisable style. It makes sense to have the full treatment while I'm here: face, nails, more face, and back to the hair for another beating. I invite Blen for injera and kitfo. The berbere spice converts the uncooked beef into hot coals inside my mouth: desensitisation begins here! At last, I feel Habesha again, from scalded stomach outwards.

I wait with Blen until 9.30pm, or half past three back on Habesha time. I can't return to my house during the day. Neighbours would surround me and shower me with shameless requests involving 'gifts for old friends': I might not even recognise the genuine claimants. They would count the suitcases and make their claims according to the perceived booty. It could take hours to throw them off. I don't have the patience and they have no concept of what I have been through. Any conversation would be wasted and vacuous.

I arrive by taxi in the road outside our neighbourhood.

'Blen, thank you so much,' I say. She has held my hand all day, and now I'm ready to rejoin the human race.

'It was a rare pleasure. If I ever have a daughter, I hope she's a bit like you.'

As I step onto the potholed street, young men shout at me, something about my haircut. Ah! How I have *not* missed the chat-eating idlers of Addis, unabashed and ubiquitous, at once both threatening and pitiable; I choose to ignore you.

An opportunistic young lad runs out to offer a hand with my new suitcase. Where's Abush? Maybe this boy is the new Abush of our block. I gladly accept.

The track to my house seems impossible to walk along at night in the virtual pitch-black. The stones are designed to trip us up: I have forgotten the trick of navigating them. Finally, I arrive at the strip of corrugated iron that I believe is a dark green door in the daylight. But in the darkness I am only half sure that it is my old home. I shout out, 'Peace on this house!' and I give the boy two birr. There's no answer.

I push on the metal until it creaks open. A single stride across our yard finds the front door, half-open, as if waiting for me. I pound on the door as I enter, my heart banging away in tandem. It's the same doorway that was so horribly obstructed by muck all those years ago.

Entering the house, I'm struck by the scale of everything and the appearance: it's a cramped, dark, shabby hole of a slum. Jesus Christ, son of God. Who could live *here*?

But it is familiar. Nothing has changed since the day I left for Lebanon. My foot brushes a metal bowl, upturned and empty, Henok's bowl. Two seated women in white robes gape at me, open-mouthed. Mum and Kidist.

'It's me.'

No words, no actions, no outside world. Crippling disbelief, in these long moments: moments of absolute astonishment, in a place where seconds are not counted. Time has stopped. We are off the clock. Time is irrelevant. All that matters is my mother sitting here in front of me, *alive*. I am in her company again. Time moved before this and time will move after this, but right now, it's postponed until normal emotions can be resumed. I can't even imagine normal emotions.

Kidist's face shifts from disbelief to jubilation. She hurls herself at me and grips me tightly.

'Meron! You're alive!'

Kidist's clinch is crushing my chest.

Mum can't take it in, her demeanour tormented, grief-filled, pain-soaked. I kiss her on the cheek but she's quite motionless, unable to understand my presence, incapable of speech.

'Three years? You didn't call . . . we thought you were dead,' says Kidist, now fully tearful.

I can't speak either. Tears trickle down my face. Completely overcome, I bury my head in Mum's lap. She strokes my hair but still says nothing. After prolonged silent weeping, she eases my head out of the way to stand up.

'I'm going to church,' she mumbles.

'But, Mum, it's so late . . . nobody's there! It's closed . . . don't go!'

'I can't stay in this house . . . I have to speak to my God.'

'And not to Tadelle?' I ask anxiously.

'Tadelle? He's dead . . . another cesspit drowning.' She winces.

'Every day, your mum cries . . . because of *you*,' says Kidist. 'Every day.'

'But I sent letter after letter. What happened to them? Madame never let me phone you. I'm sorry!'

'But three years . . . it's too much, Meron!' continues Kidist, the same aunt who abandoned us for three years.

Enough of this.

'Remember your single night of captivity with the housework freak?' I ask her.

'Yes, of course,' says Kidist.

'Multiply that by a thousand and you have my experience in Beirut.'

She is silenced. Mum stumbles outside. Two young men enter. They look familiar. In fact, they are two of the idlers shouting at me outside. We all gaze at each other. They are my brothers. Nobody knew anybody in the semi-darkness of the street and now I'm clasping two handsome young men: the wispy vapour trails of adolescence are fading fast, barely reminding me of the way they were and the way they went. But who are they today?

'So what was the score?' I ask.

'What? What score?' they both reply, pleasingly confused.

'That game you were playing when I left for the airport three years ago . . . obviously a really important game.'

I have them dismayed, their memories jabbing away at their consciences.

'Five–four,' retorts Nati boldly. 'I scored a hat-trick.'

'I know that's a lie . . . but don't worry, I forgive you.'

They laugh nervously. Actually, I *don't* forgive them, but what can I do? They are my brothers.

I see the welling up of a tear in Henok's eye, but bending over to remove his trainers for the metal bowl routine, he casually wipes it away before Nati notices.

'I'm going home. See you tomorrow, my long-lost niece!' announces Kidist.

'Still with Desalegn?' I ask.

'Is Ethiopia still joined to Eritrea?' she replies with a tone of resignation.

After a while, Mum is back, having prayed outside the church: probably the most grateful prayer of her life. At last, a smile breaks through. Mum prepares shiro wat and injera. I dribble at its deliciousness. My brothers feed me generous handfuls direct to my mouth, the Habesha sharing ethic in full flow. I try to feed Mum in the same way.

'I still don't accept food from the hand of another,' she says. 'Remember? It's been like that since your father died.

He was the last person to put food in my mouth, and always will be.'

I suck my fingers clean, just as I learnt to do in Beirut.

'Why are you eating like a Muslim?' Mum snaps. Licking fingers after food is unwelcome in an Orthodox Christian household. 'Are you *Muslim* now?'

There's anxiety in her tone.

'No, Mum . . . now, I'm Buddhist . . .'

'Buddhist?' she chokes, almost falling off the stool.

My brothers can see it's a joke. They start laughing. Mum is a few seconds behind. The very idea that I had changed religion!

'I managed to smuggle a gift out of my Madame's bedroom, for you, Mum . . . a pair of virgin white socks . . . now you can see how clean I left their floor.'

'Immaculate and untouched . . . delivered to me . . . like my daughter. Thank you, God.'

'You can wear them for church in the mornings in the freezing cold.'

'Yes, on my hands!'

As she tucks the socks away under her bed, I imagine Madame incensed, scouring her apartment for them. It is a splendid thought.

'And here she is,' I say, holding out the photo of Madame with dyed blonde hair tumbling over her corrected features.

'She's so beautiful,' comments Mum, my brothers murmuring agreement.

'Mmm . . . kind of,' I manage.

One day soon, Shafeek and Nazia will leave her: my sad Madame will have nobody around her, left alone with her luxuries, while in the slums of Addis, my mother will *never* be abandoned. I will not allow it. Her old age must be a pleasure. She will not be left to eat kale and to thump her chest like Mama.

'Like everyone, she has her imperfections,' I add.

How could I ever have compared Madame with Mum? What kind of fool was Meron Lemma over three years ago? She was the type who did not appreciate the immense force of goodness and intelligence lying beside her in bed with that ever-comforting hand nuzzled in the bend of her waist bringing on heavy blankets of sleep. As far as I can remember, her hand was there all night, every night, and like everything else, I took it for granted. I deserted her for three years, just like Kidist. Both of us had to be incarcerated before we could recognise Mum's ever-loving, ever-lasting glow.

'Sorry, Mum,' I say into my mother's tired eyes.

'Eh? What for?'

'Well, I made a big mistake and I can't really begin to explain . . .'

'So, is it amazingly rich there?' interrupts Nati.

'Oh God, yes . . . money lies around on the pavement. If you need it, you just have to bend over and pick it up. Mobile phones are made from solid gold and the litter bins are encrusted in diamonds and fried chicken is provided . . . all free for everyone.'

Nati and Henok stare at me agog.

'You haven't lost your imagination then,' says Mum.

'Just a joke. No, it's *not* fantastic there. A higher standard of living, yes, and more material things, yes, but happier? No way! Miserable people! Money is not the answer in Beirut.'

'So the secret is to make money there, return to Addis with the money and be happy with your mother and brothers . . . the best of both worlds,' says Nati.

'The secret is to look for happiness in whatever situation you find yourself in,' corrects Mum.

'Happiness isn't always on hand to be enjoyed, Mum . . . I had some difficult times in Beirut—'

'But God was with you,' she interrupts.

'Well, *yes* . . . but . . .'

'And here you are . . . eventually. He delivered you.'

'Well, true.'

'You see, He's always there for His disciples. But only if you believe in Him.'

'So that explains it . . . though sometimes His interventions seemed to be stuck on Ethiopian Time.'

'Of course they were. I was praying for you from here . . . in Ethiopia.'

We talk all night like this. I tell much about Madame and the others, concentrating on the more cheerful aspects: learning Arabic, the delectable Lebanese cooking and the experience of living within another culture. As dawn arrives, Mum wanders off to church again. Her routine remains unbroken. I go to sleep in Mum's bed, *our* bed, until breakfast and coffee ceremony at three o'clock (9am). We're back on the old schedule, time recommenced and it feels so good. Who cares if the days slip away in the shelter of this shack with the woman I love? I never want to leave her again.

Over the next few days, I spend a sizeable chunk of my

earnings. Everything is changed: new rug, two comfortable sofas, new bed for Mum and myself, a bunk bed for Nati and Henok, cutlery, plates, DVD player, CD player, cooking equipment, modern clothes for everyone and a new mirror that I hope reflects back the new Meron. Dollars stretch a long way in Addis. The front door is opened wide to the neighbourhood: we put grass on the floor, cook doro wat and hold coffee ceremonies several times every day. The house is warm and alive again. We all breathe a collective sigh of relief. I'm a successful returner.

I'm wearing an off-the-shoulder, off-the-thigh, completely off-the-scale clingy purple and white dress decorated with psychedelic squares, complemented by mauve heels so high and sharp not a ripple remains as I hop through Bole's puddles. That's right. It's daylight and I'm out in *that*. My head is up, my neck unbroken, lips glossed, eyes lined. I have the confidence. Babies burble, drains gurgle, women ogle, men jeer, taxis swerve, dogs leap, buses bump, Bole rumbles, but now I can handle myself.

'Lemma, you're better than Beyoncé now! What happened? You get an Arab?'

'Abush?'

'Who do you expect? Abush won't die. You miss me, Lemma?'

'Miss you?' I splutter, unable to contain my laughter.

I *have* missed the barrage of crude drivel from this prematurely street-aged face wearing multiple scars from flung rocks and hurled fists, with a nose smudged across both its cheeks. Perhaps he hasn't washed since I last saw him.

'I missed you, Lemma.'

'Really?'

'At one birr a day, for three years, that makes a lot of birr, maybe a thousand birr that I missed you . . . a thousand of your birr. Good to see you again, Lemma. Here . . . go spoil yourself.'

He gives *me* one birr. It is the dirtiest one birr note I have ever seen or smelt. I imagine it's had its uses beyond money.

'You see, Abush looks after his chickens . . .'

I throw it back at him, my fingers stained and rancid from the paper rag.

'No thanks. I don't want to catch anything.'

I have never thrown money back before.

'Lemma, this is Addis. Of course, you'll *catch* something! Better to catch it from *me*! Your boyfriend!'

He's still funny despite the demands of a street life, though these days his means of survival may be less ethical than raking through the garbage of others. I hand him a crisp green hundred-birr note. I now know the brutality and exhaustion of a day-to-day, hand-to-mouth, scared-to-death existence, constantly balanced on a precipice the width of this hundred-birr note, surviving only through the Habesha spirit.

'Yes!' he cheers. 'Yes! Lemma! Yes!'

'Take a day off from the street, Abush . . . please take a wash and eat some proper food. Buy it first.'

Half an hour later, walking past the Dembel Centre, I see a bedraggled ambling young woman, shockingly familiar. It's Tsehay, my old school friend. But what happened to the 'Indian' manager at Elephant Walk? That was nearly four years ago.

'Meron! It's *you*! Where have you been?'

Just for a second, I am hesitant in acknowledging her: compared with me, she seems to be another nobody mindlessly plodding along Bole, so why talk to her? And within that same second, I remember Selam and then Madame and Nazia, and all the pointless superiority acts those frightened people employ that fool no one and fail to understand the equality of life. *No, that's not me.* I greet Tsehay with a true smile and a long hug. I give her the *real* Meron.

'Lebanon . . . I was a maid.'

'How was it?'

'Well, *look* at me!'

'Wow! Can you recommend it?'

'Actually, not at all, it was a total nightmare, I was reduced to nothing . . . but you'll still go . . .'

Tsehay's envy is difficult to conceal. It's caught in her eyes, midway between the false smile and the frown.

'Yes, I might . . .'

It's *her* turn to make the mistake.

Ecclesiastes 1:9: 'What has been is what will be, and what has been done is what will be done: and there is nothing new under the sun.'

Now to find myself a worthy man.

Unbound is a new kind of publishing house. Our books are funded directly by readers. This was a very popular idea during the late eighteenth and early nineteenth centuries. Now we have revived it for the internet age. It allows authors to write the books they really want to write and readers to support the writing they would most like to see published.

The names listed below are of readers who have pledged their support and made this book happen. If you'd like to join them, visit: www.unbound.co.uk.